Further praise for

THE VOYAGE OF
THE MORNING LIGHT

"The power of the novel is in its brilliant depiction of life onboard the *Morning Light* and of the locales it visits. Endicott captures the place and time so emphatically through terrific sensory detail that the reader feels total immersion in the setting."
—CANDACE FERTILE, *Quill & Quire*

"A beautifully paced examination of what makes us different, and why that matters. It's also a travel story, and a richly layered look at seafaring culture through the eyes of a girl en route to becoming a woman."
—LIANE FAULDER, *Edmonton Journal*

Praise for

MARINA ENDICOTT

"Marina Endicott is a sweet-natured but sharp-eyed and quick-tongued social observer in the Jane Austen–Barbara Pym–Anne Tyler tradition, who can wring love, revulsion and hilarity in a single page."
—T. F. RIGELHOF, *Globe and Mail*

"There's heartbreak, there's joy, there are parts where you cry—and it's very high quality writing."
—MARGARET ATWOOD,
Giller Prize jury remarks for *Good to a Fault*

The
VOYAGE
of the
MORNING LIGHT

Also by

MARINA ENDICOTT

Open Arms (2001)

Good to a Fault (2008)

The Little Shadows (2011)

Close to Hugh (2015)

The

VOYAGE

of the

MORNING LIGHT

A NOVEL

MARINA ENDICOTT

W. W. NORTON & COMPANY

Independent Publishers Since 1923

Copyright © 2019 by Marina Endicott
First American Edition 2020

Originally published in Canada under the title *The Difference*

Interior images: (ships) from *3,800 Early Advertising Cuts* © Dover Publications, Inc.; (palm, coral) from *The Plant Kingdom Compendium* © Jim Harter; (turtle, dolphin) from *Animals* © L'Aventurine

For information about permission to reproduce selections from this book, write to Permissions, W. W. Norton & Company, Inc., 500 Fifth Avenue, New York, NY 10110

For information about special discounts for bulk purchases, please contact W. W. Norton Special Sales at specialsales@wwnorton.com or 800-233-4830

Manufacturing by LSC Communications, Harrisonburg

ISBN 978-1-324-00706-7 (pbk.)

W. W. Norton & Company, Inc., 500 Fifth Avenue, New York, N.Y. 10110
www.wwnorton.com

W. W. Norton & Company Ltd., 15 Carlisle Street, London W1D 3BS

1 2 3 4 5 6 7 8 9 0

For Timothy

PART ONE

YARMOUTH, 1911

They are higher than the heavens above—what can you do?
They are deeper than the depths below—what can you know?
Their measure is longer than the earth and wider than the sea.

JOB 11:8-9

I

The Sea

The *Morning Light* set out from Yarmouth on the early tide and ran with a light wind south along the shore before heading to the open sea. Teal-green water foamed and bit at the breaking prow in front, and a long, purling cleave poured out behind her. Kay was at first made uneasy, not by the motion of the ship, which thrilled her, but by the gradual shrinking and eventual disappearance of the pier, which had seemed to anchor them to land somehow. She had never been to sea before this.

Shifting into deeper water, the ship settled, sails filling to a taut curve, and made way. Thrumming along the narrows in a stiff breeze, they passed Johns Cove on the way to Cape Forchu. Seaweed covered the rocks there in vivid green locks, cascading, slippery—deeper strands revealed by the tide now glinting black-brown in the sun, the darkest ropes of it like rippling hair let out of braids for sleep. Like a dark head no longer on her pillow but askew in the doorway, shadow slipping sideways. Kay caught her mind's eye back from that.

Past the wave-washed rocks, there was the clean stretch of empty shore that their little party had strolled along when Aunt Lydia took them to the May Day picnic, their first week in Yarmouth after the long journey from Alberta. Kay had stood stock-still on the gravel, not even allowed to take her shoes off to feel the sand slumping beneath the soles of her feet, that graceful submission against bare skin. She did not know the point of coming to the seashore when Aunt Lydia would not let her wade at the wave's edge while the women walked the pebble path along the beach.

From the ship, the land looked different. A different country, no longer their own. Past the last bare, solitary rocks—out here in the nothing, in the expanse of green and grey, what was to pull them back to land? Francis spoke of voyages he had made without sight of land for a hundred days or more, without fresh water or milk or anything green save the scum on the water barrels, following the whales when he was a boy. Now, in command of his own ship, he would decide what landfall to make. Being careful of his new wife (still strange to Kay, that he and her sister Thea should be married) on her maiden voyage, perhaps they would saunter along the coast for a while.

Not that Kay wanted that herself. Once they passed out of the shallows into the great roll of ocean, she lost the unconfessed fear that she might be a poor sailor. Feeling only electric vigour, she pitied Thea suffering in the parlour.

They were out of sight of land now. Kay tucked in close beside a neat tri-coiled pyramid of rope and held tight to the rail, mind more at ease but fists still tight with the possibility of falling into the ice-green water. Behind her, the crew ran back and forth in obedience to orders Francis or his first mate called out, repeated by the men in a verse and response like the Litany in church. None of the shouts made sense to Kay; they were almost in a foreign language. *Belay*, she knew: at dinner at Orchard House, Francis would say *Belay that*, if he had asked for salt but found the cellar near his elbow.

An island slipped out of the clouded sky on the port side. The upper mind said left was *port*: both were four letters; right was *starboard*, for the stars must always be right . . . The lower layers of her mind were quiet, absorbed by the smooth greyness, green-ness, the gyres and eddies of the never-static sea. At a gap in the busy stream of crewmen, Kay slipped across to the port railing, her new boots silent on the deck, to see the island more closely. One boot fitted sideways into the scupper, the narrow drain-ditch along the deck, and again she stood braced to the rail, leaning into it as the ship rolled.

Over the side, green water laced with white stretched doilying across to that small rocky shore. The island was uninhabited. Wait—there was a little house. Look, a scrap of sand between great grey rocks, a rowboat beached on the shale, a path through scrubby pines leading up to a grey cabin, hidden in the trees. That would be a place to live. When she was a grown woman, she would live there, and be alone always. Perhaps a boy would come with victuals from the mainland once a week, a boy with fawn-coloured skin and understanding eyes. But she would not speak to him.

Already the island had slid past, receding into the old life. She had a sharp sensation that this was the beginning of her real life—this voyage, all round the earth to the South Seas and China. She could not live alone on an island for a great length of time still to come.

The girl stood sure-footed upon the deck, leaning into the wind, her eyes shining with the light of distant horizons . . .

As soon as you try to tell your life, it goes false. Her eyes had bleared with the wind.

Down below, she heard Thea calling from the saloon for the stewardess, her voice thready and hoarse from losing her breakfast. It would smell of sick down there, but Thea ought to be in bed, and would need help. Up the length of the deck to the fo'c'sle, Francis stood busy with Mr. Wright, his first mate. Kay looked back down astern through the intervening copse of ropes and sail, readying her feet to match the swell and rise of the deck.

As she made the companionway, a particularly good wave took the ship. She caught at the stair rail and half-tumbled down the steep stairwell to the door, standing open as she'd left it, leading

into the bright, wood-panelled saloon. An acre of sun was streaming down through the great skylight Thea had hung with geraniums. Everything shone with polish and cleanliness. This long
room, with cabins opening off it on both sides and down the little
halls, was their quarters now. Kay's cabin was down the port corridor, on the same side as Thea's.

Her face palest green, Thea said, "You must learn to close doors
on a ship."

Kay's pride rose again—*she* was having no difficulty. She went to
Thea, shrunk in an armchair with an empty basin at her feet, and
took her arm to help her to bed. Good that the basin was empty now,
because the smell of sick always made Kay be a little sick herself.

The stewardess came as they were shuffling across the long
saloon. A lardy woman, thickset and a little deaf. She took Thea's
other arm, and Thea straightened to pretend all was well, so they
made faster progress. When they had her settled into the beautiful
carved bed Thea shared with Francis now, the stewardess went away.

Between careful breaths, Thea said, "The motion is no more
than Francis gave us to understand. I don't complain! The rocking
and sidling can be borne, but this intermittent plunging—" She
put a hand on Kay's, resting on the coverlet. "I'm better now, dear
heart. Will you play for me?"

Before going to the piano, Kay fetched the basin from the saloon
and tucked it in between the carved bed and the neatly nestled
chest of drawers. That way, when halfway through O'Connor's
Nocturne no. 2 (soothing for an invalid) she heard Thea weakly
retching, she could leave her to it.

❧

Between fresh spasms, Thea listened, apprehensive. But to her
relief, Kay had gone into the music and did not hear or come to
help. Good. She would be safely out of the crew's way for an hour
or so, and Francis would not find her underfoot, at least at first.

This is the purest dream, the best life possible, Thea told her fist, inside the cave of sheet and comforter. If only she was not so queasy. But that too was to be expected. The outer motion and the inner motion, that secret movement deep inside, had overset her temporarily. She would be better soon.

∾

By nightfall they had gone a long way, so that Francis was happy with their progress when he came down to the saloon for his supper.

Mr. Wright the first mate came too. He had his own cabin farther along the corridor, and might sit down to supper with them sometimes, although Francis said he would more often eat with the boys and Mr. Best in the crew mess. Mr. Wright was a lanky man, quiet but with a firm disposition, perhaps a little unbending. He knew odd facts and delighted to tell them, and was a student of astronomy; he promised to let Kay look through the little telescope he had made himself, to see the rings of Saturn.

Saying she was stronger after a rest, Thea came out in her Delft-blue going-away dress, laughing at herself for succumbing to a weak stomach when she wished to be the perfect seafaring wife. Her ranging eye caught Kay licking salt from her wrists, where the spray had coated them all afternoon, and later again, meditatively tonguing the back of a spoon at table. Thea looked pointed and shook her head a fraction. Because even when one was twelve years old, she never would cease telling one what to do. Perhaps she ought to go back to bed for a while longer.

Kay had the middle chair, and Mr. Wright sat across from her, his back to the wood stove. But he only stayed for a formal greeting to Thea before taking his bite of beef and cup of tea back up with him. Lena Hubbard the stewardess and her husband, the steward, who was just called Hubbard, served them boiled beef and potatoes with beet relish, and summer pudding the cook had made with blueberries from Lake Milo.

Dinner was short, both Thea and Francis wanting nothing after the summer pudding but to sit talking before the stove a little while. The skylight was still open, though the night had turned cooler. They spoke softly to each other, a word or two rather than sentences. Kay was not one of them and ought not to be there at all. She went to the piano at the other end of the saloon and played a little—soft Chopin études that would not make a dent in their solitude.

Before very long, Thea got up from the armchair and said that Kay should find her bunk, and the sea air, and Francis said yes, yes, what a long day this has been for a young lady on her first voyage, so there was nothing to do but acquiesce and leave them.

Lena Hubbard came to set a tin of hot water in her little wash-basin, and showed Kay where to stow the tin on a hook below the basin when she was done, and where the pan hid, for if one did not want to go along to the head (as they called the toilet closet on a ship) in one's nightgown.

The cabin was satisfyingly trig and trim: dark wood boards fit tight together made the walls, curved as the ship's wall was curved, and the last of the August twilight glimmered in through the port, a thick, round, bolt-fastened window over the bunk. The featherbed was tucked up taut with a blue wool blanket, and above it ran a shelf with short walls for a book and a small lamp. She got a lecture from Lena (which she did not at all need, having already had one from Francis, twice) on how one could only have a lamp in a calm sea, and on putting out the flame very carefully. Kay did not mind being lectured to at first, it was only when the people ought to *know* that she would know that she grew irritable. Lena gave her a pat on the knee, saying she was already a great sailor and they would soon have her in the navy—speaking as if she was a child still.

At last Thea came and kissed Kay's cheek and left, her blue skirt filling the door and emptying out into the corridor to go back to Francis, who was her husband now, shutting the door behind her. You must learn to close doors on a ship.

Alone in her bunk, Kay stared sightless at the wooden ceiling, recounting her life so far, putting it into language: *I have bad dreams, I cannot be left.*

She was afraid to dream here, in case Francis put her off at the nearest port. Because it had happened before, at Orchard House, Aunt Lydia Wetmore's spreading white villa out at Lake Milo.

Then there had been such a clanging and a whispering and the sacred telephone being used to ring up and summon Thea, so that she harnessed Aunty Bob's pair herself and drove the wagon out from Yarmouth town at five in the morning, before the trolley car began. Kay had not slept since waking the house by shouting with the nightmare, but had dressed herself and sat stiff as a mummy on the top stair, waiting for punishment or something worse. She felt darkness as huge as a bear inside her, eating and eating, becoming larger.

Hearing the wagon's arrival, Kay had got up her courage to go downstairs.

Aunt Lydia's daughter Olive stood bandy-legged in the front hall, staring at Thea with her pale fish eyes almost popping out, her upper lip strangely trembling: "It is too much, Theodora! Too, too much—you cannot expect us to—and Forrest away, too—and the house in an uproar, an uproar, and *Mother*! Mother did not sleep one wink last night."

Fish in the eye, rabbit in the lip, light hair frizzed over her ears. Kay found Olive very ugly and was glad that she was not related to her at all, because she was Thea's cousin on her mother's side, and Kay had had a different mother who was not from this stupid place.

"It was not so bad," Kay told Thea in her bedroom, as they packed her trunk again. "I woke up in the upstairs hall, that's all. I had been shouting a little."

"What were you dreaming?"

Kay did not want to say. "The bare trees were coming down to the shore like bones walking, and we had to run, I had to warn them."

Thea bent to look under the mahogany bed. "Where is the blue valise?"

"The attic, I think—Aunt Lydia said it was too old and should be put away."

"Well, run and get it."

Kay hesitated, because the attic was full of webs, with damp-sifted dust furred over everything, but she could not bear Thea to reproach her for cowardice; and the valise had belonged to her own mama, Eliza Warner Ward, and she did not want to leave it in this house.

She went, treading carefully only on the strips of carpet and never on the black walnut boards of the floor, and found the door that led upstairs again, and the heavy Bakelite switch for the single bulb. Then up, coir matting on the narrow attic stairs sharp under her stockinged toes, into the lofty space under the roof. The light was dim, so early—but there, tucked under the eaves, was her valise. *E.W.W.* in gold letters on the side. Still clean, because Kay had only arrived yesterday morning. The only clear, clean thing in this blurred space. The valise's black bone handle fit her hand. The attic was only dusty, not haunted. The rope dangling from one rafter was not a noose, or at least not a noose for a person.

Then they all said that she must leave Aunt Lydia (who was not Kay's own aunt, but Thea's mother's oldest sister) out at Lake Milo, and go to Aunty Bob, the youngest sister, who could use a girl to run and fetch for her—terrible prospect—at the grey house with the tower on Parade Street in town.

All afternoon at the grey house they sat with Thea in the round front parlour at the bottom of the tower: Aunt Lydia and Cousin Olive, Aunt Queen the middle sister, and little Aunty Bob, all speaking in low voices as if that meant that Kay, huddled on the window seat, could not hear them. Aunt Lydia and Aunt Queen said again that they had no patience with Father, nor with their sister Maria for being so determined to throw away everything civilized and trek out to the wilderness with him, for all the good it had done either one. It was a foolish venture, and if he was so determined to help the Indians surely he could have found some nearer to home. Thea reminded them that Father had sent her home to go to normal school, as he promised, and that it was only to be expected that he might marry again being widowed so early, and history went on being retold, so Kay looked at raindrops on the curving window and found two to follow down the pane in the slowest race imaginable.

Then the aunts began telling Thea about boarding schools in Nova Scotia where Kay might be very happy. School was what Kay was not allowed to talk about—or what could only be talked about in a certain way—and she sat growing cold while they discussed nourishing meals, teaching philosophy and suitable study for young ladies, such as Home Economy or Pitman's Course in Shorthand. The aunts talked on as the room greyed into evening (no fire lit to cheer them, no matter how chill the rain, because it was August) about *difficult eventualities*, and *twelve years old, oh dear me*... At last Aunt Queen brought her mouth into a line and pushed the bottom lip out, and said that hospital treatments had been found efficacious for—*ahem*...

At that, Thea stood up so sharply that the tea cart jittered across the shining floor. She put out her hand to Kay.

"Please excuse us," she said to the aunts. "I must give Kay her drops."

"Mastoiditis," murmured Aunty Bob, who did not often align with her sisters against them.

Thea shook her head without looking back. "Only the earache. She has a proclivity."

Kay said nothing. Anything she said would be wrong.

Thea bustled with the drops and made Kay get straight into her nightgown, though it was only six in the evening and they had not had their supper, and turned down the coverlet on the cot Aunty Bob had put up in the dressing room, and knelt beside her to say prayers. She kissed Kay and said, "We have not been happy for a long time. But now we will be."

The night and day had been so jolting that, without wanting to, Kay slept.

❧

In the cool darkness of the Yarmouth night, Thea heard her sister gasp. Then a tight impending silence. She slid her feet from the quilt, darted across to the cot and touched Kay's face to wake her. "All right, dear heart," she said. "All's well. Just a dream, just a dream."

Kay's eyes were open, but she was not seeing this room at Aunty Bob's. She looked frantically to the wall, and away, and back again, staring. After a minute, she whispered, "I try not ever to think about things, but sometimes I can't help it, Thetty. I think it will escape and I will break open bleeding and die, or run away and lose you."

"And leave me, you mean."

"Yes, but then I would lose you too."

"I will always find you."

"You could not find Annie when she ran away."

(Thea saw again the bent form beneath bare branches—too late.)

"Do not leave me," Kay begged her.

Thea opened the bedcovers and climbed in beside her sister in the narrow bed. "No, no, I will not leave you. I will never leave you, or lose you, or let you be hurt," she said, murmuring and whispering into Kay's ear, into her hair and the nape of her neck, as Kay turned in the cot and gradually her shuddering stilled.

❧

At breakfast next morning, Thea announced that Kay would not stay with Aunty Bob either. There was nothing for it but Kay must sail with them. Someone (it was Aunty Bob, the one Kay had almost liked) said that some might say it was a sad thing to have a younger sister tagging along on a honeymoon, especially one ten years awaited. That was also Kay's fault, although nobody said so, because Thea had had to come out west to care for her after her mother died. Anyway, Thea and Francis had had a proper honeymoon in Halifax four months before, in May, when they first arrived. When they were first married, and Kay had first been sent to stay alone with Aunt Lydia. She had kept her dreams clamped up that time.

There was only one day left before the *Morning Light* was to leave, not enough time to assemble her kit, but Thea took Kay down Main Street to Milady's Up to Date Shop for boots with soft soles that would not skitter on the deck. Thea mourned the lack of a better clothier, but Kay yanked her braid so her neck hurt and said her middy blouse was fine, if she was to be a sailor. She was afraid of being on the boat (the *ship*, she must always say), but she would not let them see that—not the Forrests or the Wetmores or hateful old Aunt Lydia, not Thea or Francis.

Francis did not look at her askance. He nodded, as to a sailor he was taking on, and said he had a cabin saved for just such eventuality, although she would have to sleep with a crate of china at one end of the bunk. Thea laughed and put her hand on Kay's arm and said no such thing, it was only his joke.

"I meant on the way home, of course," Francis said, his eyes calm. "We don't take china *to* China, that would be coals to Newcastle."

But they do not want a child with them. They want to be by themselves.

It was foolish to think that, *by themselves*, because the ship was full of people, almost all of them men, and some very rough at that—so there was another lecture from Thea, about whom Kay was and was not to speak to. The crew was lined up to greet them that morning when they first came aboard: the tall, thin first mate, Mr. Wright, and the stout little bosun with the strong black beard; the third mate with thin pinkish hair who was a gentleman from England come down in the world. She did not remember their names, but Thea had a list to study from.

The huge second mate frightened Kay. His beet-red nose, terribly pocked from some old disease, had grown beyond the usual to take up most of his face. She looked too closely, and wished she had not, and feared that he was angry to be stared at.

Then they met Hubbard, the steward, and his wife Lena, who would see to her and Thea; and the rest of the crew, and the cook, down to the least idler, the ship's carpenter, Seaton, who was very old and lay smoking his pipe in the lifeboat when Francis did not shout at him. And the ship's boys, three of them: George and Jacky and the shy youngest boy, with light-brown eyes, who smiled at Kay: Arthur Wetmore from Port Maitland, one of Thea's hundred cousins, whose father knew Kay's own father—had known him, before he died. Arthur leaned against the foremast to talk to her, until he was shouted for, because he was new himself, only on his second voyage. So now she knew that the bitter end of the rope goes in the scupper, when making the ballantine coil of three circles in a piling, untwisting, circling round and round . . .

Roused by some change in the rocking movement of her bunk, Kay woke. She had been asleep, after all. But not dreaming.

She lay quiet. But the change in motion gave her a galvanized wakefulness that could not be ignored. The porthole only showed blank darkness.

Kay pushed back the blankets and stood, careful with the rolling, to pull on her skirt and shawl over her nightdress and slip bare feet into new brown boots. The cabin door opened without creaking. She shut it carefully, silently, and made her way along the dark corridor to the stairs and up to the deck like a cat creeping up to look out—except a cat could not hold so tight to the rope handrail—onto the deck.

Everything was moving.

Great swells raised the ship and sent it cracking and creaking down and forward, forward. As she came up on deck, the wind caught her hair and her skirt, so her bare legs felt the bite above her boots before she lifted her head to the tempest. But it was no tempest—it was only speed.

The ship was scudding fast through the darkness, everything bent forward, an italic hand racing over miles of blue-black paper sea. Sails filled the air around her, ropes taut and now shining, because now the blackness of night was broken in a blaze of moon beating down through the sails. The clouds had parted and the moon, the moon—full, splendid, huge.

The beauty of it! She was confounded, turned from a frightened, whining cat into a much larger thing, an angel of awareness. *Beauty beauty beauty*—she wept with it for a moment and then left off, merely accepting. The wind of their going lifted her hair and ballooned the sleeves of her nightdress.

Along the port side of the ship came the second mate, lurching around the wheelhouse. He was the one who had frightened Kay that morning—only that morning! at the dock in Yarmouth—with his blood-coloured bulbous nose and shambling gait. But now, in the rush of the elements, in the star-jangling wind of the night and the full moon shining ahead of them, he came rolling up beside her and said, loud enough to be heard over the wind, "Isn't it marvellous, Miss?"

She looked up to his small eyes and scurfy straw hair, the nose receding in importance in this elemental air.

Grinning like a great fool, he said, "Isn't it the most beautiful thing you've ever seen, to ride before the wind on a night with a moon?"

Kay nodded and nodded. "Yes. Yes, beautiful."

2

Boston

The ship became the world. They had a house to live in, the long skylighted saloon and their cabins, Aft; and the deck for their outdoor walking path, as long as they kept out of the way of the work. Another flight of stairs down from the Aft saloon, they were allowed to visit the trim galley, fitted out like a carpenter's bench with every needful tool on its hook, all polished copper and wood and steel-lined bins. The crew lived farther down, where Kay was not to go. Deepest below in the hold it was all case oil and coal, but Kay loved the orderly smell of the upper cargo deck: tea and mahogany, the familiar church-reek of tallow candles and sweeter beeswax, pine and cedar and other woody smells, spices she did not know. It was dark, but once one's eyes grew accustomed, the rows of pillars between boxes were like the great roof posts in the stable at Aunt Lydia's; and that was the other smell, the bleached stable smell of chickens and three well-kept young pigs, waiting to be roast pork. Sunlight slanting down through bulkheads lit upon nothing grimy or rank. "A tidy ship, no slatternliness about her," Francis said—not bragging, but assuring Thea that she would be comfortable and safe.

Still, it was a little lonely, to walk through this world a few steps behind two people who were mostly focused on each other. And not what Kay was used to, having had all Thea's attention until now.

Over the long ocean day, broken into portions by meals and the brass bell that rang to indicate changes of the watch, Kay wandered this new world, alone among the crowd of crew, shy to speak to the men but not wanting to be in Thea's pocket all day. She found a hiding place or two; in that way she was like old Seaton the ship's carpenter, dreaming in his lifeboat. In the afternoon, when the wind rose and they put on sail and the ship began to slant into true motion, Francis asked Mr. Best (that was the name of the lump-nosed second mate from the beautiful night) to show her the wooden seat tucked in at the starboard side of the fo'c'sle, where she might be safe out of the hubbub but still look out and perhaps spot land as they came closer.

Kay felt a softening toward Francis, almost tender; prickling back to caution whenever he shouted orders or was brisk with Mr. Wright or made one of the other seamen grovel or snap-to and say, *Aye aye, Sir!* He was easy in command. When he came down to supper, he began training Kay in the way of the sea, but he was never Father's sort of schoolmaster, and she understood his instruction was directed more to Thea than to herself.

"A barque can outperform a barquentine at any run, far better at sailing to windward than a full-rigged ship might be, at rising to the wind—well! Easier to handle in all seas. Perhaps the *Morning Light* is not the best runner, but we make compromise our servant and take the best elements of the fore-and-aft rig and the full, to be the most efficient rig at sea—and with a much-reduced crew—" In his enthusiasm, Francis had moved to boastfulness, which came oddly from his mouth; he was usually inclined to understatement. "Twenty-two this trip, well in hand, allowing for mishap or illness. Let's see the *Flying Dutchman* race round the Horn with less than seventy!"

Thea smiled for his keenness, and Kay saw that she held her tongue from saying *fewer* to correct him.

Kay did not care for this new entity, Francis-and-Thea. She worried over what it might mean, how her own life would be changed, or Thea's. All this time out at sea, yet her sister had not recovered her usual quiet vitality, but still sat sopping and drooping over the teapot at breakfast, and more often than not went back to lie down white-faced in their cabin, eyes shaded with one hand and her mouth in a wavering line.

Their bed was over-large for a ship; Francis had had it made especially. Carved edge boards kept the featherbed from shifting, but made it uncomfortable to sit on the side to comb Thea's hair or pat her hands with rosewater or any other thing that might be nice for her. If only Thea would get up and come out on deck into the delicious wind, she would feel better.

Nausea did not stop her from nagging Kay about lessons and her sampler and the various ways she ought to be spending her days, and demanding to be shown a page of conjugations. "*Amo, amas, amat...*" Thea said, not in a loving voice, and, "*Amamus, amatis, amant,*" Kay mouthed back, clacking like a ventriloquist's dummy, but she sighed and fetched her books. She was of course eons past the baby verb *to love*; she wondered if that was the only Latin verb Thea recalled.

Another long day slid like water through water, but the next morning was different. Kay dreamed in the early dawn, a quiet dream of a sick woman in a metal bed: white-faced, blue shadows under her eyes, a bald head. The walls were green behind her and the sheets yellow; the colours of the dream were strangely clear. Was it her mother, in heaven? She had a sweet face, not like Kay's. Perhaps if Kay were kinder. Thea said one's face only became beautiful through good deeds and loving thoughts.

The dream did not frighten Kay, but it made her worry about her sister dying, as both their mothers had died, so instead of dressing and running up the ladder to the deck, she went into the saloon.

Thea was in the saloon already, drinking tea, looking very ordinary. Kay must have slept late. The strangeness of the morning puzzled her still, until she realized—it was the stillness that puzzled her. The ship rested at anchor, tossing only lightly in the harbour's swell and seep. They had come to Boston in the night.

After she had eaten and drunk her tea and redone her copybook from yesterday to Thea's cross-grained satisfaction, Kay waited at the rail by the ladder to the boat for Francis and Thea to be finished their farewell. Thea was to have come to the shops to fit Kay out with the necessary clothing but Francis said she should lie down this morning. They were debating it still, Kay could hear through the open skylight—what Francis was to buy, and whether he should bring Thea a poultice or a tisane or something from the pharmacist.

Perhaps Thea would feel better on dry land again? Kay did not *care*, she only wanted to get on with it or begin to shriek like the gulls that wheeled about the ships. Her head hurt, and her throat hurt too. Nobody bothered about *her*, only about Thea. They had only come to Boston harbour because they were forced to keep her with them, only because of her unwelcome presence. If only Thea had not had her half-sister coming along so inconvenient, they would be on the rolling main with the wind set fair for Africa.

Kay's spirit reared a little within her chest, because she was a person, and if they did not see and understand her, she might jump off this ship into the dinghy and row to the wharf and walk the tilting wooden walkways into Boston, looming behind the dark warehouses, and disappear in its alleys never to be seen again by those who did not understand her anyway.

But Francis came up behind her, saying, as if she had not been waiting and waiting, "Now, young Kay, off we go, and smartly—Mr. Best must make the chandler's office before noon."

The dinghy went over the waves in quite a different movement from the ship, plunging and backing as the oars ploughed on, Mr. Best (he gave her a wink with one kind piggy eye) and Jacky Judge at the

oars. The back of Jacky's neck and his arms had a matte smoothness
Kay did not mind looking at, but not when he could see her. She
dipped a hand into the harbour water and let it run along, cupping
the moving wave. Behind them the *Morning Light*, all her sails
stowed, receded into a low shape in the water, a collection of black
sticks against the foggy sky.

The usual commotion of ropes and mooring held them up at the
little wharf, and then Francis went striding down the shaking boards
so that Kay had to run to keep up. Her legs were used to tilting now.
They walked (too quickly, Francis never slacking his pace) up to the
tramline. The tramcar came and plunged them down and then up
into the great walls and crackling, energetic depth of the city.

Francis was not one for talking as they went, and neither was
Kay, so that suited them both. But she was still caught between
fright and fury at being sent off alone with him—whom she hardly
knew and was half-scared of, although she would not say so to
Thea. He was older than Thea, who was nearly thirty now, quite an
old spinster to be new-married, Cousin Olive said, *and how sad that
she wasted her youth raising Kay.*

As the tramcar turned onto Summer Street, Francis pointed to
Filene's, the big store Thea had said they must visit. He ordered
Kay to look sharp and hopped off as the tram lurched to a stop,
turning back to give a hand to Kay.

She scorned to take it—*oof*, the pavement was farther than her
legs had thought. They hustled to the curb through the welter of
traffic and looked up at the brown bulk of the building, great glass
doors glowing with brass and interior golden light. Beautiful doors,
sectioned like an orange in a skin of brass hoops, went round in a
glass drum. It was like skipping rope, to find the right moment to
enter the carousel, and then take tiny, rapid steps inside the moving
wedge of floor, all your feet were allotted. Inside, the light was
startling, rays and beams sparking off myriad edges of glass and
brass. The brilliance sent Kay back a step upon the threshold,
almost back into the revolving swirl.

Francis barked, "Ladies' haberdashery?" at a nearby girl in a dark skirt and a trim blue shirtwaist with a pretty collar that Kay wished she might have. The girl (whose hair was perfectly swept into a Gibson, whose teeth were jagged, whose little boot toes peeped beneath her skirt) pointed to the moving stairs.

Kay held tight to the handrail, one step up from Francis. He had ushered her on in front, as if he was perhaps afraid of the motion himself. Or to catch her, if she panicked at the step-off and fell. But she had been on moving stairs before, in Montreal, on their way from Blade Lake; she knew to lift her foot and hop as the treadle-step approached the end. It was Francis who stumbled a little.

A fearsome woman, shaped like a prow and jacketed up to the throat, took Francis's order from his hand. "*Serge skirts, two; white waists, two; middy blouses, four*—yes, yes . . ." She ran her eye down the list Thea had written and turned to inspect Kay's legs. "Stockings."

"Very well," Francis said, like he said at dinner to excuse Mr. Wright from table. "All that you think fit. We had time for nothing but her boots before we sailed."

Kay stood it. In the close dressing room, people put blouses over her head and measured her waist and her bust, which she did not like. She told them she had no need of camiknickers, but the prow-fronted woman paid no mind and set aside six plain, ugly ones and a number of vests. The middy blouses were fetched and stacked. One of the serge skirts fit; an underling took a seam-ripper to another to let the waistband out, squatting on a stool in the corner. Then she hemmed both skirts quickly, with long, slanting stitches Thea would not have let Kay set.

The last item on the list was *white muslin dresses, two*. The underling rolled in a rack of mixed whites, embroidered or plain, sleeves small and large. The manageress picked out one that had nothing nice about it at all, and one Kay liked, which almost felt comfortable. She did not see why she could not have two just the same, and said so, and the manageress nodded. The dresses went over her head and back again too, and then two plain shifts that needed tucks taken, until she thought she might screech. But she did not let herself, because she had won over the dresses.

At last it was done. While the packages were wrapped in blue paper, Francis stood by the counter, legs wide-braced, jingling coins in his pocket. He reached over to tweak Kay's cheek and said, "Luncheon? Cake? Come, sprogget, we might as well amuse ourselves."

Because Thea was not there, he meant. His humour and his kindness were both too heavy for Kay to help him with.

Down the moving staircase, taking the view of the marble hall below; then they burst out into the street, afternoon sun now lighting the other side of the cobbles. Francis hailed a horse cab and stowed the package behind. He told the man they were starved, and the horse gee'd up. The cab jiggled over the stones, in a quiet way, to the Westminster Hotel, where the rooftop restaurant had gay striped awnings attached to a set of Grecian ladies holding up their spears. First of all, per Francis's orders, petits fours; then a dainty plate of cut sandwiches. Francis had a bowl of chowder—to test the Boston version, he said. He was pleasant company. Kay wished she did not feel a sense of caution. But she remembered how careful they had always to be with Father, who as principal of the Blade Lake School also held a position of authority. And she did not know Francis as Thea did.

"If only your sister was not having so hard a—" He stopped.

Kay took another sandwich: chicken with a spiced yellow dressing, and raisins. Francis did not start again.

"Hard a what?" Kay asked, at the end of her sandwich, which was delicious.

His face had gone stiff. Was he angry with her? "Well, perhaps she will tell you herself, when she thinks it time," he said.

He seemed to think she was seven years old instead of going on thirteen.

There was one last yellow sandwich, and a pity to waste it, so Kay took it. Before she bit, she said, "I have not had a moment's queasiness. I have my mother's strong stomach."

"Thea's mother was more delicately reared."

Thea's mother Maria was, had been, Maria Wetmore. She was Francis's second cousin—all those Yarmouth people were related—so he would not hear a word against her. Kay's own mother, Eliza Warner, was just a country girl from the land north of Battleford. But she died too, when she was about to have another baby. Kay thought about that other little babe sometimes, the dead brother or sister. And of her young mother, whom she could not remember at all. Perhaps it was her sweet face that Kay had dreamed of that morning.

When they had finished, they took the brass elevator back down to the street and the uniformed man gave them the package with Kay's clothes and whistled for another cab. They were bowling along the street when Francis leaned forward and tapped the man.

"Stop a moment," he told him, and the cab pulled up, the horse blowing wetly through his mouth as if disgusted.

They went into a little shop with gold lettering on dark-glassed windows. Francis walked up and down the glass-topped counter, peering into the black velvet depths. At last he pointed, and the clerk took out a pearl pin shaped like a new moon. Plain, but pretty. Kay approved.

"Do not tell Thea," Francis said when they were back in the buggy. "We'll keep it a secret until later." He looked confused and mysterious.

In a cascading shuffle of thinking and discarding—Thea's birthday long past, and Christmas too long ahead, *until later* when?—Kay saw that of course Thea must be going to have a baby, as people almost always did, once they were married. Once vague things had been done to them that did not bear thinking of. While Francis was paying the driver and hailing Mr. Best, Kay turned her head to the salt-smelling sea and blew through her mouth like a horse.

3

Eleuthera

From Boston, round the curve of Cape Cod, they lost sight of land and flew south to the Caribbean Sea, straight down the globe Thea had screwed into the lid of the saloon piano for Kay's lessons. Coal was the *Morning Light*'s usual cargo for Governor's Harbour, Eleuthera. Francis had been loading in Glace Bay while Kay was dreaming at Aunt Lydia's, before she ever knew she would be sailing with them.

On the globe, Eleuthera lay like a long bird with a beak, an outer island of the Bahamas that formed a barrier between the Atlantic Ocean and the Caribbean Sea. It grew closer each time Francis took the morning sights.

He was teaching Thea to use the sextant. After Boston, she perked up enough to come up on deck for most of the morning, to lie in a shaded hammock Francis got the deckhands to set up for her below the fo'c'sle. She smiled and seemed herself again, if a little depleted. She and Kay sketched seabirds and the rigging and from time to time each other, in watercolours and in charcoal, until Kay grew frustrated with her lack of skill and turned to a book instead. None of the books on board were interesting. Francis read nothing but naval histories, and Thea (even worse) only spiritual improvement. Kay's own books, quickly gathered from Aunty Bob's shelves, had lasted the first three days; now she was rereading *Treasure Island*.

Most of all, she looked: at the sea, at the sky, up into the laddered maze of sheets and tackle, up, up to the perspective-vanishing point of the crow's nest, up where Jacky Judge or Arthur Wetmore scampered at Francis's bidding. Kay wished she could climb there, so free, so high. Her arms were pipe cleaners, and as much use. At night she tried to pull herself up on the inside of her cabin door, scrabbling with her bare toes for purchase, fingers aching, but it was no use, she was floor-bound. At least she was not land-bound—bounding as she was, they were, over the main.

಄

Persistent pain on the left side still troubled Thea, and she found certain foods unpleasing; but it was true that she felt a deal better now, out in the sea air and the temperate-flowing breeze. Francis's regard for her, and the hammock, gave her a feeling of safe refuge she had not known under her father's glacial rule. Kay too was more cheerful, less likely to wear that frozen face that was Father's legacy, or to split like him into a rage. And no dreams, all this time. The rocking of the sea must be good for her poor head.

Thea put out a foot to the ledge of the fo'c'sle and set the hammock gently rocking too, the two motions and then a movement within her combining into a kind of ecstatic swirl, so that when Francis appeared to check on her, it was all she could do not to pull him down so their mouths could meet, how sweet his mouth, how cool on her mouth and on every secret part. She clasped his hand instead, and he held hers too long, yet not long enough for her desire. An unexpected fillip of her condition!

಄

On the ocean side of the island the water was dark Atlantic blue, but as they rounded the point to Eleuthera's inward side, where Governor's Harbour lay, the sea changed colour. Blue melted into sheer turquoise, a pale, translucent window to the bottom of the sea. At the railing Kay looked down, down—sixty feet, perhaps? ten fathoms, that was—past iridescent schools of fish, past shadow and shoal, to the sliding gold-green bottom of the sea. It took effort not to leap over the side, the water looked so delicious.

"Miss!" came a shout from above, and there was Jacky Judge, the quick, dark one, pointing down—where silver-grey things came leaping and sidling alongside the ship.

"Dolphins," Francis told her, gesturing Thea to come to the railing too.

A company of blunt-headed grey dolphins swam effortlessly beside them, teasing the ship, easing along the blue way faster, faster, faster than the *Morning Light* could ever go, keeping them company and arching in melodious rounds in and out of the ever-foaming sea, as if they felt the same thrill themselves that they produced in Kay. "Oh, let me—" she cried, leaning over and over to see better, until Francis laughed and Thea caught at her waistband.

Twenty silk-smooth dolphins played along for a league, and then romped off in another direction, doing their tricks, leapfrogging and whirling through the waves like—like— No, they were like nothing except themselves.

Then more surprise, more shouts—a score, thirty, fifty silver birdfish leapt from the water in formation, flying, flying, stretching the flight as long as they could, poor wingless winging things. The small heads daggered out beyond small fins that whirred like toy-mills, like tops. The fish seemed to go forward by sheer wishing it so.

So much effort toward the air—but then Kay thought, do they fly *from*?

She looked down again as they sank, only to rise again in frantic flight, and tried to see. Arthur Wetmore, going by with a rope coil, pointed and she saw—she thought she saw—nothing. A darkness.

"Shark, likely," he said. "Something big."

Then he was off, at a shout from Mr. Wright the first mate (always so quiet in the saloon on the occasions when he came in, but he had the biggest voice on deck), and the crew surged around them, around Thea's hammock even, because Francis had ordered them to reef the mainsail, tie it up so they would not go too fast in the increasing breeze.

Although the pale water seemed so clear, still you could not see what was happening under the surface, only the result of it—the flying fish that leapt, leapt, fiercely forward, arrows out of the water, not exulting in air as Kay had first thought, but driving away from danger. When they fall back, do they fall into the mouths of sharks? You cannot see, even in this glass-coloured Caribbean blue.

Kay stood looking down, down, into the sea and through it. The dolphins came again companionably along, leaping for joy—for joy this time. No shark could threaten them.

From the wharf at Governor's Harbour they went for a walk—Kay's and Thea's legs, amusingly unused to land, were unsteady at first—on the white road through the little town, past a tempting pink-stuccoed library, up over the hill-spine of the narrow island, then down to where Kay could just see a long stretch of pinkish sand. Everything was pink in this little place. But Thea stopped in the roadway and said that was a long-enough walk, they must turn round now.

Kay pulled on her hand to tell her how badly she wished to go on, but Thea closed her eyes and shook her head, her face as closed as her eyes.

So Kay could not argue and they turned away again, back into the shade of overhanging orange flowers. The day was advanced and Francis had the last of the unloading to see to; tomorrow the sugar would load. He told them as they walked just why it was most important to see that the stevedores put two-thirds of the new cargo in the 'tween decks for the best stowage, and embarked on an involved tale of cargo once shifting so that some ship or other "nearly foundered, save that the crew shovelled rock salt uphill for three days to right her!"

Thea nodded, not speaking. Kay thought her own thoughts and wished she could go back to the pink-sand shore.

They had a duty to call on the Anglican rector and his wife; Thea had a letter of introduction from Mr. Archibald at the church in Yarmouth. As Francis carried on around the little harbour back to the *Morning Light*, they stopped at St. Patrick's sign and went through the white lych-gate to a substantial grey church with sea-green doors.

The right-hand door was slightly ajar. Kay pulled on the great iron ring to open it more fully. In the tiled entry they found a woman just getting up from washing the floor, pushing herself erect with beautiful long hands that she lifted in greeting. She did not answer Thea's inquiry directly but called out through a side door in a strong, free-flowing voice, "Susannah! Tell Rector! Lady to see him, two ladies," and then turned back with an open but unsmiling face. "She tell he," she said.

Kay was happy to be thought a lady. Thea stepped forward, though, and Kay's heart cramped a little, knowing that Lady Bountiful would appear next. "Thank you," Thea said, over-precisely. She opened her little purse to find a coin, but the woman was busy wringing her cloth and taking up her pail and did not seem to notice, and indeed Kay could not say herself why she thought Thea's gesture was so rude.

A plump white woman came through the side door saying, "Yes, Rhoda?" and then, to Thea, "Oh, I am Mrs. Judd—you must have come on the *Morning Light*—I'm told Captain Grant has brought a wife with him."

Behind her followed a man, younger than Francis, but not a boy. He had an over-boned face, with a long chin and wide cheekbones on a head that appeared to take up half his body. Seeing Thea, the man bowed and smiled. To Kay he smiled more widely—the split of his mouth widening until she thought his jaw might detach. His eyes almost disappeared in the creases of his face.

"This is Mr. *Brimner*," said Mrs. Judd, saving Thea from the error of thinking he was Canon Judd. It appeared that Canon Judd was occupied, and had asked Mr. Brimner to give them a tour of the church—Mrs. Judd did all the talking, still. "Mr. Brimner is soon to be leaving us, in Mission to the South Seas. You will have to get some pointers from Captain Grant," she told Mr. Brimner. "I hope you will stay to dine with us after Evensong, Mrs. Grant? We will give you a taste of *Bahamian victuals*, if you are willing?"

Thea agreed with proper thanks, and Mrs. Judd said she would leave them to the tour and see to supper.

Mr. Brimner led them through the tiled porch into the nave, where the floor was pale-grey stone and the walls white-grey smooth plaster.

Gathering his thoughts, he began, his wide mouth over-articulating the words. "What do I know to tell you ... Well! This church is not *very* old, 1848, but the parish of Eleuthera and Harbour Island dates from 1768, and the diocese from the 1600s, so you see they feel themselves to be quite Established, no New World upstart. I have been favourably struck by the clergy's scholarship and independence of thought in my short—though they may feel not short enough!—time here, I promise you."

He did not require comment, but led them halfway up the aisle before turning to point above to the organ loft at the rear of the church. "The truly *glorious* pipe organ—I'm told it cost a hundred pounds. I do not believe there can be another so fine in the whole of the islands. The pipes, delightfully painted with flowering vines, as you see, make a tremendous noise to the Lord."

The church windows stood open to the wind. It was peaceful in the shaded interior, open and uncluttered. Stained glass windows, oblong and round, made strange dollops of colour on the pale stone floor.

"Where in the South Seas are you going?" Thea asked.

"I have a missionary post at Tonga, south of Fiji, for a year or two. Chiefly a teaching post," he said. "My arrival in Eleuthera was—a stagecoach stop, as it were. Unforeseen circumstance (well, a sinking!) delayed the ship on which I was to proceed, and I have been here three months now awaiting another. They will grow weary of me soon, and my post will weary with waiting."

Thea was about to speak, but above and behind them the bell began to ring for Evensong. They took their pew as Mr. Brimner directed them and the congregation came flowing in, dotting the other pews with their hats and coats, spots of gorgeousness like stained glass on the grey stone. In the mass of people, only a few colourless blots stood out, grey British ladies with small mouths, and a man or two in corporation clothes.

The organ swelled, indeed making a very loud noise, as Canon Judd processed into the church from the vestry door, spectacles flashing, vestments swaying, lordly in the pomp of a magnificent stomach.

"The nineteenth Sunday in Ordinary Time," he said, and pointed to the hymnal board. "*God who sets us on our journey!*"

Canon Judd was not as good a preacher as Father. He was of the brimstone variety and gave a homily on sin that Kay had no inclination to make head or tail of. Starting with a discursive tour through Nineveh, he roamed on in rolling British accents, and Kay laid her head on the high pew-back and let her mind drift until Thea gave her arm a tender pinch. Then she tilted her chin downward to look attentive, but she still was thinking of other things. Not of the bad things that she sometimes turned to in her mind, of Mary hanging, or Annie lying in the dirt under the wolf willow, but of blunt-headed dolphins racing the ship, easing along the blue way faster, faster, faster than the *Morning Light* could ever go, of silver bird-fish flying, flying— Oh, it was over. Thea was rising for the hymn.

∾

"I suggested to my wife that in the circumstances she might remain at home and rest after the exertions of this last year," Francis said, taking the chair that Canon Judd indicated, across the dining table from Thea and Kay. Thea had not wished to telegraph her condition to Mrs. Judd, but Francis seemed to be an old favourite with her, and Canon Judd too.

"But she wished nothing more than to accompany you, I'm sure," Mrs. Judd said, beaming at the happy pair. "Very proper in a captain's wife." She made her face smooth again and closed her hands together for grace to be said, which Canon Judd did at length in careful Latin. Thea pressed Kay's foot to make her sit more still.

"And was it a great blessing to leave the frozen North?" the Canon asked, to start the conversation again once he had finished reciting and left a suitable pause for reflection after their amens.

Thea felt Kay stiffening beside her, but she smiled for Canon Judd. "Not so far north. You must think we lived in harsh conditions, but the region is subject to melting winds, and snow is only rarely troublesome. We were very comfortable in the principal's quarters—and of course the students much warmer and better fed than they would have been in their teepees." But even saying this, she thought of the Stoney camp downhill from the school when the Elders came to talk while Father lay dying, the wood-smoke warmth of the women's tent, bright-faced babies tucked up together; and those two old women who walked up to the school, plaid blankets wrapped tight under belts, the fur on their beadwork mitts lifting in the wind. She thought of the children shivering in their dormitory cots last winter, even with two blankets. Twice the blankets, because half the beds were empty.

She looked to check: Kay had bent down her head and was stolidly eating, using the fish fork just as she ought.

Thea picked up her own, and said, "We stayed at Blade Lake until Father's replacement could arrive, in March, then another while to acquaint him with the running of the school, and finally we set off—and were delayed by a snowstorm at Calgary for three days."

"How I disliked that telegram," Francis put in.

"Oh, but it was spring from then on, across the country, the train moving through bare fields and into new leaves by Ontario. And then—well, then we were married, as soon as we were able after Kay and I arrived in Yarmouth."

"O happy day!" Francis was performing the courtly lover for the Judds, but also for her. If she had not felt so low, Thea would have blushed.

"You had served seven long years for your bride?" Canon Judd asked.

"Ten, Sir!" Francis smiled across the table. "I ought to have ridden to fetch her, but I'm only a man of action on the sea."

Thea said, "My father needed me, when his wife fell ill—his second wife. Kay was an infant, and I felt a strong duty to go. I was born in the West, at Fort à la Corne, you know, my father's first parish in the diocese of Rupert's Land, and only came home to the East to finish my schooling. I was glad to be of service in the school."

"But to wait, to be kept apart for so long—ten years!"

Careful not to let Mrs. Judd's overblown sympathy make Kay feel like a burden, Thea said, "I missed Francis, of course. But he was away at sea most of that time. I was happy to be back in the landscape I had loved as a child, and to come to know my step-mother and my little sister."

"It must always be a privilege to bring light to the darkness of the Red Man, but I credit Mr. Brimner's choice of climate over your father's," Canon Judd said, returning stubbornly to the weather. "A sojourn in the tropics will do you good, as it will him. If his ship ever *does* put in, eh, Mr. Brimner?"

Taken aback, Mr. Brimner's mobile eyebrows jumped. "Again I am forced to apologize, Sir." He put down his knife and fork to make praying hands, and the tall woman took his plate away and replaced it with another.

She put another plate of fish in front of Thea and offered the sauceboat. Mrs. Judd had very fine china, Thea thought, trying to distract her unruly stomach. Pretty, two birds on a branch. Meissen? One could not turn it over to look.

Mr. Brimner had turned to her. "My destination is a fledgling mission school in Tonga, Mrs. Grant. I must take instruction from you on how the education of native children may best be managed, and what errors to beware. My heart is willing, but my skills untested."

Not knowing what to tell him, Thea said, "I had no skills to speak of, sir—one year of normal school, training to teach obedient boys and girls in Nova Scotia."

"*Quite* a change, going to a wild Indian school!" said Mrs. Judd, warmly approving. "Christian service in action, indeed!"

"They were not *wild*," Thea felt obliged to say, at Kay's quick diamond glance. She tried to smile for Kay, but found her face no longer willing to obey. She rose, and said confusedly to Mrs. Judd, "Is there, may I—?"

"Oh, of course, of course, my dear, I ought to have thought . . . Come with me, right along this passage . . ."

Shut in the water closet, blessedly aware of Mrs. Judd's feet tapping away to the dining hall, Thea leaned her forehead on the wall beside the commode. She felt a sudden sweat start up on her forehead as her interior cramped and twisted, unused to and ungrateful for *Bahamian victuals.*

◌

Thea had been talking a great deal, and was tired perhaps from the long walk. So was Kay tired. These people were stuffy and there was too much to eat and too many different glasses and forks, as if they were out-Empiring the Empire. There was a long course of conch soup and then more fish, and Thea came back from the toilet and Kay thought she might go but could not make up her mind to bother Mrs. Judd.

More fish with lovely smooth slices of orange fruit around it, and after that a powdery potato stew with strange vegetables in it that Kay did not at all like, and then plum duff, brought in with a steaming gravy boat of rum sauce even on this hot day.

But Thea was standing, and then dropping, bowing, hands to her skirt as if to hide something—her face gone white looked up, caught Kay's eyes, jerked on to Francis and on again, still searching—

Mrs. Judd came around the table at a run and caught Thea from behind, putting an arm around her waist, and almost swung her to the door, saying *come come my dear come now* and then they were out of the door and gone.

Canon Judd and Francis and Mr. Brimner looked around the table as if they thought to find some answer there in the empty seats, and Mrs. Judd's voice in the distance calling, "Rhoda! Rhoda, come quick, will you?" rang clearly through the quiet night.

Nobody spoke. The wind had risen and the sound of the waves lapping at the pier was louder now, crash and ripple repeated over and over.

After a minute or maybe ten, Canon Judd sat down at the table again, nodding slowly, his heavy body making his chair squawk along the wooden floor. Mr. Brimner subsided silently into his own chair.

Francis, almost as white as Thea, said, "I should—may I go and find my wife, Sir?"

"I wouldn't," said the Canon.

Kay felt she was invisible now and wondered if anyone would hear if she opened her mouth.

The kitchen door behind her opened a crack and the soft, dark head of a little girl poked through. "Come," she whispered, reaching long fingers to tweak Kay's skirt. "Come, girl."

Mrs. Judd, coming in through the other door, nodded to Kay to go along.

Kay stood up and set her napkin on her plate, careful to make it an elegant fold. "Please excuse me, Sir," she said, but it was as she had thought, nobody moved or answered, or seemed to have heard.

As she went out, Mrs. Judd was saying, "Well, Captain Grant, you will have to brace yourself, my dear."

The girls took Kay to a long white room in another part of the house, where they were finishing their own supper on a deal table:

a bowl of sago pudding. There were three cots at the other end of the room, with mosquito nets over them.

Kay stood in the middle of the floor, not knowing what to do. The littler girl stayed with her, one arm around her now, running the other hand down Kay's long braid.

"Mamma say you are to go to bed here," the second girl said, the older girl. "Your mamma not too good and so she does not go on the ship tonight."

No one else came. Francis did not come, nor Thea. Nobody told her what was happening to Thea. If she was dead, perhaps.

After some time waiting, Kay took off her boots and stockings and her new white dress and lay down where they told her to. The older girl undid the netting and set it over the bed, and after another blank gap of time Kay fell asleep, still not knowing anything at all.

∾

Thea heard her own voice saying, *I know, oh no, I knew, I know.* Perhaps not out loud, she hoped not. Hard pain like a mass of stone slammed into her from behind. Sharp pain breaking over that, again and again, really dreadful pain. She could hardly tell where the pain came from, it was in every place, her back, her legs, her chest, her arms, folding tight around her as she tightened into a fetal curl around herself and her burden, her treasure.

Nothing made sense. Mrs. Judd stood aside from the bed where she had fallen, pulling away the skirt of her Delft-blue dress, wet and dark with blood, and the other woman put a thin hand to her forehead. Dark eyes, no smile in them. Thea felt sense leaving, again and again, but then pain came again and the darkness surged away so she could not be blessedly unknowing, unknown. This was not good, this was not the way.

If only she could faint. More blood, and the woman taking blood away. She waved her hand and asked for a pot to sit on, and made another great evacuation of the bowels—so much humiliation, with this woman she did not know, and Mrs. Judd coming in and out; but she had lost the ability to care about such nonsense as pride or civility, and only rocked in the bed waiting for it to pass, this thing that was happening. More blood, in great gouts—the bed would never be clean again. "Oh my dear," Mrs. Judd said from the doorway. "Rhoda, is she—" and the dark woman said, "More to go, but she progresses."

Nothing was progressing, there was no—hours and hours, nothing but a black blade scraping inside her and the clamping cramp of her body trying to get rid of it. Of the baby, the darling, already gone, she knew it must be. A punishment, she felt most deeply. But it was not, she told herself. *Oh God*—she told herself again that God's justice was not man's, that she was not at fault, or that she was forgiven—and then the cramping took hold again to twist her so she rose up grossly in the bed, panting on all fours and groaning like an animal in pain. Because she was an animal in pain.

At one moment she heard herself say, "Thank God I am not on the ship." The inner mouth of her mind that still could think said, Yes, indeed, you see, that would have been worse. The outer mouth said no no nothing nothing could be worse.

She opened her eyes but could not see. She put out her arms and there was a basin put in them and she vomited.

When she next noticed, she was sitting on the pot again, Rhoda holding her arms, or was it Mary, is she, am I taking Mary down from the doorway? Poor dead weight, poor girl.

No, no—she would lose her mind. This was insupportable. She forced her brain back and got up to walk, going from side to side of the room three or four times, but could not carry on and so she lay back down and turned, coiling in the effort to be still and quiet.

After some hours or some days, the woman came again to peer between Thea's legs, then pushed a hand down *hard* on her stomach so Thea cried out in shock and hurt. Holding her there, the woman slipped long fingers into her, right inside where it was—everything—flaming with blood, and there was a sliding rip and more wet, more blood in a stranger's house, this bed would never be unstained.

The pain diminished at once—a relief of spirit and body to be only hurting, only dragged to pieces, not cut right in two. And there was a little sac, lying in the woman's pearly palm, all reddened now, a red, transparent sac, and inside it a mite, a thumb-sized child, a tragedy of waste.

∽

Wake up, Kay heard. *Wake, wake, wake up, girl*, whispering, then a tweedling humming, *wake up wake up* again, all very soft and almost sleeping in her ear. The air was cool and sweet. She had been dreaming, running along a path after Annie as the dark was coming, and where was Thea? Lost, as the dream was lost on waking too.

It was the little girl Sally and her sister, Susannah. When Kay opened her eyes, they took her hands and pulled her from the bed, smiling and whispering. "Come come come," they said, and Kay pulled her white dress back on over her shift, leaving her stockings where they lay, and went with them. They went in bare feet and so did she, as if it was the old days at Blade Lake. Her feet were soft after a long summer in boots, but she did not mind the round stones or occasional prickles on the path. They went ahead of and behind her, laughing in their yellow dresses now they were outside, and Susannah said her mamma ("my sister," Kay said) was still asleep and would be most like all day so their mamma said to play along the sand instead of getting underfoot.

Susannah must be her own age, Kay calculated from her height and seriousness. Sally was only little, six or so, tagging along with Susannah as Kay and Annie had run along beside Annie's sister Mary whenever they could.

The morning was still pearly-early, only faint sounds from the town below them as they climbed on a long white path through tangled brush and hunkering flower-bushes, ducking or leaping branches as they went. A bleating, bell-dangling goat ran past them once and Sally turned to smack its rump with a stick as it went by.

The path went downhill then, and left, went right, and opened up as if through an archway.

And there was the sea again, the same particular green-white-blue-white glass that begged you to come in.

They did. The girls dropped their sacks and dresses, and ran down the pink slope shrieking. Kay took off her white dress and ran with them just in her shift, her bare feet on the bare sand, glorious.

The girls were in the water. They would drown! But no, of course they would not. They were laughing and jumping, leaping to meet the waves and leaping back, dancing into the shining water and back.

Sally ran up to where they'd left their clothes, and pulled from one sack a big glass jar. She raced back down the sand—oh! do not drop it!—and into the long, calm shallows past the waves where Kay and her sister stood. Susannah took the jar and showed Kay how to use it, waiting until the wave had passed and the surface quieted: she pressed the bottom of the jar gently into the water and bade Kay look.

She bent over and looked through a clear eye dipped down into the sea—look, fish! Transparent small fish, a school of them, flitted through Kay's and Susannah's legs and arms, invisible in the waves until the glass revealed them all. They almost made Kay want to jump back, not to be bitten, but they were small fish, after all. But when a long striped fish swam into her glassy view, Susannah said, "Run!" and they went splashing through the spray, away, away from whatever that bad fish was. The curling surf came racing up the sand so strongly, and pulled back so strongly, that you could only stand sideways and wait for it, almost shivering with the thing that was coming, and would you live?—and then *pound, pound*, the wave pummelling you over into a great unknowing mound, lost in sudden silence and green motion—and then you were set free and could jump up again. And again, again.

They ran along the water's edge till they were tired, then back along the sand, wet shifts clinging and sticking to their legs. Susannah's sack held oranges and plums and bread. They ate, and there was water in another jar to take the taste of salt water out of their mouths. Sally fell asleep with her head in her sister's lap, and the older girls sat drawing pictures in the sand with a stick until they got hot again. Then Susannah woke Sally (bright eyes clear as marbles, the lashes tangled black velvet) and they ran back down into the purling, constant, ravelling-unravelling sea.

The surf was higher now, and they went straight through it to walk in the chest-deep water past its edge, Sally leaping up to ride Susannah's jutting hip. This time the best thing happened. Susannah pointed and pulled Kay's arm to turn her to the south. Not twenty feet from them she saw two long grey shapes slide shining through the shining turquoise surf—two blunt, brainy heads, silk-grey skin, one fin with a notch out: two dolphins, strayed into the little bay. How long were they? Nine feet, ten—and they swam close, so close!—their bulbous foreheads, the sweet long line of mouth and nose. The notched one's face looked up, his eye intense in focus, then away again—her existence did not impinge on his.

Susannah went closer, closer, both sisters sidling nearer and nearer to swim beside the dolphins, wanting to be closer, as Kay did herself. Susannah waved *come on*!

From the ship she had wanted to jump in and swim with them— but now it felt impertinent to think of touching that grey flank without an impossible permission. The dolphins were not like a fish that you might want to eat, but like a big dog coyote looking back at you from a stubble field. His coat the colour of the grass, as the dolphins were deep-sea-coloured.

But this was Sally and Susannah's place. Maybe by living here always and knowing the place, they had the right to touch, to swim along with the dolphins.

No place was her place, it seemed to her for a bleak moment. Everywhere was places she had been taken to, or barged into. Even the *Morning Light*.

Thea lay all day in Mrs. Judd's guest chamber, still bleeding. The world was made of blood. Still more was coming; they said it would go on for another day or so, like the worst of one's womanly time. Solid clots like portions of fresh liver ready for the pan, sliding smoothly out as if it was an ordinary month, no pain to speak of.

Mrs. Judd said one must not repine; God's will, she said. She said she and the Canon had been disappointed time out of mind—four times, that she knew of.

She left Thea alone so she could think again, but Thea did not want to.

Francis came and sat on the end of the remade bed, clean-looking now so he could be spared her pain. He stroked his hand along her leg. "Never mind," he said, "never mind, my dear," and she nodded, to relieve him. But of course they minded.

∽

Nothing was said to Kay, that morning or ever. Rhoda said Thea was still too sick to talk and for they girls not to be *at* her, and continued going to and fro with bowls and basins. She did a great bustle of washing in the hut past the kitchen: a bower of sheets and cloths hung swaying, bleaching in the sun. Kay stayed with Susannah and Sally in the back kitchen, and Francis did not come.

Kay thought, not knowing what to think, that Thea might have had an apoplexy, like their father, but survived; they would say if she was dead, wouldn't they? Not tuberculosis—Kay had seen many people die of that, and it took a long time before they wasted into death. She had not died from the baby, since there was no baby crying or demanding. Kay would have looked after it, if Thea died, as Thea had looked after her when her mother died.

Lying in the little white bed that evening, Kay reasoned it out, from the sadness in the house and the noise and now the silence. The baby itself must have died, as a calf will sometimes die and be pulled dead out of its mother.

On the third day, able to carry herself without showing weakness, Thea went into the empty church in the afternoon. She knelt to pray, but found the usual words sticking in her throat.

After a time Mr. Brimner appeared at the pew's end. He bowed minutely, in his over-formal way. "I fear Canon Judd has ridden out over the island ... But if it would help you to have spiritual counsel, or simply company, I am at your disposal."

Thea moved her stiff mouth to courtesy, and said she was very well, thank you.

He nodded. "This morning I found myself refreshed by the words of a collect in the early baptismal service—the 1549, you know—which I thought might be of use to you. Of course, all still-born children are welcomed into the sight of God, there can be no question otherwise, but still, the language here ..." He waited, as if for permission, and at her silence dipped his head and took a card from his vest pocket. "*Receive them, O Lord, as Thou hast promised by Thy well-beloved Son, saying Ask and you shall have: seek and you shall find ...*"

Mr. Brimner looked up again, as if to be certain she was attending and allowing him to continue. Receiving no stop from her, he did so. "*Saying, Ask and you shall have: seek and you shall find; knock, and it shall be opened unto you. Give now unto us that ask—let us that seek, find. Open Thy gate unto us that knock, that this infant may enjoy the everlasting benediction of Thy heavenly washing, and may come to the eternal kingdom which thou hast promised, by Christ Our Lord, Amen.*"

At "heavenly washing," Thea felt her eyes open and tears flood briefly out. She had a fresh hanky but could not find it in the unfamiliar pockets of the skirt Mrs. Judd had lent her. Mr. Brimner waved a large white one at her nose, and she caught it and turned away for a moment. Only a few tears, quietly shed. Like a deposit on her grief. It was not true release, it was not that she had forgiven God.

Walking down the gravel path beside the church, Kay heard someone weeping. She stood on tiptoe to look in the window, but it was
too high. Instead, she slipped into the vestry porch, silent in bare
feet, shadowy against the white walls in her white dress, no longer
spotless, softened by sun and salt water. Thea was praying and crying,
a hanky pressed to her face. It must be hard to have a baby inside you
and find that the baby died, and perhaps Francis would be angry.

Mr. Brimner looked up and saw her standing there, and he
smiled again at her as he had the first day, face creasing into an
excess of kindness. He waved a hand at her as to a friend, an equal.
She nodded back and went on cat feet, out again.

There she was still, wandering in the graveyard, when he came
out. She saw him casting about for a glimpse of her. He started over
the grass, stepping over graves just as if a person was not rotted
away to white sticks under each one.

"Miss Kay," he said, when near enough.

"Mr. Brimner," she said in turn, since he kept waiting for her to
speak.

"I have been— Well, do you know, Captain Grant was so kind
as to suggest that I might take passage to Tonga on the *Morning
Light*, and I wished to say—I have been accustomed to earn my
keep. Your brother says your schooling has been neglected. He
thought we might study together, as we go, to lessen the burden for
your sister. And perhaps increase your skill in algebra." At her gri-
mace, he said, "Hm! Or we could study the English poets—Spenser,
Donne, Milton? I am myself now engaged on a work of— But no,
I see you are unmoved by poesy. The Latin tongue, then? I could
benefit from polishing my Catullus."

Kay looked at him. Her father's Hebrew Bible, thick and backwards, blackest ink on thinnest paper, lay in the bottom of her
trunk. "Could you teach me Hebrew?"

He smiled again, lesserly, without the creases. "Sadly, I am no
hand at Hebrew. What would you think of Ancient Greek?"

Her heart leapt.

"Cyrus and Xerxes, the three hundred— I believe I saw a *First Greek Book* on Canon Judd's shelves. We might persuade him to part with it . . ."

Kay said, "Would I learn the other letters?"

"The Greek alphabet? Necessarily."

"My father did not have time to teach me yet, and then he died."

"Well then, I believe it is a bargain." Mr. Brimner put out his hand, and Kay took it. His smile as usual broke his head in two, this time the neck jutting out to add emphasis to his pleasure. Kay took her hand back, but she was pleased.

∾

Mrs. Judd gave them a sad fare-thee-well, sobbing into her lace-edged cuff; her tears lent Thea stoic resolve. She was grateful for the care that Mrs. Judd had given and caused to be given her, and thanked her as warmly as she was able to do—not very well.

That morning Rhoda had brought her a small box, six inches long and three across. Inside, on a piece of satin, lay a wrapped clump of matter. Thea did not unwrap it. She pulled the white ribbon from the hem of her trousseau petticoat, from which the stains would never be got out, and tied it round and round, seven or eight times, with a tight knot and a careful bow. Making the bow became the only job she had.

When Francis came, bringing Jacky Judge and Hubbard to carry her bandbox and Mr. Brimner's trunk, she asked him to walk with her down the beach before they went aboard.

They walked as far as Thea could manage, and at the end of the long pink spit, Francis dug a deep hole in the sand, where it would be some time before the beach wore away, and buried the box. No marker. Thea put a stone on the heap of sand and prayed for a moment, and then they left that place.

4

The Atlantic

Mr. Brimner came aboard like a sailor, jumping handily over the lip at the top end of the gangplank, all courteous enthusiasm for such a shipshape vessel. He nodded to Kay but did not linger on deck—perhaps having been long enough at Eleuthera. He only clapped his hands together and went below to oversee the stowage of his trunks. She watched him go down the stairs, thin legs trotting cleverly below his portly body.

Mr. Wright bellowed the order to cast off, long lines ran snaking back, and the ship slid from the wharf on the afternoon tide. Jaunty at the rails, the boys whipped ropes into neat coils and called fare-thee-well to Susannah and Sally, who stood waving from the jetty. Kay waved her own handkerchief, but could not look at them.

Francis settled Thea into a deck chair on the shady port side with a fine white shawl, and she huddled in it as if she was cold, hands bunched together though it was a fine, hot day.

Alone by the rail, Kay stood stiff and silent. This was no choice of hers. She must always do what other people decided; she was a prisoner, in fact. If she could, she would stay with Susannah and live on this island forever, swimming in the sea instead of sailing over it to some terrible place or other. The temporary world of Eleuthera was like heaven set down on the earth.

And very likely there was no other heaven to wait for, it was all a lie; or if there was, Father would be waiting there for her, as if she had been sent to his study for a whipping. But her mother would be in heaven too, half-seen, a soft cheek and a wing of dark hair visible around an ivory pillar. So then Kay might best throw herself over the railing and drown or be eaten by a shark and get on with it. Except she did not think she could make herself die on purpose; she would fight it like the fish flying fiercely out of the maw of a shark.

You cannot see from what they fly, Kay said in her top-mind, the one that pronounced.

In the Pacific, Arthur Wetmore had told her, they would see whales. Their dark, curving tails and their spouting—perhaps that would be a consolation. Francis too had spoken of their vastness. Still in the turquoise-pale Caribbean transparency, the sea that she had swum in herself, Kay looked down into the water and through it. The dolphins coming companionably along were now quite ordinary, although her eyes searched for the particular notched fin of the one who had been with them at the shore.

She did not mention swimming to Thea, who in her duty to Kay's correct upbringing was like Aunt Lydia. In their ladies' prison of propriety, they could not know how good the water was, how holy—how, after hours of tumbling in the sea, you felt washed bright again, a better, nobler person. In the same way that sailing in the ship, this little piece of world broken off from the main, made you feel braver. Like a voyager, an adventurer.

The beauty of the filling sails filled her eyes; they were putting on sail now, white acres lifting and lifting into the giddy air. Not unhappy, Kay gripped the rail as the *Morning Light* swayed on a strong wave of moving sea and caught the wind to sweep round into the darker Atlantic blue, the true deep ocean.

At the wheelhouse, Francis stood absorbed in charts, with Mr. Wright roaring an occasional command to hearten the crew after their three-day rest. Every shout rang in Kay's ears because it must hurt Thea's. Kay did not want to look at her, in case it hurt her to be observed in this condition. Thea's face looked foreign. She could not truly be thinner in only three days, but the pale skin was drawn tight over her forehead and her eyes were blue-shadowed. But it would be worse if Thea had died, and Kay had to sail on alone with Francis forever, whom she hardly knew.

Mr. Brimner trotted up from below, where Hubbard had been settling him in his cabin. He smacked his linen-jacketed chest with both hands and searched a moment in his pockets, then pulled out a pair of dark-glass spectacles and exhibited them to Kay.

"Guard the eyes from strain!" He pulled each rounded crook carefully over his great ear-tops. "My physician's strict orders," he told her solemnly.

A crackpot. She was stuck with him now.

Thea tilted the brim of her straw hat to see him better. "Did you have them specially made?" she asked.

"In Oxford," he answered. "Ground and smoked to my eye's idiosyncrasy. They answer very well. But some things shine strangely through them—" He looked about him as if to prove it. "Rainbows and glories. The sun itself. Some colours—reds, greens—glow with a ferocious beauty that tempts the eye."

Gazing out from his portable darkness, he looked like that villainous kidnapper, blind Mr. Mole of "Thumbelina," in Kay's childhood book of stories. It was strange to have another person now in the world of the ship.

Mr. Brimner took the chair beside Thea, fidgeting for a moment with his glasses case before drawing out a small green book. Then he sat quite still, instantly absorbed; or perhaps only pretending, to be less of a bother.

Setting her own book aside, Thea beckoned to Kay to come beside her chair, and leaned to interrupt his stillness with a frown of apology. "I cannot seem to find the gumption, Mr. Brimner, to get down to serious work while at sea—but my sister's school work—I know Francis spoke to you, and I would be grateful. She is a clever pupil. Although not much interested in grammar or arithmetic, she has a great facility in Latin." Thea smiled at Kay, who moved her own mouth in echo, slanting up very slightly.

Mr. Brimner said sadly, "Great Latin, has she? She'll outstrip me, very like. But Miss Kay and I have determined that our chief work is to be wrestling with the Attic language. We feel, with Scaliger, that not to know Greek is to know nothing."

Thea did not reply, and Kay could not, because she did not yet know Greek.

Smiling anyhow, Mr. Brimner seemed to feel no reserve. "My intention is to do some serious study during the voyage. My Greek is rusty too, much in need of burnishment."

Burnishment was not even a word. Crackpot, oddball.

Thea reached out, hand and wrist thin and white, to touch Kay's black middy cuff. "You will like that, won't you?" Her eyes were puddles of darkness.

So Kay could not stay sullen. She nodded, eyes pricking with tears for no reason, except the reason she could not say: Thea weeping in the church. "Yes, thank you," she muttered, bobbing her head in Mr. Brimner's direction.

"Our father," Thea said to Mr. Brimner—how Kay disliked it when Thea said *Our father*, as if it was the beginning of the prayer— "was a scholar of ancient tongues, you know, and Kay has his keen mind. Greek and Aramaic, of course, and Hebrew too. But he had too little occasion to use his knowledge, his charges needing instruction in ordinary English, you know. It was very difficult to make them relinquish their childhood language, requiring the strictest discipline and watchfulness."

A familiar pinch of hatred cramped Kay's chest. She screwed her eyes tight against Miss Ramsay's stick crashing down on brown fingers.

Mr. Brimner gave a slight cough, like a spinster might. "Last evening I persuaded Canon Judd to relinquish the language of *his* youth." From another pocket he pulled out a book: bright red, holding the mystery of language. Gilt letters read *First Greek Book.*

As Kay took it, Thea put a finger on the embossed cover—it was a lovely book, it made you want to touch it—saying, "Mind you do not let your Latin suffer . . ."

Over the thick pages ran the beautiful code of new letters, dark black squiggles—almost known, almost readable. Greek was a thing Thea had never learned, so *ha-ha,* Kay laughed to herself, though that was childish. If continuing with Latin conjugations paid the toll for learning Greek, very well. Latin took no effort, it was just English tilted to the side. She had a facility.

At the rail, Mr. Brimner said, "See! a school of dolphins gives us escort for the voyage! Plutarch tells us, *To the dolphin alone, beyond all other, nature has granted what the best philosophers seek: friendship for no advantage."*

There, a notched tail—was it? She could not see.

"Perhaps you are a scholar of Plutarch already," Mr. Brimner said. "With your facility."

Was he laughing at her? Working with Mr. Brimner would require facility of a different kind: the determination to be, to remain, herself. *I am inside here, I am, I.*

The open Atlantic behaving tender as a lamb (Francis said when he walked down the deck), Kay and Mr. Brimner worked on deck for the rest of the afternoon, leaning together over the *First Greek Book,* leaving Latin and arithmetic for later. Thea left them to it and went down to the shadowy saloon. In the portside shade of the round-house Kay's eye and hand moved over the familiar/unfamiliar Greek letters to learn the alphabet and understand the breath markings, beautifully gone into another world that was more real than this.

But on the *Morning Light* no world seemed quite real. They travelled the changeless, ever-changing ocean between everywhere there ever was; it seemed so today in this peaceful sea, anyhow.

When Mr. Brimner finally begged for rest and went down to his cabin for tobacco, Kay got up and went to the side, leaning into the railing until it cut her gut in two, till it threatened to halve her. She would go back to the book in a moment, to ἐφήμερα, *ephemera*, which was the dailiness of things and came straight into English as *ephemeral*, like a butterfly that lives only for a day: from ἡμέρα, *hemera*, which meant day, and ἐπί, *epi*, which meant over or close upon; and to ἀγορά, *agora*, the marketplace or the open air.

There was such a thing as *agoraphobia*, a fear of the open air, Mr. Brimner said when they were thinking of derivatives, English words that had been formed from Greek words, but she did not suffer from it herself. Openness was what she liked. He said there was another condition, *claustrophobia*, and he hoped she did not suffer from that either, because it could be horrific. But that was not a pure word—it came from Greek in the *phobia*, the fear part, but the first part was from Latin *claustrum* (a shut-in place), from *claud* (I shut, close; I imprison, confine). A coffin, a confining. That she did not like.

The bell rang for dinner before Mr. Brimner came up, so Kay ran down. In the saloon, Hubbard had pulled the table leg out and added the extra leaf that they would have to use all the way to Fiji now, to accommodate Mr. Brimner. Lena was laying the silver and setting jars of relish and mustard on the white linen cloth—and a platter of beef, very rare, as Francis liked it. Kay thought the blood oozing from the meat might make Thea feel sick, but she got up from the daybed to sit at the foot of the table. A knot still stitched in her forehead, yet she smiled at Mr. Wright and Mr. Brimner as she arranged her skirt.

Mr. Brimner said grace, gabbling slightly as one who is often called upon. "*Benedic, Domine, nos et haec dona tua, quae de largitate tua sumus sumpturi, per Christum Dominum nostrum.*" He paused, flicked his great eyes up at the company around the table and repeated in English, "*Bless us, O Lord, and these thy gifts, which we receive by Thy gracious bounty, through Christ Our Lord, Amen.*"

Francis nodded and Thea unclasped her hands. After a gargantuan slice of beef to tame his first appetite, Francis looked down the table, the benevolent captain. "You are fortunate, Mr. Brimner, you are fortunate! Normally we'd be no use to you, bound as we are to Hong Kong, because we'd nip up into the China Sea and then on eastward through the Banda Sea—but this trip we have a cargo of case oil for Auckland and Fiji, so we'll tack south along Australia and come round New Zealand slow and safe."

"Oh!" Mr. Brimner was surprised. "I rather thought we would swing west around the Horn—is that not the shortest route?"

Mr. Wright and Francis laughed, and Francis said, "No, no, we don't do the Horn the wrong way round! That is never lightly undertaken, and I'd be reluctant to put Thea through it. Prevailing winds and currents run west-to-easterly, you know—and the Horn is scarifying enough in that direction!"

On the globe, Thea had shown Kay how the *Morning Light* would speed eastways round the bottom of the world—her narrow, blunt-tipped, needle-bitten finger resting lightly on the downward slope, sliding around the tip of Africa as she made the earth spin with her left hand. On a flat map it was harder to see the sense of the route.

Mr. Brimner made noises of comprehension and horror that Kay thought were put on, but Francis reassured him: "Oh, the *Morning Light*'s a tea wagon, slow as a barge, but from time to time she can put on some speed, I promise you."

"I suppose there is some commercial reason not to use the Canal?"

"No Suez for sail," said Mr. Wright. "That's what's let us in for all this h'mmed steamer traffic. We still struggle around the Horn— or on the outward leg, round the Cape of Good Hope." He bent to his beef again.

Francis nodded. "September is an even-tempered month around the Cape. We'll saunter along in the friendly forties over to New Zealand, and give my dear wife an easy voyage for her first time out. And Kay!" Francis added, as if he had clean forgotten her until his eye caught hers.

"We ought to have stayed at home," said his dear wife. "Kay and I both."

Francis looked down the table, silenced.

"But every wish beckoned me on board," Thea added, to show she had not meant to complain.

Kay felt her cheeks getting hot and put up her palms to cool them, not exactly liking Thea to be sentimental.

"If you'd stayed at home, you'd have had to join the Crypto-sporidian Club," Francis said, to lighten the air.

At Mr. Brimner's uprising eyebrow, Thea smiled, and leaned to push the mustard within his reach. "The *Krito-sophian* Club," she said. "It is a signal honour to be asked, and I won't be, till I prove myself a suitable candidate! I am told the name is based on a Greek word meaning *council of the wise.*"

"Well, *de*based, perhaps!" Mr. Brimner dobbed a large spoon of mustard next to a little pyramid of salt he had spilled on his plate from the cellar. Kay watched him dip a piece of beef first in the mustard and then in the salt, until it looked like an iced petit four. "Is the club intended for intellectual improvement?" he asked.

That made Thea laugh a little. "I believe they are quite force-fully improved by Mrs. Adah Murray, who oversees the reading programme."

Francis smiled down the longer table with the unexpected sweetness he from time to time displayed. "Your own intellect could hardly be improved upon, my dear!"

Kay did not mind when it went that way, when Francis was soft to Thea.

While Thea and Francis and Mr. Brimner drank their tea after dinner, Mr. Wright went to relieve Mr. Best at the wheel, and Kay ran up behind him to fetch the books she'd left on deck. An orange line above the indigo of the western sea marked where the sun had gone. Soon it would be dark night, although still so balmy and warm.

But the books—had they been swept overboard? She had felt no heavy swell. Not on the table, nor the deck . . . Kay looked about her in the gathering twilight, almost despairing.

Old Seaton the carpenter leaned over the edge of the lifeboat above the roundhouse, one bare, ink-drawn leg and foot pointing with a great grey-callused toe to a deck box, and there she found books and papers stowed safe away. In a rough whisper Seaton warned her that she "orter take more care," so she supposed it had been he who stowed them.

She looked up to the brown fingers clawed over the boat's rim and said, "Thank you very much."

He beetled his brows at her in mock annoyance, spat tobacco juice in a long arc to the sea and lay back down into his sanctuary.

∾

In part payment of his passage, and as his bounden duty, Mr. Brimner held Morning Prayer on deck on Sunday, inviting any of the crew who might like to attend. A surprising number did haul up from their bunks, to stand or kneel on scrubbed planks as the service prompted. Francis ran a Christian ship, Thea thought, watching the men. They followed the readings well, though on this Fifteenth Sunday after Pentecost, the Epistle was a complicated piece of Revelation.

She and Kay were left in a pew circle of their own, and Kay (never a natural religious) seemed to receive the lessons in good part. Mr. Brimner's green stole for Ordinary Time was delicately embroidered with birds. Someone at home must love him.

He had very thin legs, thin right up to his waist, it seemed. Fixed on those sticks, his body was round-set like a bug's. His deep, mellifluous voice was so pleasant that Thea sometimes found it easier to close her eyes while listening to him, not to see his guileless, guiltless, pug-dog look. His voice was more intelligent than his face. The slight bulge of his eyes and the portliness of his carriage made him somewhat ridiculous. But he was a serious person, and she was coming to appreciate him. The reading was from Job II:

> *For then shalt thou lift up thy face without spot;*
> *yea, thou shalt be steadfast, and shalt not fear:*
> *Because thou shalt forget thy misery,*
> *and remember it as waters that pass away:*

But she did not forget her misery. Since her father's death, she had receded from God. The effort of handing on the school, and the long journey home to the reasonable, long-awaited, yearned-for but still unsettling fact of her marriage: all this had kept her from thinking why she was not praying. She said her prayers, of course, but they were rote. Comfort, or poetry. Until the pains took her; then she had done nothing but pray, and prayer had done no good. If she could consult him now, Father would no doubt say the outcome had been a calling home, that the child had been spared travail, God's mysterious ways.

This is why I do not pray, Thea told herself sharply. As the crew dispersed to their work, she sent her body on weak, betraying legs to climb down the companionway and put the saloon in better order, and to water the geraniums in the skylight. To do what she could.

∽

Days passed with no difference between them but the way the dimpled morning sea ironed out to a steadier pattern of uncombed waves by afternoon, and the sun swam up and down, sharper or less sharp in focus. Days and days passed, almost unregarded, dots in the seven weeks the crossing would take.

This life was not so different from their old life. Early in the morning, once Francis had gone up on deck, Kay could still creep along to Thea's cabin and climb into bed with her, could still have another half-sleep cuddled beside her or watch through half-opened eyes as Thea began the ritual of dressing. Kay loved to watch her strong, thin fingers, quick and deft at buttoning, her sweet back bending and rising for stockings and petticoat-ties, exchanging nightdress for day, skin powdery pale in the filtering, shifting light from the port, the brief underarm hollow as her arms raised to lift her dress over her head. She was easy in movement, elegant by nature, and Kay loved her very much, more than anything.

As they went farther and farther south, early mornings were so good that Kay woke earlier and earlier, kneeling up on her bunk to peer out the tiny port window and see what the sea was doing in the dawn: melted silver, molten lead, shifting mercury, then warming and transfiguring into deepest green.

Those mornings she would not disturb Thea at all, but pull on skirt and middy and sagging stockings (Thea had decreed she must *never again* go up on deck unless fully dressed) and climb quietly up into the soft, shining air, markedly warmer as they sailed on into the south.

Some mornings she emerged into a forest of empty masts, bare sticks like the sticks of teepees before the skins are draped over. Some days the rigging was already full of white sails billowing and bellowing, and the invigorating race of wind. It still made little sense to her why the sails were up or down, or what the cries and answers meant, but she liked to watch the long line of men straining to sweat the ropes, raising the sails as the wind fought to fill them, snapping in the shrouds.

Each morning she was greeted by the sailors, the ones she knew well: Mr. Wright the first mate, monstrous Mr. Best the second mate, shy, red-headed Mr. Quick the third, and Mr. Cocker the bosun, expert in marlinspike seamanship, the art of rope tying and coiling. The ship's boys, Arthur Wetmore and of course Jacky Judge and George Bayard, were always on the run and only threw a *hallo there!* back over their shoulders before racing down the deck or leaping for the shrouds to nip up aloft on some urgent, mysterious purpose.

It was warm enough to eat their breakfast on deck, so Francis could sit with them and still attend to matters; Kay saw that he had arranged it that way so Thea would have reason to come out into the sea air. Francis believed every ailment, physical or otherwise, could be cured by exposure to sea air, and perhaps that was so. After they had eaten their porridge and kippers, or a boiled egg with toast soldiers, if the hens were laying, Mr. Brimner and Kay would read Greek for a while beside Thea's hammock, only going down to the saloon when the heat of the day overtook them.

Mr. Brimner had two Greek books with him: the *First Greek Book* from Canon Judd's shelves and *The Frogs*, by Aristophanes, which was a play. While Kay wrestled with translations of Xerxes and wrote declensions of verbs and derivation lists, Mr. Brimner read *The Frogs*. "To improve my idiom," he said. From time to time he laughed aloud, which made Kay want to read that book instead of hers. She had been taught by Father that it was unforgivable to ask a reader what had made him laugh—at least, she had been taught that by Thea, in Father's service. Father rarely answered a question put directly to him, but relied on Thea to answer, to translate his silence to his younger daughter. He considered answering a question to be a form of capitulation. His dead-blank eyes would slide off her face and course around the room, coldly suffering, until Thea told her to hush and not disturb his sacred train of thought.

"πομφολυγοπάφλασμα, *pompholugo-paphlasma*," Mr. Brimner said beside her, derailing Kay's own huffing train.

He lifted his round head to the wind and recited in rolling syllables the rest of the verse, building to that long, bubbling word again: " . . . πομφολυγοπάφλασμα . . . the sound of bubbles rising from the sea."

He pointed his pipe hand out over the rail, where there were indeed bubbles rising and rising. Some sea creature not yet visible beneath the surface. The ship went cantering on over gentle waves with a breezy, careless air. Kay left her page unturned to stare down into deep green, remembering turning in the turquoise

Caribbean water's effortless lifting buoyancy, how under the water she had opened her mouth to shout and heard in the deafness below the wave that bubbling release of air.

Mr. Brimner, perhaps because it was Sunday, opened his own mouth now and called forth to the waves the singsong verses from Job he had read in the service earlier:

> *Canst thou by searching find out God?*
> *Canst thou find out the Almighty unto perfection?*
> *It is as high as heaven; what canst thou do?*
> *deeper than hell; what canst thou know?*
> *The measure thereof is longer than the earth,*
> *and broader than the sea.*

It could not all be Greek and Latin. Sometimes, when Mr. Brimner did not want to work, Kay ran out of knowledge and had to stop. Then she would gently vanish so that Thea did not notice her idleness and bring out the loathsome sampler.

Although she loved the galley, with its clever cabinetry and nooks and hooks, Kay could not like Dent, the ship's cook, a thin man who had once been fat and still lived in his old, sagging suit of skin. There was something wrong about him; he did not smell good. But he was welcoming, even anxious for her visits, seeming to want her youthfulness in some medicinal way. And he always gave recompense in jam or candy, or at least a sponge rusk.

"I scraped the bottom of the barrel," he confided once, so dolefully that she felt even more obliged to listen. "Born to a good life in Upper Pubnico, and look what's come of me." Not much, it looked like, but he had a cozy curtained berth here in the galley, and a closed stove (kept lit in all but the worst weather) to keep him warm as toast all day long.

Dent carved in bone—the art called scrimshaw. In the empty galley one long afternoon, quiet at that hour save for random screeches from the poor moulting canaries he kept in a wire cage, he showed Kay his trove. He had built a shelf on which to array his bits and bobs, each bone thing penned in by a tiny wooden bar. Kay shuddered inside as she stared up at them. The biggest was a whale's tooth carved with a clipper ship in full sail, an infinity of black lines composing the picture; the smallest was a tiny box that opened, with a red bead for a handle. She did not like scrimshaw. The carving was rough, not at all expert.

But she felt sorry for him, so she gave some effort to praising it, enough that he found a button to bestow on her. A crooked yellow bird hooked one tiny-clawed foot to the cage wire to watch as he rummaged.

"Here ye go," Dent said, putting the three teeth remaining in his head on display. His hand sought after hers, pawing almost, so it took a good deal of effort to hold out her hand and let him deposit the button there. His lips were wet and his wet eyes almost lost within grey folds of skin and grey wisps of hair on his brow.

She would sew it onto her hair bag, she promised him. The bone button was carved in slices, like an opened orange or a flower. It was cool in her hand, but she imagined it kept a trace of the cook's rheumy substance, and she could not wait to put it down.

In her cabin, she set the button in the washbasin and poured water from the jug until it was submerged. The refraction of the water (at first bubbling and disturbed from pouring, then gently shifting as the ship shifted) made the button loom and recede, its darkness enlarging. She scrubbed at it with her fingertips and water fell from it as she pulled it out again and dried it quickly on the linen towel. Milky bone with darker channels, polished and gleaming. Two dots of darkness to sew it on with. Very well, darkness was hardly foreign.

She found her chatelaine and took up the hair bag, and set to work.

༄

Francis had promised Thea that she could sight Saint Peter and Saint Paul's Rocks: tiny islands, dead mid-Atlantic, sixty miles north of the Equator, used by ships to check their bearings. Francis said (Thea found herself repeating *Francis said* too often, and laughed at herself for that feminine inanity) that Charles Darwin had stopped there in the *Beagle* and listed all the fauna he could find—a booby and a noddy or two, a large crab that stole fish intended for the booby's babies; those might all count as visitors. For permanent residents, only beetles and a number of spiders, which he believed must be scavengers of the waterfowl. Not one plant had he found on the rocks, not even a lichen.

By this time Thea had grown expert in helping with the sights, and she took her task seriously. When the ship's chronometer (most carefully guarded in its sheep's wool bed on the saloon mantel) registered noon, she would call Greenwich time out the skylight while Francis, above, measured the angle of the sun with his sextant. A complicated equation then revealed the latitude, and Francis would estimate the local time.

She enjoyed feeling useful in this daily task and fairly sang as she took the time, and Francis made a great show of relying on her. Once in a while he switched places to let her use the sextant instead, telling her she had a dead eye for it. She loved his partiality.

The rocks appeared soon after breakfast, a dabbling of grey along the horizon, and as the wind was negligible, the ship hove to for a kind of holiday. They tacked closer to the islands so that Thea could see and say she'd been there. Francis let her use his good spyglass, and called Kay to come and look too. In the round eye of the glass, Thea still saw nothing— Oh, there. Yes, rocks. An uncomfortable clutter to stub a ship into in the dark, the way the Portuguese had first discovered them.

The islands were not volcanic, Francis said, but a lifting of the seabed. The tip of a very tall mountain down below. How strange that in the middle of the waste of ocean this set of stones had been raised up, granted by God for the pure purpose of giving aid to navigators.

To cap the holiday they had a visitor: Captain Davison from Windsor, Nova Scotia. Rounding the southern rock, they spoke a schooner, the *Moskwa*, and since the wind was very light, Francis put the boat out to bring the captain back to midday dinner. He toured the ship and said all the right things about Thea's arrangements. His own chickens were a failure, he told her. "Two dozen, and they have never laid an egg!" Thea had Hubbard crate up one of their older birds to send back to the *Moskwa*, in case a maternal presence might persuade the others to lay, and told the captain to enjoy some stewed chicken if that did not avail. She sent back with him also a sack of potatoes, for which he was pitifully grateful, in exchange for the books and newspapers he had brought over in case they'd worked through their reading material by now. Kay and Mr. Brimner pounced on those.

∾

The Windsor captain had a monkey for a pet, which went with him everywhere. The monkey sat behind him at dinner, on the back of his chair, reaching for food with childlike fingers, observing the conversation with watchful eyes. A consciousness in the room. A soul.

Mr. Brimner petted the little creature, who put its head on one side and listened intently as he spoke to it in Sanskrit; but Kay shivered and drew back when the monkey touched her hair with its pale-skinned hand.

Later she asked Thea what the monkey would think of being at sea, and was it not unkind to keep him? Because what right, what right, had the captain to hare that little person with him around the world?

Francis laughed, and said it was a very lucky monkey, living the life of Riley, well looked-after and fed by hand by that doting fellow. "And what would you do?" he asked Kay. "Let him go into the wilderness and be eaten, after he's been tamed?"

But even when Thea reassured her that the monkey did not have human ideas of home or family, Kay was not comforted.

5

The Doldrums

The crossing of the Equator next day was marked by hijinks down below. Arthur Wetmore and George Bayard were first-timers, prey to the initiation rites practised by sailors for those crossing the Line. Mr. Wright begged a place at the saloon table in the morning to write out his secret certificates, and later came through again to bow to them attired as King Neptune in a long rope wig and beard and salt-stained velvet robes. Mr. Wright was Neptune for he had crossed the Line full forty times, twice what Francis had himself. Neptune invited Kay and Thea and Mr. Brimner up on deck for the baptismal rite, which involved sprinkling them with a ladle of sea water from a bucket brought up by Jacky Judge, who grinned and gave Kay a squinty wink, and ducked his head when Thea asked how he could do it—how he could betray them so to King Neptune. Francis gave the required alms, which went into the tin for the crew's jollification, and they were released.

Francis himself took no part in the ritual. He never did, not liking much in the way of physical jests, but he went down below to watch the crew's performance that evening (which he said Thea and Kay were not to think of attending), to keep some semblance of order around the edges. "It will be jolly enough for a tar, but very bad for a lady," he said as he left them. Mr. Brimner was not invited either; he said sadly that his cloth often excluded him from revelry.

The noise continued long into the night, with a deal of shouting and at one point even running feet overhead, until Kay was quite worried for poor Arthur Wetmore, who was only fifteen after all. But nobody was thrown into the drink that she could hear, and eventually she slid down from her porthole watch and fell asleep.

∾

Dent the cook fell ill and died—all his scrimshaw left behind. Kay fingered the button on her hair bag. She might take it off now, but that seemed cold-hearted, so she endured it. The cook's ill-fitted body was sewn into a canvas bag made of torn sail and sent overboard after a brief funeral service, which Francis conducted, because he was the captain and it was his duty, although he did ask Mr. Brimner to say a prayer toward the end. Kay shut her eyes as the bag slipped loose of the ship. She waited for the splash, which when it came seemed not very much for a person. Because they were sailing so very slowly, she watched the canvas bag still bobbing on the waves for quite some time before it sank.

After the first dinner cooked by the Hubbards, Thea went down to the galley and put on an apron, saying Hubbard might continue to cook for the crew but she would see to the Aft meals herself, with Lena to help as necessary. Kay followed, to be of some use. The familiar work of lunch making and cake baking sparked useful energy in Thea, so that she was herself again, hair curling against her temples in the close heat and rush. It was laundry day, too; Lena Hubbard did the crew's sheets in the big boiler in the galley, grumbling and shouting for her husband to help as she wrestled them in and out.

Thea washed their own clothes and the good linens herself. Kay helped, wringing and pulling and taking pillowcases up on deck to flap with a snap into the hot, still air. They strung them on a line run from the wheelhouse to the roundhouse, and then sat for a rest inside the double line of sheets that formed a radiant white hall inside the deck. Thea sent down for another bucket from the boiler and washed Kay's hair and her own. In the wind and sun they walked the white alley, combing their hair and singing as they used to do in happy times when Kay was only a child. Francis poked his head through the white walls and said, "Hello, mermaids!" when he saw their combs, but Thea sent him packing until their hair was dry and shining in the sun. Then she set a black velvet band about Kay's forehead and went down to the galley, because supper needed tending and she could not trust Lena not to burn the fowl.

Mr. Brimner was sound asleep in a deck chair on the sunny starboard side. He'd set his straw hat over his face to shield it, but a triangle of pink skin at his throat was coming to red grief. Kay woke him with a light tap on his arm, and when his hat fell askew and one globular eye stared up, she tapped her own throat to show him where the burn was.

"Thank you!" he said. "I am a martyr to the sun, dear Kay. Four months in Eleuthera to harden, yet I am still boiled beef. However shall I function in the South Seas?"

And indeed Kay wondered.

༄

On an afternoon when it was perfectly calm, no wind at all, Thea sat reading in the stern of the ship. Hearing some small sound, she looked out at the sea, and to her surprise saw Francis rowing about, having a fine time all by himself. They had put the boat over so quietly that Thea had not heard the least noise of it. She hallooed, and ugly, kindly Mr. Best ran to put the ladder over for her to climb down and join Francis, who rowed with a will and soon had them far out over the glassy sea.

Looking back, Thea saw Kay wave from the deck. After that, she looked back at the *Morning Light* frequently, just to be certain it had not sailed off without them. Away from the ship there was nothing.

Nothing at all. No wind to carry the ordinary noise of the ship. Out on the water, in a small boat, ears perked by instinct, what one heard was nothing. So still, one might think one were dead.

The sun was warm, but Thea's bonnet kept her head and face shaded. Francis sent his line whizzing out over the mirror-flat sea to bounce, bounce, touch and dip. He caught three fish that Thea did not know, and promised they would make a fine supper. One was very nasty-looking. They lay in the boards flopping until Francis clunched them on the head with his—that thing, his—marlinspike, was it? She would not ask. She ought to know by now.

While they were out there, a whale blew, not a hundred feet away. If it were to come under this little boat, it would capsize them like a leaf on a pond. Thea told herself that she enjoyed the row very much, but it was not like rowing in the ponds where trees are on all sides. In any direction, look as hard as her eyes would try, the ship was the only thing to see. And the whale.

Two weeks after the Equator, when they still lay in doldrums, angling to catch enough wind to make way, Francis discovered that he had miscalculated their route. He had taken the streams too low in latitude, and they were going to lose time—perhaps as much as two weeks.

He was angry with himself, so angry that Thea retreated from him a little. Even in those limited quarters it was easy to distance oneself from the captain of the ship, since there was always another call on his attention. She had only to employ her natural reserve. On deck she shifted her chair slightly so his glance did not meet her eye, to prevent him striding down to fume again about his error. Her distaste for this extravagant self-reproach was most likely because she did not yet understand how much an untimely delivery would cost them.

She did not want Kay to notice the slight dissent or distance between herself and Francis, and kept it from her by the occasional use of—not outright lying, but prevarication. Francis was kept very busy; and Kay was immersed in Greek with Mr. Brimner, learning as quickly as she might.

Still, the error set them all on edge.

∾

Seaton, whom Kay had rarely seen out of his lifeboat, came to the saloon to show them his model ship, which he had worked on for many years, he said. It was a large model of the *John Stuart* out of New York in 1881, which Seaton had sailed on in his youth and remembered "every splinter of," he said.

To Kay it was a miniature version of the *Morning Light*, but she had the good sense not to say so, knowing that Seaton would be shocked that she could not tell the difference. Perhaps sensing it, he used one long brown talon to point to and name each of the sails: "Above the topsail, the skysail, the flying kites; above the sky-sail she carries a main moon sail, and above that, consecutively, a cloud-cleaner, a stargazer, a sky-scraper and an angel's footstool."

Mr. Brimner's fancy was caught by that. "Angel's footstool!" he repeated.

"That latter sheet, however, being set only in dead calms, when the watch on deck were not allowed to cough or sneeze, for fear of carrying it away."

With that, Seaton carried away his precious model to some below-decks place of safety. His legs were like twisted oak posts, muscle overlying bone, overlaid in turn by a thin skin of ink.

He was the strangest mixture of a person Kay had ever met—hardly human at times, scurrying below decks or vanishing around the side of the wheelhouse, bare shanks covered with ungodly ink-drawings that shimmered and moved over the extraordinary clench of his calves. Mr. Wright told them that Seaton once batted for Australia, and Francis said he believed it.

One calf was mangled by an old wound, and his tattoos were barbaric, but Kay felt perfectly at home with him, perhaps partly because Thea did not. His accent and speech wandered from clear English to mumbling incoherence in many other tongues. He had at times a surprisingly educated turn of speech, was athletic, reserved, even courteous; then in an instant, a fit of boastful grandiosity would hit and he would loudly declaim his superiority to all there present, until Francis snapped, "Seaton!" and he stopped.

∽

At dinner, when Kay asked about the sails, why the *Morning Light* did not wear moon sails and stargazers and cloud-cleaners, Francis replied shortly, as if insulted: "We do not need the speed. A case oil cargo does not go bad, and excessive risk is not in my nature."

Thea looked at him: her passionate correspondent of the last decade, whose letters had sustained her through terrible loneliness and pain. Who became, from time to time, this short-tempered, scowling man. She held in her heart the truth of his inner nature. Thought of his mouth, beautiful lips rosy from lovemaking, now invisible in the firm lines of his face. Both things were true.

He tucked his chin in, to soften his shortness. "Case oil is not my preferred cargo, but it will do. I will be easier in my mind once we are unloaded in Auckland."

Then he told Mr. Brimner the horrifying story of a ship's fire he'd witnessed as a lad, the captain's wife tossing her babies over the ocean to the boat—dear God!—and then jumping herself—and the loss of the ship. All survived, Francis promised, glancing at her.

In fact, there were so many ways to die, Thea thought it might be a relief never to have a child of her own. She'd worried for so long about children dying, sickening and then gone. And poor Mary, dangling limp from the transom window-latch, unable to carry on even for her sister's sake—how is one supposed to think about that?

∽

Then for four days there was no wind at all. Simply nothing.

The *Morning Light* sat dead in the water, gently-very-gently rising and falling only on the ocean's sleeping breath, and the life of the ship carried on at a suspended pace. Nothing happened. Nothing. The watch changed. Nothing happened.

The boards of the deck glowed soft and white with holystone scrubbing, from Mr. Best finding work for the boys to do, and Mr. Cocker the bosun put them through their paces with the ropes until their hands blistered.

Kay's own skin peeled in the constant sun, onion-paper sheets curling off her forearms as she sat at the table Francis had caused to be set up again on deck, puzzling out a sentence of Pindar.

Thea looked over her shoulder: τὶ δὲ τίς; τὶ δ'οὐ τίς; σκιᾶς ὄναρ ἄνθρωπος. She put a finger on the place, and Kay sounded it out for her: "*Ti deh tis; ti d' ou tis; skias onar anthropos.*"

"Yes indeed, a dream of a shadow . . ." Mr. Brimner's head did not turn to them as he spoke; he continued to stare out over the unmoving sea.

"You might as well have waited for your own ship," Francis flung back as he stalked on in the obsessive rounds the doldrums induced in him. "We will never get to the Pacific at this rate."

"*What is a person? What is not a person? Man is a dream of a shadow,*" Mr. Brimner said, bending to check Kay's exercise book.

6

The Boston Seaman

The weather blew up finally as they neared the coast of Africa, later than Francis had wished because of the wind, and his error. He'd stopped bemoaning that—to Kay's relief, because she saw that it was making Thea impatient. It was the same when Father fell into the megrims: for a time Thea would sympathize kindly, as if there was an allotted time for self-pity; then she withdrew in disapproval. Francis seemed to pay no more mind to this withdrawal than Father ever had, yet he did stop. Perhaps the relation of a husband and wife was different from a father and daughter; or perhaps he was too busy to mope.

With the wind came driving rain—three days and nights, and no abating. The saloon, so spacious, now seemed cramped, but there was nowhere else to go save one's bunk. As they caught their books from sliding off the table once again, Mr. Brimner quoted Homer in rolling accents: "πολυφλοίσβοιο θάλασσης—*polyphloisboio thalasses*, the loud-roaring sea . . ."

"Ah, well, we have had easy weather until now, my love!" Francis told Thea. He was in good fettle, clapping his hands together as if this was the sort of thing he lived for. Up he went to bellow on deck, he and Mr. Wright vying for volume, louder than the roaring of the waves.

Rain increased, clouds scudding over racing seas until Francis had to shed sail, and they all felt the sudden slackening. After a sullen night the storm broke properly, such heavy going through the troughs and valleys of the waves that they were forced to spend most of that day in their bunks being relentlessly rolled and slammed, until toward evening the wind slackened. Thea and Kay and Mr. Brimner remained pinned down in the weather-buckled saloon, but at least set free of their cabin-prisons.

This general discomfort was complicated by quarrels below decks: one of the crew, a sailor from Boston, had taken grave offence at something a Yarmouth man said and was causing difficulties, turning resentful and quarrelsome to every other man aboard, even to Francis. The man had to be disciplined, and Francis went up after dinner, thunder-browed and curt, to give the order to Mr. Wright.

Kay had a nauseating memory of Father and Mr. Maitland thrashing it out between them which child must be beaten and why—of sitting beneath the dining table watching their black-clothed legs pace about, deciding.

She knew better than to mention this to Thea, but in the over-heated saloon, in the strain of the weather, it became burdensome to carry the memory alone, not to be able to discard it by speaking of it.

What Kay was not allowed to talk about, or what could only be talked about in a certain way: the children who had died last winter, and the ones who'd died the time before that. She was not allowed to think or talk about it, Thea had said she must not. Kay did not see how Thea could have stopped the sickness; but if there had not been a school at all, if the children had been with their own families, maybe they would not have become sick, maybe they would not be dead. But—Thea had told her this many times—maybe the children would have starved to death the winter before, without the school to feed them.

On the train travelling to Nova Scotia last spring, when Kay had dreamed again about rows of empty beds and woke up weeping, Thea said they would never speak of it again, that they were leaving all that behind. Her eyes shone with angry tears. "Do not forget, they invited us to Blade Lake," she said, looking out the window into the dark landscape running by. "They wanted the school, it suited them for their children to be fed and given an education."

That bitter statement had sounded to Kay like Miss Ramsay talking rather than Thea; and it was not at all what she had seen herself. She did not know who *they* might be—the children's parents? But Annie's mother had not wanted her to go to school.

"The school was doing such good work," Thea told the dark window. "It was only a bad year. First tuberculosis, and Father's illness, and then the flu . . ."

Lying in her cabin in the *Morning Light*, staring at the wooden roof above her head, Kay thought it was not the procession of ailments that had caused all the trouble. It was Mr. Maitland. And Father, yes. A blight of English people bringing bad things west with them. Miss Grace Ramsay, also from England, with an elevated opinion of herself. She knew even better than Father; *her* father had been master at Saltcoats, a very superior prep school, as she was always telling them.

Kay's principal worry, although there was some competition among her various fears, had been that Father might marry Miss Ramsay, and she would have a stepmother. Thea had had one, but Thea loved Kay's mother; Kay hated Miss Ramsay. For her pinched mouth and vengeful nature, for her pinching fingers and the way she brought the belt strap slashing down on even the littlest girls' hands. For the dainty way she sat with her legs to one side, ankles and wrists carefully crossed, as if she guarded some treasure in her lap.

The only truly bad person Kay knew was Miss Ramsay. Young Mr. Maitland was quiet, but he had dreadful headaches and when he was in the midst of one he could be terribly hard on the boys. Spare the rod, he would say, and then proceed to flail about him. Thinking about it now, Kay saw that he was also a bad person, perhaps worse than Miss Ramsay, for the things she had seen him do.

Bad things were done. Done and done and done. Discipline, dignity, diligence, Father said. Courage, he would add, before he whipped the boys, demanding that they *took it well*. If any cried out, he was whipped harder, on both hands or on his bare back. Kay saw Benny Twoyoungmen's back when he ran into the wash house, long lines black-edged, red-edged, frilled skin pale and shrinking between the edges.

She felt her own back shrinking, sitting under the skylight in the saloon, listening to the great howling that had set up above as Mr. Wright brought the quarrelsome sailor up on deck.

Thea got up and used the metal ratchet to close the skylight window more tightly. "Francis has to have the seaman whipped," she said. "But we do not have to listen."

"Which one is it?" Kay asked. "What is his name?"

Thea looked at her. "What does it matter? Not one of *our* boys, someone hired on in Boston. Francis cannot have fighting below decks, you know."

"But what did he do?"

Thea took the watering pot and attended to the flowers, answering without looking back, as if it was no matter at all. "I told you, he has been fighting with other men. That is not permitted on board ship, it can lead to terrible trouble. It must be—nipped in the bud, you see? Discipline must be maintained."

From the corner, where he had seemed to be immersed in his book, Mr. Brimner said quite quietly, "The ship is a *microcosm*, Kay—from which words does that word come?"

"μικρός," Kay answered automatically, seeing the word in Greek letters. "Tiny. And— κόσμος, *cosmos*?"

"κόσμος, the world, yes." He exchanged his long, thin legs, one for the other, the left now resting on top. "κόσμος, everything that is the case. In this world, we develop rules for living with each other, so we can depend on each other. We agree on those rules,

generally—although the debate has been going on for centuries as
to what civil behaviour may be. In this small world of the ship, if
one person tramples over those rules, we all suffer."

Kay looked at Mr. Brimner, without acquiescing.

∾

As the weather let up, Mr. Brimner took sick, his first bout of seasickness—or perhaps it was a bad pot of Gentleman's Relish—and
was compelled to keep to his cabin. He sent Kay's Latin book with
exercises marked, set two more translations in the *First Greek Book*
and included a note: "Composition has been neglected. You may
write me a story—write three or four pages about your best friend.
In a fine hand, mind you."

The exercises were quickly done. Even the Greek set piece; she
was not as confident of it as of the Latin, but with liberal use of the
vocabularies at the back of the book she felt sure it was close. There
remained only the story. Kay filled her pen again, and sharpened
her pencils, thinking whether she ought to write about one of the
colourless girls who had been invited to tea with her in Yarmouth,
whose names had slipped out of her memory along with their
faces. And what could she say of Susannah and Sally except *They
took me to the water . . . ?*

In her notebook she wrote,

> I had a friend who was kind to me. Her name was Annie
> Salter.

For a time it seemed enough of an effort to write that down,
to say that she had had a friend, to name Annie with her whole
name. But Thea would never read this book; Thea had never yet
looked at her school work since they came onto the ship. So she
went on.

When my mother got sick at Blade Lake, Annie's sister Mary looked after me. She was ten, when I was a baby. Then Thea came, but while she was teaching, Mary still came across to the House to be with me. In the nighttime when I was afraid Mary sat by my bed and sang the songs she knew. When I was sad or angry she would click her fingers at me from across the room in a certain order to make me laugh.

Then her sister Annie came to the school too, when she was six and I was five. Annie was in ward B, where the younger girls slept. She was the third bed from the end. I was not allowed to go in the ward but sometimes Mary had to take things to Miss Ramsay, clean towels and flannel, and then I went with her quickly and came back quickly, so Mary did not get in trouble. But then Mary died.

She did not want to write about that, so she crossed it out.

~~But then Mary died.~~ I was forbidden to go into the School because of sickness. Many students brought consumption with them and Father said I was susseptible, since my mother's family all died of it. I had to stay in the study with him for many weeks. ~~and he did not speak to me at all.~~

Later, when so many people were sick, Annie tried to go home. She came from far away, so far she did not know the way to go home and Thea found her but it was too late. She was buried behind the school in the small lot by the horse graves.

That filled up three pages. Kay shut her book. She would tear those pages out later, before Mr. Brimner was better.

That night Kay had a bout of earache, the first since Yarmouth. Hearing her sobbing in her bunk, Thea came from the saloon where she and Francis sat talking to see what was amiss. The drops had leaked in the medicine chest, giving a mentholated smell to the whole kit. Kay did not want them, but could do no more than weep slowly against the prospect. Thea sat on the bunk with Kay's head on her lap, gentle fingers smoothing the hair away, holding the lobe in a soft grip. The liquid trickled down and wound its way through her ear's whorls, cool and unpleasant. Kay lay staring at tiny tucks in the waist of Thea's purple dress. She had not realized that it was Thea's beautiful blue going-away dress, dyed darker. Rhoda must have dyed it, to better hide the stains.

Kay slept, but dreams pursued her, a dream of boxed ears, a box of broken ears, broken eardrums, ears running with yellowish fluid, of the rhythm of four great slaps, back, forth, back, forth—and a pause, and four great slaps again, and again, and then feet pounding down the echoing wooden halls and Miss Ramsay chasing them, her big red chapped hand reaching and ready. She followed after Annie, down behind the shed with the broken window, behind the shack, behind the trees—following, was she Miss Ramsay or herself, Kay?—the path open past the falling-down byres where calves huddled in the storm, and then an opening in the brush, the slit through which we slipped down to the bottomlands, down the long slant into the coulee, a long path down, wolf willow parting and the path widening, earth tamped by deer or by buffalo in the olden days, where in the earliest spring paths were marked through swampy slough, wet pools and pockets, fire smell and smoke smell from the camp where trappers scraped furs, rot and leaves and earth and the dark-green darkness roofed over, circling to a hut—the ghost of a hut, the hidden place—the man there, what was he really? The bootlegger, the still man. Satyr dog-sailor Satan Saviour Seaton, with his dirty child and a dead porcupine, quills and quiver, he pulls a handful, offers us the hooks, the sticks, the spines. Annie said he was not people. The wagon open, a mound up there, what is in there? What is under the wolf willow branch?

She woke to Thea clutching her arms, saying, "Stop—Kay, stop!"

Oh no—she had been dreaming again. She pulled away from Thea's hands, which were hurting her arms, and shut her mouth and held her breath, afraid to speak. Her face was wet.

Thea said, "What were you dreaming? What was it?"

"Annie," Kay said, when she could make her mouth open. The wood above and around them was solid, the dream was a dream. She put her elbow across her eyes to shut out the light from the lantern Thea had brought.

"I want you to stop this," Thea said.

Kay nodded, eyes still shut.

"Look at me," Thea said. "You are not to think about her any-more," she said, her face unyielding. "Not to dream about her."

"But I cannot *choose*—"

"You can. You are to put that away now. You are not a child any longer, it is time for you to curb your temper and control your outbursts. And to stop this everlasting—"

"You are unkind."

"No, I have been unkind not to stop you before now."

A gallon of water was forcing its way up in Kay's chest, was going to burst out of her now. She did not, did not let it. "It was unfair! She wanted her mama and her little brothers—she wanted Mary, but you could not save her."

Thea stared into Kay's eyes, her own eyes like black coals burn-ing in her white face. "I did the best I could to save Mary—you saw me take her down and work on her, you saw me."

"You should have sent Annie home then. Father should have let her go."

"Well, he would not. He could not, and she could not. It was the law that she must go to school, Kay. And it was better for her to stay. She was a clever girl and could have made something of her life— if she had been educated."

"She wanted to go home and talk with her mama the way they talk, and tell her about Mary."

"It was too far to go, and nobody to take her, and it was winter. She would have starved up there, I've told you. You never saw the way they lived in the bush, the terrible hardship—she would have starved, or died of cold, or been beaten, or fallen ill and died."

Kay's chest dissolved, because it was that or break. Because of death. "I am just sorry," she said. She was surprised that tears did not come shooting out of her eyes and drown them all and sink the ship.

∽

Thea did not know how to do better for Kay, how to help her to overcome this obsessive grief. She had tried not to look ill or tired or sad, not to allow her sadness to intrude. But Kay must have known about the baby. Of course she did—she was there at dinner, and staying in the house! But as was only natural for a child, she seemed to have forgotten all about it. So it was a surprise when she mentioned the baby one afternoon, after Francis had stomped back up on deck in a temper to deal again with that sailor who was still making trouble.

"Why did your baby die?" Kay asked, abrupt and cold, as if she had screwed herself up to it. Her sunburnt face was tight-clenched. A nightmare on its way again.

Thea answered, without adornment, "It was not meant to be. God decided."

"*God* decided."

Thea looked up, again surprised. "What do you mean?"

"I do not understand how God decides things, or why, by what measurement. Does God decide when everyone is to die, each person?"

"Yes," said Thea, shortly. Mr. Brimner was at the other end of the saloon, lost in one of the Windsor captain's months-old newspapers.

"Each person—but also each animal, each thing?"

She had hoped Kay was finished with this line of questioning. "Come and wash for dinner, and I will think how to answer you."

∾

The shouts were louder in Kay's ears, after dinner. She sat at the piano, staring at music she already knew. While Mr. Brimner and Thea finished their stewed prunes and talked and talked, Francis was above, watching as Mr. Wright flogged John Cherry, the Boston seaman. Arthur Wetmore had told Kay his name.

If she had a measuring device like the roll meter for waves, the arrow would point at 7 or 8, although the shouts had started lower, at what might be called a 4. Was there a sextant for measuring sound? She could not let herself think about the man's skin, brown and bare beneath the lash. Or the shouts of the boys being beaten in the shed. Some of them weeping. One boy laughed—little Silas, the one Annie liked. That made Mr. Maitland hit him harder.

There was nothing to think and no room to not think it. She turned the leaves over and over, searching for a new piece to learn. They would wait for half a minute between each lash, and there were to be ten lashes, because this was John Cherry's second offence.

Between shouts, Lena Hubbard came plumping in with the big china teapot, making an impatient to-do with her skirt and a table that had been shifted and got in the way.

"Your experiences must have expanded your faith," Mr. Brimner continued, after Lena had set down the tea and gone away again.

"Sometimes it is very hard to understand God's purpose." Thea glanced at Kay. "I trust the will of God, but I do not always—" She turned her mending. "There was an accident just outside the school grounds one day. A family from Scotland, breaking land. The father was hauling logs, and stopped the wagon with a lurch at our gate. He got out in time to see a log roll down onto his son, who had been running along behind."

Kay remembered that, from when she was very young. The man's white-rimmed, staring eyes; the boy lolling, head and legs limp and misshapen, a crater in the chest under his grey shirt. Thea's long white apron touching her black boot-tops.

"He was holding his son in his arms, but the boy was clearly dead." Thea stopped, and put thin white fingers to her upper lip.

Swinging the piano stool a quarter turn, Kay glanced at her sister.

Thea said, "I took him into the back kitchen and laid him on the table. I prayed over the poor boy. I thought if I had enough Christian faith I would be able to ask God to bring this child back to life, like Lazarus. I felt guilty for years, wondering why I had not had enough faith. I had a hard time getting over that."

"Yes." Mr. Brimner nodded, his several-times nod of understanding.

"And again, when the tuberculosis came, and so many of the children succumbed—I prayed and prayed, I did my utmost, and nothing . . . And then there was influenza."

Mr. Brimner did not speak at once. No longer pretending to play, Kay heard the pause extend over several bars, linking phrase marks pulling it on and on . . . Then he said, "There is a comfortable idea that death comes when we are ready, or that prayer can be efficacious against it. I have not found either to be so."

Thea turned away, practical, tight, controlled. She was always like this, after speaking of Blade Lake. Kay's throat hurt.

Thea said briskly, "Well! I no longer take so much pride in my prayers."

Mr. Brimner rose, as if he might go to bed. Instead, he said, after a moment, "My own dear friend, a priest and poet I respected and admired with all my heart, was stricken last winter with the influenza. His work was very fine, very fine. I cannot begin to know what he might have accomplished in this life, but he was taken, without the least—"

Then it was Mr. Brimner's turn to stop. A hitch, a slight, calm breath. His voice came again, dark and light at once, like rubato in music. "It is my task to bring his work to a wider audience. I have corresponded extensively with his sorrowing mother over the editing of his poems, and on this voyage I hope to complete the manuscript for parcelling off to Cambridge."

Thea turned a cup upright and checked the teapot's warmth with her palm.

"I cannot convey how beautiful a soul he was, how extraordinary his poems are," Mr. Brimner went on. "But if I can see this through, I will not have to tell you—you will be able to read them yourself."

"I read very little modern poetry," Thea said, and pressed the bell for Lena Hubbard to bring hot water.

Mr. Brimner turned back to retrieve his book. She had dismissed the story, Kay saw, and hurt Mr. Brimner. Perhaps because it involved poetry, which was not religious, or for some other reason Kay could not see.

Thea was too straight, she had no understanding of other people's sideways-ness, and did not see how difficult it had been for Mr. Brimner to talk about his friend. On the piano stool Kay cramped into tight dislike for her sister's composure and self-satisfaction, for her believing that she was so close to sainthood that she ought to be able to call back the dead—she was like Jesus Himself, she was so noble and pure.

Seeing her sister's eye on her, and as if she were party to Kay's interior mind, Thea said sharply, "We are put here to do what good we can, and to leave the rest to God."

Still rebuking Kay for dreaming about Annie—a thing she could not help, no matter how Thea might think a person could control everything inside their own head and body—perhaps *she* could, because she was a cold holiness, a head without any human misery in it.

Thea snapped the mending taut, pulling it into true, examining her firm, invisible work with satisfaction. "Whatever our feelings might be, we cannot know God's ends, or explain why it is necessary for someone to . . . to be called home."

It rose out of Kay, coming up like a thunderclap from her deepest parts: "Annie was called home—if you had let her go *home*, she would not be dead."

Thea turned in her chair to look at Kay with hurt, accusing

eyes, all her certainty sunk into a sorrowing, deep-bruised soul. From her tower of rightness, she said, "I will pray for you to be granted greater understanding."

I will pray for you. Because you are nothing but a child, with no intelligence or heart.

It was in Kay's mind to say, *And what about your baby, was your baby called home?* She caught herself at that, it scrambled in her throat, and because she was holding back so hard, it came out instead in a screeling, insufficient hiss, a quiverful of arrows racing toward Thea's eyes. "You are the cruellest, coldest— You are horrible!"

Lena barged in again with the drinks tray, making a bustle out of setting it on the lipped table. She made a face at Kay, warning her to mind her manners.

"*Sic loquendum est cum hominibus, tamquam dii audiant,*" Mr. Brimner said absently, not to any point. "We should speak with people as if the gods are listening."

That quiet aside almost caught her back, but then Thea said, "You know nothing about it. Have a care not to go too far."

Already too far over the threshold of temper, Kay leapt up from the piano. No longer caring who heard, she shouted at her sister, as loud as she might, "I hate you—I despise you!" In her hatred, *hatred*, of Thea, she turned to run—and kicking out at whatever was in her way, she caught the round back end of Lena Hubbard, edging away.

"Oh!" Lena cried, and scuttled from the room.

Kay's foot stung with the force of the kick—it must have hurt Lena very much.

That inflamed Kay's fury so that she cried out herself, she shrieked, beating herself on her chest and arms with her own balled fists, in a flurry of despair and loathing.

Thea gathered up her Kashmir shawl and flew across the room to wrap the cloth about Kay tight, tight, almost smothering, so tight that she could not breathe for a moment, could only gulp and stop, and stop.

Then there was silence in the saloon for a blessed instant.

In the silence they could hear Lena Hubbard crying outside in the passage—a plain fat woman who had never done Kay any harm, but only cleaned her chamber pot. Kay burst again into a storm of damp, useless sobs and sank down into her own welter on the floor, too strongly despairing for Thea to hold her up.

After a period of reflection in her cabin, she went to apologize to Lena Hubbard, which was very uncomfortable, so now Kay hated her, as well.

She came back to the saloon to find Thea and Mr. Brimner playing cards.

Moving his chair to make room for her at the table, Mr. Brimner said, "I have been reading Melville, you know, and you remind me of the opening to his whaling novel: *when ever my hypos get such an upper hand of me, that it requires a strong moral principle to prevent me from deliberately stepping into the street, and methodically knocking people's hats off—then, I account it high time to get to sea as soon as I can.*"

Kay felt some lightening of spirit at the methodical hat-knocking. "I told Lena Hubbard that I was extremely sorry, and she said well fine then there's an end of it. I begged her pardon, and told her that I have an ungovernable temper, but would work to be better."

"No need to exalt yourself," Thea said. "Every Christian born is subject to anger. We simply prevail against it."

"If I were a better Christian, I would not have tantrums," Kay said. "God ought to help me be a better Christian."

Thea looked at her without pity. "Please try not to be morbidly introspective."

Mr. Brimner laid his hand on the table, sighing regretfully. "Gin!" He gathered the cards together. "My dear Kay, I'm afraid it is a false conception of religion, to be selfishly preoccupied with our own betterment, our personal spiritual expansion. The object of religion is neither the improvement of our own character nor the service of our neighbours. The object of religion is to love and serve and glorify God."

Kay had not thought him so priestly before. His fingers were clever with the cards.

In her plush chair, Thea folded her hands but stayed silent, though Kay expected her to protest re *the service of our neighbours*, which had been the guiding principle of all her life.

He shuffled the pack, making a fluttering bridge. "Of course, we could hardly reach this object—the end for which we were created—of loving and serving God *without* living a life of love and service to those we live among. And we certainly cannot reach it except by—well, by personal holiness. But we cannot achieve it at all if we allow our religion to degenerate into a vague philan-thropic enthusiasm, or a mere attempt at self-improvement! I feel this strongly," he said, seeming to surprise himself as he spoke. "That all genuine religion is directed to God as its sole end, with-out reward or fear of punishment."

Thea's hands moved to the polished arm-ends of her chair, but she said nothing.

To Kay, Mr. Brimner's face looked more definite and beautiful than usual. She found his argument convincing, too. But all the same, she was not happy to be lectured to.

After a moment he said, "For me, there is no need for morbid introspection—the answer is the contemplation of the person of Jesus."

He smiled at Kay, long, creamy teeth emerging and emerging through his smile as they did when he was truly amused, or wished you to be comforted. "For others, perhaps like you, Miss Kay, it is the contemplation of the world, and the beauty therein."

He knew her very well. She saw it now, that was the way for her.

7

Port Elizabeth, South Africa

The *Morning Light* breezed past Cape Town in a stiff easterly. Francis took full advantage of it, racing around to Port Elizabeth, where they had cargo to load for Auckland. That loading must be prefaced by unloading of Bahamian sugar, and the redistribution of material below decks—which Francis told Thea would take three or four days at the least. He thought she might wish to occupy the time in the company of some Nova Scotia ladies: Mrs. Hilton and her young daughter were moored along the Dom Pedro jetty, on the *Abyssinia* out of Yarmouth, and others as well—old Mrs. McGiverin, from the *Restigouche*, for one.

Shy at the thought of other women's experienced eyes somehow perceiving her recent loss, Thea felt unwilling to initiate visits with captains' wives, as Francis pressed her to. But she was finally feeling well again, and longed for a chance to stretch her legs on land. On their first morning in port, she went to Kay's cabin to rouse her, and found her bunk neatly made and clothes folded, for a wonder. Trying to lessen Lena Hubbard's lot? Perhaps the tantrum had been a step to some maturity of mind. That would make life easier. Or perhaps Kay's uneven temper was a sign of her body's maturing, the changes of womanhood—and then life would *not* be easier. Casting her mind back, Thea thought she had been twelve herself, when her courses started. Or thirteen? She dreaded the pain Kay's monthlies must produce if she was like Thea—which she would not suffer at all quietly. And more laundry, and extra disturbance for Francis, who had no experience of sisters growing up, or any womanly weakness. She would have to impress upon Kay a seemly discretion.

That made her laugh at herself—the chance of Kay's seemliness seeming slim. She tied a kerchief round her neck against the sun and went up to persuade her sister to a walk onshore.

Under the awning, Kay and Mr. Brimner were bent over the *First Greek Book*. That had been providential, at least. Thea was filled again with gratitude that God had sent this peaceful scholar to them.

"Will you come with us and walk up to the promontory?" she asked Mr. Brimner, on the theory that a bland assumption that Kay was coming might produce compliance.

"No!" Kay screwed her eyes against the glare. "We are not finished work yet!"

"Well, you are the first pupil ever to say so," Mr. Brimner said. "This African sun calls us out from under the awning, and we will work better for a constitutional stroll. Unless you feel a need for solitude, Mrs. Grant?"

"Oh no, but do not feel obliged, for Francis tells me Port Elizabeth is safe as houses now. He says there is a little stand just up the hill with fruit and ices, which I thought Kay would find refreshing."

Kay tied her hat on with no more grumbling, and they went over on the next harbour lighter. At the jetty she nipped down the ramp between trips by crew and longshoremen, a good deal faster than Thea or Mr. Brimner could manage on legs which had forgotten the knack of ordinary land, and stood laughing and boasting on the broad concrete.

"We are strangers here," Thea told her, "and must behave so that we do credit to Francis and the *Morning Light*."

A nudge being always better than a direct command, Kay curbed her spirits. The long seafront negotiated with decorum, they set off up the broad main street toward the tower visible in the distance above. Elegant stone shops and offices faded into plainer buildings as the street curved upward.

Seeing a black-lettered sign ahead, and pointing it like a duck dog, Mr. Brimner paused, saying, "If you do not mind, Mrs. Grant, I will diverge from you and Miss Kay after all. It has been many months since I've taken a turn in a bookshop. An hour's refreshment among the dust of ages will do me the world of good!"

Thea thought Kay might pull to go with him, but the idea of ice had taken hold on such a sultry morning, and she only held her flat hand to help her hat make shade, peering up the rise to see where the fruit stand might be. Thea pulled out her little purse for the silver English shillings Francis had supplied, and they boarded a double-decker trolley to higher ground, where they would be able to look at all the ships and the town laid out below. The trolley was painted green, with always-open louvred windows below. Thea held Kay back from climbing to the open top level, since she could see only rough workingmen up there.

As they rose, the louvres revealed an attractive city, much of it new-built. At supper last evening Francis had told them how the city had been so infected by bubonic plague brought in by Argentinian rats that there was nothing for it but to burn large sections to the ground. The affected communities were razed, and new buildings set upon sanitized ash. "While they were about it, they built a segregated suburb for the blacks, the Xhosa," he said, making a strange clicking-sucking sound to start the word, "who were most affected by the destruction after the plague. New Brighton, it's called. Now they can live with their own kind—and be happy together," he'd added, seeing Kay look up at him, her mouth the straight line it made when she was considering. Thea had learned to dislike that line, which reminded her of Father. In Kay, thinking too often took a contrary stand, for no reason but the natural contradictory bend in her soul.

There was the ice stand, bright with fruit and flowers, and a swivelling telescope on a pedestal to see the sights. While Kay ate her ice, Thea swung the scope down to the harbour to find the *Morning Light*, like a toy ship, brightwork gleaming in the sun. At her turn, Kay sent the telescope searching back into the hills to the east, to a shantytown huddled behind the opulence. At any rate, she told Thea, pointing, that dusty, dark place could not be New Brighton!

She does not understand, Thea told herself, schooling her own impatience. She has seen nothing of the world. If some do not serve, others cannot have flowers and ices.

༄

Kay's insides felt numb from taking in this strange world, Africa. Every person they saw was odd, and some were surprising. Going back down from the hill, she wanted to stare at the people with the click-sounding name—their tidy faces and limbs going about their work. The man selling ices had tiny black knobs of raised freckles or moles all over his brown face; the trolley driver had no fingers left but steered his machine with the L shape of his thumb and palm. The eyes of the woman seated across from them darted left and right unceasingly, in a terrible inexplicable worry. Not-staring, although of course correct, was irksome, and the effort of not letting her own eyes dart in sympathy made Kay anxious.

When they stepped up onto Dom Pedro jetty to wait for the lighter, Kay could see Lena Hubbard's busy rump roiling along ahead of them, and Hubbard in tow, pushing a barrow. They had gone past the lighter's steps, though. Good, because she did not want to see Lena just now.

Beside the steps, Mr. Brimner stood waiting for them. He presented Kay with a small package: a pocket *Odyssey* in cloth binding, much worn with thumbing but still perfectly legible, if one could λόγος it. λέγειν, Kay corrected herself.

"We cannot make real headway if you are stuck with Cyrus all the time," he said.

It was small and green, with thin gold lines picked out on the cover. She opened the book and saw that it was in Greek on the right-hand pages, with a literal translation on the facing pages. The paper was delicate, clean, and the Greek letters crystal clear.

Kay's eyes pricked and filled. She scowled into the pages, hardly listening to Mr. Brimner telling Thea (who could not read Greek at all, poor thing), "We might call it our *Second Greek Book*."

Back at the ship, they found Francis at the top of the ramp, his face stiff and dark. He addressed Kay in a cold captain's bell-clap: "Well, Miss! See what comes of rampaging behaviour!"

"What is it, my dear?" Thea asked, putting a hand on his arm to gentle him, which Kay very much appreciated.

"Only your greater discomfort, I'm afraid! Hubbard and Mrs. Hubbard have left us. They've moved over to the *Easthaven*, bag and baggage, to take service there for England rather than continue another day with us. Can you tell me why that might be, Miss Kay?"

He hated her. Most likely he had always hated her—coldness in her limbs had foretold it when first she laid eyes on his accusing face, because she had kept Thea from him for ten years—and then she had been foisted on the voyage. He was right to hate such a bug, such an ugly girl, a devil, who could kick a poor fat woman for nothing at all, nothing but being in the way.

Shame piercing through her chest, Kay cried, "It's all my fault!" She raced past Francis and almost fell down the hatchway in her haste to attain her cabin. There she fumbled with the catch on the door, gulps of sobs tearing up out of her stomach to almost make her be sick with the force of them, her own stupidity and guilt nearly cleaving her in two until she could smash her head down into the cold, clean pillow and cry as quietly as she could into the pillowcase, which now Thea would have to wash because Lena had left them, and it was all her fault. She hated Lena even *more* now, while also darkly hating her own unbridled temper.

But beneath the turmoil of her heart, clutched in her hand still, was her new green book. The *Second Greek Book*, the gate to the untravelled land.

~

Because the Hubbards were gone, Thea made the supper for both crew and Aft. Kay emerged from her cabin to find nobody in the saloon, and went on silent feet, boots gentle on the boards, to peek into the galley. There was Thea cutting in lard for biscuits, flour on her violet dress where the makeshift apron had come loose. A great copper pot of stew on the cookstove sent up fragrant steam, an offering to the gods.

Kay swallowed to keep down whatever might come spouting up, a shriek or a spume of bile and fruit-ice. She was hungry, but per- haps, since she had made Francis so angry, Thea would be even more angry with her than Francis was. She crept back to her cabin and climbed into the bunk again, the odour of disgrace clinging to her hands.

Nobody came to knock on the door.

After an eon, an eternity, came four bells, meaning six o'clock, the time for dinner in the Aft saloon. Soon after, she heard Mr. Brimner go swinging by, whistling.

At last Kay got up and smoothed down her skirt, and for good measure changed into a clean middy blouse—only remembering when it was over her face and trapping her arms that, now the Hubbards were gone, the laundry would all have to be done by Thea too. Well then, Kay would help without complaining. Tears started to her eyes again at her own goodness, but she gave them a knuckling and patted her face with water from the ewer, which Lena Hubbard would not fill tonight.

She opened her door without a sound, stole down the corridor, and peeped in the saloon door: Francis and Mr. Brimner sitting silent at table, no sign of Thea.

Then a call came from the galley: "Kay! Come and help, please!" and Kay ran.

Thea had no time to be cross. She was supervising as Mr. Best lifted the great stewpot and directed his underlings, Jacky Judge and Arthur, to manage a loaded tray of cutlery and a basket of biscuits.

"My boys will take on kitchen duty directly after supper," Mr. Best told Thea over his shoulder as the little procession made their way below. "They'll leave everything spotless, or I'll take the hide off them. Good hands with the china, don't you worry about that." He shouted ahead to warn the sailors of the stewpot, "Gangway, lady with a baby!"

Thea turned to Kay, who had been worried that the whole of dinner had just gone down to the men, and took up a large dish, footed and lidded. "Here, I will take the tureen, and you look lively with the biscuits and the mustard."

A second tray was set out with a white cloth on it, and a mountain of risen biscuits like Thea used to make for Sundays in the old days. Kay followed, obedient and vestal as the Virgin Mary.

Francis was in a temper, but it was the Boston seaman, John Cherry, who had provoked him, not Kay. Mr. Wright came in during supper to whisper in his ear, and Francis looked up to the skylight with dark eyes and a jumping mouth. He sent his first mate packing with a harsh command, "Make it so!" which they had not heard from him before.

"When seamen are accustomed to the rule of violent mates—who in many cases could qualify as prizefighters, and are as eager to ply their fists—and happen to sail next in a ship where force is not so dominant, they are apt to be troublesome, Mr. Brimner," Francis said, as if to the clergyman; but really he was speaking to Thea, in explanation of his temper. "The necessity of imposing discipline falls first on Mr. Wright, but in the last instance upon myself." With that, he tore the napkin from his lap and banged out of the saloon and up the companionway. Because this was the third time, Francis would now whip him with the whole crew watching; that was what captains did. Because discipline must be kept.

The crew were called up from their supper, and the man was strapped to the mast in irons and lashed again. They heard the commands, and the screams, quite perfectly through the closed skylight for a very long time. Thea stayed motionless at table, not eating. Mr. Brimner applied himself to his stew in silence. Kay saw that though he split a biscuit, the two halves remained on his plate.

Time passed. The air in the saloon became thick and heated. No tea arrived—well, of course it did not, because Lena Hubbard and Hubbard were on the *Easthaven*, making tea for those people. Since the lashing was finished and the screams had stopped, Thea got up and opened the skylight again, and then they sat again in silence.

After some length of time Arthur Wetmore and George Bayard appeared, with Mr. Best in charge. They picked up all the dishes very neatly and vanished again.

Twenty minutes later, there came a knock at the saloon door.

Mr. Brimner looked up, but Kay was closer, and she went to open it as Thea called, "Come in!"

In the doorway stood a short, lean fellow in a brown tunic, his front hair shaved high and a black braid over his shoulder. Neither old nor young. "I, cook," the man said, tapping his chest with one finger. "Liu Jiacheng. I bring tea." He bowed, turned and—like sleight of hand—produced from a small cart behind him a tray with the silver teapot, and the best teacups. The tea smelled of flowers.

"Oh dear," said Thea, coming forward. "My husband—the captain does not like China tea, I'm so sorry—"

"*Nonsense!*" came Francis's voice thundering down through the skylight. "I am entirely indifferent to tea! I will drink any sort you have."

The man nodded to Thea. "India for captain, it is made." He bowed and took his trolley up the stairs, lifting it without effort.

The thin cups, so old that they had no handles, rather burnt Kay's fingers, but the white flower floating and opening in her cup made her feel much better.

That night she woke, sitting bolt upright, clawing her way out of a dream. She could not breathe. The whole of the world was full, a swirling vortex of multicoloured specks, from the ship out to the horizon as far as she could see. Broken china? But that would not float—this mass of sluggishly moving fragments rose and fell with the waves, seeming to tamp them down in a great whitish blanket . . . miles in every direction, thousands of miles. It choked her eyes and her mind and her throat. She drank the water left in her little jug and sat up in her bunk, afraid. In the dream it was all her fault. Somehow she had done this terrible thing to the world. It was an hour before her heart stopped pounding and she could lie still again.

∽

The Boston seaman, made an example of, was sent packing on the next lighter. He would find another berth, Francis told Thea—not that he himself gave a straw whether that was the case or not. "Any infection of spirit below decks must be rooted out like a bad tooth," he said.

They were lying in bed, beneath the last clean counterpane. But after supper Jiacheng had inspected the linen closet with Thea, and assured her that he would launder for Aft as well as Below. She assured him, in turn, that she and Kay were accustomed to helping on laundry day and would be happy to continue, and with slight but multiplying mutual bows they finished the first skirmish at a draw.

Francis was in a strange mood, both elevated and despairing, tight-strung unhappiness combined with satisfaction. As if he had not been sure he would be able to deliver such a punishment—and at the same time, as if the act of beating someone into lawful submission had a kind of pleasure to it, the pleasure of physical prowess. As if men were made to, meant to, fight each other with their hands.

Thea was wary of this mood. The woman in Eleuthera, Rhoda, had said she'd best hold off her husband for six weeks. "Till you are all healed up, all the body from the turmoil—if you don't want infection or to make it so you have no other baby." Thea had not told Francis this, but he had made no demands on her as yet. Only in this exalted, unhappy mood, it seemed that he wished to; he lay close behind her, pressing against her, wordlessly seeking entry. That thing that wants, wants, without thinking, that cannot tell what is seemly and what is rash. In truth she had a yearning herself, because the day had been fractured and the city was strange and then the man shouting above, and her darling Francis—who was both soft and hard, who kept the ship as he had to keep it, like it or not, though it was perhaps harder for him than for some, to do that. Let him revel in it, then. It had been five weeks, and at his blunt, unvoiced beseeching she felt an answer rising inside her after all, which she had thought she might never feel again.

∾

Next day Mrs. McGiverin, the captain's wife from the *Restigouche*, moored on the Dom Pedro jetty, rowed out to visit. She wore a great blue peaked hat, which she said kept the sun off her face in these lower latitudes and saved her from showing her age. Which she then instantly told Thea was forty-eight.

She had a wealth of theories and superstitions and advice. No children on board now, but she had raised four sons at sea, all now in New England; none in the ocean business. "They had their fill!" Mrs. McGiverin shouted up to the skylight, and Francis looked in from above to salute her smartly.

Speaking confidentially, but still in a perfectly penetrating voice, she listed closer to Thea. "I hear you lost your stewardess to

Easthaven, but you are better off without a complainer in the saloon.
I won't have 'em myself, another woman on board ship is a nui-
sance. I run a tight ship, you ask Captain McGiverin! No second-
guessing, altered orders, *oh I thought you wanted*—none of that for
me. Fair's fair, and I suppose the steward was useful, but good rid-
dance is what I say."

Kay said it too, but she said it under her breath. Because—and
here was the sting of it—as soon as Mrs. McGiverin began slagging
Lena Hubbard, Kay was forced to see Lena's side of it. How she
ought not to have kicked her, no matter what; and how she could
not go on indulging in tempers. Could not ever again lash out.

From the corner of her eye she saw that Thea was watching her
face, which was most likely scowling dreadfully. She smoothed it
out and asked Mrs. McGiverin if she would like to see her sampler,
which made Thea flush and smile.

There! It was easy enough to be civilized.

∽

As the *Morning Light* was making ready to leave port, a ship out of
Halifax arrived, bringing mail from Yarmouth which included a
letter for Thea from Aunty Bob. She read it out loud at breakfast,
exclaiming as she read.

> You will be sad to hear that Lydia has suffered a small
> stroke, not anything to worry you on the other side of the
> world! but it has slowed her down a trifle. Her mouth drags
> on one side, but she is still able to plauge poor Olive

"Her spelling is worse every year," said Thea, aside.

> and make all and sundry dance to her bidding. Queenie
> and I go out to Orchard House once or twice a week to
> give the girl a rest; last week she had hystericks and cried

on my bosom, 'Now I may never leave Mother!' Am afraid
you will have some trouble reading this. Love to all and
Francis and to poor Kay, I hope she has—

'Well, none of that is important.' Thea folded the letter and ran up
to ask if Francis would let her write quickly in answer before they
sailed, to send her sympathy back to Aunt Lydia, with some over
for Aunty Bob and Queen and of course poor long-suffering Olive.

∽

The emptiness of ocean, after port.

Along the forties on a still night, the stars bent near the earth.

It was too bright for sleep just yet, and only eight o'clock. Warm
and safe by Thea's purple-indigo skirts, Kay leaned on the taffrail,
looking into the heavens and the long-spreading veil of the Milky
Way. When you stare deep into the dark, the sense of up and down
dissolves—everything is out, out, outward.

Mr. Brimner paused in his nightly circumambulation.

"Infinity," Kay said. "What is it? What comes after *infinite*?"

Thea moved, turning slightly away from the glory. "Oh—it is all
God's love, I think—expanding, transcending."

Going off his watch, Mr. Wright offered to bring up his old telescope, to show them "the wonders of astronomy, et cetera . . ." and
went below to rustle it out.

Mr. Brimner took up a portion of rail beside Kay, because really
it was impossible not to stop and stare. "What is the boundary of
the universe?" he asked, perhaps not speaking to her. But went on,
after a moment, "In an old Hindu tale the earth rests on the back
of elephants. Who stand upon a great tortoise."

Thea said, "What absurdities people once believed!"

"William James tells of an old lady in America who told him
that story, as gospel. To enlighten her, after the Socratic method,
he asked, and what does this turtle stand on? Another turtle, said

the old lady. And on what does that turtle stand? A bigger turtle! But my dear lady, James asked, what holds up *that* turtle? Oh it's no use, Doctor, said the lady, waggling a finger at him: It's turtles all the way down."

Half-listening, Kay looked up into the reaches of blackness stretching out on either side, on every side, into never a border, no end to it, because what could be outside? There is no outside—everything is here, revealed, the deepness shining to tell us.

8

A Change of Heading

Mr. Brimner gave Kay back her notebook one afternoon after checking her declensions of the aorist, with one finger stuck in an earlier page, which he then opened to.

She had forgotten to tear out those pages about Annie. "I do not wish to discuss it any further," she said. Giving him *such* a look, so that he would never refer to the story again. Because if Thea heard, or Francis, they would know Kay could not be trusted. She had been very stupid to write it down at all.

Mr. Brimner nodded, closed the book and left it beside her on the table. He did not ever push against one the way some people did.

A true storm overtook the *Morning Light* as she crept along the forties below Australia, reaching for New Zealand. The first real storm of the voyage—more like a prairie blizzard than the thunderstorms they'd weathered so far. All hands on deck; Jiacheng the cook was pressed into service and worked his full rotation with the rest, binding his braid round his neck so it would not be caught in a rope twist.

Early in the forenoon of the first day, the wind increased until the mainsail must be furled or be torn to pieces—or have the ship over. After Arthur Wetmore tore open his leg on a marlinspike, even Mr. Brimner was called up to help haul rope. Kay watched, tucked in close by the lifeboat, as ten men struggled high above with the furling, and a dozen below kept haul on the ropes. The men above were like ants strung out on a laundry line, so small and helpless against the whipping of the wind.

At last they had the great sail furled; then the ropes had to be made fast. Mr. Best's shouts were thrown back into his mouth, but the men knew their work and stood firm to it. When all was tight, they shimmied one by one along the spar, back to the mainmast and down, down, safe except for new howling of the frustrated wind. Kay scarpered below before Francis could catch her up on deck.

As the gale worsened that night, Francis not only ordered them to keep to their bunks, he said they must be strapped in. Thea worried that Kay would be lonely and afraid, so he strapped both together into their bed, his and Thea's. Kay did not want to go in with Thea—it was babyish, and beside Thea she could not do the things she did at night to make herself sleep. And she was afraid that she might have a nightmare and make Thea angry.

If she did, the storm overrode the dream. No other sounds could match it. They spent twelve hours in the full grip of wind and wave, clutching one another when the pitch and yaw was at its worst, talking a little (or trying to), drowsing from sheer nervous strain and waking, with a startled groping for each other, at some fresh banging shriek or paroxysm of the ship.

During the blizzard last winter in Blade Lake, Kay had shivered alone over a stoneware hot water bottle, wearing all her warmest things, huddling in the bedclothes for two days while Thea came and went and ice grew like ferns on the windowpanes. But this shuddering seaquake was stranger and longer, and far louder than the whining ghost-wind around the school. The frantic bucking of the *Morning Light* in massive seas was sometimes dreadfully frightening, and the constant creak and groan of wood made one worry that the boards would pop apart and spill them all into the ocean to drown.

At one lull, a momentary silence, Kay woke in semi-darkness. Beside her Thea lay at the far extent of the strap, her back curled into the side of the curving wooden wall, weeping silently. She must be thinking about her little baby. Kay touched her closed eyelids, stroking the fine skin as gently as her fingers would move, until Thea took one arm from the blanket-trap to stroke Kay's cheek in turn. In a while they slept again. They had turned into animals, sleeping to heal themselves from fear.

No food came, since Jiacheng was on deck; Francis had left a tin of biscuits and a cask of water near. Sick from the pounding motion of the hull, Thea could not eat, but she drank a little when Kay carefully poured out half a metal cup, only spilling a very little. Once or twice they struggled up to sit on the chamber pot, clutching at the bed rail and snatching the lid back on as quick as could be.

One of those times, as Kay clambered back over to the far side of the bed, Thea opened her eyes in the semi-darkness of the storm light and said, "I am pleased to see how hard you are working with Mr. Brimner. He says you make marvellous progress."

Kay felt her face heating. "I do not work hard enough," she said.

"Well, I dare say, but you have a natural cleverness for languages and learning. You take after Father in that way." She meant that Kay did not have to work to understand things, as other people did; as Thea did herself. It was a way of criticizing someone, in fact, for being facile and lazy.

"I think *you* are more like Father than I," Kay said, at first meaning to wound Thea back, but finding it was true. "You worked with him, and he talked to you and admired your skill, and when he was ill, you ran the school—you were as good at it as he was." And Thea had Father's spiritual insight too, which Kay knew herself to lack.

"If you put the same effort into your other studies, you could perhaps go to normal school one day—not that I believe you would enjoy teaching."

Kay did not think so either. "I will not be a teacher," she said. "Perhaps I will paint . . ." But that was childish boasting; she had no skill, she was of no use in this world at all.

"You certainly lack the patience to teach."

"Well, what am I to do, then?" There was some pleasure to this, to Thea's attention on her future, even if it was a sore-tooth kind of pleasurable pain.

"Perhaps you will marry, one day. Or find some other calling. You need only submit to God's will, but you are too fond of your own ideas," Thea said. "It is not a bad thing to feel so certain about one's own opinions, I suppose."

"Mary submitted. She said, *Behold the handmaid of the Lord.*"

"Well, you will not be asked to be the mother of God," Thea said, in the dry way that meant she thought Kay ridiculous.

A strong awareness of her own hugeness, her possibility, rose up in Kay, contrary to Thea's damping. "There could be some other task, that someone might one day have to do?"

Thea turned away from Kay to lie facing the door, no longer willing to discuss nonsense. But she left her warm feet behind her so that Kay's could still be warmed.

The door opened and Francis came in to check on them, as he had from time to time when he could be spared.

Kay lay quiet, breathing as if asleep. Behind a tangle of eye-lashes, she watched him bend to kiss Thea. It was so strange to see Thea lift her face to meet his mouth. That happy yielding to her husband, even in the midst of the storm. As if they had always been together—as if all the years Kay had had Thea to herself at Blade Lake were a story, or a lie.

It went on and on, twenty hours, thirty . . . nearly forty hours before the storm spent itself and spat them out the other side. Thea stayed the whole of the storm obediently in bed, but after thirty hours Kay found it physically excruciating to be swaddled all the time, and convinced her sister that she must creep quickly back to her own bunk, just for her Greek book, or begin screaming.

Each step across the bare and battened-down saloon was dangerous. The passengers—all she and Thea could ever be—had been ordered to stay below, but how could anyone notice? It was six o'clock and would be dark again soon; she must find some brief respite in the air.

In her cabin, Kay dressed and put on her mackintosh. She climbed slowly up the companionway, gripping the handrail hard, stretching her neck to reconnoitre before she stepped up on deck. It was not *so* bad, not anymore. It was cold but not raining, and the motion was only the predictable rhythmic rolling of heavy seas. She pulled the mackintosh tighter about her neck and slipped around the port side, out of the mate's eye.

The water was black, except where it wept or ached into dull gunmetal grey. Holding tight, Kay leaned against the rail, hip bones crushed into the wood until it hurt. Everything hurt all the time anyway, her head, her throat. Her insides, those wormy guts, and the bottom of her back.

Thea was wrong about her being so clever. She was too stupid to learn Greek. All she could do was read music and make her fingers go in a certain way at a certain time on the piano. It did not even sound good, only correct—nothing like the beauty of Thea's own playing. And now the piano was out of tune, along with everything else.

There must be something I can do well, some work I can do, Kay thought, desperate in this darkness and storm about the course of her life. Well, but why must there? God had no use for her, no reason that she was good, or anything, or any thing.

On a sighing subsidence, the cloud that had wept over them parted and the moon shone through, a thin, bright, painful light, showing you the path across the sea. Which you could never walk on, or you would drown. A swell came again, and the wind rose into a shrieking roar, racing over the water to dive into the reefed mainsail and the tiny storm jib. Kay grabbed at the rail, her knees bending to take the roll. It was fresh!

As the ship plunged back into the trough of the wave, her feet came off the deck, and she was for a moment airborne—her fingers closing round the railing more fiercely and her heart lifting like her body.

Never mind misery. She laughed to be there, after the places she had been before. The scrubby prairie had not confined her, nor the hills and the mountains, beautiful as they were too—and these waves were more than mountains.

The ship's heading changed, making the deck tilt again under her feet, as Francis and Mr. Wright set the wheel to lessen the force of this new blow.

A screeling voice cut through the water and wind. "Catch your death!" Seaton cried, like a seagull shrieking. Kay spied his beaky head peeking from the lifeboat's tarpaulin.

One finger pointed back to the companionway. "Lubber," he named her, and she bowed, conceding, and scrambled below.

$\backsim$

They made land at Auckland in good time, the storm having blown them ahead of schedule. Francis proposed deputizing Mr. Brimner to take Thea and Kay for an afternoon's outing to the famously beautiful Nihotupu Falls up by Waitakere while the *Morning Light* was being unloaded in Auckland harbour. But that proposed jaunt stretched into a longer excursion when Francis was approached on the pier, not an hour after they moored, by a hustling, importunate dentist from Ottawa who was searching for a ship to take kauri logs to New York, and wanted to show off his new tramway. This perilous line carried logs from the forest on a steel-rail track winding around the cliffs to a loading wharf at Whatipu beach. The dentist hoped to convince Francis that kauri logs were worth a stop on his way back from China.

Although doubtful about lumber from a tree he wasn't certain he could sell, Francis accepted Dr. Raynor's offer of a conveyance over to Piha, and a pleasure jaunt on the tramway. He was too willing to respond to a stranger's advances, Thea thought.

Next morning, Dr. Raynor rolled up in a brake, sharp to time. He secured Francis a seat beside him in the front of the brake, where he must listen to the dentist's unending stories. Sooner him than me, Thea thought, stepping up into the back to compose herself for a jouncing ride. But there was no escaping that penetrating nasal voice. Raynor told Francis that he was determined to bring the local logging industry up to date. He had built a sawmill and, in order to make it a paying proposition, fashioned a tramway from the Piha valley along Karekare beach all the way up to Whatipu, where boats waited to ship the logs to Australia.

Through the heat of the morning, Thea, Kay and Mr. Brimner sat silent, still pale and testy from the rigours of the crossing. The dentist provided an ostentatious picnic lunch, which they stopped to eat at Piha. Thea waved Kay off to walk in the sand, when she had eaten enough sandwiches and was reaching for a third cake. Mr. Brimner sat upright, watching Kay go down the slope of the shore. Taking mercy on him, Thea said in his ear, "Please do go, Mr. Brimner. I'll explain to Dr. Raynor that I do not like Kay to walk alone."

He set off gladly, clapping his odd straw topi on his head. Thea lay back in the very comfortable folding chair and un-listened to Dr. Raynor rhapsodizing about the uses to which kauri lumber could be put, and his innovations re efficient distribution. "We gather the logs in gullies in the hills, sluice 'em down to the beach at Piha, load 'em on my train, *tockety-tockety* round the beach to the wharf—Bob's your uncle, and my aunt Fanny!"

Although Francis enjoyed him, Thea found the little dentist's practised sales pitch coarse. While Raynor held forth, she watched Kay and Mr. Brimner stroll out along the beach, faces turned to the sea wind, their footprints making a curving line in the shining wet sand. They were in step, those two. Thea watched them with quiet pleasure. What a very good thing it had been to take the priest on board. God had sent him to relieve her burden.

Then the source of that burden, the loss of her son, sprang back to her mind, as it did from time to time, from day to day, hour to hour. She shut her mouth tight and turned back to Francis and the dentist.

∾

On Piha beach the waves seemed to argue with each other, not rolling in long, inevitable curlers but going every which way, crest crashing into crest, confusing. Even on land she was at sea now, Kay thought. She felt a little weary.

The beach stretched out in a wide half moon, bounded at one end by slow-rising hills and nocked on the other by a giant, solitary rock, which one could imagine to look like a lion couchant. Beyond the rock, more beach. Oystercatchers skittered in the surf on bright-orange twig-legs, long orange beaks sifting sand. Surf-pound mingled with the steadier sound of falling water sparkling down from the hills.

Boots and stockings tied round her neck (she had paused behind a rock to do it, once Thea's attention drifted), Kay ran ahead over the glistening mirror-surfaced sand. She had not been on a beach since Eleuthera. This was a wilder, rougher place—the water not at all welcoming—but the sea wind shocked her hair from her head enough to liven her blood, and she sprang in exultation over the gleaming rind of dampland between wave and rock, feet leaving a pleasing, impermanent record of her presence on the earth.

Mr. Brimner carried along behind, black oystercatcher legs holding up his plump middle. Like the birds, he did not want to get his feet wet, and moved in a diagonal, up out of the tide-swelling surf-eddies. They had no need for chatter, the wind was enough. Kay saw his lips moving—praying to himself, most like. To God, she supposed she meant. When she got closer, however, he turned to her with a brilliant smile and said, "βαθυδείελος! *bathydeielos*—is it not a lovely thing, after the last few days, to be *steeped in sunshine?*"

She had become very fond of him.

The luncheon was cleared away by the two men who had driven them up, and then they all climbed back into the brake for the short trip to the railhead. Kay was determined to ride the tram. She wanted Thea to come too, but once the little track came in sight, they could see how rough it was. The tram was a dinky, ramshackle thing, bolted-together steel plates making a basket on two of the carriage beds. But the kauri logs! As wide as houses! A single barkless log, twelve feet or more in diameter, had been tied to each of seven carriage beds, making the tram look even more like a toy.

Scale occupied Kay's mind as they drove on: little, big; how each thing has its long-ordained suitable size, and how a difference in that size sets our perception of importance zinging and swings the world upside down. There was God in that thought, somehow, the way that tiny things assume importance: the way a change of view, when one crouches down to look properly, turns an ant's leaf into a landscape.

The tram terminus stood in a little camp, with a few ramshackle huts of various purposes: a smithy, a saw house, a cook tent. Thin dogs and mangy chickens roamed the dust, nosing for food. Kay held out a last corner of sandwich from the luncheon basket and it was snatched at a gulp by a tall white-and-brown dog. Men loitered about the place, dark-clothed, touching their hats to the dentist but not behaving subserviently. They had long legs and strong faces, some with black markings. A few horses stood about, listless in the heat. No women to be seen; this was a working camp.

With cautions and precautions and shouts of *way!* the little tram (the engine was called *Sandfly*) juddered off, making a tremendous pother about it all. The logs swayed in their lashing and the human occupants shook along with the tram, each clutching for tighter hold on the slanted sides.

The rails ahead tilted around the rocky edge like a long smile of broken teeth, ties higgledy-piggledy and rails clinging to the cliff. Twenty feet below, surf pounded the great dark rocks. Kay stood up to peer over, knowing Thea was too distracted to tell her not to.

This rail carriage was pinned together with rivets and string. Its wheels made a shrieking screel to accompany the ride, but even that noise was overpowered by the building cacophony of the waves. The engineer turned back to wave a filthy hat and smiled, blackened teeth very like the broken railings.

Kay loved it. Thea did not, and told Francis so, loud enough to be heard over the screech of metal on metal. Mr. Brimner kept his thoughts to himself, merely clinging tight to the steel wall of the basket, the tips of his pink fingers gone starry white.

Seeing her joy in the trip (when Francis put out a warning hand to stop her craning farther over the side), Dr. Raynor shouted bois-terous approval of Kay's bravery—which was not courage at all but some giddy form of self-torture. She loved the deep-carved sensa-tion in her guts when the cars rounded the bend, perhaps loving too the possibility of death. It could all be over in an instant, and then there would be no worrying to do at all!

At Whatipu, Kay and Thea stayed in the bucket, still trembling from the journey. Thea closed her eyes and sank down in a puddle of skirt to the bottom of the carriage, but Kay watched the men unload those giant logs. Each one must be pried up onto rollers set along the narrow wharf, and coaxed along—then the short tumble into the boat, a bit sickening. Each time, Kay thought the boat would sink, but each time it bobbed up again, adjusting to the new weight. She hoped Francis would decide not to take this lumber. She would hate the *Morning Light* to wallow with it. Once the logs were all off, with a good deal of sidling and hitching, the tram ground back again more slowly along the darkening cliff.

Disembarking after the loud, discombobulating ride, they scrambled back up the scree from Piha. The brake's thick earth-bound wheels and sturdy boards felt like staid luxury after that harum-scarum tramway.

"Here," the dentist said to Kay, reaching deep into an overcoat pocket. "Got something for you, Missy." He handed up into the carriage a handful of fur—a muff, was it?

The muff turned and stretched, and opened a pearl-toothed maw to yawn. Inside, the roof of its mouth was ridged, pink, brown-speckled like a trout. It was a puppy, half head, half paws.

"One of the camp dogs whelped a month ago, and this is the only pup that lived. Comes of a good breed, I dare say, what'd'youcallit, a mountain dog of some kind. Will do for an ocean dog, I dare say. A companion for a good brave kid."

Kay looked down at the moving mass of fur on her lap. A pink tongue showed between black lips and spiky teeth. Its breath smelled of skunk: a wild, clean smell.

"There, Kay," Francis said, turning to admire the pup. "Say thank you to Dr. Raynor—this little fellow will be a good pilot for your journey."

Names fall so easily, with an idle word. Pilot he was, her good dog Pilot.

Hugging the puppy to her chest for safety, Kay was glad to be gone to sea again, into the air and wave; land-borne life was not for her.

The *Morning Light* pulled out of her berth with a graceful sway, buoyed on the true home. Pilot reached up and bit her chin gently to say she was squashing him, so she let him down, now that they were far from the wharf.

They left Auckland harbour in a graceful spray, and Kay raced the puppy around the deck, in what Father would have called an access of animal spirits. She won—Pilot's lumbering legs were too short yet to bear the burden of that great head, and he was not yet a sailor and tended to fall over when the ship rose to a swell. He tired quickly, poor pup, but that was good, for work had still to be done. The school table was set up on the foredeck, Mr. Brimner already ensconced but not yet absorbed.

"You are walking on air—ἀεροβατεῖς—today," he told Kay, looking up. "Which in your derivations list should be related to those who walk on the heights, *acro*bats—instead of your more usual ὑπνοβατεῖν (*hypnobatein*, sleep-walking), which also helps us to remember ὑπνολογεῖν (*hypnologein*, sleep-talking)."

Kay could not tell if she should be cross with Mr. Brimner for mentioning her nightmares, but not feeling anger, she did not invent some. Pilot slept at her feet—on her foot, in fact. If he found that leathery pillow comfortable, she would not move it.

The dog turned out to be a great deal of trouble, both on deck and in the parlour, because he was not yet trained to civilized behaviour and would from time to time embarrass himself; it was a good thing the carpets were rolled up as they left port. He always seemed so sorry—who could blame him? Even Thea could not, and they always cleaned it up before Francis saw. Jiacheng tolerated him; Kay had been worried about that.

It felt unfamiliar and perhaps unfair to be happy, but she was. They were flying north on a bright sea, in a blue line stretching from Auckland, on the north tip of New Zealand, to Tonga— where in three days Mr. Brimner would leave them.

Wanting to work hard during the last of his tutoring, Kay bent to her *First Greek Book* with alacrity.

RELATION OF WORDS TO OTHER WORDS
877. It is of great *practical* importance to note and fix in the mind the relationships of Greek words.
    In acquiring a Greek vocabulary, do not commit words to memory as separate units, but group the Greek words together that show affinity in form and meaning, and associate with them the related Latin and English words.

But how was one to remember the words if one was also not to commit words to memory? Except that it was not exactly memory;

it was knowing, rather than recalling. The way one did not have to recall Thea's name, or think of the word for a stone. Mr. Brimner would read great slogs of Greek as she followed along, listening and seeing, and then would set her to reading herself, out loud and in her mind, and every day she went farther and farther into what had at first seemed a forest of bent sticks and now was becoming familiar paths through her own place.

The papers were held on the table with stones from Yarmouth, large stones that used to fill the bare hearth of the saloon fire until Thea fetched them up, having seen how fluttering the work was. These stones were far from home. Round, worn-smooth grey granite, each one the size of a baby's head.

Across the table, Mr. Brimner worked on his dear friend Prior's poetry, marking up the lines in thick black ink. His left cuff had a great smudge on it.

She turned back to her own page.

1. The bowmen shot birds and wild asses in the plain.
2. The army was cut to pieces by these barbarians.

Barbarians always cut you to pieces, if you did not fight them. Everyone always thinks the other people are barbarians, Kay thought. Mr. Brimner had said the word only means *strangers*. Everyone always thinks the strangers are savages.

3. It was not safe to be among the barbarians.
4. The soldiers were still in plain sight.
5. This was not true.
6. But the birds were black.

The birds were black, like the birds in Blade Lake. No singing from the birds there, none of the meadowlarks that Thea and Father could imitate so sweetly from earlier days in Fort à la Corne—*o-chayt-o-tiddlyboot*. Only *caw-caw-caw* in Blade Lake.

Bright crow eye staring at you from the fence post. Hawks pelting down like arrows out of the sky, soldiers in plain sight. It was not safe to be among the birds.

A hand on her neck—what? Oh, she was sleeping at her book. The sun was too warm. It was Francis, finger to his lips so she would not wake Thea, dozing in the hammock.

He gestured her to follow him to the rail. "See?" he said, pointing. Two long black shapes.

Then another, rising and curving, wet-shining between them. Then a spume of water, and another, with a sound like a coughing sigh, *ahhhh!* They were whales—she had been waiting so long to see them.

"Humpbacks," Francis said. "Two of them, with a calf."

Kay looked and looked, following the black lines and the low, aerodynamic fins that showed, and winked away beneath the wave.

The water felt empty without them.

"There! Gone. They'll dive for an hour now," he said. "Magnificent, hey?"

Good, that they were gone. She thought of the harpoon that hung over the mantelpiece in the mates' parlour. She did not want them to be caught.

αἰσχρός, aischros, *shameful, disgraceful.*
βιός, bios, *life.*
ἀπαλλάττω, apallatto, *abandon, rid oneself of; mid. depart, go away.*
χρόνος, chronos, *time, season, period.*
ἀποθνήσκω, apothneisko, *die off, die, be killed.*
θνήσκω, θανοῦμαι, ἔθανον, τέθνηκα (cf. θάνατος), thneisko, thanoumai, ethanon, tethneika, cf. thanatos, *die; perf., be dead.*
πέπονθα, pepontha, *experience, suffer.*

All will experience, all will suffer. All people will die off, be killed, fall in battle. Be dead. Not just Father, and her mother, and Annie, and Mary. Thea's baby. A long list.

Kay shook her head to push the shadows out of it, and dipped her pen again. The ink-pot lid had to be pried off each time, which was a bother, but if it was not lidded tight, any rising wave set it slopping out to where it might stain the clean cream-and-brown fur of Pilot, flattened at her feet.

Beside them, Mr. Brimner lay sleeping in a wicker chair beside the table, his face flushed apricot. Even his eyelids were pinkish. He was not cut out for southern climes. He had said for her to wake him if she ran into difficulties, but she would not.

The end of the afternoon watch rang—four o'clock, she could not help still thinking in landsman's language—eight bells and all's well: the day's work shipshape, a light breeze and a limpid sea, so all the sailors were at rest, one way or another. At the fo'c'sle, Mr. Best held the wheel while Francis, leaning against the bulkhead, looked through his spyglass at nothing. Thea went below to confer with Liu Jiacheng over what was to be done with a non-laying hen. Nothing disturbed the sleeper's peace.

How would Mr. Brimner make do in a strange place like Tonga, where no English ship would arrive with black-bordered letters, and there would be no English marmalade at the breakfast table or Gentleman's Relish at the dinner? He might find someone in Tonga to teach Greek to—but perhaps, like Father, he would be too busy teaching them English and Scripture.

It was hard, even after so many Sunday services, to think of Mr. Brimner as a priest. He did not wear vicar clothes, but cool grey linen shirts and jackets; he saved his clerical collars for best. Passing his opened cabin door, she had seen a cupped set of them lying on the bunk. The foot of the bunk was taken up with books, row after row, like Francis had threatened to set a crate of china on her own bunk. Mr. Brimner must curl very tight to sleep, or pack them all away each night. He was more scholar than cleric.

593.   1. The gods will show us the way.

2. He was considering what answer to make.

3. There they remained a week and collected supplies
for their journey.
4. Considerably later (the cloud of dust appeared) like
a sort of blackness in the plain for a great distance.

That was an exciting development, that cloud of dust appearing
in the great distance. She did not feel she was making any very
great progress, yet Greek words had slipped into her understanding as things themselves, not just other names for the things.
Realness was gathering like a cloud of dust in her mind, still in the
distance, but perceptible.

Mr. Brimner opened one teal-blue eye. "Enough!" he croaked.
"Walk the rail, jump in place, school your dog, be a child! There is
time aplenty for the dark cloud *work* to crouch on your head in
future. Go and ask your brother if you may climb to the crow's nest."

Kay laughed, because Francis would never let her climb that
high. And then shivered, because she did not want to!

9

Tonga

Early next morning, the *Morning Light* crept up on an island, a high green hill humped up out of the ocean. Beyond it they could see larger land, misted to grey in the early morning air.

Through the morning they rounded the point of the first island, which Mr. Wright told them was 'Eua. They were not stopping there, but made for Tongatapu, the largest island of the archipelago of Tonga. The map in the saloon called it *TONGA or FRIENDLY Iˢ*. Mr. Brimner, who had read up in readiness for his post, said that was because Captain Cook had found the people willing to trade and kinder than other islanders, whose first instinct had been to kill the interlopers. And perhaps that would have been a better idea, for Mr. Wright said many islanders had died of diseases brought by Europeans, before they gained resistance to new germs. Like tuberculosis, in the West.

It was a soft, murky sea around these islands. Near Tongatapu the water lay quiet, variegated from blue-green to brownish in patches, from some vegetation on the sea floor. The main town crouched on a slight rise: scattered white buildings around a larger official mass, also white. Yet everything was a little greyish, and dirty too. A fitful wind blew across the deck.

"The draft is shallow," Francis said, coming to sit for a luncheon on deck, in honour of the gentle weather. "Here at Nukuʻalofa we will not dock at the wharf, but anchor well out and take the tender in as we need."

That was a strange, unaccustomed name for a town. Kay said it under her breath to get it right. Nukuʻalofa, Nukuʻalofa.

Across the water she could now distinguish a large white building, a pepper-pot red roof on a stubby white tower; next to that, a church. A double avenue of low, feathery trees hid the buildings from full sight, but there looked to be lawn there, and park grounds along the waterfront.

Near shore in the shallows, submerged to their chests, dark-haired people moved along a line of basket weirs, threading something through the water and peering down to run hands along. Eels? Kay hoped not eels, for she had a horror of them.

"They soak the fibres for their mats, *taʻovala*, their waist-wraps," Seaton said from the lifeboat above her. "The women soak them in salt water for days or weeks, and come to check to see how pliable they are for weaving. I had a mat, long ago . . . My grandmother's father's *taʻovala putu*, that I wore to her funeral."

Was this where Seaton was from, then? His strong hawk nose lifted into the air, seeking, as if this land would have a different smell. Kay breathed in too, but could detect no special flavour.

Mr. Brimner dawdled in the companionway as if unwilling to go up on deck, his dark spectacles flashing in a subdued way. "I hope you will all come to tea with Mr. Hill, if invited?" he asked earnestly. Perhaps he was a little anxious.

Thea said, "Of course!" and turned back to her cabin for gloves.

For the heat of the day she also brought a sunshade. Kay did not want to stay in its irksome shade, and was told she would soon have a headache, and warned not to muss her good white muslin dress, laundered to a turn by Jiacheng. "The laundry is not suffering the lack of the Hubbards, at least," Thea said. "That is good luck, or I should say God's hand, although why God would use your foot in Lena Hubbard's bottom end as His instrument I really cannot tell."

A soft giggle rose in her throat. Kay had not heard her laugh in ages.

The tender tied up at a long wharf, with steps cut up one side. Kay's spindly arms were elastic enough to haul her up a ladder quickly, and she had no fear of her good boots slipping through rusty rungs, but stairs were quicker, and meant Thea would not have to spoil her best white lawn on a ladder climb.

First at the top, Kay looked about her, inspecting it for Mr. Brimner's sake. Rubbishy kind of place, and hot in this late September afternoon.

A gaggle of ragged young men loitered at the pier head, sitting for hire in brakes and open carts, none in good repair and some showing the road right through their floorboards. It was all a bit fly-blown and deserted, for the main town of a place.

Then along came bowling a neater carriage, an open trap with a white horse pulling it. A clerical gentleman, small and dark, sprang out and came toward them, taking hands one at a time as if this was Sunday morning after church, his mouth making a polite pink triangle. He greeted Thea first, and Francis, and then found Mr. Brimner again and pumped his hands together over and over.

"We had your telegram!" he cried, seeming more excited than was fitting. He turned to bow to Kay, lifting his old-fashioned hat. "And this young miss?"

She was prepared to dislike him, or anyone else who stole Mr. Brimner away. With a very slight pressure Mr. Brimner put an arm along her shoulder and said, "May I present the Reverend Mr. Hill, incumbent here in Nukuʻalofa town. He is an old college mate of mine at Caius, and one of the reasons I entered the mission."

She yielded, since he wished it. "How do you do, Sir," she said. At least polite.

Bowing correctly, Mr. Brimner turned to Mr. Hill. "Let me introduce Miss Kay Ward, younger sister of Captain Grant's wife.

An apt pupil of classical tongues," he said, giving her a dignified collegial nod, "and a sound maritime companion."

"Capital, capital! Do all of you come along. Mrs. Hill has got a luncheon ready, with tea as good as one may obtain on this benighted isle."

Francis took himself back to the ship, but the others climbed up into the trap and found a handhold as Mr. Hill shook up the reins and shouted at his poor thin horse. They wheeled off over dirt roads that soon yielded to grass tracks, a little crowded with a quiet jostling of traffic in the town. As they went, Mr. Hill pointed at a number of buildings, which all turned out to be churches.

Not far from the wharf, a dog darted across the street before them, heavy dugs swinging below a starved-looking belly, and was caught—a terrible sound!—by the wheels of a heavy cart going the opposite way. The dog rolled and shook herself, whimpering, and limped off into an alley.

Kay had left Pilot in Jacky Judge's charge. She looked down the alley, but the dog had vanished. Perhaps it would live.

Leaving the crowded market area, they turned corners very confusingly along empty, dusty alleys lined with whitewashed walls and scrap-wood fences in front of little ramshackle houses, and after some time pulled into a short gravel drive before a yellow bungalow with a roof of thatched straw. A woman waited on the porch, fair-haired and tired-looking.

Mr. Hill announced, with endearing pride in this nondescript lady, "My wife!"

"We are hoping you will stay to tea," Mrs. Hill began, as they climbed down from the cart. "And maybe take a walk with us this afternoon, before Evensong . . ." Her voice was light and hesitant. A girl and a small boy clung to her sagging yellowed-muslin skirts, the boy peeping round and hiding his face again. He had pretty gold curls like bedsprings. The girl's duller flaxen hair was pulled into taut triangles by braids at her temples.

Mr. Hill handed them down from the cart, stopping to display his imported British flowers ("Carefully packed, and of course hand-watered in this climate, shoots do survive!"), and ushered them in, all the bodies bustling round in a swirling of people and steps and light and shade.

Kay stood still in the quiet garden, in the greyish-white light of Tonga, staring at palm-frond leaves and a ragged rooster ranging in the yard, and the horse still harnessed to the cart. In a foreign place.

∾

Mrs. Hill had brought out her wedding china. "Only coconut cake," she apologized, setting down small, thick cakes arrayed on a platter of flow blue undoubtedly crated with them from England. Understanding the honour paid her, Thea said they looked delicious.

Mr. Hill had gone into full clerical spate, informing Mr. Brimner of things he likely already knew: "Our small Anglican congregation in Tonga originated as a breakaway from Methodism. We might perhaps characterize our flock as Anglo*phile*—it was at first named for Queen Victoria!" Mr. Hill chuckled at that. He amused himself too easily, Thea considered.

Mr. Brimner sat quietly taking in the house: the open expanse of bare oilclothed floor, two chintz-draped chairs, a short row of books in rough shelves below the front window.

"By the grace of Bishop Willis, our church has been attached to the new diocese under the higher jurisdiction of New Zealand," said Mr. Hill. "We have a gentleman's agreement, you know, not to seek converts from among those already baptized by the Methodists or the London Missionary Society, and we *do respect* that."

"Oh yes, yes," Mr. Brimner said gravely, as if accepting vital dogma.

Thea suspected that perhaps Mr. Hill, busy with his family and his garden, did not mind having a limit placed on his conversion labours.

He had none of the uncomfortable religious zeal she remembered from missionaries they had known in the West. He reminded her more of Mr. Hinch, the finicky curate in Yarmouth, an authority on Gregorian chant who was happy to gossip in Aunt Queen's parlour. Perhaps zeal was for missions in the wilderness. Tonga could not be called wilderness; its ancient people, its long history and the presence of quite so *many* churches all precluded that.

∽

The girl came out to the porch with her brother to call Kay in for tea and cakes. They were named Muriel and Peregrine—a silly name for a boy, but Kay did not say so. Inside, the house was stuffy and dark, with a smell of church over must. Thea and Mrs. Hill sat drinking tea at the table while Mr. Brimner and Mr. Hill talked at the other side of the room in the only other chairs. Mr. Hill had lit a pipe, another reek. Muriel took Kay to sit on a bolster against the wall with a plate of quite nice cakes, if you did not mind chewing.

They sat silent; Kay was listening to the others talk, and Muriel seemed to have no conversation. She was twelve or thirteen, taller than Kay, but not by much. She kept watch over Peregrine and did not allow him to have another cake, after two. He looked as though he might pout but was distracted by a toy donkey cart he found under a cushion, and spent a long time going back and forth on the linoleum, murmuring *clip-clop clip-clop* to himself. Muriel said he was six, but the golden curls made him seem younger.

The burden of going on and on like this, sitting in rooms listening to people talk, weighed down on Kay. The thought of living for perhaps eighty more years, or even fifty—or until she had a baby and died of it like her mama—when even one year or one day more was unbearable. More of this and then more, all of it tedium and irritation. The same feeling descended on her at the start of church, at the first *Dearly beloved*. This house was infested with churchiness. What was the use of going elsewhere in the world when you brought everything dull along with you?

The ladies were rising. By the window, Mr. Hill and Mr. Brimner turned, staring as if they were surprised to see them still there.

"Will you walk with us toward the harbour?" Mrs. Hill asked Thea, which meant Kay would also have to go and walk in the heat. "I am going to call on Mrs. Rachel Tonga, a great lady of the town, and I believe she will be glad to meet you."

They left the men in the shadowy house and walked out into one dusty lane after another, and soon went diagonally across a long, scrubby promenade of grass, like a street but with no paving, and then along a withy fence toward the harbour once more.

The great white house with red roofs they had seen from the harbour was the palace, Muriel said. It had not looked like a palace to Kay; it was not even as large as Aunt Lydia's house at Lake Milo.

As they walked, Mrs. Hill did most of the talking. She knew all the royal family, and all those who were related to royalty, in which exact degree, who had done what to whom many years ago, and what that second person had done about it—as if she had transferred an English interest in monarchy straight over to Tonga, with all the reverence attached. Kay found it impossible to fathom the story of the king's second marriage, or its ramifications for Princess Salote, who had been sent away last year and was now "practically exiled" in New Zealand to attend what sounded like a very ordinary girls' school, while the people waited for her father's new wife to have a son, who would be the heir.

Mrs. Hill told them that Mrs. Rachel Tonga (with whom Princess Salote had been lodged before her exile) lived with her sister Sela and Sela's husband Sione Mateialona, who had once been the premier. Rachel and Sela, she said, were "real Tongan ladies—certainly the most intelligent and best-mannered I have seen." She paused to chide Peregrine for jumping and creating dust that might coat the ladies' muslin.

Mrs. Rachel Tonga lived along the Beach Road in Kolomotuʻa, west of the palace. West also of the British consul and the Residency, which Thea told Mrs. Hill she was most interested to see, although when Kay wanted to know why, she could not say precisely.

"Oh, because of Empire, I suppose," she said, and laughed a little.

Kay looked up at her sideways. She said nothing impertinent but allowed her gait to slow so that she walked behind Thea.

"It is a handsome building, is all I meant," Thea added.

Then Kay wished she had not asked why. She did not intend to be a disagreeable person, even though it sometimes came out that way.

"Mrs. Rachel Tonga keeps proper house, you'll see," Mrs. Hill promised as they came closer, on this hot and too-long walk. "Very grand and clean. They are *fakapapalangi*, living in the European style, unlike some of the locals."

"They have a little dog," Muriel told Kay. "A pug dog."

"*I* have a dog," Kay said, and went back to worrying about Pilot, and whether he might have slipped off the deck and drowned in the sea.

The house was a low white bungalow with a handsome veranda decorated with angular gingerbread. Mrs. Rachel and Sela sat on the low stoop in their shirt sleeves.

"You have caught us resting from our washtubs," Mrs. Rachel told Mrs. Hill, laughing. She was a strongly built, warm-faced woman, bulky at first glance but graceful when she moved. A comfortable presence, calm in her own powerful good sense, and she spoke English perfectly well.

Another woman, Miss Winifred Small, came as they were standing on the steps. She too was kindly welcoming when Thea and Kay were explained as connections of the new Anglican missionary.

Kay liked Miss Winifred, who was youngish, and prettyish, although some might call her plain. While the ladies talked, she looked like she was thinking of interesting other ideas. Miss Winifred had lived in Tonga from childhood, among the Wesleyan people. She had with her a friend, Lisia Fifita, a round young woman in a straight blue dress, and Lisia's little girl Eponie, all dark eyes and glowing skin, perhaps three or four. A lovely child, with a deep dimple that came and went, although she was shy to smile. She put a warm hand on Thea's knee, patting gently in welcome, and soon Thea pulled her up to sit in her lap, where she settled in so comfortably that Kay could almost feel the tender weight herself.

As the women talked, Kay took off her hat to let the little girl try it on. Liquid, velvet-brown eyes looked up from inside the brim, absurdly happy. When Kay asked for it back, Eponie took it off at once and held it out, but her eyes filled with great tears that spilled over and tracked down her darling cheeks. Thea shook her head. "That is Kay's only hat," she said. But she kissed the little girl's soft cheek.

In their height and strength the women were interesting to look at, but their conversation might have been ordinary lady-chat in Yarmouth, and Kay wished they were at least still with Mr. Brimner, rather than on this strange visit.

When she glanced up and saw Peregrine toddling out over the lawn, she followed as if she was looking after him, although she did not intend to bother fetching him back.

They wandered along the expanse of grass and sand, stopping when Peregrine wanted to. Muriel came after them, even though Kay was finished talking to her. She was an insipid girl, perhaps not a dolt, but not interested in anything of the mind. She talked about ribbons, what she had eaten for breakfast and what there would be for tea. Peregrine did not talk, he merely put a rock in his mouth from time to time, which Muriel would hasten to make him spit out. He was not clever either. Kay felt quite alone.

They wandered for some little time over the gentle swell of grassy park, until they were far out of sight of the women. The landscape was not empty, but the few men scattered about seemed to be taking rest, sitting under trees with their arms folded on their knees, gazing into the middle distance.

Seeing some landmark, Muriel stopped, and said that they had got into the palace grounds, where they should not be. She pulled Peregrine back, but he did not want to go, his attention was fixed forward. Ahead of them on a shadowed path lay a shadowy shape. As they looked, the shape began to move. A rock or boulder moving—how strange. Oh! It was an enormous turtle, quite a yard high.

"It is the Tu'i Malila," Muriel said. "The oldest tortoise in the world."

Kay took a step toward it.

The turtle's head lifted, pointed and tiny. Its narrow eye regarded her.

After a moment, it blinked. One wrinkled stump of a leg lifted, and it took a step toward them.

"It is hurt! Look, the marks on its back?"

"No, that is very old. Captain Cook carved his initials on it, they say, when he gave it to the Tu'i Tonga— No, no, Peregrine, come *away*!" Muriel caught at Peregrine's hand and pulled.

Kay expected the boy to complain, but he did not. It was a very strange tortoise. Perhaps it frightened him a little, as it did her.

Muriel came back and plucked at Kay's sleeve. "Come, come away, I am sure you will see him again, he is the king of Malila, the oldest tortoise in the world. He was given to the king very long ago. When you go to the palace later, you will hear all about him."

As Kay lingered, wishing to go closer, the tortoise took another step. It was a moving hill, red and black, a bulge in the fabric of the earth. As old as the stones at the edge of the sea.

Francis was busy aboard ship, taking advantage of their stop for painting and refurbishing, mending sails torn in the great storm, and all the domestic duties that had been waiting his attention. Kay was glad Thea did not decide it was time to turn out the saloon as well, so they could come ashore every morning and spend the last days with Mr. Brimner; except that they did not see enough of him, because Mr. Hill commandeered him.

On their last day, Mr. Hill arranged an excursion out to a famous landmark, a standing stone like Stonehenge, but (Mr. Hill said) "not so ancient, but still very old for this part of the world." They drove out two carts; Kay went with Miss Winifred and Lisia in their cart.

It was a relief to Kay to be alone with them. Not only because she had tired of Mr. Hill, who was a tedious gabster, but because— because Thea walked everywhere, in every company, as the most superior person in the room. It was not egotistical of her, it was simply her perception of the reality of things, her calm under- standing of the strength of her character and education and the protection of her religion. Kay thought it odd that she herself had not received that same certainty from Father, spending so much time in his company. Her sense of her own position in the world seemed to come out as—not lower than other people, precisely, but off to one side.

Kay had once or twice seen Thea's sense of superiority register- ing with Miss Winifred, kind as she was and accommodating to the foreigner's odd opinions. Travelling alone with them, Kay could enjoy Miss Winifred and Lisia, could talk to them and listen to them talk together of people they knew and new babies and the king and other interesting matters.

They drove past groups of drowsy men sleeping on the side of the road or anywhere a little shade could be found, out some dis- tance to the village of Niutoua. At last, there it was: a great lintel and doorway standing in a field.

It was very large, certainly. They all got out of the carts.

Mr. Hill had the facts at his fingertips. Thea did not seem to mind listening to him, though most likely he had been talking ceaselessly during the whole journey.

"Ha'amonga 'a Maui—the Burden of Maui! Constructed from three limestone slabs, nearly twenty feet high," he told them. "Built at the beginning of the thirteenth century under the eleventh Tuʻi Tonga Tuʻitātui, for some purpose of determining or celebrating the solstice, or as the gateway to his royal compound."

Kay wished he would be quiet.

The thing was large, fine. Made of spongy stone, like a lintel for a temple—mainly interesting because the lines of the interior were so straight, after all those centuries. What she liked better was the strange slab stuck into the ground farther down the slope, in a little grove. The throne.

"This is the *ʻesi maka faakinanga*, stone to lean against," Miss Winifred said. She too had wandered away from Mr. Hill's lecture, perhaps having heard it many times before, or knowing more about it all than Mr. Hill did, since she had grown up here. She set the palm of one large, smooth hand against the green-black rock, higher than her head.

"They say we were giants in the olden days. They say this was the old Tuʻi Tonga's throne—his name, Tuʻitātui, means King Strike the Knee. With his back to this great stone, he was safe from assassins from behind, and with his long stick"—she lunged at Kay!—"he would strike out at the knees of every enemy in front. In the oldest times, they say, they burned the bushes, so that from this place he would be able to see enemies coming from over the sea."

She had said *we* were giants. Was Miss Winifred a Tongan, then, too? She had dark hair and strong bones; she did not look like Lisia, but perhaps that did not matter.

Kay never knew what one ought to do in the presence of old things. She touched the rock. A man had once sat pressed against this rock, in fear of assassins—and had lashed out with a stick and broken some knees.

She tried to feel if the Tuʻi Tonga's ghost still sat there, but could not sense it. But it was, all the same, her favourite thing she had seen all this time in Tonga: its flat, unembellished surface, out in the little grove that had grown up around it, hidden away from the world because the places that enemies came from had changed.

In the early afternoon they travelled on to Fùa, the village where Mr. Brimner was to serve, and the people there laid out a welcome feast for them on tablecloths of palm leaves: roast pig and chickens and white yams, wrapped in more leaves. Some girls brought round the packages of food, and some girls danced.

Lisia took Kay close to the dancing floor, where a girl was being dressed for the dancing. "My cousin Lotoa," Lisia murmured in Kay's ear.

"She is beautiful," Kay whispered back.

Lisia stroked her arm, tenderly agreeing. "All my family is beautiful."

An old woman crept around Lotoa's feet, anointing them with some substance—Lisia said it was coconut oil, mixed with fragrance—smoothing the oil on Lotoa's calves and shins and on her legs, far up, even under her tapa cloth skirt, until they were glossy. Rising to her feet with no seeming effort, the old mother oiled Lotoa's arms and shoulders. Lotoa spread it on her neck and bosom and across her upper arms, smiling to herself as she became the shining one. Kay felt it in her own arms and breast, cool oil sliding down the front of her own chemise.

All the girls were burnished with coconut oil by their mothers until their arms glistened in the dance, which was both modest and immodest: the girls kept their legs at all times carefully close together, bent at the knees in a docile crouch, but they swayed intoxicatingly, and moved their shining hands in a complicated series of meaningful gestures (which Kay invented translations for, all ocean voyages and pledging allegiance and yielding to love). The dancers were accompanied by two old men and an old lady, singing at one side of the dance floor in cracked, almost shouting voices that were nevertheless very sweet.

There was always singing. Late at night, even in her cabin on the *Morning Light*, Kay heard the singing carrying from the shore. Men's voices and women's, so close-blended that she could not tell if they were singing harmony or all the same notes but in different shades of voices. Church went on all the time too, all night it seemed. It was a strange country, but more real to her than other places she had been. The people were not setting their best face to the water, pretending for guests. The whole island, as far as she had ridden by cart and pony trap, was the same, people living exactly as they had lived for a very long time, except with more churches.

That day, Bishop Willis made harbour from Christchurch. When they returned from the village feast, he was awaiting them, an elderly, bony, straggle-bearded man, large hands and feet out of proportion to the amount of meat left on him. Kay disliked him strongly. Perhaps he had some flavour of Father in his knitted, protruding brow. He was all rigged out in black, ancient black gaiters coming down over his boots in frog-pads, and he wore a balked expression. As if ripe to do some balking of his own.

Beside him sat a small, neat man with a brown Vandyke beard, so tidily combed it looked false. Kay had an urge to pull it. In a tone of gloomy triumph, the bishop introduced this fellow as Mr. Piper-Ffrench, late of Christchurch, New Zealand, and the new incumbent for Fùa.

But that was the village where they had just been feted—Mr. Brimner's new parish. Kay did not understand.

On the dining table the bishop set a thick paper, with printing and writing on it. "There is yet a niche for you, Brimner, never fear," he intoned, as if reading the litany. He pushed the paper across, saying, "Your new orders, my dear sir."

Mr. Brimner bent to examine the sheet, taking out his spectacles and polishing them as his eyes raced over the page. He did not need his glasses for close work, Kay knew, only for time to think.

"Spare me your recriminations," the bishop said, holding up one knob-knuckled hand.

Mr. Brimner had made none.

"The island archipelago of Ha'apai has been underserved, although the worthy Mr. Fruelock has established a school on the main island, Pangai. Dr. Barnes of Christchurch believes it will be wise to expand our diocese into the islands nearby. Ha'ano is the island he suggests, and he has travelled there often enough to be sure you would be welcome. The Society has purchased a rudimentary house, with an outbuilding suitable for renovation into a school, which we will consecrate in the spring, once you have made the desired changes."

Seeing Kay's attention, Mr. Brimner slid the sheet over so she could read it. The parchment was signed at the bottom with a huge flourish: *Alfred Tonga.*

Kay looked up, questioning. Not moving his eyes from his reading, Mr. Brimner murmured, "That is how bishops sign, using their See as their name."

Pomp and *ceremony* unfolded in Kay's mind like a shabby velvet carpet rolling out to a set of marble steps. She squinted up the steps into the expanding darkness of one kind of universe—then turned her mind away from all that, because it was a sham. In her experience God was interior, or vastly exterior, not bothered with position or hierarchy. But some poor silly folk did think it mattered.

ᔆ

Thea was disappointed on Mr. Brimner's behalf, but proud of their friend. His courtesy never faltered, upon being informed that he had arrived too late to take up the post he had been promised. Was the bishop using the royal *we?* In his old-fashioned black gabardine, he looked to Thea like a great mangy vulture, squawking. Like that vile Mr. Drummond who came to Blade Lake, visiting the school and demanding a reduction of their budget . . .

She stopped, her attention turned inside. She had begun to feel uncomfortable during the ride back to Nuku'alofa, and now a strong interior cramping made her forget Mr. Brimner's trouble in her own.

Dodging through the back kitchen and down the moonlit garden to the outhouse, Thea lifted her skirts and sat just as a wave took her over. *Oh,* she thought. *Oh my dear.*

And then a flooding out. The pain was nothing, no more troubling than was ordinary for her courses. She almost wished it had been more, to register the fact of it. Two months' delay—she had been allowing herself to believe that God had forgiven her.

It felt like the bottom had dropped out of everything. But Mrs. Hill had left a basket of rags there, and after some time of spasmodic flow it was possible to clean herself and rig a wadding for her underclothes, to avoid stain or discovery. She did not like to think of the tiny homunculus down there in the cesspit, but since there was no help for it, she pushed that from her mind, and also whether the child already had a soul, and whether she should pray, and why she could not do so.

She did not cry. After a few minutes to compose herself, she walked back to the house, the bright moon making it easy to see the path. It was over, that was all.

At the wharf, Francis came over with the tender. He was surprised to find Mr. Brimner returning in the trap with them, but quick to put a kind face on it. "Sailing on, eh? Ha'apai—well, well, that lies on our way, not more than a hundred miles north," Francis said, at Thea's hand on his arm. "Farther to travel, eh, Mr. Brimner? It is often the way."

After these several days' delay, Francis was impatient to be on their way, but not at all ill-tempered with it. Thea pressed his arm and resolved never to tell him of the—the newly lost. A little clot of blood, that was all.

∾

The full moon shone so ferociously from the heavens that the night was bright as day. Mr. Brimner was down below unpacking, readying for the next thing.

Kay kicked the leather ball again for Pilot, who raced down the deck to catch it before it went into the scupper. He overshot the mark, and his nose went smack into the metal ditch, but he shook his head and caught the ball in his sharp white teeth, and trotted off to take it to someone else, as was his annoying habit, flag-tail waving at the prospect of another chase.

She looked after him down the length of the ship, hoping it was not Arthur Wetmore he aimed for, because that might make Francis cross.

Mr. Brimner materialized out of the not-darkness beside her. "What a moon," he said. "σελήνη—*Selene*," he said. "And on a night like this, πανσελήνη—"

"*Pan-selene*," Kay said. "All-moon—full moon?"

"That's it." He pulled out his tobacco pouch and lit a cheroot, which he saved for special occasions. "Your progress has been splendid, my dear Kay. I have no qualms about abandoning you to work alone. But I wonder if from time to time you would perhaps write me a letter, perhaps in the original Greek, so that I can enjoy your further progress?"

Kay felt her mouth stretching, that kind of smiling that is more like pain.

∾

When they emerged on deck into the bright morning, Lifuka lay before them, the largest island of Ha'apai, reached during the night. Francis had already sent a boat to the wharf at Pangai town with a message for Mr. Fruelock, to whom Mr. Brimner was to report, and had had word back inviting all who cared to visit Pangai to come ashore. Kay wanted to go, of course, and after the restorative tea Thea agreed; she too was curious to meet Mr. Brimner's colleague.

He was waiting on the wharf—easily recognized, a black crow in the crowd of white-tunicked men, wearing stovepipe trousers rather than a mat round his waist, with a very wide vicar's hat. He looked almost Tongan, so brown was his skin from sun. He had the black hair that goes with an olive complexion, and looked a good deal healthier and more reliable than Mr. Hill, Thea was glad to see.

Mr. Fruelock shook hands generally and welcomed them all to Ha'apai, and to the village of Pangai, and begged them to set forth with him on a short walk.

"My wife is at the school but will break off when we arrive, for she is eager to meet you, Mr. Brimner. Mr. Hill has sung your praises these many months, and we are delighted to have a scholar of your proportion, although you may find little exercise for the mind at first, beyond learning the new tongue. Do not be astonished if you find pupils who can engage to— Ah! here we are, and here is my dear wife. Dorothy! Come and meet Mr. Brimner, and of course Mrs. Grant and Miss, um, her sister . . ."

They had arrived at a low-walled house on a quiet lane removed from the main road. The woman at the door wore a welcoming smile on her broad, clever face. She came out to greet them and took Thea's arm in a friendly way, exclaiming that they had never thought to have such a treat today, a visit from a captain's wife!

Thea pressed Kay's hand, and she slipped behind Mr. Brimner to let him greet Mrs. Fruelock, who was as tall as he—a good deal taller, standing on the step.

"So this is Mr. Brimner!" she said, looking down in a satisfied way. "We are fortunate, and I hope you will count yourself to be so too, once you have found your feet here. I hope your voyage was supportable—are you a good sailor? I am not, myself—the voyage here was misery, I tell Eric I will never make another . . ."

Still talking, she led them into the interior darkness and along a tiled hall to a large sitting room. There were actual chairs. Clean and airy, white-curtained, the room had a comfortable feeling, and made Thea feel well-disposed to Mrs. Fruelock. Mr. Fruelock saw to his guests' disposition while his wife poured water into tall glasses; the day was hot enough to make that very welcome. Three girls emerged, each with a plate of biscuits and cut fruit, which they set down carefully before curtsying to the newcomers.

"Back to school now, girls," Mrs. Fruelock told them. "We will come in a few moments, to see how well the children are coming on, and then we will have some singing."

Kay stayed standing by Thea's chair, perhaps a little shy of the girls. One looked to be older than Kay, Thea thought, and the others a year or two younger.

"Let me congratulate you, sir, on your assignment to this diocese, and to this mission," Fruelock said formally, and shook Mr. Brimner's hand all over again. He sat, stood, bustled a little, rummaging for a paper, and sat again. "Well! Here is a map to show you— Oh, you have? Well, no need to look again, then." He set the map aside. "You are on a two years' gift, I believe—the bishop has no doubt told you that this is a mission post?"

Mr. Brimner nodded. Still a little pale under his sun-pinked skin from last night's upset.

Mrs. Fruelock nodded with him. "No church. No. But teaching!"

That seemed odd to Thea. What was the point of a mission without a church? Mr. Brimner was looking off to the long white wall, where the jalousied blinds let in slits of light in a shifting pattern on the plaster.

Mr. Fruelock stood again, and sat again. Crossed his thin legs. "Yes!" He crossed his legs the other way. "It is a delicate business here in Ha'apai, between the Wesleyans and the relatively new Free Church of Tonga—which is also Wesleyan, the church to which the king belongs. But the rift, for we must call it that, allows of movement. I do credit Bishop Willis, his judgment is acute. He presents, or rather *we* present, here in Ha'apai, a kind of wedge that may drive through—although always in a Christian sense!—to bring more converts into the comfortable fold of Anglo-Catholic worship. The bishop fears the Latter Day Saints will return with the Samoan mission. In fact, they have already established a school in Neiafu, and there are rumours of property purchased for a church in Nuku'alofa."

These machinations were not unfamiliar to Thea from the Indian missions in Canada. But there seemed to be an embarrassment of churches involved here.

"But the LDS are not our chief concern. Assuredly, the Roman Catholics will arrive in force! We hope equally to save these poor islanders from the excess of the Romans, as we instill the principles of Christian love in the heathen heart."

"Not that there are actual *heathens* left in Tonga!" Mrs. Fruelock struck in. "Because the Work has been strong!"

"Yes, ah! Yes, it has, my love. But delicate, as I say. And so—no church here, as yet, but we make inroads. My dear wife runs the infant school, and I take pupils in the middle school, but we believe, that is, the bishop believes, a school in the hamlet of Ha'ano will provide a foothold on the island and strengthen our position in all of Ha'apai . . . This entails considerable responsibility for you."

It seemed Mr. Fruelock was a schemer, a political animal. Mr. Brimner would never be that. But he was a very good teacher, Thea knew. They were fortunate to have him.

Mrs. Fruelock patted a firm, kindly paw on Mr. Brimner's knee. "Eric has secured you a house. The outbuilding, in need of some repair, will do for a schoolroom . . ."

"Yes, yes, he will see all that soon enough," said Mr. Fruelock. "Now we must pray, Dorothy, and perhaps you can show Mrs. Grant and Miss Um the school? We have Shirley Baker's printing of the Book of Common Prayer in Tongan, Brimner—a Wesleyan, but a man of parts, Anglican in his outlook, moving toward conversion, I believe, in his later years. Anyhow, his translation will do until Bishop Willis finishes his own, next year . . . Gracious, Dorothy, are you still here? Do proceed, and I will strive here with Mr. Brimner, and then take him to see Baker's grave—a side note to our current struggles . . ."

Prayer was a working mechanism for Mr. Fruelock. They were still following Mrs. Fruelock out as he bent his head fiercely forward and began, *"O God, who hast made of one blood all the peoples of the earth, and didst send thy blessed Son to preach peace to those who are far off . . ."*

"Eric is not un-devout," Mrs. Fruelock was saying, "you must understand, dear Mrs. Grant—but he is single-minded. The task is the establishment of solid ground in Haʻapai, which nothing but zeal can accomplish. And even then—well. We shall see."

She led them out into a sunlit enclosure, tamped-down earth and a few parched weeds, and across into a building with jalousie windows, a long porch giving shade to the windows. Inside, in two classrooms, were twenty or thirty children, one half repeating a vocabulary list from the board under the direction of an older girl with tidy braids, the other reciting by rote as another older girl—a pale, pretty girl, who must be another Fruelock daughter—pointed to pictures pinned to the wall. All the children were neatly turned out in long green tunics. Some of the boys wore mats, but not all. Perhaps they were not all well-connected, Thea thought, since the mat seemed to be a mark of rank or prestige.

They poured out of the rooms and mustered into rows under direction from the two elder girls, crying greetings from group to group until hushed and orderly. "*Mālō*," they said in unison, and then broke into a laughing discord of "*Mālō! Mālō e lelei!*" Miss Winifred had told them that *mālō e lelei* meant "it is good to be alive," but the people seemed to use it as both "hello" and "thank you." Mrs. Fruelock translated again: "Congratulations on being well, they are telling you. Being in good health is worthy of gratitude to our Lord!"

The children sang a greeting song, bathing their guests in good nature, and then gave a display of poetry, including recitations of "The Boy Stood on the Burning Deck" and Rossetti's "Up-Hill" and other famous works, made charming by their great enthusiasm for the task. They laughed at each other and prompted the speakers when words failed, and were equally happy to be dismissed at the end of their demonstration.

One little boy came directly to Thea, and stood beside her, patting her knee with his hand. Five or six, perhaps. He was serious, and looked up into her eyes with complete trust, as if he already knew and loved her. "*Mālō*," he whispered, leaning closer.

"That is Sione, don't let him bother you. Be good, Sione!" said one of the Fruelock daughters, Thea did not know which.

She laughed and said, "He is perfectly good, are you not, Sione?"

He lifted his eyebrows several times, such a funny little man, as if trying to tell her something secret.

"That means yes, he is saying *yes, yes*," said the Fruelock girl, and Thea bent and raised her own eyebrows back at him, *yes yes yes!* Refreshing to see her look less forbidding than usual.

She and Kay clapped with as much vigour as they could, and were swarmed with more children come to give a special *mālō* before they ran off and out the green wooden gate.

Mrs. Fruelock waved them away and set her daughters to tidying the schoolrooms, and said that after such a strenuous morning she felt the need of her dinner, did not Mrs. Grant? She called her daughters to order and they came at once, the youngest one slowly, because she had skinned her knee and was weeping a little, but still with good nature.

Dorothy Fruelock ran both the school and her household with such efficiency and lack of fuss that Thea felt ashamed of her own efforts at Blade Lake. No emergency fazed her. While attending to the daughter whose knee was skinned and needed ointment, she directed other daughters to the putting on of the kettle and the setting out of linens and cake tins, so that very soon the midday dinner was spread out neatly on the board, although Mrs. Fruelock's attention had remained fixed on her task and she had never raised her voice or become cross, as Thea might have done. Knee mended, she patted the daughter off to the garden with her sisters and Kay, and settled back in her chair for a cozy and leisurely visit with Thea while they waited for the gentlemen to join them.

∾

Mr. Fruelock's wife was lovely, Kay thought. Her name was Dorothy, the same as Thea's name Theodora, but backwards, and much more modern. And she was a teacher too, but with all those girls of her own, identical in white smocks, identically well-scrubbed except for the bandaged knee of the littlest one.

Kay did not mind being sent away with the girls. Mr. Fruelock had Mr. Brimner closeted in his study anyhow. In a little while he would go down to the wharf with them and board the *Morning Light* again for the short trip to Ha'ano. The mission boat, upended in the back of the garden awaiting repairs, looked like it would be some time till it was seaworthy, but Mr. Brimner would not be trapped on the smaller island: Mr. Fruelock said he could borrow a Wesleyan boat for the asking, and promised he would be out himself within the week to see how things were going on. So that was all right. And it was only for two years—he had only promised to stay that long in mission.

Some of the girls were younger than she was, their names all flowers, hard to remember. Rose was the eldest, four years older than Kay; she had been teaching the native children. Then Violet, Lily and Pansy—or was it Daisy? It must be Pansy. In former years, when Kay had sometimes made lists of the children she would have, there was always a Daisy on the list; sometimes she had a twin, called Buttercup. The girls were undemanding company, sufficient in themselves, content to continue a long-running, complicated game involving a pattern scraped in the dust and the tossing of a stone and jumping to and fro. Kay stood at the edge of their marked-out turf, looking away into the gardens. Small birds flitted through the trees, twittering to each other, *mālō, mālō e lelei*.

Mr. Brimner had sent a message to Francis, asking if he could be ferried on to Ha'ano, and Francis himself came in answer. He had discovered a minor leak on the *Morning Light*, a matter of caulking that should be done before setting out for Fiji, and had left Mr. Wright to oversee it while he came ashore to fetch Thea. The Fruelocks offered beds for the night, but there was no need for that, Francis said. The work would be done today, and they might as well wait till morning to take Mr. Brimner on to Ha'ano; but he intended to take Thea back to the ship for a proper rest, if she was willing.

Looking at Kay, who shook her head violently, Thea laughed a little. "You may spirit me away, dear Francis, but I think Kay would like to stay and spend the day with the girls, if she may?"

Mrs. Fruelock said of course, and that they would undertake to get her back to the ship with Mr. Brimner after supper. Kay loved her even more.

"I am grateful, Captain," Mr. Brimner said. He looked pinched about the eyes, tired perhaps from the indisposition of the previous night—perhaps from the strain and delay in reaching his destination. Anybody might find it difficult. He did not know the language yet, and was to be sent to a separate island without English company at all or anyone to talk to. Kay would be frightened, if it was her, going there all alone.

Mrs. Fruelock smote her hands together and said they must go to market now, to send provisions with Mr. Brimner. The girls took the plates. Swept up in their industry, Kay was given a tea towel to dry with. When they came back to the sitting room, the adults were ready to walk out.

Taking a little pull-wagon, sufficient for Mr. Brimner's needs, they walked to a market lot where trays were laid out in the sun with a straw awning over them and a woman or man sitting behind each; there was a shack with shelves inside it, on which were two or three jars and a few canned goods. Mrs. Fruelock spoke in Tongan to each person, warm fluid syllables, beginning each conversation with *mālō, mālō e lelei, mālō aupito*. One of the older women asked them "*Na'a ke kai?*" which Mrs. Fruelock said was a very traditional greeting meaning *have you eaten?* From an olden time when perhaps you might not have, Kay guessed. She wished Francis had brought Pilot ashore. With a rope to keep him, he would find this market interesting, and there did not seem to be any wild dogs to worry him.

Mrs. Fruelock told Mr. Brimner she could provide flour and sugar from their own store, and the people of Ha'ano would give him white sweet potatoes and fish, but he would need sorghum, corned beef and various other things—tea, and tinned milk, for there was no fresh milk on the islands. Mr. Brimner declared he had no need for milk, being a plain man who took his tea in its natural state, so (murmuring, "But guests!") Mrs. Fruelock contented herself with two cans, and went on heaping bananas and melons into a bushel basket. She promised him a brace of good-laying hens before Christmas, and he said he would be glad of eggs. So they continued in a bantering promenade around the various stalls.

Kay and Rose followed along, the younger girls darting off through the market to see their own friends.

Rose said, "Is he your father?"

"Mr. Brimner? No! He is my teacher."

"Oh. I thought he might be—I knew the captain could not be."

"No, he is married to my sister."

Rose looked at Kay through her lashes. "He is very handsome."

Kay was startled.

"Captain Grant, I mean," Rose said. Her mouth pulled into a considering moue. "Your sister is quite old."

People had interior selves, Kay already knew. But this secret wickedness was a surprise.

"She is no older than he," she said. "They were engaged for ten years, because he was at sea and she was teaching the Indians."

Rose shrugged. "She looks old. Many captains stop here. Many of them have lovers here, so perhaps that is why your sister travels with him now."

Kay turned away from that girl without saying anything more. She walked back along the dusty road to the jetty and stood there for a time, waiting for a boat. But it came to her that they could not know on the *Morning Light* that she wanted a boat yet, and might not see her standing there. Eventually, after walking a good deal farther than she might have, she found the Fruelocks' house again, recognizing it by the green wooden gate into the school-yard. She stood about in the back garden a while longer, watching through the window where Mr. Brimner and Mrs. Fruelock were carrying on a laughing conversation, while Mr. Fruelock worked irritably at a desk. She did not go inside when the girls carried the supper dishes in, either. Rose was as sleek and proper as always, her eyes down-turned.

Kay decided to wait until Mr. Brimner came out to walk to the jetty. Mrs. Fruelock must think she had already gone back to the boat. Perhaps Rose had told them so.

You cannot know what is inside people's heads, Kay thought. And Rose was older than she was, fifteen or sixteen. Kay could not fault her for it, though she did dislike her. Girls thought of love at that age, and in this strange missionary landscape she had no one to think about but the visitors.

Kay told herself she would not treat Francis differently because some girl thought him handsome. It prickled her, though, that Rose had not asked about Mr. Brimner, who was much younger than Francis and, if not precisely handsome, a very good sort of person.

Dusk had fallen as it did here, too early and too fast, and the night garden became soft and strange. Birds flew above—or, no! They were *bats*, great bats flitting in the branches in black silhouette. Nothing was wrong with bats, anyhow, but that they had a wrong or a different tempo, when you were not expecting them.

A feeling of unreality settled over Kay, the human part of life shown up as unreal, unreliable. Or merely unimportant. The bats moved quickly, shadows in the sky. Like voles in their movement, going swimmingly across the patches of dark-blue sky.

In an hour or so, Mr. Brimner came out, trundling the wagon of supplies behind him, and Kay fell into step beside him. He did not seem surprised to see her.

"There you are. Found the company of all those biddable girls trying, did you?"

Kay nodded in the darkness.

They went on in companionable steps, not speaking, the moon giving enough light that they could have walked all night. But they soon reached the jetty. Mr. Brimner lit the lamp to signal the boat to come out for them, and they arranged themselves on the stones to wait.

"October the fourth. This is the anniversary of my ordination," Mr. Brimner said. "I therefore indulged in a tot of rum, in lieu of the venerable sherry in the MCR. It makes me friendlier, I do notice that."

Was he unfriendly, usually? He seemed to Kay to be an entirely serious person, separate, solitary. But easy to work beside.

"I am rather reticent in the social niceties. Not shy, only restrained. But I must tell you, my dear Kay, that I will miss your good company."

His face burst or blossomed into his beaming smile, the excessive beam that broke his face in half and stretched his mouth—a great many large teeth showing, caught in the moonlight. His forehead was damp, but the smile was sweet, refuting the glistening jumble within.

Kay smiled back, or tried to; she was not much good at it. She had dreamed last night, she now remembered, that it was possible to love someone who is conventionally ugly. (But it was not Mr. Brimner in her dream, it was a larger man, with a bald head and a tender face.)

"Most beautiful," he said—and the words hung for a moment in the air. "*Most beautiful I leave: the light of the sun. Second: bright stars, the face of the moon—but also: ripe cucumbers, apples, and pears.*" He bowed in some vague easterly direction. "Praxilla, a poetess! The shades in the Underworld asked her what was the most beautiful thing she left behind . . . *Most beautiful I leave: the light of the sun.*" He paused for a moment, and then recited it in Greek. "κάλλιστον μὲν ἐγὼ λείπω φάος ἠλίοιο, δεύτερον ἄστρα φαεινὰ σεληναίης τε πρόσωπον, ἠδὲ καὶ ὡραίους σικύους καὶ μῆλα καὶ ὄχνας."

Kay nodded. No cucumbers in this place. No apples, no pears. The boat came toward them out of the inky water, and they descended the stone stairs to meet it.

In the morning they set off for Ha'ano. A mere jaunt, as it turned out: an hour's easy sail along the in-curving western coast, with a light breeze to make it pleasant. Kay and Mr. Brimner did not open a book, but leaned together on the port-side railing. At the near horizon, a perfect triangle of a mountain rose, occupying a whole island.

"A volcanic isle," Mr. Brimner said, pointing it out to Kay. "I believe that must be the island they call Kao. The one to the left, that is Tofua, an extinct volcano, with a crater cutting off the top. Mr. Fruelock tells me there is a lake within, and that someday we will take an expedition there, to visit the sole resident."

So he would have an excursion to look forward to; Kay was glad to think that.

"Not to convert the old person—of course not," Mr. Brimner added. "Nor to school him. I suppose he must have learned everything he needs to know already about how to live in these parts."

Seaton pushed his frowsy head up out of the lifeboat behind them, saying, "There's some as have not enough to do and must rouse workingmen too early."

Mr. Brimner touched Kay's arm to bring her attention back, and pointed out over the sea. "There," he said.

She looked. Nothing. The water was calm, a mirror for the sky.

Jacky Judge came pelting down the deck on silent feet, waving an arm. He reached them and pointed too, mouthing *there*!

Again she turned to the sea, and waited.

The volcano in the distance, the quiet motion of the ship. Nothing.

And then, *there*.

A huge shape melted upward out of the water, and another

behind it, melted into air and back into water in a rounded, elon-
gated gleam of wet black skin.

Nobody spoke.

Two of them, one large, the other immeasurable. Black gloss in
blue gloss.

Kay looked and looked, until her eyes were stretched.

Out of the nothing, out from under the ship and out into the
water that was all the water always, up came another great shape in
a thundering rise, twisting into white underside, falling into a great
foam—breaching—*breaching*, that was the word.

"Are you afraid?" asked Jacky Judge, and Kay looked scorn at him.

Francis, coming to watch, told her, "I started out on a whaler,
twenty years ago—lucky to come safe out of it."

"But they are so—gigantic, so beyond our ordinary scale, I do
not see how the first person decided to kill a whale."

"Fear! Some are afraid of anything larger than themselves, and
want therefore to kill it. The world is full of bad apples," Francis
pronounced, and went back to his work.

The women in Ha'ano had made a special mat for Mr. Brimner,
of white straw with the word T E A C H E R spelled out in darker
fibres. They were standing at the stone jetty when the *Morning
Light* sailed into view. How had they known to come out? Someone
must have been keeping lookout for the stranger arriving.

The stone jetty was just thirty feet long, and as they followed the
welcoming people up the slight rise beyond, they saw that the village
held only a sprinkling of little houses. Straw roofs, tiny windows,
garden plots around them. One house near the shore was a little
larger; beside it, a long, low building stood with windows open to the
air. That was the building that was waiting to be the school, but it had
no tables or desks yet. The floor was dusty, and in one corner a broken
crate bled sea-swelled Bibles. Every book, every piece of paper in
that place was salt-damp, soft and swollen, almost unreadable.

Kay stood in the doorway while the women showed Mr. Brimner over his house—two plaster rooms, with a small roof out back over a cooking place. A dirt floor, but the sandy dirt was well packed down. The first room held a table and a chair, and the women were evidently very proud of them.

They opened the door to the other room, revealing a long bed, fit for a Tongan, with a long white net over it to cheat the mosquitoes. It was clean and pretty. This would be his place, for as long as the bishop said so. The wooden step outside the door was covered with slippers. The women had taken theirs off as they went in. Only Kay and Mr. Brimner still wore their boots.

They all went back out to the schoolhouse, where more women and men had gathered, bringing food. Always food when somebody visited, in this place. Children kept appearing round the corner of the house or climbing the low stone fence, interested, and trim in worn, well-laundered white shorts or dresses. Ten or fifteen of them, and a trickle more. With ceremony, the gift mat was pinned to the schoolroom wall.

There would be some difficulty, living in a place where nobody spoke your language and you did not yet speak theirs.

Mr. Brimner gave a short speech anyway, mounting the one step to the long porch of the school building. "*Mālō e lelei, mālō aupito,*" he said (they laughed with pleasure at this brave attempt). "I am sorry not to speak your language yet. I am told there is a man in another village—Fakakakai, or perhaps in Pukotala?—who speaks English, having lived in New Zealand. But we will not rely on him. I have my Tongan dictionary and am eager to learn. I am fortunate to have come home to this place, *mālō, mālō aupito.*"

The little crowd clapped their hands, although they could not have understood him very well, and then they ate, and drifted away into the fields again about their usual business. Each person a person as much as Kay was, as much as Mr. Brimner was. Each one thinking his own thoughts or singing an unknown song inside her head. Maybe, in the two years he spent there, Mr. Brimner would come to know what the people were thinking, maybe he would find someone else to teach Ancient Greek to, or to teach him Ancient Tongan.

The sailors brought Mr. Brimner's trunks up to the house. The last mothers shooed the children out and helped unpack; even though each item must be exclaimed over, it was quickly done. The women looked at the neat house with satisfaction and left them alone.

Mr Brimner hung his plain silver-and-ebony crucifix on a nail on the wall, and set four or five books, including *Meditation and Mental Prayer*, on the table.

"I will keep most of the books stored away until I need them," he told Kay. "Having seen the damp-damage at the school."

The house door hung a little awry, but he shut it carefully behind them anyway and latched it with the rotating piece of wood, and walked with Kay down to the little stone jetty. The boat had gone back to the ship to take back the sailors, so they stood there, silent, alone together in this odd place. Ha'ano.

Well. Arranging her pinny behind her so as not to muss her dress, Kay sat on the edge of the jetty, little stones pressing into her legs and rump. She would have pebbled dimples on the back of her legs from the rough concrete.

"Keep up your derivations list," he said absently, scanning the variations in colour in the shallow sea.

"Yes," she agreed.

"This is a pleasant haven where I find myself," he said. He turned to look back at his house, and the other houses laid out along the interior road, and the forest of palms that reached almost to the ocean, along a thin edge of sanded beach. "It will only be lonely at first."

The boat was crawling across already from the *Morning Light*. Kay stood and fluffed her dress around her again. "I will write to you," she said. "I promise I will."

The boat bumped up against the jetty. Mr. Best was waiting. She held out her hand, and Mr. Brimner took it gently and shook it with grave attention. He doffed his hat.

In the boat she sat facing the shore so she could wave to him again. His long, thin legs, his round body, his large head and smoked spectacles. He stood on the stone wharf, waving his handkerchief. Then, so that she could leave, he turned and wandered off down the beach, pale-grey jacket flapping a little behind him.

10

Ask and You Shall Have

As the ship moved over the deep sea and her bunk moved likewise, beneath her and supporting her, Kay dreamed and dreamed. She could not wake from dreaming of Blade Lake; it seemed she dreamed for days, years, the whole length of her life. She turned away again and promised not to see or speak of the children in their lines, shivering in the long, deep shudder of winter in the North, wrapped in grey blankets torn in half, ice on their eyelashes, standing in the snow for fire drill. That was a good thing, though: Father instituted the drills after a school in Saskatchewan burnt down, and many children died.

Many children died. Standing in lines again to be tested for TB, turning their heads to watch the snick of Miss Ramsay's knife, making no cry. Thea told them she was proud of their courage.

Kay hated her saying that. It hurt them just the same—it was not all right to hurt them, because they were brave! Some were too afraid to cry out, some of them hushed the others. John did not like the cut, but Annie pinched him to be quiet, and then he went out to do the evening milking after all, since it was Rota C that day. And Thea sent Annie back up to scrub the ward floor, because she was still being punished.

That was Kay's fault. She had run faster than Miss Ramsay's

approaching heels, and let Annie take the blame for being in the pantry. It was true that Miss Ramsay would blame Annie even if Kay stood there with a mouth full of bread, molasses on her chin. But she should have run back to say, to shout, that it was her, it was her all the time, taking what she wanted, it was not Annie at all. But she did not.

Worse than that. In the study she had let her head nod when Miss Ramsay told Father that Annie was stealing bread. She was afraid, was she, of Father?

She could not look at herself for that, she could not think about it. She had been staring at what he would do to her that she had seen him do to others. The big strap slashing down or a furious shaking or a long time in a cold, dark, confining place. She could not make her mouth move to tell.

Nor could she come out of the dream. In four o'clock twilight Miss Ramsay stood over Annie with the pointer from the upper classroom, and when Kay said no, no, she swung harder again and this time with the many-pronged five-chalked music-line-drawing stick, scoring five dark-red lines into Annie's winter-pale arm when it clawed down with long brass fingers.

Then Kay did wake. She pulled herself out of the dream and climbed up through twisted sheets into the close-wrapped wood of her bunk, breathing in rhythm with the slap-slap of the waves on the side as they ploughed through the long sea up to Fiji.

She knew where she was now.

It was because they had left Mr. Brimner at Ha'ano that her nightmares were back. She could not be left.

Mr. Brimner would not claw anyone, he never would. At the worst he might look at them questioningly. Ha'ano was too small for the children to be kept from their parents. They would run home even in the middle of the day for their dinner of fish soup and taro. If the teacher beat them—but Mr. Brimner would not beat them—but if anyone ever did, any other teacher, like Mr. Maitland, or some Mr. Fruelock or other, the children would tell, and a large father would walk over the field and pick up the cruel teacher with one big fist and shake him like you might shake a misbehaving cat, only until he was dead.

Since Thea had not come to wake her, she must not have cried out with the dream. She had not cried out in life either, watching Miss Ramsay slash at Annie's arm.

In her bare feet she stole up on deck and found Pilot curled tight in his box close by the stove vent, and buried her cold hands in his fur. In the distance, Mr. Wright called quietly to a seaman, and the seaman answered. The only sound in the world. The ocean was quiet and there was no moon. She picked Pilot up and carried him down to her bunk, which was not allowed.

Even then, she dreamed again. Perhaps because of being at sea again, after a break of several days. Miss Grace Ramsay, black dress, staring owl eyes—four strong slaps back and forth, and a pause, and when Annie does not give in and cry, she slaps again, one-two-three-four, and again, and again, until Father comes and stops her, Thea running in the hall outside and Miss Ramsay stiff neck and eyes still staring, utterly right right right right.

Kay forced herself to lie back down. Pilot had curled on the floor on her discarded dress, but he looked up and then bounded back onto the bunk, where he turned six times around his own tail and nestled again into her knees, and with that steadying weight she could lie still, thinking and remembering, but at least not dreaming.

At breakfast, unable to contain her thoughts, she asked Thea, "Why did Father first go to Blade Lake?" That was a thing she thought she was allowed to ask.

"To bring succour to the Indians, of course," Thea said, frowning. "As was his duty. He had worked hard at Fort à la Corne, and to be offered the school was an honour, proof that his efforts were recognized, that the bishop saw his success with the community there."

"But why was the school there at all, why did they not just have schools of their own, with their own people to teach them?" After

Tonga, the schools and churches there, and men like Mr. Fruelock and Mr. Hill, Kay now saw the whole arrangement as false, wrong—silly men, caught up in ambition.

Impatient, Thea said, "You forget, they *asked* us to come, it was part of the treaty! Why do you always forget that part? They understood that their children needed education, in order to be part of the white man's world, to be part of civilization. And they needed medicine and treatment."

"The children did not want to be taken away," Kay said, into her collar. The medicine did not do them any good, she did not say.

"That is a very common thing, all over the world. Father was sent away too, you know that. In England, it is the privileged classes that are sent away."

Didn't do him any good either, Kay thought. Once, when he had drunk more port wine than Thea liked him to, he told Mr. Maitland a story about when he was fag (which meant a kind of servant that the younger boys were to sixth form boys) to a much bigger boy who tormented him. A tic fluttering at the edge of his eye crease. "That fellow is now in Parliament. *Hartlingford!*" He spat into the stove, not looking like himself at all. Kay did not know whether Hartlingford was the name of the boy or the name of his seat in Parliament. Sometimes the name came to her in the middle of the night, with blotches around it.

∾

Thea watched Kay carefully, the first days out of Tonga, in case she was missing Mr. Brimner too keenly. She was disturbed, clearly—caught up again in useless thoughts of the old days. But she continued to do her work, Pilot on her lap or curled at her feet, covering notebook pages with (blotched, yes) declensions, lists of derivatives and crossed-out, struggled-through translations. In Shanghai or Hong Kong, Thea had promised Mr. Brimner she would find a Greek-English dictionary, the smallest Liddell & Scott, or the next one up. He had entrusted her secretly with a five-pound note for the purchase, saying, "The Great Scott is beyond my purse, but the Middle Liddell, or even the Little Liddell, will do perfectly well." It was kind of him to think of it.

They all missed him, in fact. Francis was busy on deck most of the day and tired by eventide; even at supper, he and Mr. Wright made very little conversation without Mr. Brimner's gentle prompting. Kay was silent by nature, and Thea was tired. She ought not to be! This life, with the luxury of Liu Jiacheng's quiet service, was practically a rest-cure compared with the unending physical labour at the school, with Miss Ramsay too patrician to ever lift a pinky in the kitchen or, God forbid, the barn, so that a good deal of the rough work fell to Thea.

A lassitude had settled over them with Mr. Brimner's departure, that was all. In the mornings they still sat at the deck table under the awning, but Kay (bent over her papers, working alone in a concentrated, crabbed way that reminded one of Father) had blue shadows beneath her eyes. If that did not mend soon, Thea would insist on a liver dose.

༄

Kay did not give much conscious thought to Mr. Brimner. Except sometimes at night, to wonder what his little hut was like, now that he truly lived there—the way that places become your own and are then entirely different. The ship, for instance, had seemed first like a pretty toy, and then a kind of factory almost; as she came to know its nooks and crannies and to live her life here, it expanded to become the world.

The two rooms of Mr. Brimner's house would have expanded and filled with his presence by now. He would have more books on his table, but perhaps he'd still keep the very best wrapped in oilcloth against furring from the damp salt air. He would be sitting in his one chair, but he might have carried it out onto the little tamped space at the back, to look out over the ocean and watch the sun setting, as they had always used to do on board the *Morning Light*. And then he would fold up his book and knock his pipe against the door frame, and wash the cups in his kitchen before the village woman came to cook. He had never liked to leave a mess for Lena Hubbard or for Jiacheng, and always made Kay help to set the room to rights at the end of their working time. She would continue that orderliness, in his honour.

On deck in the morning heat she thought of him too, when Jacky Judge sped by with a wink, and Mr. Brimner was not there to call some responding jest after him; when Arthur Wetmore came to sit by her for a moment, because she seemed lonely. Not that she could ever be lonely, having grown up in Blade Lake— she was used to her own company for long hours and days; used to people who did not talk to you (Father) or disdained speech (Miss Ramsay) or were too busy to talk, like Thea, or not allowed, like all the rest of them.

Arthur called her to the side, where he stood peering down. "Look, look," he said, and she looked where his finger pointed, to the black sleekness rising from the wave.

She could never have her fill, however many. A group of humpbacks this time, four or five of them. The ship flew on above, the whales flew on below—they would collide! Except the whales easily shifted their trajectory and played tag away from the moving shadow of the ship. But the smallest of them came alongside, curious, looking up from the depths, and Kay saw it was only a baby, the size of a dolphin.

Arthur said, "Aww, reminds me of my baby sister Kitty," and Kay laughed out loud, because she had met that little Kitty and she did have a very long, flat face and a curious eye.

You could not be lonely in a ship, surrounded all the time by thirty others—and in the ocean, living and breathing, the beautiful, responsive creatures of the deep.

The wharf at Suva was serious business, bustling and bright-hot. Draymen loading copra, tall women pushing barrows of brilliant fruit, freight of every kind. When they had made fast and Francis gave permission for them to go ashore, Kay and Thea walked down the street that led from the wharves to the Grand Hotel, and had tea with beautiful cakes on a white veranda overlooking the sea.

That long street, with the sea to the right and its shambling line of dishevelled and crowded shops to the left, might have been an illustration: "A Town in the Tropics." On their way back, a sudden burst of hot rain came down in sheets, pounding down as hard as a prairie rainstorm, and they stepped into a doorway to wait it out. The rain did not wash away the strong, exciting smell of the street, but strengthened it: sea and flowers, spice and dirt, all sweet, hot, close.

The next day being Sunday, they went to the cathedral. A dull service. Kay kicked her heels very quietly beside the others, and almost did not go up for Communion, but Thea gave her an impatient look, so she kept herself in check and walked obediently up. She put her hands in place, but she did not close her eyes, and did not pray while she ate her bit of wafer-bread. Thea could not get at what went on inside her head.

During the necessary days in Suva, Thea and Francis made a practice of going for short walks ashore—at first so that Thea could show Francis the handsome hotel veranda, and then on the way home from church. They went again next day, calling it a constitutional, but Francis had an itch for curio hunting, and often as not they came back weighed down with paper-wrapped parcels tied with red string. They went by themselves, not inviting Kay to go along, and seemed to enjoy these outings as a kind of courtship spree. It was only fair that they have some time to talk to each other without the constant accompaniment of a mere child; and in fact Kay found it a relief to be out of her sister's searching eye for once, to stay at the deck table working even while the ship went into shore mode and the swarm ran to and fro, unloading and loading. Perfect freedom, to retire to her cabin and spend all afternoon in her bunk if she liked, training Pilot to do tricks.

———

One night, in a great ruckus, a herd of cattle was loaded aboard the big steamer at the next mooring, a cattle boat bound for the islands farther on. It took all night. While the world slept, the wharves and the ships were wide awake with work. Voices shouted from the dark sheds, answered by shouts and loud laughter from the boat. Cows stamped and bellowed in the scows; Kay could not blame them, they must have been horrified and bewildered by all this turmoil. The winches screamed as they wound and groaned as they unwound, and the people on the steamer's deck (where islanders bought cheap passage, sleeping in bedrolls in the open air) cheered as each poor creature came swinging over the side. Cheering for a future good dinner, Kay supposed.

On one swing the rope slipped, so the cow hung head downward, dangling between sea and stars, and there was such a tangle of shouts from the hold when they tried to right her that Kay feared the poor thing's neck had broken. She vowed she would not eat beef again, and was grateful for the comparative peace aboard the *Morning Light*, where only Mr. Best shouted—and only when required to by Francis or Mr. Wright.

Francis found their own loading, by skilled longshoremen from the Indian contingent, very satisfactory. As they sailed away, he gave Kay and Thea a history lesson on Fiji's Indian population, to which neither paid much mind. Thea was making a written list of the trinkets and surprises she had found in the stalls at Suva to send to the aunts at home; Kay wandered to the piano and began to play, in a dutiful and clumping way. Since she had not practised for days, or maybe weeks, she did not take offence when Thea called to her to put the soft pedal on, and to find some other tune than "Rondo alla Turca." And please *not* to thump.

———

Coming up one morning as they meandered along eastward, north of the Solomon Islands, Kay found seven giant gull-looking birds tied up under the bridge. Mollymawks, Mr. Best said they were, their wings six or seven feet in span; only a wandering albatross would be larger, as much as eleven feet, Mr. Wright said, from there to the mizzen-mast. Jiacheng had caught the mollymawks with a piece of pork on a hook, and was going to fry up their livers for tea.

When the dish arrived, Kay felt too sad to taste it, but Francis said they were splendid. "You cannot tell the difference from bullock's liver!" he told Jiacheng, who bowed in the particular way he kept for Francis: measured, deliberate, not low.

Kay had seen him bow lower for Thea, when they had one of their tussles over the way things should be done. Sometimes he bowed to admit defeat; sometimes he bowed even lower, in ironic acknowledgement that she was the boss-lady; he bowed lower still if he had won the right of it and appreciated her understanding of that fact.

The mollymawks were splendid-looking birds. Seeing them hanging dead, spread out like that, wingtip to wingtip, Kay found a tear welling in the delicate niche of her eye, and touched it tenderly, so that it dropped down her cheek and slid into the corner of her mouth.

Another day, an albatross flew round the mainmast, too wily to be lured by a lump of pork fat. Kay thought of Mr. Brimner, and of Coleridge, and felt herself to be quite erudite.

While the ship wore on through warm, restive seas, the sailors fished from long lines to augment the dinner table. They caught a large shark, which Mr. Wright pronounced too old to eat even before Jiacheng could refuse it. It was a queer shape, like a clumsy drawing, rough and broken-skinned. Mr. Wright judged that it might be more than a hundred years old; Thea said it looked *antediluvian*. Mr. Best sent it overboard to feed the other fishes.

All day long, schools of fish of many kinds passed round the ship, visible or invisible, or the ship passed through them, or both—two separate consciousnesses, Kay thought, staring over the side. They cannot see or know us, as anything but a large shadow; and we cannot know what moves them or goes through their minds, except perhaps *danger!* or *food!*

Thea would say that the fish had no consciousness, no souls, but watching them dart, stagger, turn and sway in their schools, Kay could not believe that their eyes and brains were not as active as her own, or Pilot's. They did less pondering, possibly—but then there was the Tu'i Malila, who had had so many years to think, and moved so deliberately, exactly like Father caught on a thought, waiting between one leg and the next for it to formulate, and be considered, and to dissipate. If Kay ever broke in and interrupted that process, Father would be in a pet for the rest of the day. The thread of his consciousness was more delicate than the Tu'i Malila's.

One afternoon Francis called Thea and Kay up from below to see a large scattering of whales—fifty or sixty of them. They passed right by the *Morning Light*, and one went off with Francis's best hat. He had given the hat to Thea to shield her as she ran back to the stern to see them better, and a spit of wind tipped it right off her head onto the rising rush of a black, spouting back. Away it went— Thea cried out *oh no!* but Francis laughed and said not to mind, as it was the only thing he had yet lost on the voyage.

∾

Shanghai, four thousand nautical miles away, was the next port of call. The journey took on a strange pace, a slow, lingering sail through thick heat north of the Solomons, a place of myriad islands and low winds, and then north of Papua New Guinea. That pace suited Thea and Kay well enough, who had no reason to rush to Shanghai, and did not mind the days following one after another with no variation except what Jiacheng should find to feed them.

After the noisy activity of Suva, Thea spent the long days doing nothing much at all, standing at the rail staring into the middle distance. With the aid of the noon sights for their latitude and the mileage chart for longitude, she helped Kay trace their route with drawing pins on the globe; once the scattered islands of the Solomons diminished, they had no land in sight for some time. They might not have seen land anyway, for low clouds filled the air, and then heavy rain squalls filled their water tanks. Francis was pleased to avoid sending sailors ashore to find and carry water; less pleased when, at a drop in the wind, they drifted back and lost all they had made for two days, the currents against them all the time. That drifting took them closer to Papua, the large island. Next afternoon Arthur Wetmore sighted Jayapura, and they passed within a mile of the harbour. The land was very high, just there. They could see the beach and the huts down along the shore. As it grew dark, they saw the fires all along.

Prey to sudden primitive trepidation, Thea insisted that they retreat below decks as night came on, but before going below, they saw canoes in near the shore, and a small vessel. This land looked truly foreign to her—and wild, as the Cape and Auckland, and even Tonga and Fiji, had not.

∾

That night Kay could not sleep. The moon had come into her port window, and the air was radiant and strange. She pulled her middy over her nightgown and slipped up to breathe for a moment in the luminous night air, warm and heavy even well off from the land.

Someone came aft, walking along the rail in his bare feet. It was Seaton, who Francis had told them was often taken with madness at the full of the moon. He stood clasping and unclasping his hands in ecstasy, carrying on a one-sided conversation in a confidential undertone, nodding his head at intervals in vigorous confirmation of some eerie confidence. He would smile and then grow serious, gazing with rapt, listening attention at the streaming road of pure light the moon set over the sea. After a few moments of this communion he turned on the rail and walked away in perfect balance, receding and blurring so that he took on the quality of the moonlight, and Kay went down to her bunk.

Early in the morning, Kay was back on watch, hoping they might sail close enough to see the islanders. The trees were giant, surprising, rising from the low islands in great formations. About noon they saw what looked like boats coming off an island that Francis said was Bras Island, or Berasi, but they had been disappointed many times before—but in half an hour they had three canoes alongside. Thea said it was worth the voyage to see "true native boats."

The people came to trade, their canoes loaded with pyramids of coconuts, bananas, sweet potatoes, even a basket of lemons. Thea said fruit must be out of season, because everything they had was small and greenish. They had trinkets to sell too—shells, braided and woven mats, boxes, hats—great lumps of coral, and a red parrot who squawked louder than Kay expected and made her jump. Its beak was a sharp scimitar, and its black eye looked at her so assessingly that she hoped Francis would not take a fancy to it.

The man pointed at the lace handkerchief tucked in Thea's waistband and offered her the red parrot in exchange, but to Kay's relief Francis said, "No, no, no birds, thankee, unless you have brought chickens!"

They wanted anything, anything: shirts, trousers (even though none of them wore any), blankets, tobacco—they were loud in asking for that—knives, iron, wire to make fish hooks. The head man spoke a trade pidgin Kay could almost make out, with six or seven English words salted through it. He called himself Cap Paul. He was tattooed even more thoroughly than Seaton, every inch of him painted in shapes and marks, all seeming full of meaning, though Kay's unaccustomed eyes could fathom none of it. They all had long, bushy hair, and though small in stature looked strong and clever.

In one of these boats there were six or seven children, one a small boy about the size of Lisia Fifita's little dimpled daughter in Tonga. Thea said he was far too young to be out without his mother. The men brought the children up on deck and let them run about. Francis said these people must be accustomed to trading with passing ships. The boys ran up and down the ropes in swarms like monkeys and made an awful noise, all shouting together, so loud, until with loud cries of goodbye they put off again in the boats.

The *Morning Light* sailed on, keeping the breeze just long enough to get out of sight of land—when it left them semi-becalmed again.

"We are just two thousand nautical miles from port now!" Francis said at supper, after his evening calculations.

They had turned north, to strike up around the Philippines for Shanghai. When he predicted it would be cooler soon, Thea said, "I will never complain of the cold again!"

In her well-washed white muslin (stockings and shoes left off, as they had been since Fiji, now that Thea had forgotten to scold), Kay did not feel hot at all. She leaned out to catch the last of that receding wind.

∽

About four in the afternoon, Thea was walking with Francis along the port side when he sighted a small island that on inspection of the map turned out to be Pulo Anna, or Anna Island, half a mile in circumference. She never wearied of seeing an island on a map and looking up to see it in reality, lying before them.

While the *Morning Light* was still about ten miles out, they saw two boats coming off. Large boats, so big that Mr. Wright thought they might be ship-boats which had been wrecked there, and Francis ordered him to reef sail so they might linger—but as they came nearer, it was clear that they were natives.

The boats were full of men. Looking up from his map, Francis told Thea they must want something pretty badly, because it was already growing dark and looked like squalls. The boats came up alongside and hailed. After taking a look at the men, and exchanging a few words, Francis let them come on board. They all came, perhaps twenty of them.

The poor things looked to be almost starving. They didn't have a morsel of food in their boats to sell—nothing but mats, and splendid fishing lines, and shells. The men said they were "poor, poor," and repeated it, pointing to their stomachs.

Among them was a young boy, seven or eight, or perhaps older, but not large. He stood bravely on the deck, a little man already, with a clear interested eye to all about him. When he raised his hand to Thea she caught it, and their hands clasped, neither larger than the other—he was truly very thin.

She turned the little hand over in her own, touching the strong knuckle-bones, and looked into his eyes. He looked back into her own, and seemed to find pleasure in the exchange, for he smiled with affectionate welcome.

She sent Jacky Judge down to ask Liu Jiacheng to bring up bread. When he did so, the men ate and ate, and more was brought up, until they had downed a bushel of bread among them.

Thea took the boy on her lap to feed him, since he did not push forward to ask for a piece and she feared there might be none remaining. His knees were too large on his skinny legs, and the fine skin stretched taut over them. So young, but wide awake to the world too. Sitting tranquil on her knee, he ate the bread neatly, and when she smiled to reassure him, he smiled in companionship again. Not a baby anymore, but a person already. He had a quality of stillness, of attention, that surprised and touched her. She touched his forehead, and he laid his head back to rest on her shoulder.

The men spread out their wares before her, and showed fine shells to tempt Kay, too. They would take nothing for their mats but tobacco—the other word they all knew, besides *poor*. Mr. Best brought up what they had to trade, setting up the tins in a short pyramid that made the men shout appreciation.

"Tobacco, tobacco," repeated the thin-legged man who was the leader, whom the others, when he shouted to them to back him up, called the king.

They were crazy for tobacco—mad for it. Several of them spoke to the king, and he turned to Thea and pointed at the boy on her knee, and then with four fingers at the tins of tobacco, and then to the boy again.

Francis said, "He's offering to sell you the boy, my love."

Thea looked at him, and then at the king. *Ask and you shall have: seek and you shall find.*

Everyone was quiet.

"Four pounds of tobacco for this boy?" she asked the king.

He nodded, and the men beside him nodded too. The other men rustled among themselves and pushed forward a couple of other younger fellows, but Francis waved them back. "No, no," he said. "I have no need of crewmen."

It seemed to Thea that all the men would have stayed on board if they could have. They must have been near the end of their resources—so many of them, and such a small island to support them. What could their lives be like? She looked at Francis again, one arm still around the boy on her knee.

"I can probably get them down to two pounds of tobacco," he murmured.

She shook her head.

"Four it is, then," Francis said. He pushed the cans across the deck with his foot.

∾

Kay had backed away from the shell-sellers, a little afraid of their hunger. She watched this bargaining unfold from the shadow of Seaton's lifeboat. It did not feel— She thought that there was something wrong here, some misunderstanding from the lack of common language. It gave her a dizzy feeling to hear Thea say that,

"Four pounds of tobacco for this boy." Confused, Kay watched the men agreeing, and she watched the boy. What would Mr. Brimner say to this?

From his canvas nest above her, Seaton muttered, "There's many worse lives than boy on a decent ship."

The boy slid from Thea's knee and stood patiently on the white-clean deck, waiting to go home. He was so young, looking about him. Not knowing.

Aren

Once the deal was done, the men left the ship, going past the boy one by one, rubbing noses with him. Kay had heard it called that, but it was a wrong expression, for what they did was press their faces to his face, soft and deep. Forehead to forehead, they looked into the boy's eyes and clasped his arms. The last of the men pressed his face into the boy's face over and over, not wanting to go, so that Kay thought he must be the boy's father, or perhaps his elder brother—it was hard to tell how old the people were.

Thea held out another can of tobacco, urgently. "For the boy's mother," she said, and Kay ran to the side and handed it down into the canoe.

The king man took it. Kay pointed back and shouted, "For his mama!" but did not know if the man understood her.

Then they settled to their paddles and oars and set off back to the island. It was almost twilight.

It was full dark by the time Mr. Best had brought up a washtub with fresh water, and by lantern light they stripped the boy and put him into the bath. Mr. Wright held him while Mr. Best cut his hair short, so it would not be so tangled.

The boy made no protest or cry, but submitted peaceably to

whatever was done to him. He kept his eyes on Thea while it was done. Jiacheng brought up a white shirt and the smallest pair of trousers from the slop chest, the store of clothing left by former ship's crew. The boy was put into these things (much too big) and set down again barefoot upon the scrubbed planks of the deck. He looked around, intently examining everything he saw, up in the ropes as well as around at all the people, shadowy in the torchlight.

Then he cupped his hands over his eyes and stood very still.

Thea went to him and put an arm around his shoulders. "Never mind," she said, as if he could understand her. "You are safe here. We will help you and teach you, and you will be our boy."

Francis watched her carefully, but said nothing. Kay did not know what he could have said, after all.

Of course, the boy did not have any idea how to go down stairs, and at first tried to lean forward and scale down them on his hands and knees. Thea caught him back and showed him how to take a step, and called Kay to help her walk him down into the saloon.

The saloon surprised him very much. Through his eyes Kay saw it fresh herself, how odd it was to find such a place below decks in a ship. The brass gleaming quiet and calm in the lamplight, the bird's-eye maple panelling, the darker polished mantelpiece, soft sofas and chairs. The piano! That must be infinitely strange to him—wait until he heard her play, perhaps that would comfort him. She went around to all the various fixtures, pointing out their purpose, until Thea begged her to stop and sit still, and to be quiet for a little, for pity's sake, so she took a wicker armchair and instead watched Thea lead the boy from place to place—doing no better with her laboured miming.

Jiacheng brought the evening pot of tea, and tinned milk for the boy in an enamel cup.

"What is your name?" Thea asked the boy. He looked at her but said nothing. She pointed to his chest and asked again, "You, you?"

Could he even speak? But Kay had heard him talking to the men as they left.

"Thea, Thea," Thea said, pointing to herself, and then, pointing, "Kay."

Kay nodded and pointed at her own chest, "Kay, Kay!" and back to her sister, "Thea!"

He said something very quiet, and they leaned closer to hear. Sighing, he said again, "Ah . . . Reng."

Or maybe it was Aren? Or A'rang . . . Αρεγγ, it would be, in Greek, Kay thought. With the double *g* that makes an *ng* sound in ἄγγελος, messenger. Angel.

"Aaron!" Thea said.

The boy looked at her again, and after a moment his face spread into shy agreement—or acceptance or capitulation, who could say. He said nothing, but when Kay put out her hand to shake his, he caught at it, twining thin fingers with her as if in some children's game, and he smiled, his eyes full of tears.

After a warm supper of bread and milk, they put him to bed in Mr. Brimner's old cabin, which was still made up. Tucking him in, Thea told Kay, "You will have to help me make Aaron some clothes, since we have lost Mrs. Hubbard."

Did she have to remind one of one's sins *every day?*

Kay sat on the end of the bunk, watching the boy's eyes dart about the cabin, watching his fingers feel the softness of the white sheets and the warmer spring of the navy woollen blanket that Thea had tucked in too tightly.

While Thea knelt beside the bunk to say prayers, Kay quietly used her boot toe to loosen it a bit, wondering, what am I going to do with this boy? She guessed the boy would be wondering too. Wondering and wondering, what are they going to do with me?

———

In the middle of the night, Kay dreamed of a line of children and a line of their mothers and fathers. Two separate lines stared at each other, at first across a rope barrier, and then the earth was splitting between them, wider and wider, a coulee crack in winter, each line now walking in snow on a separate dirt cliff, snow flittering down between them. Or it was railway tracks, those lines separated by longer blacker lines of the rails.

In her dream she heard the boy singing. She heard and was awake at once—it seemed she had only rested, floating on the surface of sleep.

Bare feet on the cool planks, she opened her door, taking great care not to let it squeak. The saloon was empty and tidy, nobody awake, so she moved down the corridor to the next cabin door and inched it open. The boy looked up from where he was singing into his fingers. His clean, dark-rimmed eyes shone in the small moon-spill coming through the porthole. Bare naked again, he squatted on his skinny haunches on the bunk, swaying as it swayed.

He stopped singing. His cheeks were sticky-damp with tears.

She put her fingers to her lips.

He put his to his.

"Shhhh . . ." she whispered. "Not at night."

Although he could not have understood her, he raised his eyebrows two or three times, as little Sione had done in Ha'ano. That meant agreement, in Ha'ano. Maybe for him too.

If the boy was noisy or unruly, if he had nightmares, would Francis put him off at the next island, or find a boat or a canoe that could take him home again? That seemed a terrible thing. Kay could not quite think Francis would do it, or that Thea would let him; but taking him away from his home was terrible also. He might be weeping for his mama, as Annie had wept for hers. She could keep watch for him.

Pilot nosed at the cabin door, and she let him in. The boy put down his fingers for him to smell, and the pup jumped up onto the bunk, circled as he always did and settled into the blankets. Thea need not know.

Kay sat on the end of the bunk. This had been Mr. Brimner's sanctum, his own place, but now it was all right for her to go in. She was the elder sister now.

"I will tell you a story," she said. "Then you will be quieter and go to sleep."

The boy sat up against the headboard with his thin legs hugged into his arms and watched her face, sometimes her mouth as she spoke, sometimes glancing up into her eyes and then letting his gaze slide away again.

She told him about Odysseus, the man of many ways, who was beleaguered and travelled about the seas, but at last, after ten years' wandering, wound his way home again—

At least, she began to tell the story, but the sound of her own voice spouting an incomprehensible mix of English and Greek (when she could think of the words) dampened her spirits. It made her see how little she knew, or ever would know now, without Mr. Brimner to teach her, and how impossible it would be for Aren to learn English and speak with them, and then she thought of how Annie had not been able to speak in her own language, the muting of that . . . Soon Kay was too sad to speak at all.

When he put a hand on her knee to urge her to go on, she told him instead something soft and ordinary, one of the first things she remembered: once, when she was very little and went running after Mary into the cow byre early in the morning in new spring snow, to see a newborn calf there, its crooked, woolly legs struggling to get up and stand, its large, wet nose nudging at her chest by mistake, and Mary's soft face laughing and dimpled as she showed Kay how to push the calf toward its mother. The soft warmth and dampness of that woolly fur, the warm closeness of the mother and the byre, and the soft woodsmoke smell of Mary.

Sometime while she spoke, the boy turned back into the pillow and went to sleep. Pilot made a nest for himself between their legs and they were warm and safe, and the ship sailed on through the night without hurry or haste, through safe old dreams that nobody would tell you not to say.

But next morning there was trouble. Down in Thea's cabin, drinking morning tea with her before Jiacheng had brought their porridge, Kay heard a commotion of running feet above. She ran to check while Thea was still pulling on her linen shirtwaist and tucking it into her skirt, but the boy was still sound asleep in his bunk. Aren, his name was. Curled tight as a fiddlehead, fingers in his mouth, and so still that Thea, coming after, was worried and felt for the rise and fall of his chest. She sat on the edge of the bunk and said, "No, no, it's all right," when the boy woke, startled.

Something up on deck, then. Kay sped up the companionway, and as her head rose over the ledge, she heard Francis shouting to "Stay back from the rail, in case they have projectiles of any kind."

Who did he mean by *they*—and did he mean blow darts, or harpoons? Now she saw the boats, heading out from an island not far off. Many, many canoes. Perhaps they were coming for the boy, to buy him back or take him. She was afraid to ask it out loud. She slid into the shadow of Seaton's lifeboat and stood mute, not wanting to be sent away.

Mr. Best told Francis they'd made forty miles from Anna Island overnight, and this ahead was Sonsorol. These islands were so small and poor, Mr. Wright had not thought them inhabited at all anymore. Francis put down the spyglass, not needing it anymore because the canoes were so close. Kay saw that the ship had already turned, and sail was being raised to put away at speed, but even so, they were soon surrounded by canoes, skimming over the water as if in a race, going a good lick—six knots, perhaps. Kay counted fifteen canoes, with ten or twelve men in each.

Sailors stood stationed along the deck, armed with sticks and staves, one or two with knives out. Jacky Judge was twisting his in

the sun to make it glint. Arthur Wetmore stood in line too, sturdy
as could be, though looking a good deal concerned.

Mr. Wright shouted to them to look alive for boarders, and then
his shouts were drowned by the men from the canoes, all crying at
once, "*Tobac! Tobac!*"

They were bound to come on board. From the lifeboat's shadow,
Kay saw their skinny arms reaching for the ropes as the canoes
bumped alongside and jostled each other for water space.

Calling again to Mr. Wright and his men to 'ware climbers,
Francis shot his pistol into the air—once! twice!—and the noise
diminished a little as the invaders paused.

Then Francis called another order, and Mr. Best threw open a
box and tossed a tin of tobacco across to him. Francis went to the
side and shouted down to the boats to desist, but seeing the tin he
held, they clamoured all the more.

"*Tobac, tobac!*" they cried, in many voices—there were so many
of them, and they looked so desperate, that Kay was certain the
ship would be overwhelmed. She thought what she must do, where
she could hide Thea and Pilot and the boy.

Francis drew back his arm and hurled the tin of tobacco far
behind the canoes, and two or three of them did turn back for it.
One man, not waiting for his canoe to turn, leapt overboard and
swam for the bobbing tin.

In the meanwhile, Cocker the bosun had been harrying his men
to sweat the ropes fast, and the ship at last began to make real way—
but still the canoes pursued, and one or another would come up
with a bump and a scramble. Then Francis or Mr. Best would send
another tin tumbling back through the air, and again the onslaught
would be distracted as men fought with each other to reach the
tobacco before it sank.

Thea came hastening up, alone, to find Kay. She whispered that
she had left the boy shut in the cabin. They stood tight-clasped
together by the lifeboat, fearful to leave or stay, and when a canoe
slammed right beneath them, they looked down into the blearing

eyes of a man who was climbing the side of the ship with fingers and toes as if it was a coconut palm. Then along came Jacky Judge with an oar and bashed cruelly at the man's reaching hand until he fell off into the sea and was hauled back into a canoe by the others.

The screaming for tobacco never stopped, that was the worst of it. The men were delirious in their desire and pain—Thea said it was like poor wretches crying for morphine in a hospital. Kay was afraid, and afraid for Aren, down below. Then she saw his shorn head peeping over the companionway ledge—he was clever to have figured out the door fastening!—and he ran to the rail beside them to see who beleaguered the ship, staring over into the roiling confusion of canoes. The cries (he must have known that word *tobac*) were growing a little less violent, but were still enough to frighten Kay.

Aren looked down at the men but said nothing, and did not call out to them to come and fetch him home to his mama.

Thea caught at the back of his shirt anyhow, as if she thought he might jump over. "Come down with me," she said into his ear. "We'll find Liu Jiacheng and get you some bread for breakfast! This is no matter for us."

He pulled a little against her hand, but she persuaded him down the steps again, cautioning him to take care with his footing.

Since nobody told her not to, Kay stayed on deck until the last of the canoes had been left behind, the men in it waving and laughing.

"We may be thankful for the breeze we had," Francis told Thea later. "They'd have made short work of us if they had got aboard in that mood!"

But in fact, as the canoes tired of paddling and dropped away, to Kay's surprise Francis had called out an offer to trade with the last two canoes, and made a great haul.

"I don't know where I will be able to stow all these things!" cried Thea, when he showed her the treasure: a barrel of splendid sponges, beautiful shells and more of the exquisitely woven fishing lines.

"They'd have followed us yet, if we had not traded," Francis said in excuse. "All they would take was tobacco. I got a lot of their arrowheads—and nine turtles!"

"Turtle soup and fried turtle for supper," Thea said, looking them over.

Kay disliked eating turtle extremely. She knew a tortoise.

Aren had not had a word to say to the men, although they were from an island not forty miles from his home, and he did not seem to want to look at the things they had traded. That was interesting, Kay thought. Perhaps they were bad men who marauded along these waters and troubled his own place. When Kay pointed to the water where the boats had been, he looked vague and said a word she thought might be *rengalack?* Or perhaps it was his name again, only with something added.

However were people to understand each other when words were not written down? This was impossible. She went back to her Greek books, all shuffled and out of order because of the commotion of the morning.

He was not a bold boy, but not fearful either, Kay thought. Once they left the vicinity of the islands, he slowly emerged—not from hiding, precisely, but from where he had stood inconspicuous, melted into a shadow by the mizzen-mast. He stood watching her at her books now, his strong, broad feet easy on the deck, no need to wait for sea legs. Jacky Judge, running to make adjustments to the mainsail, caught him and slung him easily up to his shoulder, and then *oop*—up into the mainmast shrouds.

Not rising from the hammock, Thea put a hand to her eyes to watch him climb, crying *Oh!* but making no real protest. Aren laughed and grabbed at the ropes and scrambled up ahead of Jacky, easily beating him. Sad again for her spindly arms, Kay turned back to her now-orderly books and opened to the exercise for today.

TRANSLATE INTO GREEK:

1. If I had known that you were there, I should not have gone away.
2. Do not give anything to anyone till I come back.
3. You ought not to have sold that horse for so little money.
4. I thought that I should not be able to wait for you.
5. I sent a messenger (ἄγγελος, *angelos*) to tell him to come tomorrow.

She looked up from her work to find Aren staring at her books again—long lashes opening wide those clear eyes. He rested an arm on the table, casually, and leaned nearer to see her page. Checking to see that it was all right with her, he pressed a small finger gently onto the page, and looked a question at her.

"Greek," she said. "It's Greek, the language I was telling you the story in last night . . ." Then she said, as if she was a ninny, "I already know *quite a lot* of Latin."

If it had been anyone but he, she would have blushed at this ridiculous boasting. But he looked at her lovingly and lifted his eyebrows in understanding. He had a companionable way of keeping his mouth closed that was agreement, acceptance.

In the evening after supper, Kay sat with Aren swinging in the hammock while Francis and Thea promenaded along the deck. No islands in sight, no worrying flotilla of canoes. Not far enough away (but of course Aren could not understand him), Francis asked, "What do you expect me to do with the little chap—train him for cabin boy?"

Her violet skirt swaying as she turned, Thea answered him shortly, "No, not at all. He is our boy now."

From the still look of his face, Kay thought Francis was not in agreement, but he said nothing.

⌒

Thea began to teach the child proper English. He was a responsive little fellow, and had picked up a smattering of words already in these few days, at least to understand. She sat with him at one end of Kay's table, making letters on a piece of scrap paper and sounding them out, as if Aaron was one of her early pupils at Blade Lake. How different these circumstances! The sea air wafting around the deck and the comfortable bustle of the crew both tempted him away from the table, but he seemed to have a strong desire to speak to them, and did not tire quickly of repeating the words she taught him, pointing to the pictures she drew.

She drew the alphabet, which had been of some assistance in training the Indian children, and got him to trace the letters on scrap paper and erase them until they were perfect. In Shanghai she would try to find a child's primer; she missed her old books.

"Ship," she said, and waved her arms around them and at the little boat she'd drawn.

"*Shit*," he said, and Kay bent farther over her books to hide her laughter. Thea kicked her ankle beneath the table; mockery would not help the pupil. She said the word again, drawing his attention to the difference in the making of the *t* sound and the *p* sound. Both were present in Polynesian languages, and he learned quickly.

When he'd had enough of schooling, Aaron helped Seaton mend sail, followed Jacky Judge up into the rigging or sat with Kay, feet through the railing, watching the crew scuttle around the ship. In the afternoon they had another session, and Thea drew more pictures of ladies and houses and bears and cats to illustrate the words she was teaching him. He had a quick mind and a good ear, and he liked to please her. He loved to play *this is the church and this is the steeple*, especially when her hands turned inside out to show all of the people inside them, or twisted into the parson going upstairs.

The days grew longer and warmer, and even slower. Francis said they would be out of sight of land now for some weeks, and out of danger from marauding canoes. Seeing that they were also out of chickens, and had not been able to barter for more, Thea decreed it was time to butcher Mr. Dennis. The pig was always called that, it being considered unlucky to mention the word *pig* on board ship—Thea still did not know why.

Liu Jiacheng managed the butchery before she came up in the morning; but a great harvest of blood had been saved in buckets lined up along the deck, for making blood sausage and headcheese. Shuddering at the smell, Kay declared she would do her work in the saloon. Not being so dainty in his sensibilities, Aaron stayed on deck watching interestedly while Thea and Jiacheng portioned and dressed the meat and Mr. Best, bustling in, set up the smoker at the rear of the House for smoking sausage.

A long, busy day. After a good dinner of roast pork, Thea found herself genuinely tired by evening. So was Aaron, it seemed. While she played lingering Chopin nocturnes in the twilit saloon, the boy crouched to watch her feet go up and down, pressing on them gently as she pressed the pedals, before rising when she paused in the music to climb up into her arms like a baby. Kay had not done such a thing for many years.

His skin was warm and clean, his bones light as air. Thea reminded herself that he was very young. Francis had settled on eight years old, given the small stature of his people, and had given him the day of his acquisition, December 1, for a birthday. The birthday of his new life. His head, pressed into her shoulder, was all over soft and sweet-smelling. Eyes still hidden, he reached up and stroked her cheek with one hand. She held him tighter, glad that Francis had gone up to speak to Mr. Wright.

What his life must have been like, she could scarcely imagine. Poor, certainly, and hungry, but he was a loving child, and that is learned from loving parents. She tried to turn her mind away from thinking of his mother. Life on these islands could not be easy. Perhaps Aaron's mother had too many children to feed, and would not notice—well, hardly that, but perhaps be glad that one was well taken care of now. Perhaps she had died, as women so easily did in these cultures. The father had had no qualms in selling him, after all!

A benevolent God had given her the chance to save this one soul at least from poverty and starvation—to bring him up as a Christian, in love and kindness, and as part payment for the deaths of all those poor Blade Lake children—and she would do her best.

12

China

The *Morning Light* docked in Shanghai, and the discharging of her case oil cargo began. The harbour smell hammered into Kay's nose: intoxicating, almost suffocating—she put her hat over her face for respite. The land wind carried spinning odours of sherry wine or Hollands gin, fruit-laden as it came in old fruitcake, with a following assault of fish paste and fetid meat. The cleaner snap of mace was left behind in the islands; complicated, darkening rot now crawled in at every breath. The harbour was clogged with putrid things; little catamarans and push-boats picked their way through the watery mess even while adding to it; every boat had on it someone tossing a basin of slops or night soil over the side. Kay shivered to think of falling into that dark-moving murk.

While Aren helped Jiacheng and Arthur Wetmore turn out the kitchen and restock, Kay and Thea spent a whole day housecleaning the cabin: taking screws out of tables and chairs so they might move about the room again, rolling out the carpet, finding summer slipcovers for the settee, et cetera—all the dainty things that make life comfortable in port. Since they would stay in Shanghai for a month, pictures and photographs came out of the lazaret, old china Kay had never seen, and all the other treasures Francis had picked up in various places, including the famous Hundred Faces fan that had been given to his father by their Shanghai partner, Mr. Yen, in 1880. On the fifty two-foot ivory sticks of one side, fifty faces were carved, and on the other side, forty-nine; the face of the one holding the fan became the hundredth face. With these things set up in their accustomed positions, the Aft cabin looked fully dressed, quite different from when the *Morning Light* was at sea.

When he came back from the market, Aren roamed the room, touching every new thing with a careful finger. Inspecting it with his skin, Kay thought. Once he had made the place his own again, he surveyed the whole room and, with a conscious look at Thea, nodded his head in the English way of agreement, saying carefully, "Very nice, shipshape!"

But he could not keep his eyebrows from lifting, lifting to Kay, as they did when he wished to say *yes*.

The harbour water still moved and shifted and moved as the sun set, but the night sounds of little boats rowing and people chatting to each other were almost soothing. Lying in her bunk, almost asleep, Kay pressed one hand against the wood. Outside that wooden barrier, the China Sea pressed back.

Francis spent the thirty days in Shanghai on business arrangements, working the local shippers to find charters for this trip and the next several projected voyages. Between company visits, the city was a splendid place for shopping, with streets and streets of little shops, each for one purpose and one purpose only. Still wearing hand-me-downs, Aren was left on the ship, happily learning knots and ropes and carving with Seaton; Kay went along or did not, as the mood took her. More often she stayed with her books, especially after Thea presented her with the Middle Liddell, found in a crowded bookshop with spectacularly packed shelves stretching up thirty feet, and a spindly ladder to reach the highest, as high as a crow's nest.

Kay found the city strange and a little frightening. So civilized, the apex of humanity and learning, but so crowded, all dirt and cacophony. And backward, as Thea pointed out, in very many ways. A hodgepodge of the possibilities. Jiacheng, knowing the lie of the land, had advised them where to find the book, and escorted them to the very street. At home here, he absented himself from the ship at strange hours, and might be seen slipping up the gangplank from shore like a wraith in the pre-dawn, emerging from the crowd of other Chinese people to enter the ship's world as himself, known among all these unknown.

One day they travelled by cart to the famous Yuyuan Garden, which had been damaged in the Opium Wars but was still worth seeing, Francis said. He had been visiting this place since he was a little boy, with his own sea captain father. Many of the statues were broken, and the little pavilions had sad holes knocked in their walls, but the vegetation had recovered from that long-ago assault. After walking, they sat to rest on a litter of gold beneath an ancient ginkgo tree, said to be three hundred years old, whose autumn drift of fan-shaped yellow leaves was the most beautiful thing Kay saw in China. "The earth repairs itself," Thea said; Kay wondered how much damage it would take to be irreparable.

During their long stay in harbour, Thea and Francis walked every afternoon, dipping into various promenades, Jiujiang Road and others. Francis believed in acquiring nice things—investments that might grow in value, Kay supposed he meant, china and ornaments and curiosities. But Thea was interested in the ordinary things of daily life, pipes and shoes and games. Kay liked both. She was sadly materialistic, as long as somebody else fetched the things; then she was happy to look at them in peace, in the cool-shaded saloon.

Like Aren, Kay was happiest aboard the *Morning Light*. She did like to stravaig along the first stretch of the Bund, where all the great ships lay moored, but only in daylight, and only if Aren went with her. He was a good companion, and they could tell Thea and Francis they had been practising English, even if all they did was jabber *hello how are you I am very well I thank you what a nice day is it not* back and forth and point out oddities to each other.

She had a dream, several nights running, of a port—not here at the Bund, and not the *Morning Light*, but quite another ship, made of iron. She dreamed of falling from a high wharf or pier into low-tide water, falling between the pier and the great black ship tied up there, into oily black water far, far below. The water sucked and churned at the pilings and the ship swayed in its chains, and she knew she would be crushed before she could drown. The dream ship went out to sea then and was attacked, or sometimes it blew up in harbour, leaving her clinging to the dark, rotted wood of the pilings.

Because Thea did not mention it, she thought she must not have cried out with the dreams. The only respite was work; but Cyrus was now too familiar, and the *Odyssey* still too difficult for her skills. It frustrated her to be without Mr. Brimner, whose casual guidance she had not appreciated enough while she had it. Then, breaking out of scholarship, she would hie up Pilot for a race down the deck, or go below to find Aren where he sat listening to Jiacheng.

Jiacheng was teaching Aren rudimentary Chinese phrases, to the comforting sound of his elegant and efficient knife working its way through whatever was to be for dinner. Aren was allowed to chop too. Kay was not; the first time she was let, she managed to snick her finger and bled a little. Although she swore it was no matter, Jiacheng did not give her the knife again.

Listening to Jiacheng and Aren speaking Chinese made her think of Blade Lake. There was no pleasure for Kay in listening to language, she liked to see it written down—that seemed to be the only gate that opened for her. But she kept seeking meaning in what they said. "I don't like foreigners," she had heard Miss Ramsay tell Father once. "One cannot grasp the nuance, the thoughts behind words. The cues, you know, are missing." It was unpleasant to feel that same dislike, listening to Jiacheng talking rapidly and confidentially to Aren. She would not be like Miss Ramsay.

Kay shook her mind and went back to Ancient Greek, which was always text, and never spoken aloud anymore unless one was learning. Next, she would like to study Sanskrit. She was beginning a list of words repeating in Homer. Often they were long, with rolling syllables: πολυφλοίσβοιο θάλασσης, *polyphloisboio thalasses*, the loud-resounding sea, or ῥοδοδάκτυλος ἕως, *rhododactylos heos*, rosy-fingered dawn—she had heard Father say that, standing at the morning room window on a red-sky winter morning in Blade Lake.

It was Aeschylus, not from Homer—found in a footnote in the Middle Liddell—but she liked the sound of κῡμάτων ἀνάριθμον γέλασμα *kumaton anarithmon gelasma*, 'the innumerable laughter of the rain.' And best of all the lovely one Mr. Brimner had given her long ago: πομφολυγοπάφλασμα, *pompholugopaphlasma*, the sound of bubbles rising from the sea. She remembered leaning on the rail with him. She would never forget that day, and the sea sound of that bubbling word.

No cargo charter materialized for the *Morning Light*. Francis said the advent of steam had made things so bad for sail in this city that it might be some time before they received one. He looked frustrated, but still went about the city finding walks that might deliver some beauty. They all went a second time to the Yuyuan Garden and sat beneath the giant ginkgo trees overlacing the pavements, their golden leaves now falling in a slow-descending rain. Kay and Aren gathered them up in handfuls, small fans flared on a tender stalk, their delicate vein lines satisfying to Kay's fingertips.

A week later Francis did receive orders to proceed to Manila within thirty-two days to load sugar and hemp for New York. In the meantime, he had secured a half load of hand-reeled silk for Singapore, and told Thea they would set out as soon as the silk arrived and the required ballast had been got in, more a matter of hours than of days.

13

A Cough

They celebrated Christmas in Singapore: an unseasonable feast. Singapore was *hot as Hades*, Kay said to herself, as Mr. Brimner was not there to understand her—Thea would rebuke her for using that word. To go with Aunty Bob's plum pudding (kept wrapped up since Yarmouth), Thea made roast chicken with raisin bread stuffing. The pudding was dense and sticky but satisfied nostalgia in Francis, its prime purpose.

He was fond of Christmas, and delighted in giving presents. On his excursions he had found toys for Aren—ivory tangram puzzles, a travelling set of Chinese checkers, and a climbing-man toy; and for Thea, a treasure: a *famille rose* platter depicting an emperor's hunt. She scolded him terrifically for buying it, weeping a little with plea-sure, and said she would keep it wrapped in lambswool whenever the ship was not in dock. Although Kay expected a book, Francis gave her a length of creamy silk to be made into a long dress "for parties in New York," and a pearl pin like a new moon.

Kay knew that pin; it was the one he had bought in Boston many months ago, when he let slip that Thea was going to have a baby. He had never given it to Thea. He must have decided that it was not bad luck to give it to Kay, since she had no need for a child.

The day after Christmas they went out into the country on a train, to give Aren the pleasure of the great machine. They stopped at the Woodlands railway station for luncheon and Francis hired a guide who took them on a long ramble into a forest park, too groomed and tamed to be real jungle. But there were still monkeys in the trees and wild-calling birds, and one had to watch out for lizards. Aren enjoyed the train very much. He could not be persuaded to sit for a moment, preferring to hang his head out the window and watch the landscape rushing past. Francis took him to the engine car to see how the thing was run, and they came back covered with smuts, so filthy that Thea would not kiss them.

But after their excursion to the Woodlands, Aren developed a cold that settled into the lungs, and began coughing in a very distressing fashion. Kay took it from him, and soon they were both bundled in their bunks and subjected to alternating doses from Jiacheng's and Thea's medicine cabinets. For a few days fever gripped them. Aren went very quiet and slept most of the time, hot and dry to the touch, his mouth slack.

Kay took it in delirium—she felt herself to be a whale calf descending under the sea, the fever an almost pleasurable sensation of letting go and submerging into another element. She had ferocious dreams, too many and too confusing to think about. One bad night the dreams were all of rows, long rows of naked bodies, pale on dark ground; rows of dead trees in mud. Then of children in rows and rows of cots, of walking through the ward with her hand clenched on the back of Thea's pinafore. By that, she understood it must be the first tuberculosis epidemic, not the last one.

She woke with tears washing her face, remembering for the first time in a long while Mary's body hanging from the doorway, and Thea's frantic efforts to save her, the worst thing Kay had ever seen in her life. Thea lifting, straining, stronger than she really was, to unhook Mary and bring her down onto the white-sheeted bed and labour over her. Annie came and huddled with her at the foot of the bed while Thea pushed a great needle into Mary's arm or chest—the dream would not let her remember which, but the needle did no good. Thea standing quiet at last, nothing more to be done. The great quiet in the room when it happened, and Annie silent beside her on the floor.

Kay got out of her bunk, crept along the corridor to Aren's cabin and climbed in beside him. Without waking, he shifted to accommodate her, one arm over her middle. It comforted her to be with him, though the dry heat that radiated from him was strange.

Another plague, from the general filthy conditions in Shanghai harbour: the ship was overrun with rats. Before leaving Singapore, Jiacheng found two cats to hold them down, but both died—he thought from eating too many rats. He would get a better cat at Manila. Kay protested she was afraid to go to sleep at all now, having a dread of one running over her chest. One night two large rats fought inside the piano! Kay shrieked, feeling them writhe over and under her feet, until Mr. Best flew down like an avenging demon and killed them both.

Having heard that cayenne pepper scattered around would keep them away, Thea tried that, but the drafts swept the pepper into the air. It acted on the humans like the very best snuff, and they were all seized with violent sequential sneezing and strangled coughing until she gave up, opened all the skylight vents and damp-dusted the room.

Loading in Manila was very quick, less than a day. Properly baled, sugar and hemp had little tendency to shift, making the organization of the hold less particular than for case oil. Jiacheng went ashore and brought three great ugly mousers to live below decks as a scourge to the rats. He also installed piglets in the big pen: two to eat soon as roast suckling, one to fatten into the new Mr. Dennis.

Then they were off, away from bustling, feverish cities, headed for the open seas again, provisioned for the next long leg, round the Horn and up the right side of the Americas to New York. That evening, Thea allowed Aren and Kay up on deck for an airing. The steamer *Egremont Castle* passed close by and the men on board waved to them where they lay bundled up in wicker chairs at the rail.

Kay felt sorry for the passengers swarming the deck, who had to travel by steam instead of in the lovely rush of air. She felt a quickening in her midsection, the giddy sense of going forward. A relief to feel it, after all this tedious sickness.

∾

Thea nursed Kay carefully, but was privately more afraid for Aaron. Or *Aren*, as he and Kay had decided the name should be spelt; Thea saw no point in arguing with them in this fever. Her experience with consumption in Blade Lake had left scars, not on her lungs (she was luckier than poor Mr. Maitland, who died that last hard winter with the children) but on her spirit. She searched for signs of infection in both, although Kay had proved resilient in the old days, but could come to no conclusion. The coughing, which had been hard to bear, tapered off, and when the fever abated, a little colour came back into Aren's cheeks, but he was listless.

Even Francis was affected by the change in him, saying quietly to Thea after looking in on him one evening, "Such a bright spark just last week! Terrible to see what it's done to the poor sprogget."

Aren was flagged out by this fever; but there was no blood in the sputum, and he did not complain of pain. He had enough fluency in English to let her know where it hurt, and he did not hold his chest or show weakness that Thea could see. She relaxed her vigilance, and rather than fearing the worst, as the complaint worked its way through the men below decks, blamed one sailor or another for bringing back a hacking cold from shore leave.

Seeing the children still flat-spirited, Thea decreed a bath day to revive them. Instead of setting up the hip bath in the saloon, she asked Jiacheng and Mr. Best to prepare a barrel bath on deck for Kay to hop into. A good soaking would revive her interior mood as well as cleansing her exterior. Riding the last wake of illness, Kay was ornery, but Thea persisted, and she did at last consent to strip down to her shift and climb into the barrel.

Mr. Best had set the barrel close to the railing, for ease of emptying later, and had hung a jib sail at both sides of the barrel for a modesty drape.

Shucking off her blouse and skirt, Kay stepped up onto the little stool Jiacheng had thoughtfully brought up from the galley, and into the barrel. She shrieked a little, saying *too cold!* but after a moment allowed it to be refreshing. Relaxing, she turned this way and that so her shift ballooned in the water and made pleasing patterns. Enjoying the coolness, she let Thea scrub her back and give her hair a good wash, with more water from a jug to rinse it. Wanting vinegar for the last rinse, Thea went to the companionway to call down to Jiacheng.

She looked back to see Kay standing with eyes closed, dripping but content, dreamy in the pleasure of coolness, and close by, up on the railing, Aren. What did he hold—

He was inching along the rail, one hand above in the ropes to steady himself and one arm and hand wrapped around a wriggling little— Oh dear. He had one of the piglets.

He had almost reached her now . . . Kay was turning, she would see. But her eyes were closed. Ought she to have some warning?

Francis, behind Thea with his Brownie camera, put his hand gently across her mouth in case she might call out. She could feel him behind her, shaking with silent laughter as Aren crept along, somehow keeping the piglet quiet, until *ploop!* into the barrel went the pig.

The squealing was enough to raise the dead from the bottom of the sea.

Kay lifted off, a shrieking seabird rising from the wave, three-quarters out of the bath before the piglet touched bottom and scrabbled its way back up.

And all the time Francis was clicking and forwarding the film, as well as he could for guffawing. Men were such children!

The sailors watching from behind the jib screen laughed—Arthur Wetmore, Jacky Judge and Mr. Best, even sober Mr. Wright—and Francis louder than anyone, and Thea could not help but join them, hoping Kay would not take one of her fits of umbrage.

Now she was up on the barrel's edge and out of it, still shouting, shift plastered around her—crying "What? What?" like a banshee, and now she turned to stare into the barrel, where Aren was laughing so much he almost fell overboard, and Jiacheng leapt in to haul the piglet back out of the water before it drowned.

"You!" Kay shouted at Aren. "You! What?"—as if she had lost the gift of language.

"You!" he cried back. "You you you *you*! You, pig, *surprise*! I surprise you!"

Thea rushed forward with a towel to put round her, and held her tight, still laughing, until Kay could laugh too, and put out a hand to tickle the poor little pig, the replacement for Mr. Dennis.

"I'll make sausage out of you," Kay swore, but in good humour again she lunged to grab Aren's ankle and dump him into the barrel in turn. Then they were all wet, and the barrel fell over, of course, and everyone on deck got well splashed, even Francis, before Jiacheng caught the pig and carried it off to restore it to its siblings in the peaceful pen.

A little slice of piglet hoof made a moon-shaped scar on Kay's arm. After it healed over, she liked the pirate look of it.

14

A Passenger

In early April, the *Morning Light* berthed again in Suva for a couple of days, to take on water and supplies and to give the men a last shore leave before the long leg round the Horn. Suva was a safe place to do that, Francis said, being small enough that none of the men could lose themselves. Jacky Judge and Arthur Wetmore got roaring drunk, and rolled home at three in the morning to wake first the watch and then the rest of the ship with their singing and roistering, but that was nothing to write home about.

Next day, looking pale about the gills and emitting occasional muted groans, they holystoned the deck near where Kay and Aren sat at their books. Arthur told Kay earnestly that he'd never do such a thing again in his life, or if he did, it would be in better company than Jacky and at a better establishment, where the vile drink would not poison a man. Then Thea came up to work with Aren, and Arthur evaporated back into silent swabbing. Jacky, less badly off, twinked Kay's boot toe as he swabbed by and gave her a sorry kind of grin.

Aren had progressed from the baby school of learning his letters to writing words and simple sentences, and wanted to do more, but they'd found no primary-school books for him in Singapore, so

Thea carried on in her own way, drawing pictures for him of any-thing he asked for, and then setting him to write the name of it below: a coconut palm, a bat, a church, the *Morning Light*. Then he would write a story describing the thing, and the stories were sometimes very amusing to Kay for what he had got wrong. "Bird of night with arm wings," for the bat—in Singapore they had been startled by a sudden exodus of goose-sized bats from a warehouse as they walked by. She shivered, remembering their arm wings. And then shivered again, thinking of the bats in Pangai, flitting in the darkening leaves while she waited for Mr. Brimner outside the Fruelocks' house. Before they even knew Aren.

He wrote, "What we climb and drink and eat, it is very tall," for the coconut, and for the church, "The house of the god who saves us." Thea corrected him to use *G* for the one true God, and he looked at her sideways.

Kay thought he might be wondering what made one god God and all the others gods but did not have the vocabulary yet to ask that. She was just as glad, preferring not to listen to Thea, as she had to Father, on the innate superiority of Christianity over all other religions.

"What is this?" Thea said, pointing to scribbles on the side of Aren's work paper.

"Jiacheng teaches me Chinese," Aren said. "I teach him ABC, he teaches some Chinese letters me. I teach Kay," he offered, in case Thea might be angry with him.

Kay looked over. "What is this one?" A funny little square, with a peak and a squiggle.

"House, pig inside, see? It is *home*."

She laughed. "Or *bathtub*!"

Francis had had his photographs developed in Suva. Kay did not like the way her hair looked streaming wet, but even she could see the joke now—her leaping up out of the barrel open-mouthed, like a whale breaching, and the poor piglet scrambling his sharp hooves at the other edge, desperate to get away.

Aren put his hand over the pig-house letter. "No more joke."

Kay patted his arm lightly, to show that she forgave him. "It was funny."

She remembered the exhaustion of listening to another language, watching the rows of children at the school suffering the sharp barrage of English from Miss Ramsay. Nowhere for the ear to rest, nothing to hook onto. She remembered their bird voices, their dusty-dirty hands moving as they spoke, and Thea coming and calling the class back to order, the voices halting, reciting un-English English in rote and rhythmical voices, reeling off a long line of poetry about an incomprehensible English landscape. *Men may come and men may go, but I go on for ever* . . . She remembered being glad to go into the study with Father because it was silent.

Aren did not seem to feel that weariness; it was a game to him, one he was good at. The way she was good at Greek and Latin, at solving that puzzle.

Thea was still examining the Chinese characters ranging down the side of the page.

"*Jia*," Aren said, pointing to *home*. "One-th part of Jia-cheng, his name."

"First part. Yes, I see," Thea said. She traced the house, and the pig inside.

It being Easter, they went ashore on Sunday to go to the cathedral in Suva, and there they found a great surprise: Mr. Brimner, assisting with the service.

As the clergy processed in, Kay saw him, and the surprise was so great that she jumped up, and Thea had to pull on her elbow to make her sit again. She could not even whisper to Aren what the great thing was, but spent the rest of the service anxiously jiggling, unable to bear the wait. If it had not been Easter, if Thea had not been sitting right beside her, she might have called to him or run up to greet him, her friend!

At Communion she knelt at the rail, hands held out, the right palm properly above the left, but she could not close her eyes for long. Following after the celebrant, who had the Host, Mr. Brimner came along the rail with the cup. His best chasuble swirled about his knees, the one embroidered by the nuns at Wantage, near Oxford, that his dear friend Prior's mother had given him for his missionary posting. Birds and vines and holy insects on figured gold damask. Kay looked up and held the edge of the gold cup, gold all around her, and God alive again today, in a sudden veil of joyful piety—and Mr. Brimner smiled down without surprise, because of course he had seen them in the congregation. He spoke the usual blessing without ceasing from smiling at her. She wanted to point to Aren, who knelt on the other side of Thea with his arms crossed for a blessing because he was not yet confirmed, but that would have to wait. She said *Amen* and took a great gulp of wine by mistake, but did not choke.

After the service, there was tea in the hall. Thea would not be hurried, but Kay managed to thread them a way through the great crowd of every-coloured people to where Mr. Brimner had come out of the sacristy, now in his ordinary grey suit again. Every part of him agreeably ordinary and the same, all these months later: his pale, bony forehead, the slight bulge of his eyes, the comprehending warmth of his whole unselfconscious being.

She took his hand and held it, as the other people were doing with the other priest, but could not think of anything to say.

"*Ave, quondam* pupil," he said, speaking for her. "What joyful news to be met with your shining face below me as I came to read the Lesson! Dear Mrs. Grant, a great pleasure—you will be wondering what I am doing here. I have not been passed along to Fiji as a reject, I was only sent by the bishop to be locum tenens, the interim replacement for Canon Crake, who was sent to Auckland for a restorative holiday. My duty ends today, and I will be back with my own people at Ha'ano by the end of April, if I can get a ship before too long."

Aren stood beside Thea, one hand grasping the folds of her violet skirt. Mr. Brimner looked down and asked Thea to introduce him to her young friend, and then Francis came with two cups of tea and found them a flimsy table. On her flimsy chair Kay tried to sit still, in an agony of anticipation and frustration.

"Aren, say good morning to Mr. Brimner," Thea prompted, and Aren did so.

"God bless you," Mr. Brimner said seriously, setting a hand on his head as the priest had done at Communion, and Aren looked as if he was not certain about any of this.

Francis, going back for more tea, snapped his fingers to Kay to come and help. "We'll leave Thea to tell the tale of her purchase of this little fellow."

At that, Mr. Brimner's eyes snapped up to Francis's face, as if he checked for a jape or jollity, but he schooled his expression quickly to one of objective interest.

Thea drew Aren into her arm so that he leaned against her, saying, "One could not credit how desperate the people were . . ." as Francis pulled Kay away.

If only they had known Mr. Brimner was here, she thought, they could have been talking to him all these last four days. It made tears rise behind her eyes to think how she had wasted those days. And the saddest thing of all—they might not have seen him at all, for the *Morning Light* had been loaded by Friday, only ships never leave on a Friday, especially not on Good Friday. Then Thea had asked to stay for Easter service, but they must definitely leave on the early tide tomorrow.

Francis handed Kay a plate of cake, lifted two more cups and made a channel for them through the crowd like a tugboat in Shanghai harbour.

"Francis," she said, hurrying to catch him up. "Francis!"

He turned with his head cocked to one side. "Mm?"

She could not remember asking him for anything before. She did not have the courage to ask now. "Never mind," she said.

His stern, lipless mouth twitched in amusement. "Never mind, yourself."

When they had settled at the table, and as Mr. Brimner addressed himself to cake, Francis leaned across and said, "Now, Brimner, you're in need of a passage home, and I have need of a Greek tutor for a few days. Shall we do a trade?"

Mr. Brimner's mouth was cake-full, but he nodded, beaming without his usual prodigious display of teeth, and behind his handkerchief said that nothing could suit him better, if the *Morning Light* could let him off at Pangai without divagating too far from their route. Thea said she was very happy too, and Mr. Brimner rose to prepare for second service. He regretted that he could not dine on board that evening, being unavoidably shackled to the bishop for the Easter feast, but would come faithfully at first light with his baggage. "Only a valise, I promise!"

So Mr. Brimner's stick legs and grey linen coat and battered hat strolled the deck of the *Morning Light* again, as they ran out to sea on a light breeze, Francis saying that if this kept up, they might make Ha'ano in four days rather than five. Which made Kay hope that it would not keep up.

Without the slightest ripple, she and Mr. Brimner settled back into their routine, three chairs pulled up to the table now rather than two, with Aren set to copy all the words he knew in a fair hand. Once Thea had sharpened his pencil for him again (he had a way of pressing very hard on the leads that soon wore them to nubs), she went down to turn out Aren's things and set the upper berth for him in Kay's cabin, to give Mr. Brimner back his own.

Kay showed him how far she had got in the *Odyssey*, and turned the leaves of her notebook over and over to try to find some really good translation.

Mr. Brimner saw through her. "Fresh fare is what you need. Anyone tires of a diet of dark wine and fire-seared lamb. You need some lighter fare. I have with me Lucian's *Vera Historia*, his Hellenistic novel, parts of which are often set as excerpts for young scholars. Other parts of it are laughably unsuitable, but you may safely explicate the Voyage to the Moon."

Kay worked all the afternoon, employing her Middle Liddell with industrious abandon, and before sunset was able to present Mr. Brimner with her translation, which she read out loud for his approval. On the step beside the hammock, Aren crouched to listen; between whiles he pushed the rope to rock Thea gently to and fro where she lay reclining, a little wilted after the long, hot, still day.

"*For seven days and as many nights,*" Kay read, "*we sailed through the air, until we saw a great country like an island, shining and spherical.*" She broke off to explain to Thea, who had only come up when the afternoon cooled, "They have gone to the moon, you see?"

Bending again to her paper, she read, "*When we reached it and came to anchor, we disembarked. Exploring the countryside, we found it to be inhabited and farmed. That day we saw nothing more, but many more islands appeared nearby when night came on. There was a land below, with cities and rivers and seas and forests and mountains, and we supposed that it was our world.*"

She looked up at Mr. Brimner. "So they can see the earth from the moon? I think you could not, or at least it would be very tiny, the way we see the moon from here."

"You are *entirely* correct," he said, and motioned her to carry on.

She read: "*It seemed good to us to travel farther, and we met the Horse-Vultures. Their men ride on great vultures, and treat the birds just like horses. Learn their magnitude thus: each wing was larger and thicker than the sail of a great ship.*"

Aren found this profoundly funny. He laughed, quietly, as he always did, and so much that he had to rock back and forth. All he could say, when she asked why it was so funny, was, "Horse-wing, arm-wing!" which made her laugh too, from his description of bats. He was such a good rememberer of conversations.

But back to her story: "*These Horse-Vultures were commanded to fly about the land and, if they should find any stranger, to bring him to the king.*

And indeed, taking us captive, they led us to him. When he looked upon us,
he guessed who we were from our appearance and raiment, and said, 'Are
you Greeks, O strangers?' We assented, and he asked, 'How did you arrive
here, coming so far through the air?' And we told him the whole story. And
he in turn told us of himself, that he too was a man, by name of Endymion.
He had fallen asleep in our land and was snatched away, and arriving at
this country, he ruled it as king."

"*The moon sleeps with Endymion,*" Thea said, and it was such a
strange thing for her to say that they all looked at her. She blushed
at their regard and sat up quickly, becoming straight again. "It was
in a book at school—it is—oh, Byron, or some such."

"Shakespeare, I fear," Mr. Brimner gently put in, to spare her.
"*Merchant of Venice,* and entirely fitting: Portia, discoursing on a
calm and lovely night." He knew all the things, every book and
work of art, and all the languages, and Kay wished the Voyage to
the Moon of Ha'apai would take forever.

Mr. Brimner had been told the story of how they acquired Aren,
but he asked Aren about it himself, one hot morning while they sat
in the shade under the lifeboat. Seaton's long mahogany leg, vined
with black images, dangled above them in the afternoon sun,
twitching from time to time as he dreamed his strange visions.

Mr. Brimner had a notebook and pencil on his lap. He did not
make notes, but simply sat still, his eyes on the dimpled surface of
the waves, talking as if it was of no importance, even though he was
so interested.

"What did you do before you came onto this ship?"

Aren looked up from the brass oarlock he was polishing for
Cocker. His eyes roamed the rigging, as if he could scarce remember another life. "I did fish," he said at last.

His voice was thrummy and soft, but at her table Kay heard him
clearly. She always could hear him, from wherever he spoke.

"What fish did you fish for?"

"Not should—" Aren faltered for the word. "Not allow-ed to fish with hook only yet."

Kay hoped he would find the proper words, she hated him to be frustrated.

"Fish, fishing, round hook in—soon," he said, making a hook shape with his finger. His English had made such leaps that it was odd to hear him fumbling for grammar again. "*Teach* to fish?" he said, testing it.

"Learn?" asked Mr. Brimner. "You learned to fish?"

"Yes," Aren said with relief. "I learn-d to fish."

"What kind of fish did you catch?"

In answer, Aren leapt to the table and his own pencil, and drew a very detailed picture of a fish with a bumped-up head and a frilly top fin, which Mr. Brimner did not know. Mr. Wright, drowsing at the rail because there was no wind at all to deal with, perked up at the mention of fish and came to inspect it.

"That's a blue-lined sea bream, that is," he said.

Aren pushed the paper to Mr. Brimner. "This, I am let to fish!"

"Or perhaps it is a dogfish," Kay said.

"And who did teach you to fish? Was it your father?"

Aren looked at him without understanding. Thea had not taught him that word.

Kay wondered if she had taught him *mother*.

Because Thea asked him to, and of course in accordance with his own understanding, Mr. Brimner agreed to baptize Aren. He did this on deck, at noon on the third day of their sailing, reading the form of service from the prayer book he had always with him. Mr. Wright and Mr. Best, both churchmen, stood godparents, and spoke their responses loud and clear, promising to keep Aren from the World and the Devil.

Afterwards they had cake, and all the crew toasted Aren's health with a rum tot. Then, while Mr. Brimner changed out of his surplice and stole, and Aren ran about the deck training Pilot to retrieve a piece of salt beef without instantly eating it, Kay sat with Thea in the hammock, cool and soft in the slight shade its awning made.

Thea said, "There—I am thankful to have that done."

Because Aren's soul would be safe now, she meant. Kay did not like that. His soul was safe because God loved him, because there was nothing but goodness in him. Not because of the words being said over him, or the holy water. It was hard to see why everyone must be baptized, when we already believe that God will take care of the lilies and the mice in the fields. But Thea had told Kay before that she was not the arbiter of doctrine, and should simply accept the teachings of the Church.

"Do you remember me being baptized?"

Thea smiled, enjoying this kind of nostalgia. "No, for I had gone back to finish school in Yarmouth before you were born. But I remember your mother being baptized."

Kay was surprised. "When she was a baby?"

Thea laughed. "No, no, she was a little older than I! But she had lived in the country, you know, and there had never been a chance for her to be baptized, so in our first years at Fort à la Corne, Father baptized her."

"And then he married her."

"Yes." Thea was silent a moment. "She was lovely, your mama. Easy to be with. She had a peaceable nature."

"Not like me."

"No, you take after Father, I think. But she was strong-minded, too. I left for Yarmouth confident that they would deal very well together, although she was so much younger than he. It was the happiest I had ever seen him, on their wedding day, and I was happy too."

"But then she died, and you had to come back to care for me."

"No, I had already come back—after normal school I came out to teach at Blade Lake for a year. I was there when she died."

"Oh yes, tell me again."

Thea's head tilted to check Kay's face, but she was patient enough to retell it. "She was tired, after church, and she went up to lie down. She asked me to bring her a cup of tea in an hour—"

"And when you took it up, there she was, dead."

"Yes."

A flood of tears pricked at Kay's eyes, wanting to flow forth, but Aren had come back and was looking at her. Thinking of his mother never seeing him again, she was distracted from self-pity. She got up to run along the deck, her bare feet almost as fast as his.

In the ideal hour, near the end of the watch on a slow afternoon when the work was done and the men slept or sat carving in the shrouds, low sun brought a lessening of the heat. Everyone she loved was here, Kay thought.

Silence spread like oil over the unmoving sea. Then up from underneath came a blue-black swell rising in a long arc, longer than thought, unthinking, unknowing, unknown. Kay waited, immensity pressing on her, hovering in the difference between herself and the whale.

While Thea and Francis took a turn about the deck in the early morning heat, Mr. Brimner asked Aren, "Shall I tell you of Arion of Methymna, a name close to your own, who was carried ashore at Tainaron upon a dolphin's back?"

Aren nodded, and Kay said, "Yes, oh yes, that would be perfect." Which sounded as if she knew the story, which she did not—but Father had read him, therefore Herodotus was manly reading, and a historical account rather than mere fiction.

Mr. Brimner adjusted his dark spectacles (Kay was happy to see his portable darkness unbroken) and began: "This Arion, they say, was a great harpist, the first, so far as we know, who composed a dithyramb!" He gave a courteous nod, as if Kay at least would certainly know what a dithyramb was. She smiled at him, knowing he knew by then exactly what she knew and did not know.

"He had sailed to Italy and Sicily and made a great deal of money—he was the Caruso of his time. Wishing to return home to Corinth, he hired a ship with a crew of Corinthians, whom he trusted. But out in the open sea, those rascals announced their intention to cast Arion overboard and take the gold for themselves. He offered them all his wealth if they would spare his life, but the sailors insisted he either slay himself on deck or leap straightway into the sea. Being driven to it, he promised to put himself to death if they would let him sing one last song."

Aren looked to Kay; she mimed the playing of a lyre-harp to show what was meant.

"Thinking it good to hear the best harpist alive, for the few moments he remained alive, the men settled themselves on deck to listen. He dressed in his full singer's robes, took his harp and sang the Orthian measure. At its end, as he had promised, he threw himself into the sea, and they went on sailing away to Corinth."

Mr. Brimner sat back in his deck chair and took his spectacles off to polish them.

"That cannot be the end," Kay protested.

Aren said, urging him, "Then? And then?"

Mr. Brimner sighed. "You are too wise for my narrative ploy. Yes, and *then*—and then, as Arion struggled in the waves, a dolphin came and swam beside him, and then beneath him, and supported him on its back across the water and brought him to shore at Tainaron, which is very near to Corinth."

Kay could have said, I once swam where dolphins were. She remembered that grey smoothness, the clear eye watching her. And how she would not have touched him without his permission. It did not seem impossible to her, this tale.

"And when Arion came to land, he went to Corinth and told the king what had happened. The king set watch for the rascally sail-ors, and when they came, he inquired of them if they had any report to make of Arion, his famous harpist. Oh yes, said they, he is safe in Italy, they left him at Taras faring well . . . At that, Arion appeared before them, in the same singer's robes as when he made his leap from the ship, and they were struck with amazement and no longer able to deny their crime."

Aren laughed and laughed. Kay was not sure if he understood it perfectly, or if he merely laughed to please Mr. Brimner.

Who laughed as well, and added, "Herodotus says this tale is still told by Corinthians, and there is at Tainaron a bronze figure of a man upon a dolphin's back."

The voyage was too quickly over.

They stood again on the little stone jetty under the rise of Mr. Brimner's house, Francis having good-naturedly said they would pull for Ha'ano, no need for cadging a second lift at Pangai. Thea sent a basket of supplies and two chickens over in the boat; Kay went along to hold the chickens, and to say farewell.

Mr. Brimner pulled on his thin nose. "Well, my dear Kay, good-bye again, for a short while at least."

"Yes," she said.

The pier faced a flat, beige-blue stretch of sea with nothing much to interest the eye.

"Your brother tells me another voyage is planned, not next year but in 1914."

Kay nodded. Her braid had come loose; she pushed her hair out of her eyes again and rubbed them.

"When people are fast friends, it is immaterial whether they visit in the flesh or in the spirit. I have been following your work and travels with great interest through your letters— Wait, let me think . . . Have I yet received a single epistle from you? No?"

She blushed.

"Ha, I do not mean to shame you! The price of a seafaring life is that one is always busy, and correspondence suffers."

"I will write to you faithfully now," she promised.

"And I to you," he said. He shook her hand on it.

She went down the pier and hopped back into the boat. The boys pulled on the oars, and once again she left Mr. Brimner's bundled, bird-legged body standing at the end of the pier, waving his handkerchief to them as the boat separated from the pier at Ha'ano and made way to the *Morning Light*, back out into the blue.

15

An Eclipse

On April 28, they sailed through an eclipse of the sun, the first that Kay had ever witnessed. Mr. Wright, a great amateur astronomer, believed it must be the first for Aren too, since he could find no note in his almanacs of a full eclipse occurring in this hemisphere during the boy's lifetime.

The sun was bright and ordinary when they went up on deck for breakfast, but Mr. Wright rushed round with pieces of card and instructions for creating a pinhole viewer, and dire warnings about blindness, not only for Kay and Aren but for all the crew. Aren was in the lifeboat playing knucklebones with Seaton, and leaned over when called. He watched the perforation of the card with interest, listened gravely to the cautions of Thea and Mr. Wright, and then leapt back up to finish his game, crowing whenever the bones fell in his favour.

Kay took her book up to the roof of the Aft cabin, letting her bare feet dangle down through the open skylight. Thea had quite stopped remembering to order her to wear either boots or stockings these days—everything was much freer now that Aren took up half her worrying time.

At a sudden feeling Kay looked up, scanning the yellowish sky, but could see no portent. And yet everything felt strange.

The ship was nearly at a standstill, the wind having dropped completely, and Francis directed Mr. Best to set the sea anchor so that all the crew could stop their work and watch the phenomenon.

Finishing with the bones, Aren appeared again over the lip of the lifeboat and made a game of coming to sit by Kay by the most devious route, ending with a drop onto all fours beside her. He sat close, looking at her book, which was *Treasure Island*, for the seventh time.

There was no point in attempting study when something enormous was about to happen, but Kay read to him, pointing at the words, and his finger raced ahead to find words he knew: *ship, island, table, ocean*. She stopped reading to him and made him read to her, helping him when needed.

> Though I had lived by the shore all my life, I seemed
> never to have been near the sea till then. The smell of tar
> and salt was something new. I saw the most wonderful fig-
> ureheads, that had all been far over the ocean. I saw,
> besides, many old sailors, with rings in their ears, and
> whiskers curled in ringlets, and tarry pigtails, and their
> swaggering, clumsy sea-walk . . .

They were getting on very well, Kay doing a good deal of prompting and Aren very concentrated, when that feeling of quiet alertness came over them again, as something odd happened to the page. It was muted, darker.

Aren looked up first, and then Kay. All the men had gathered on deck, even those who ought to have been sleeping. All were looking up into the sky.

Pilot came out of his shady spot by the wheelhouse and stood looking up too.

"Not direct at the sun!" Mr. Wright called in general warning. But the temptation was strong! Many of the crew put up their hands to shield their eyes, but most continued looking generally up.

The day—darkened.

Nobody spoke.

The eeriness of it, and the stillness of wind and sea, took hold of Kay in her deepest heart. Aren had moved imperceptibly so that he was very close to her. Kay whistled for Pilot, and he came, moving quietly and crouching a little as if afraid, and hopped up onto the saloon roof. Aren made room for him and put an arm round his neck.

Thea came with the pieces of card and reached them up. Kay adjusted them to show Aren how the sun was looking—a bite taken out of the top of the disc. It had turned into a horned thing. Then there was a slow progression into dusk. The men eventually went back to a desultory kind of work, until in half an hour or so the twilight was pronounced. On the card the sun showed like a crescent moon lying on its back. Then they had to look up.

The air around them had fallen into purple, eerie evening. Kay realized that half its mystery lay in the absence of a preceding exit of the sun, no redness in the west, no lingering light. The whole sky darkened equally.

When Cocker called eleven o'clock, the sun was only a bright thumbnail left in the sky, like a bit of evening star come early. The sky had tinted from cerulean down into Delft and Prussian blue, and then lower, into a shining indigo.

In the starboard shrouds, Jacky Judge called down, "Sir!"

Francis turned, and Jacky pointed out to the sea. Kay and Aren stood to see better—to see the strangest thing imaginable.

In the weird descending twilight, the water was full of shapes. Whales, many of them, had come to the surface, their heads gazing up. Then more, smaller shapes.

Aren said a word and Kay said, "Dolphins, dolphins . . ."

A head, and another head, another—dotted across a wide space, twenty or thirty dolphins and whales had risen from the deeps, all looking up into the heavens together to where the sky was growing murkier, yellower, more sombre and burnt umber every minute— no longer normal darkness in the least.

Again, silence fell across the ship. Thea had crouched down by the railing and Kay thought she might be praying.

Darkness fell then, as quick as a blind. They could see the shadow-edge of it skimming toward them across the sea, and in two minutes it was night.

Kay let out a little shriek and clamped on to Aren, as he did to her with both his thin, strong arms. The darkness came with a wave of vertigo—everything was wrong! This was not how the world was to work!

The darkness, which was not night but a tarnished-silver sadness cast over the world, lasted four minutes. Kay breathed, of course she did, but she could not make her chest open as usual. She and Aren both kept tight hold on Pilot, who shivered uncontrollably all through it, and on each other. When the light came back, as if it had never gone away, they saw the other observers diving down, dispersing like darkness, going on about their usual lives. And so did the *Morning Light* sail on.

Aren was interested in everything. While Kay sat reading in the morning, sitting on the roof of the Aft cabin, Aren poked about the ship and asked *what? what? how?* wanting to know how the ship was steered, how the pulleys worked, how the scuppers drained, how the holystone ground the boards to that clean white finish. He was quiet, but infinitely alert. Timid and brave by turns, very loving to Kay, whom he had adopted as his partner. For a time he would sit with her at the work table, printing his own letters at Thea's direction; then he would race around the deck, laughing with the boys. He could swarm up the ropes faster than any, but Francis had commanded him to stay out of the way when orders had been given, and he obeyed. He was fond of Francis, which surprised Kay a little—she thought he might have been shy of him, as she sometimes had been herself at first. His affection was quiet, a matter of a hand trustingly laid on Francis's arm, or of standing side-by-each at the chart desk, in undemonstrative harmony.

But he was sad, too. From time to time it seemed that the weight of learning things was too much for him, and tears would well into his eyes. Then, tired of new knowledge, he would go and knock on the hull of the starboard lifeboat and be taken up by Seaton for a rest.

One afternoon Arthur Wetmore called Kay and Aren to come quick, come to the side. "Sharks!" he said, not so loudly as to alarm them. Looking over the rail, they found shapes milling in the dark-green waters—long, thin, grey, muscled in their movements. Liu Jiacheng had just dumped a basket of scraps, and the great fish had come to feed. Six upright fins, circling, looking for more. The thick grey skin had a rough look of badly moulded clay.

Aren stared out over the water. "I wish for my *taod*."

"What is that?" she asked.

He made a strong motion. "I stick the—wood—stick in fish. Stick, stick . . ." He lifted his arm and slashed it down, again and again.

In his own place, he would have been a fisherman, Kay thought. What would he become now, in this place?

16

The Horn

Off the western side of the Horn at 6 p.m., the wind was blowing hard when the starboard watch came on deck to haul up the mainsail. All hands went aloft to make it fast—an operation that Kay always watched if she could, because it was so terrifying: twelve men at intervals along the mainsail, hauling, and six below, sweating the ropes even harder, to make the wet canvas compact into a long roll fit for tying up. She stood in her oilskin coat, tucked into the shelter of the House, staring upward into the clouded twilight overhead. They had furled the sail, all but the clews, and now came the tricksy part.

Arthur Wetmore was the outside man, way out at the end of the cross yard, sitting on the footrope ready to pass a turn of the gasket around the clew—when somehow he lost his balance, slipping forward of the footrope, and came down.

He held on to the gasket, but it was a small rope, not two inches across, and it slid through his hands so that he fell into the sea. It must have hurt his bare hands terribly—it made Kay's hands hurt as she watched.

They all saw him fall. Francis rushed aft, and as he ran, he was calling to the man at the wheel—it was Mr. Best, for the starboard watch—"Put the wheel hard down!"

Kay felt the instant change in their course, the ship responding even in this turbulent sea. Francis had already grabbed the lifebuoy. He threw it to Arthur, and it landed not ten feet from him—his arm reached out and clutched at the log line, but that too slipped through his fingers. When he came to the log, he held it for a moment, but that towed him under and he had to let go—but then Kay saw him take the few strokes, swimming hard, and he caught at the lifebuoy. Her heart was clamouring in her chest. Suddenly everything was awful. But he had the buoy.

Francis shouted, "Let go, t'gallant halyards! Let go, topsail halyards! Jacky, you there! Up aloft to watch for Arthur . . ."

Jacky swarmed up, faster than Kay had ever seen him go, and clung fast to watch.

The other men were working their way inward from the mainsail to safer positions and then all scrambling down, knowing what must be done. There was no time to take in more sail—Francis tore the covers off the gig, Seaton leaping from his station in the lifeboat and helping to unfasten the mooring, and six or seven of the men carried the boat over the deck to the lee side and threw her over the rail with a single line in each end. The gig was longer and stronger than the lifeboat, it would fare better on these bad seas.

Mr. Best and four of the strongest men, Douglas, Anderson, Lynch and Thomas, started out from the ship. Francis gave Thomas a tin of oil as he went over the side, for the sea was very heavy and now breaking badly.

Kay watched in terror, seeing the boat almost standing on end. She was still standing there, fists tight-clenched about the rail, when Francis spotted her and sent her down below. She did not protest, but went as she was bid.

In the saloon, Thea sat reading to Aren, as if nothing at all was happening. Kay told them, words clogging in her throat, and they waited together for a very long time, not wanting or daring to intrude up above. Then Thea stood and said she must—they could at least—ready things for the men returning.

She went to find Jiacheng, and they together made up the fires in the narrow forward saloon, while Kay and Aren fetched extra blankets from the lazaret and set them round the stoves to warm.

"Hot water too, please," Thea said, and Kay and Aren fell to as Jiacheng's bucket brigade. They were glad to be busy down below, while Thea went up—Francis had sent word down that they'd lost sight of the gig boat.

She came down shortly, saying the sea was dreadful, that she had seen nothing like it since the hurricane. But she did not pack Kay and Aren off to bed, perhaps realizing that Kay would not go, and thinking it best to keep Aren with them anyhow. Or perhaps even wanting their company, Kay thought. Kay sat beside her at one of the mess tables for a little while, holding her cold hand and kissing it to make it warm.

It seemed a very long time until they heard glad shouting and noise up on deck—then Thea sent them back to Aft quickly, to make room for the chilled men coming down, saying she would soon follow. Kay tucked Aren under one quilt with her on the banquette at the end of the saloon, far from the lamp, and he had fallen into a doze before Thea came.

In a little while Francis too came to the saloon and told them all that had happened. At least, he told Thea, not seeming to be aware of Kay and Aren in the shadows behind him. Even Thea had forgotten them.

"After half an hour the dark had come down so that we lost sight of the boat. I wore ship at once. We had clewed the topgallant sails up and the upper fore topsail down—" He caught himself up. "But that is for my report. Find me my inkwell, will you, Thea?"

She hastened for it, and some sheets of rough paper, and he sat at the table to tell the rest, scribbling a note now and again as he went through the tale.

"She was in a dead drift, as I wished to keep the boat to windward to give them a square run before the sea coming back. The rain squall had set in, blowing hard. The risk was terrible, and I set the ensign to recall the boat, but for—oh God—for an hour and a quarter, I tell you, we saw no sign of her. I gave her up."

He stared across at Thea, his hand stilling on the page, silent for a moment. "One must go through the experience to realize how horrible is that feeling. Jacky Judge was in the main crosstrees all this time, trying to sight the boat—I sent him down for warming too, poor lad—and at last I saw her, right to windward, as the squall cleared, steering for the ship, running as much as ten feet of herself out of the water in those seas! They got under the lee of the ship and pulled alongside, the boat half-full of water, but no Arthur. He's gone, poor fellow."

Francis stopped again. Kay thought he was going to weep, and she was afraid to watch. He sat silent, his thumb twisting around his finger, over and over, and then continued, still dry-eyed. "Best says that, twice, the water was up to the thwarts as the sea broke over them—had she filled, they all of them would be gone. He says the oil saved them, smoothing the water around them and keeping the sea from breaking."

Thea did not speak, but touched his hand where the thumb was coursing, coursing, tightening and releasing. The skin had gone white under the lamplight.

"One man—it was Douglas, I think—saw an empty lifebuoy on the top of the sea. They went on, on, until they lost sight of the ship in the squall, and then started back. Poor Best, he said it was the hardest thing he ever had to do, to come back without him—and he did not think it possible then that they could save even themselves."

Francis bent his head so Kay could hardly see him in the shadow. He breathed slow, through his mouth, and then went on. "I must make a note. The last Jacky Judge saw him, Arthur was on the weather quarter. He did have the lifebuoy around him, but several seas had broken over him. He could not have lasted long, the water is ice-cold . . ."

Francis wiped his face, which was all over wet with sudden tears Kay had not seen him shed. Thea knelt beside his chair, taking his wet hand in hers.

"The men are exhausted, they were out there two hours. I will never risk a boat's crew again in such a sea—only Providence saved them. We waited till nine thirty, in no occasion of hope, you know, but through my inability to form the order, and then wore ship."

Thea was weeping now. Kay did not know why she did not cry herself. Aren moved slightly in his sleep, and she tightened her arm about him.

"I do not see how some people can call sailors *dogs*," Thea said. "The sea those brave men started out into, to try to save Arthur—if they could see them starting out in that gig boat, I am sure they never would call them so again."

Francis nodded, and stood, and said, "I must go and make sure— I'll write it up tomorrow, and we'll put into Montevideo to report."

He mopped his face once more, and touched a hand to Thea's shoulder where she still crouched, and started back up the companionway. "You will have to cable to poor Arthur's mother," Thea said after him, but he made no reply.

Kay took Aren's hand to wake him gently, and led him to his bed. As she tucked him into his blue blanket, he said, "A dolphin must come up out of the sea and carry him now, Kay," and she nodded and kissed his cheek. His arm tightened around her neck and then it slackened, and he was asleep. He was very young still.

So was Arthur young. Arthur, who had gone into the sea.

Kay went to her own bed, expecting to dream of looking overboard into the grey scalloping waves, but did not dream at all.

In the morning, Francis wrote it up in his logbook. Sitting beside him at the table in the saloon, her own books disregarded, Kay read the account:

> 1 bag, 1 quilt, 1 pillow, 1 pannikin, 1 cup, 3 shirts, 3 prs. socks,
> 4 prs. dungarees, 2 pr. trousers, 1 coat, 1 pr. shoes, 1 suit oil

clothes, 1 cap. In addition to personal belongings, Arthur was owed $56.47 in wages.

Francis dusted the page with sand and closed the logbook. It was not much, to be all that was left of Arthur, who had showed her how to ballantine a rope.

17

Corcovado

On Thursday they saw a raft with a man fishing; later in the day they could see detail on the coastline of Argentina. Three steamers passed by, going south, their engines untroubled by wind or tide. But Kay thought the passengers must feel the heavy seas, at any rate, even if the captains were not worried. A man standing by the rail of the third lifted his arm to Kay and Aren, and Kay felt a squashing fright that he might be washed overboard next, and how would a steamer stop in time? But the man stayed tight to the rail, and as he passed them, he turned and went inside. Safe for now.

The *Morning Light* anchored at Montevideo to report the loss of Arthur Wetmore—the first port where Francis could send a cable to Arthur's poor mother, a task he said took a sad toll on him "but would exact a sadder on the recipient"—and their departure was held up for a week by protocol concerning the death.

∾

It seemed to Thea that their voyage was cursed now. Two days after leaving Montevideo, they collided with a large sperm whale, a jarring bump that rattled the windowpanes and threw the books onto the floor in the saloon—and an hour later the duty man came up to report a stern leak. There was no word as to how the whale had fared in the encounter, and Kay mourned it in an excessive way until Thea almost boxed her ears for her.

Francis went down to inspect and came up with brows like thunder, not willing to be coaxed out of his ill temper for a moment. He took his evening meal in the wheelhouse and did not come down to sleep at all, that Thea was aware of. The leak occupied every instant of his attention, and caused a great deal of extra work for the men, who were put in rotation at the pump.

Then they had headwinds most of the week, and a storm on Friday—the cold wind the Brazilians call the *pampero*. "They do not last long," Francis promised Thea, some of his equilibrium recovered by the exhilaration of dealing with the weather. "But the wind blows very hard, with thunder and lightning."

It was *very* rough. Aren loved it. He made a game in the saloon, sitting against one wall and sliding down the sudden slope of carpetless floor to the other wall. Thea laughed and caught him up before he banged into the baseboard with his boots, and he wriggled around in her arms and hid his face for a moment—perhaps he had been frightened after all?—before raising his head again to cough. His cough was back.

She kept his hand and went along for the medicine chest, and called down to Jiacheng for some of his soothing tea.

On Saturday, one of the sailors caught a big albacore, weighing about eighty pounds, and they all had an excellent dinner of it, Aft and sailors alike. Francis said it was all that kept the men from mutiny over the constant operation of the pump.

The *Morning Light* entered the mouth of Rio harbour on Sunday morning, past the beautiful promenade, which would have been a delightful sight had not the weary crew been on their last legs, and had Francis yet been able to throw off his sorrow and anger over Arthur Wetmore. Here would be a cable waiting him from Arthur's mother, and Thea knew how much he dreaded reading that.

He came back from the cable office and down into the saloon with a grave face, which Thea at first attributed to grief—but it was not that, or not only that.

"There's yellow fever here," he said. "Captains with families are being advised to send them to Corcovado, a resort high on the mountain. Gomes in the shipping office recommends that we comply, says he's never seen an outbreak like it, even after all their attempts at greater sanitation in the city. I dislike sending you, but we cannot chance it with the fever. I met Hilton, from the *Abyssinia*, you'll remember him from old Yarmouth days—he's sent his wife and daughter up ahead, so they'll be company for you, and there are one or two other women you may count on. Gomes has arranged a trap to come in an hour to convey you up to the railway."

Thea took his hand. "We'll go," she said. "What might it be—two weeks?—before you've finished the repairs? Too long to take the risk." She was thinking of Aren's cough.

"They are taking it very seriously, these fellows. Their own wives and children are already gone from the city."

She'd meant to find Aren shoes, and he had gone right through his other pair of trousers; all that could wait. Thea turned to her cabin, calling for Kay and Aren to come at once and help her pack.

❧

After three or four hours by pony trap over a bone-rattling road, they transferred to a cable car to get up to the mountain refuge. Kay had never been on one before, and of course Aren had never even heard of such a thing as a cog-and-wheel railway. He sat against the red leather bench with a hand on Thea's knee for safety, eyes intent on everything around them. His ears almost moved, straining to catch the inflections of Portuguese. What an interesting life he was having, Kay thought. He would have liked the train around the beach at Piha, and she could hardly wait to show him the escalators at Filene's in Boston! She was having a curious life, too, of course—full of sights and sounds one could not have imagined, in Blade Lake.

They were comfortably settled in a long rear seat, with the window open onto the passing greenery, when partway up the cars suddenly stopped and ground their gears. Pilot's head tensed under Kay's hand, but he did not move or bark.

A group of nuns, black, voluminous birds on their way to the monastery, fell noisily to their knees and prayed in unison, with astonishing vigour, until after a few moments the train shuddered into motion again. Not speaking or understanding Portuguese, Kay assumed they were passing some religious shrine, until they arrived and were met by Mrs. Hilton, the Yarmouth captain's wife, who told them that a few weeks earlier a train had crashed down the mountainside when the brakes failed to hold. Kay was glad not to have known that before the trip.

Outside the little station, signs in Portuguese (tantalizingly almost translatable, from its kinship to Latin) directed visitors to the zoo and a botanical gardens. Above the station, higher up the mountain, stood a large church and the small monastery, to which the line of nuns hurried in a straggling queue.

Mrs. Hilton and her daughter had been at the retreat for a week already, and had learned the ropes. She took firm charge of Thea and the luggage, steering her into the reception area of the *pousada* to find the manageress, explaining the protocol and meals and so on. She spoke a little Portuguese, Captain Hilton having been many months in Rio over the years, and helped translate room rates and other details for Thea. She introduced her daughter Marion, saying, "She's just your Kay's age, and will look after her all right. You go explore the summit, girls, and see you're back in time for supper."

Marion was shorter than Kay, and wearing a much fancier dress, tobacco-striped taffeta with blue ribbons daubed on it here and there. Her yellow hair shone in separate curling locks, and her pretty boots were blue Spanish leather. As her mother turned back to carry on helping Thea with the accommodation arrangements, Marion obediently led Kay out to walk around the square.

Seeing Aren following along with Pilot, she asked, "Is that your boy?"

Kay nodded, then realized what Marion meant. "He is my—" She had not had to explain him before. Nothing seemed exactly right. "He is Aren. My sister has adopted him. Come on, Aren!" She took his thin hand and drew him close, putting one arm round his shoulders.

Marion laughed. "What an odd thing!"

"It is not odd at all." Kay was furious now. She did not know what to say without shouting or kicking, she did not know how to protect Aren from what this girl was going to say. "He is my brother."

Looking at Kay as if she was halfwitted, Marion laughed again. "Well, he's a darky!"

"He is my brother," Kay said again, quickly, her words tumbling over Marion's to mute them, and she turned in a different direction and pulled Aren along with her, walking as fast as she could away from Marion.

Aren followed after, but she could feel him still turning back to look at Marion. "She waits," he said, pulling her arm. "Slow . . . do not go . . ."

"No."

"She wants us to talk!" He pulled harder, coughing.

"She is a mean creature and we will pay no mind to her," Kay told him.

But she could not race on when he was coughing so. She found the handkerchief in his pocket and applied it to his mouth, which he could never remember to do, not having grown up with one always being thrust at him.

Marion had followed after them and stood nearby, not coming too close. "Does he have the yellow fever?" she asked. It was the most cowardly thing Kay had ever heard.

"No! He—we have both had a bad cold, we are still getting well, that is why Thea wanted to bring us up here."

"I didn't mean it," Marion said.

"Mean what?"

Marion did not seem to know what to say. "I mean, he is a nice little fellow—does he speak English and everything? I was only surprised, that's all. That he was your brother."

They looked at each other, measuring how this would go.

"I speak English," Aren said. "And a little bit Chinese. Kay speak-es Greek and *quite a lot* of Latin."

Kay was not going to laugh. But then Aren did, so she could not help it, and laughing made him cough again. He said, "May I?" and reached for the hanky she had stuffed into the pocket of her serge skirt.

Marion was quicker. She held a big pocket square out to Aren before the next cough took him. She gave him a grin, her podgy face becoming more interesting, and Kay decided to forgive her, for now.

They climbed together to the next landing, where a little window of the monastery sold bread and pastry. Marion bought a paper bag of Benedictus, which she said was gingerbread stuffed with strawberry jam, and gave them each a piece.

Up there above the clouds, the landscape was eerie—like a surrounding Yarmouth fog, but these trailing scraps were sky-cloud, not ground-mist. Marion said they could climb right up to the summit, where there was a lookout, so they went on, a little slowly, because once Aren had started coughing, he could not seem to stop.

At the summit lay a tiled area and a stone railing where they might look down from the height onto the city and the sea surrounding it, like Christ looking down from the mountain where Satan took him to show him what he might have.

It would be hard to refuse this. Far below, the city and the land streamed out from the base of the mountain like arms reaching out to the sea, the pot shape of the hills repeated and repeated, rich in the wet green jungle they had stuttered up through on the cog train. The ocean swept on outward from the end of the land until it melted into grey haze at the blurred edge of the horizon, the almost indiscernible border of water and sky, very far away. Where they themselves had come from, at early light this morning. Kay turned around and around, the world reshaping below her with each revolution, dream islands and a dream sea, and fine strands of mist still caught in air around them.

∾

Cora Hilton had brought her unmarried sister along on the voyage. Edna had been seeing a man of *the wrong sort*, Cora confided in Thea, and the family decided that the best cure was an extended course of "out of sight, out of mind" and the benefits of sea air.

"I hope very much that she will not take fever," Cora said, looking over to where her sister sat playing at Chinese checkers with Aren. That little travelling set was serving him well.

Thea had briefly explained Aren's presence, and Cora made no immediate comment, although Thea sensed a glimmer of "must write to Mama about this!" in her regard.

Aren bent away from the game and reached one hand to Kay, sitting at the next table with Marion. Kay had her hanky ready. He coughed again, and coughed, distressingly, and bunched up the hanky.

Thea saw, though. The bright-red splotch on it.

She was up and moving before she understood what she knew. She took the hanky from Aren very gently, and laid a cool hand on his forehead. And then she went out to the lobby to seek the doctor who had been visiting the monastery earlier.

It was tuberculosis, the doctor was certain of it. A lean, thoughtful Portuguese, a gentleman, with a sombre manner that inspired belief. Not that Thea had any hope of not believing. He listened to the chests and hearts of both Aren and Kay, and pronounced Kay perfectly recovered from a slight cold. Aren's sputum test would have to be taken to the city, but he had no real doubt, and he saw that Thea had none either.

"You will have to arrange for treatment," he said. "There is nothing to be done at this hostelry here, but I might find a suitable place in the country, if you would like to leave the boy in my care . . .?"

He had left the question of their exact relationship delicately unasked.

"No," Thea said. "We will—" She stopped and flicked a tiny drop from her right eye. Not a tear, precisely, but an irritation. "I have some experience of nursing. Sea air will be the best remedy, until we can get to New York."

"Of a certainty," the doctor said. He did not bow, but gave off the sense that he would have, in the last century. "New York, indeed. They are making—strides, as I believe one must phrase it."

Language was a surmountable barrier, when people were educated—but it was still a barrier. "Can you tell me where I should take him?" she asked bluntly. "Which hospital?"

"My true expertise is confined to yellow fever, at which we have strided far, and cholera and the like, which have also bedevilled our city. But I shall inquire. Let the name of your ship be sent to me and I will cable ahead and discover for you the best facility. In the meanwhile, let him not be confined in any low-lying, dark or humid place, and be certain that he is fed liberally."

Thea shook her head, unable to face the task of assuring the doctor that Aren was no slave or servant to be bundled into steerage.

Across the room, Kay was watching them, her eyes strained. Thea let the doctor go out without further question and turned to comfort her.

∾

They spent ten days up in Corcovado. After the diagnosis, Thea kept close by Aren and left Kay to go off with Marion on expeditions of their own along the jungle paths. The girls spent long hours perched on the stone wall at the very peak of the mountain, looking down through strands of cloud upon all the kingdoms of the world and the glory of them, telling stories of high adventure in the South Seas (Kay) or the scandalous and apocryphal history of Aunt Edna (Marion), inventing dresses or (Marion again) imagining future husbands.

Kay expected, without allowing herself to examine the idea closely, that she would not marry now, because her future husband had already died. She had taken it for granted that one day she would marry Arthur Wetmore, not because of any real romantic attachment, but because that was how the world operated: you eventually married a person known to your family. And he was kind. She told Marion about his drowning, and Marion (who had been to school with Arthur) cried all afternoon, which weighed in her favour.

Although they would not have been friends in the ordinary way, it was good to have a companion for the long, cloud-wreathed days. Thea was in such a state that there was no hope of talking to her. She sat with Aren endlessly, not hammering away at his English as before, but reading to him and letting him read with her any book from the *pousada*'s shelves that caught his fancy. In the afternoons, sometimes she would let Kay sit with him while she drifted away to sleep for an hour. She was becoming pale too.

Kay was happy to sit on the long sun porch outside their room, the curtains beside Aren's couch billowing in and out on each breath of wind. There was a very old children's book in the library that Aren took a fancy to—*Nursery Lessons, In Words of One Syllable*—and asked her to read with him over and over. It had lovely illustrations, especially the one of a two-masted boat (that even Kay could tell was rigged all wrong, like no boat ever seen on this or any other ocean) that he liked to look at even when he was too tired to read. The text below it read,

> *How hard the wind blows!*
> *and how the little boats rock to and fro!*
> *It must be sad for those poor men*
> *who have to earn their bread on the sea.*
> *I hope they will bring home a good net full of fish*

> *that they may buy food and warm clothes*
> *for their poor wives and little ones.*

Sometimes, as they read it, Kay would find herself almost crying with sorrow for those poor men who earned their bread, and their poor wives and little ones. Then she would turn to her own favourite page, which read,

> *Ann's papa had a large dog,*
> *of which she was very fond,*
> *and when Ann had a bun or cake,*
> *she would give some to Dash.*
> *One day, Ann fell into a pond,*
> *but the good dog did not let her sink,*
> *but sprang in and drew her safe to land.*

"Good old Dash," Kay said, patting Pilot's head where it was jammed into the fold of her knee.

One page made both Kay and Aren laugh:

> *See! Here is a fine nag.*
> *And that is a good boy who rides on it too;*
> *for he reads his book so well, and is so neat and clean,*
> *that his kind aunt gave him this nice horse;*
> *and I am sure James takes good care of her gift.*

"*See here is a fine nag,*" Aren repeated, laughing again, very gentle, suppressed laughter, so as not to provoke a coughing fit.

Kay said, "And you are a good boy who rides on it too, and reads his book so well."

At Corcovado, Kay grew used to Aren's illness, and to the telltale white sputum cup always in his hand, which Thea guarded jealously and washed with vigorous care. When they left Rio, the cup came with them, the badge of TB. There were other provisions for the journey: new sheets and a dozen warm red blankets (plenty of those, to accommodate the inevitable night sweats) reserved to Aren's use for fear of infection; a reclining wooden deck chair in which he would spend the days outdoors; and a metal hospital cot that could be lashed in place each night, for sleeping on deck.

It was all much nicer than the crowded ward where the Blade Lake children had breathed and coughed and sipped at their gruel. Kay sank into almost-panic, remembering that. She wished she could sleep on deck too, and secretly planned to keep Aren company.

Jiacheng went to market to find fifteen chickens instead of the usual dozen; three good eggs per day was the doctor's prescription for Aren, shaken up with plenty of cream. Luckily, Brazil was a good place for cattle, and by bartering and bargaining, Francis secured a nice-natured little cow, guaranteed to give a sufficiency of milk to sustain the poor child.

Without drawing Thea's attention to it, Jiacheng also dosed Aren with a concoction of his own, which he had puzzled out in his little book of cures. Kay loved the delicate vertical strands of words in that book, drawn by some meticulous hand. Aren had coaxed Jiacheng to draw out some elementary letterforms for him to copy, but Kay was content to simply look, since she already had the unending task and burden of gaining fluency in Greek.

She gathered that the book held recipes and advice for all things, not unlike Thea's *Fanny Farmer*, but it was more mystical than that practical text. Jiacheng said it required interpretation, but would not elaborate further. He made a wormwood tea, as bitter as bile, and had to add Lyle's Golden Syrup to each cup to convince Aren to take it. The cream-and-eggnog was easier, especially when Kay gave it to Aren saying, like the *Words of One Syllable* book, "See here is a fine nog" to make him laugh. But even then, the poor boy often gagged at the viscous richness before catching himself into better bravery and swallowing it down. Once he had taken it, Kay would pronounce, "And that is a good boy who drinks it too."

∾

There was nothing to be done but the things that were being done, Thea told herself. She spent the long weeks of the voyage up to New York in constant half-buried trepidation, not allowing her mind to race ahead to the inevitable, familiar conclusion of tuberculosis. Not dwelling on the many stick-thin bodies whose eyes she had closed, and carried down the long stairs and delivered into the earth.

In the first week back on the ship, she found she had been ashore too long—her stomach betrayed her again and she had some uncomfortable mornings before she grew sea-wise once more. She had no time to suffer nausea, anyway, for Aren needed her. And the weather smiled on them; if only she could have given those poor Indian children this sea air, this fresh wind and beating, hygienic sunlight . . . But she would put aside regret, and instead set about making one of the three good meals a day that Aren must have, or fetching him the next glass of milk. She became quite fond of the little cow, who did diligently produce milk at a rate that, well beyond Aren's capacity for drinking, allowed for puddings on the Aft table almost every day, and quite often junket for Below.

The dreams were back again, and no wonder. Thea heard Kay crying in her bunk, and went barefoot down the corridor to catch her before she woke Aren, sleeping inside in this miserable weather. Rain pelted on the little port window when she opened Kay's door—perhaps it had entered her sleep and provoked the nightmare.

"Hush," she said, and Kay turned, startled, and sat up.

"I am sorry!" Her eyes a little wild in the dim light. "Did I wake him?"

"No, no, but you must try to be quieter."

"Yes," Kay said. She wiped a hand across her eyes.

The lack of argument pierced Thea's defences. She sat on the bunk and took Kay into her arms. "Dear heart, what were you dreaming?"

Kay did not burst into crying again, but only whispered, "You know."

"The children dying, I know, this pulls us back there. But listen, Kay, if you think only backwards, if you think so much about them, you cannot help Aren now. I think of them too, but it is too late for us to help them. They are with God now—we have to wipe that slate clean and make a different ending for Aren."

"But are you sorry?" Kay asked, her eyes boring up to search Thea's face.

"Oh, how can you ask me! Of course I am sorry, of course I am. But what about forgiveness, Kay? Do you think we can never be forgiven?"

Kay looked and looked at her face, as if she would never stop looking, and Thea had to gather her thoughts and self together to carry on. "I believe God knew our good intention, and how sorry we are that it all came to naught. I would give anything for it not to have happened, for all those children to be safe and warm and well now. But I must believe God has forgiven us—forgiven me, I mean, and Father. And I believe the way to make it right is to keep Aren safe."

Kay still stared, her eyes unable to wake completely from the dream. It always took her a little while to come back into herself. Thea pulled the blue blanket over them and rocked her sister gently until she calmed into sleep again.

∾

Although he was so sick, Aren was not downcast. His cheeks burned with red flags and he talked more than before, to Kay, but also to

Mr. Wright and Jacky Judge, and particularly to Seaton. He asked that his deck chair be put close to Seaton's lifeboat, and they kept up a running conversation, more intelligible on Aren's part than Seaton's. Kay did her work on deck even when the weather was cool, wrapped up almost as well as Aren was in his chair, and got her only exercise trotting up and down with his empty glasses (and helping him totter to the head as necessary).

Most of the time their talk flowed along under Kay's consciousness, but some things poked up from the streaming surface. "When I am-was fish in the old place, I would make a net by now," Aren said, and Seaton growled some answer from above. Kay did not ask, "Do you mean *if I was fishing?*" but left it alone.

One afternoon he made the sound of his father's canoe for Seaton, scraping a ruler along the side of the deck chair. "Then we know to come help bring in over the sand," he was saying when Kay began to pay attention. "It is the inside sound of our own canoe. Almost the sound . . ." He scraped again, adjusting it, trying to make just the right noise.

Another time he made a different sound, this time with his hands, which had grown so thin! He was not satisfied with the sound he achieved, and was growing angry with himself, when Seaton said, "Ay!" and tossed down two pieces of coconut shell. He must have a little treasure store up there, Kay thought.

The coconut pieces worked much better. "It must not be thum-thum-thum-thum," Aren told Seaton, "but must have-be surprise—thum-thum . . . *thum* thum-thum . . ."

"What is that sound for?" Kay asked.

"It is to call *echarivus*," Aren said. "Then with a white rock I go up and down, a string on it, in the water . . ."

She did not want to make it difficult for him, so she nodded as if she understood.

Then, from the boat above, Seaton's mahogany arm descended with a boiled egg on a string, bobbing slowly up and down, and that made Aren laugh. "Fishing *shark*, Miss," Seaton said. "First

they calls 'em with the rubbing sound, then lure 'em with something they can see from a ways away . . . That what that fish-word
means, boy?"

Aren said, like Kay with her Greek vocabulary: "*Echarivus*, bites
white stone."

∾

After long and useful discussion with the Brazilian doctor, they
had decided against dosing with syr. iodide iron or maltine, which
had been shown to have no real benefit, although cod-liver oil
could not hurt. The doctor had spoken seriously to Aren, explaining that while his physician for the voyage—Thea—must be
"determined and forceful," the ideal patient must be "intelligent,
earnest and obedient."

Thea was not certain Aren understood, but it did not matter; he
had those qualities innately. Her aim was to keep him perfectly
rested and fed, thoroughly invigorated by exposure to sun and
wind; then, when he had regained some strength, to give him as
much exercise as could be managed on board the ship.

But no matter how much milk the little cow produced, no matter
how many eggs Kay found in the chickens' nests, Aren's arms and
legs still grew thinner, and his face acquired the tight patience that
she remembered from Blade Lake, that she was not allowed ever to
forget, however much, or if, she ever was forgiven.

And then, before she was at all ready, the *Morning Light*
approached New York, where he would be taken out of her hands.

18

New York

At Presbyterian, they were taken on a tour through the TB ward. Kay kept very quiet behind Francis, not wanting to be left in the waiting room. Miss Burgess, the charge nurse, said they would admit Aren today, but it was possible that a stint in the Shively Sanitary Tenements, a facility designed for patients who could be cared for by family, would be more productive.

Miss Burgess told them she had a high calling for this work. She was a medical philosopher, with theories and authority. "I have occasionally had to reprove an intern who forgot that his hospital patient was more than an interesting study. They look on this class of patient as a curiosity, rather than as a human being!"

Thea had slowed, feeling Aren's steps flagging. Francis picked him up and carried him, and Kay took Aren's place beside Thea, sliding a hand softly into her sister's.

Nurse Burgess looked back and smiled, stiff lips not revealing her teeth. "I feel it is *my* responsibility to provide the atmosphere of refinement and culture my patients need to get well. I encourage nature studies—I am in the habit of bringing a flower to each bed patient, and I recommend that our nurses read good literature aloud to our patients. I have acquired decorative china and tray cloths so food can be attractively presented. It is the task of our nurses to see that the sanatorium experience be a civilizing influence. Sanatoriums should not resemble prisons! Each of our patients, I hope, returns home with a knowledge of the essentials of a true home life."

"If," Thea said, "they do not have that knowledge already."

Nurse Burgess smiled again, with pity this time, and shook her head. "All too few," she said. "All too few."

They had reached a large set of japanned double doors with a window in each one. Miss Burgess pushed the doors so they flew wide on loose hinges, and they were in a long, echoing ward, green-painted, open windows down one long wall. It smelled of strong disinfectant. Each bed was occupied by a skeleton in white clothes.

A young nurse came toward them, but Miss Burgess waved her off. "I know I do not have to explain to *you*, Mrs. Grant, how desperately essential cleanliness, of the person and of the home, is to disease prevention."

She struck out to the left and they followed her past twenty or thirty cots to a space with an empty bed, freshly made, with a thin blanket thrown across the foot. Very clean, very clinical, Kay thought.

"Here we are!" Miss Burgess raised a hand and an orderly came with a list. She dictated: "Bed 39, Grant, Aaron, eight years of age, male, Negroid."

Thea's head lifted. "What is this list for?"

Kay could hear how angry she was, her boundless anger about everything to do with this.

"Dr. Shively's great project is to begin tabulation of the statistics of the disease. It will be of great help in future delineaments of treatment."

Thea said, "He is Micronesian, if you care for precision."

Kay looked at the woman's spotless uniform and self-satisfied face. But perhaps, perhaps, this place could cure Aren, so they must endure it too.

Aren climbed down from Francis's arms onto the expanse of bed. He looked very small, standing there. Thea helped him into the bedclothes and sat stroking his arm, smiling with him in her way, and Kay and Francis leaned against the wall beside them, letting Miss Burgess's talk run over their heads like a sluice of bilge water, effusive but not important.

"Dr. Shively says our advanced tubercular patients need the same kind of attention lepers do, and for the same reason: our lepers are nursed and cared for, not *altogether* out of sympathy, but because they constitute a menace to the community."

Kay remembered Miss Ramsay, at the worst of the sickness, declaring in disgust before she took herself off, "I might as well have gone and worked amongst the lepers!"

∽

Then there was the tedious process of having Aren's disease classified. Eventually he was declared Moderately Advanced, which Thea translated in her head as Stage II, according to the terms Dr. Bryce had used in the West. She was trying to remember everything Dr. Bryce had ever told her, in the bad time. *Moderately Advanced.* Next would come *Advanced.* There was no further stage, only death.

She looked at the little head slumped against the propped-up pillow. Strands of black hair lay plastered to his head in a day-sweat of exertion and emotional strain. His eyes were closed, and blue stained the skin below the tangled lashes. His mouth, small and delicately outlined, seemed to her never to have smiled once since she'd met him.

She sat by the bed, one hand uselessly set on the sheet beside him, and wished she could make sense of anything.

∽

Aren stayed in the ward for three weeks. For four, and five. Thea spent every day there. Francis saw to the unloading of his cargo and began to seek another, in a half-hearted way. He acquired a boy called Jimmy Giles, fresh from New Zealand, to replace poor Arthur and keep Jacky Judge company in the rigging; but he could not have the whole crew eating their heads off for nothing, and would have to discharge some of them soon if they were to be in dock for much longer. He had been offered a contract for Belgium, if Thea thought she could manage without him—a short run, a month or a little more, and it would do if Thea could be comfortable alone in lodgings. Kay listened to their conversation, but she had no stake in the matter at all. Thea would stay with Aren, and she would stay with them.

It seemed to be a case of waiting for the inevitable, a feeling Kay remembered from the old days, which she put aside by taking Pilot for long walks along the Hudson or by going down to the galley to beg Jiacheng for a job to do. The empty saloon was not fit to be in by oneself these days, and after that first day she had not been allowed back to the tubercular ward. She was lonely.

She wrote to Mr. Brimner, sending him a translation from Lucian, of the inhabitants of the Island of the Blessed who wear clothes made of spiderweb "very fine and of a purple colour" because she thought New York was a bit like it:

> They have no bodies, nor flesh, nor can they be touched; but yet though they have the form and semblance only of men, they stand and move, and think and speak. It seemed to me when I saw them as if it were the bare soul, clothed only with a certain likeness of the body, that did these things ... For these people, though they are shadows, are yet shadows that stand upright, and not such as we see here cast upon the ground or upon a wall. In this country none grow old, but whatever a man's age may be when he comes hither, at that he remains.

Of course, it was not like Thea writing home to the aunts; with mail to Haʻano, nobody could say when he might receive her letter, or if he ever would.

One afternoon, just before Francis was to leave for Belgium, Kay accompanied him out to the East River to tour the Shively Sanitary Tenements, also called the East River Houses. The tenements were not a medical clinic, Nurse Burgess had explained, but housing designed with tuberculosis patients in mind, built the year before by Mrs. William Vanderbilt to a plan devised by Dr. Shively, who ran the TB clinic. There were still suites *genuinely* untenanted, Nurse Burgess had hastened to say. "The building is new, and the concept still experimental, so you would not be in a set of rooms where—well, where any former tenant had passed on."

"It can't be long until Thea clocks that prune-mouthed old biddy with a bedpan," Francis told Kay as they took themselves off in a cab to the East River—an area which Francis said was not generally thought wholesome. "We'll reserve judgment, I promised your sister," he said, and told the cabman to stop at the corner of East Seventy-Seventh and Cherokee Place.

Kay had thought *tenement* meant a crowded lodging house for the poor, but the place looked very respectable: a large, modern yellow-brick building, bandbox new and handsome. Each apartment had lacy copper-green metal balconies and large windows looking out onto the river. Kay thought it was pretty. And less frightening than the hospital.

"Handy for shipping," said Francis, pointing downriver past the bridge to the long strings of docked steamships and luggers. "Might get a berth there . . . Let's go up and see."

Tiled tunnels led them in from the street to a central courtyard with a little garden. Mrs. Prince, the manageress, met them in the lobby and took them up, asking them to "Notice, please, the wide corridors and generous stairwells—Dr. Shively believes this lessens the risk that healthy family members will succumb to the infection." She directed their attention to carved seats built into the stair landings, resting places for easily winded residents as they went up and down. It all smelled of fresh paint and fresh air, almost to the point of wind.

At the fourth floor, Mrs. Prince unlocked 4B and let Kay and Francis step inside. The pale-green walls of the little foyer matched the green balconies outside. They walked through four large rooms, opening into one another but arranged, at least in this corner apartment, so that each room had two or three windows—those on the interior side opening onto the central court, so that Kay could feel the breeze on her cheek. This was the most like a ship of any house she'd ever seen.

Mrs. Prince threw open the windows to the balcony on the river side and they heard the bustle of the street, only as a cheerful rumour this high up. There was a small kitchen in black and white; more black-and-white octagonal tile in the well-outfitted bathroom. Past the kitchen lay a little room with one diamond-shaped window—just the size for an elder sister. Kay thought that would be her room. She saw for a moment her old iron bedstead from Blade Lake half-filling the room. Then her inward eye shut and opened again, seeing Aren in this good place.

"Only thing is," Francis said, as they descended again to the street, "it won't be easy on Thea if he is discharged." Because that would mean the hospital had given up, had decided he could no longer be treated.

And would they be allowed to keep Pilot in the apartment? She would walk him herself, every day, three times a day—and Aren was supposed to have lots of outdoor exercise. One of the doctors advocated eight hours a day outside! Francis had suggested that such a regime might be easier to manage back in Yarmouth than here in the city, but Thea had not answered him at all.

They were walking down a street lined with trees. Kay bent to pick up a pale gold leaf opening out in a fan shape. "Look!" she said. "It is a ginkgo tree—like the one in Yuyuan Garden in Shanghai!" The tree there was three hundred years old. These trees looked spindly and young, but the beautiful shape of the leaf was there, halfway around the world. Kay did not know why a leaf should make her feel less miserable. She would send it to Aren.

Francis glanced at it but kept walking, preoccupied with thinking, assessing, making arrangements in his mind for cargo and contracts and what would have to be done. Kay walked on beside him, taller than she had been last year, so that it was no effort to keep up with him. She put an arm through his navy-blue wool sleeve anyhow.

At the corner there was a fruit and flower shop. Francis put a hand out to some white narcissus, slender, fragrant things—and then, abruptly, picked up the top one of a pyramid of coconuts, old, brown, hairy things, not at all like the young green ones at home. At Aren's home, she corrected herself.

"We'll take him one of these," Francis said.

∾

Thea had never sat beside a child at Blade Lake with such fierce concentration. That, she saw now, was her true fault. She had existed in different relation to those children: their caregiver, their guardian, but not their—family. She did not for a moment call herself Aren's mother; the word did not even spring to mind. But she was his family now.

Those children had had mothers of their own. Mothers who came to the school too late, to ask where were their children. It was very hard that she must live through this again, must see what she had done and what (being younger, unprepared, untrained, selfish) she had left undone. Again she told herself what the doctor had said in Corcovado: six months to cure, patience, do everything you are doing, this is all that can be done.

Nurse Burgess came down the ward and stopped.

"Mrs. Grant," she said, a genteel, tittering canary. "I'm afraid we are going to have to discharge this little fellow on Monday, according to Dr. Shively's advice."

Aren was sleeping. Thea stood up slowly.

Burgess continued, "We'll have to go over some indications, of course, and there will be papers. It's a terrible shame, poor little monkey!"

Thea turned on her, very angry. "Do not speak of him in that degrading way again."

"Oh! I meant no harm, I'm sure!" Pink squares flashed hot on the bunchy cheeks. "I'm sure, he is quite *civilized*!"

There was no point in saying more. Thea turned away and knelt beside Aren, putting her face down into the blanket over his chest, the good red blanket that they had bought in Corcovado. She would pray again, pray better. Perhaps that would help.

She bent her mind to the humblest prayer she could remember. "*We do not presume to come to this thy Table, O merciful Lord, trusting in our own righteousness, but in thy manifold and great mercies. We are not worthy so much as to gather up the crumbs under thy Table. But thou art the same Lord, whose property is always to have mercy*—"

Where she was pressed against the bedstead, Thea felt a small interior motion. A ribbed movement, a finger raking along damp tiles, a fish turning in the riverbed.

It did not take her an instant to understand—it was as if she had told herself already but had failed to read the note in her own hand. She looked back over the last several months and realized that she had not even thought, had not for a moment—

Oh no, no, she thought, pressing again more deeply into the bed, her cheek on Aren's arm. Do not do this—dear God, I beg you, I'm sorry, please do not take this child away so that I may have one of my own.

There was no punishment she did not deserve, but she could not bear that. She knew—she told herself again—that God in His great mercy did not operate by vengefully tallying, but she could not trust that now.

Aren's hand touched her hair. "Are you weeping?" he asked.

"Oh, I am only tired," she said. "Just a little."

"We will go from this old place," he said.

She nodded. His eyes were half-closed, but they had sense in them. He held the little yellow ginkgo leaf in his fingers, not quite dried out, that Kay had put in her letter.

"Kay says the airy place is good," he said.

After a minute she said, "Shall we go there, to the apartment?"

He answered, "Yes."

∾

In the afternoon-shadowed room with windows wide open to the street below, Aren lay resting on the low camp bed. Pilot yawned and leaned slowly against the shape under the blankets, exhausted from his walk.

"I am very brave," Aren said.

Kay nodded. "I know that you are." She sat against the foot-board, feet tucked up.

"It is a thing that I have . . ."

"A quality," she said.

"A quality that was given to me. But now I am aferrad."

"*Afraid.*" It was hard to stop correcting.

"Yes."

Yes. The high room was as quiet as birds flying above the mast, not speaking, no wind carrying their cries.

"I am afraid too," she said. Then she wished she had not, but Aren smiled at her, skin stretched over small bones.

"That is good company!"

He curled himself into the crescent of her knees as Pilot had curled into his, and they waited for Francis, or for Thea, or for the next thing to come along.

PART TWO

YARMOUTH, 1922

τοὺς ζῶντας εὖ δρᾶν• καταθανὼν δὲ πᾶς ἀνὴρ γῆ
καὶ σκιά• τὸ μηδὲν εἰς οὐδὲν ῥέπει•
Do good to people while they are alive.
When each man dies he is dust and shadows.
What is nothing changes nothing.

EURIPIDES, *FRAGMENTS*

I

Yarmouth

Some nights Kay dreamed she was still on the *Morning Light*—in the tilting corridor, mahogany doors shut tight in a long row, searching for Aren or Mr. Brimner. Standing in the shifting, swaying darkness, wondering which door to open. If she could see up the companionway to the small lamp burning to light the stairs, she could go back to sleep. But often she was all in darkness, uncertain which way was fore or aft, adrift below decks, trying door after door.

She dreamed it again, coming back from Olive Wetmore's wedding in Bar Harbor. In her thrumming bunk on the *Prince Arthur*, a wide-bellied steamer that pitched slightly, stiffly, on the late spring tide, she woke in the dark to the smell of old vomit on old metal. Not right.

Still night. She lay with eyes open, nothing to see but the dim glow of the porthole. Teak, spice, wet canvas: that's what she wanted. Nothing was right. The hard metal edge of her bunk had pressed her arm to sleep. It tingled into life again.

Francis had the next cabin—you couldn't call them cabins, just boltholes in steel. She heard no snoring. Perhaps he was lying awake too; sad to be a sailor home from the sea, ferried in a tub like this.

She lay for a long time trying to return to the dreaming world, which so often seemed more real than this world. Even when they were bad dreams, she often wanted to stay there, in the place she felt at home in, more than anywhere else. Where did that world go when she woke?

The next time she opened her eyes, it was lighter. Sitting up, she looked out the round, yellowish porthole, in case they'd entered the narrows already. Not yet. Grey seas, grey skies, grey paint cracked around the porthole's edge. Morning, anyhow.

The snack bar would be open. She brushed her teeth at the little steel sink with the nice red toothbrush she had got in Boston. Then she quickly dressed, tidied and locked her case, and went to look for a cup of tea.

She was standing mist-damp at the rail in the fish smell, in the gull scream, when they docked with a clanking clunk that shook the whole ship into shudders. The Halifax train was waiting, and most of the *Prince Arthur* passengers streamed onto it.

Shouting a farewell up to Cocker, the first mate, who had been bosun on the *Morning Light*, Francis took his suitcase and shouldered Kay's golf bag with his own. She had only her small dressing case otherwise, and could manage that herself. They bulled through the crowd, and found that the pony trap had not come.

Crossing the tracks, they trudged up the wharf to the cotton mill office, where Francis got onto the telephone. After shouting quietly into it for some time, he said the cart would be out directly; Thea had mistaken the day. He looked very tired, and Kay did not ask anything more, but set her case on a rickety chair by the window looking down onto the factory floor.

The noise was ferocious. Looms racketing back and forth, belts and levers shaking as they were pulled and shoved, girls in white smocks standing at the ready to grab for discard. Seven in the morning and all those girls looked worn out, more tired than Francis. Boys too, of course, and men—inspecting spindles, checking the warp. Roland Spinney from her high school class was assistant floor manager now; there he went, long and dark, running down the aisle beneath the flying strands of thread. Clouds of feathery dust choked in Kay's throat; she did not know how Francis had stood it, when he was managing the mill last year. She went to join him at the open back door where he stood in foggy sun, talking to Abel Muise, the mill foreman, who had also sailed on the *Morning Light*. Back in their real life.

Then the trap came and they climbed up and Jerry Melanson clicked to old Blackie, who strained his poor thin spine and jigged along, not home to Elm Street, but out toward Lake Milo. The grass verges were green and springing, dirt bright and damp with the night's rain. A pleasant place in springtime, everybody always said.

Finding no one she could bear to talk to in the house, Kay went to the woods. Spring-dressed branches parted to let her through with the sharp-rotted nose of wood that never dries, fresh shoots, clear brown water, crushed moss—dead leaves revealed from snow, waiting to fall into leafmeal in the usual pattern of seasons.

Kay walked along the worn paths wanting the not-difference, the seasonless Pacific cycle of never-ending growth, dry sand, wood that crumbles in hot salt air, the transparency of water. Eleuthera, Tonga, Fiji—even Singapore or Manila, though she'd wilted in that unchanging weight of heat.

Funny to see Cocker on the *Prince Arthur*, grey-headed but sturdy, doing well for himself. What ship was Liu Jiacheng on now, reading his ancient book, smoke from his thin pipe rising thinner? He could not have died, he was catgut, indestructible. Or Seaton— but Seaton must be dead by now, he had teetered on the brink even then. From her present great age, twenty-two, she wondered if he might have been only forty or so, back then.

She must answer Mr. Brimner's last letter, four months old already when it arrived in April. She had it in her coat pocket, meaning to answer it from Bar Harbor. His two years of mission had stretched into ten, his friend Prior's manuscript was still not sent to the publisher—she imagined drafts accumulating, curling poems pinned to the wood round the door of his bure to weather until he might be satisfied that he had read the true intent of his dead friend; a careful file of black-bordered letters from Prior's mother, agreeing or disagreeing with an editorial note, open on the desk; and Mr. Brimner busy at his ink pot, teasing out the golden thread from all those drafts.

Or else he had lost impetus, lost his compass bearing. But he was not as feeble-spirited as she was. And he had real work to do, which she lacked. Some peace could be found in a long walk alone round the golf course, moving there with an easy rhythm she could never find on a dance floor. No satisfaction at all in company, in the society of one's peers.

She had no peers here, if peers meant people who knew the things she knew. Only Aren knew those things. And things she did not know, too. Kay put out her hand to touch a young birch's paper-flimsy bark, the thickness of a white petal, already beginning to peel. She peeled more, slowly, slowly, to make a page to write to Mr. Brimner on. Destroying it as if it was her stupid discontent. She wished she could talk to Aren. She could go and visit him in Halifax, she supposed. If he would talk to her.

Coming back along the creek to the old orchard, still frilled and scented with late blossom, she heard a quiet call: "*Too-wheee!*"

There was Roddy, up in the king apple tree, hidden except for his boots. The oldest tree: their refuge and their hiding place, whenever she and Aren were sent to stay at Lake Milo. She knew the branches like a spiral staircase at the trunk, and the wind-ruffled swaying of the crow's-nest branches at the top. In the last slow weeks of summer you could read up there all day, reaching for an apple when you were hungry.

Roddy's narrow elf-face moved through the new leaves, behind a tattered haze of cloud-pink petals. "There you are!" he called.

"Here I am," Kay answered, cheerful as she could be. "We thought you'd gone with Thea."

"I ran away when she said we must go visiting. I did not want to go when you were coming home." Roddy stopped on a branch to cough—he needed his belladonna drops. "Did Cousin Olive get married off?" he asked, wheezing.

"She did. She is Mrs. Braydon Dawlish now."

"She was pretty old, to be married."

Kay remembered Olive saying that about Thea marrying Francis: *quite an* old spinster *to be new-married, and how sad that she wasted her youth raising Kay.* "Not so very old, really." Not that she had any desire to defend Olive. "Your mama did not marry till she was twenty-nine, and Olive was only thirty-two."

"She was lucky anyone wanted to marry her."

Kay laughed, but could not disagree. "He is a little older, I think, but Dawlish seems to like her pretty well. Francis says she deserves some happiness after dealing with her mother for so long."

"Did you win the hotel tournament?"

"I did. A nice silver cup. They said it's worth fifty American dollars. I'd rather have the cash, but nobody offered to buy it."

"If they had given you the money, though, you could not be an amateur champion," he said. "You are good enough to be."

She laughed. "I'm not. Alexa Stirling was there, she won the ladies' amateur cup last year, you know. She said if I went touring, we should chum around. But it was just for fun, or for advertising, because Dawlish owns the golf course."

"Olive will have to play with her, then. She will be terrible at it, I think." He was busy sliding down the tree. One skinny calf came into view, smeared green as an apple from new bark, apple-sap-green. Lena Hubbard would be angry with him, but it was Thea who had knit the stocking, after all.

On the ground, he dusted bark off his rump and carefully folded his knife before stowing it away in a pocket.

"You'd better watch that, you'll cut yourself," she said.

"Sharp enough to cut a hair on water, sharp as sharp," he boasted. "I sharpened it on Jerry Melanson's whetstone, he showed me how."

"It would be a good mariner's knife, to match your marlinspike."

He took her arm—at nine, already as tall as she was—and they walked down the aisle of trees, their feet scuffing the gentle petal dust.

∾

Thea saw them coming over the meadow. The grass had been mown down by sheep over the last month, but now the lambs had been moved to pasture, it was growing up again. She must tell Jerry Melanson to send his nephew Hubert out there again with the scythe.

There came Kay and Roddy, good, because Aunty Bob was driving out from town for dinner, bringing the Krito-sophian ladies to discuss the next lecture series. The ladies were attempting to secure Aimee Semple McPherson, so very interesting, with her mission life and wide experience. Thea found the idea irritating, but she was tired, after a long week alone with Aunt Lydia. Now Olive was married and never coming back, and this care would be her duty for some time to come, years perhaps. And the weather was oppressive, too warm for May.

Francis had gone down to the stables. Back again, more or less in one piece. She could taste the silky mother-of-pearl skin inside his mouth, the tender inwardness that she loved—even at this advanced age, forty next week. She could let go his hand in the morning knowing she would lie with him again at night. Why are we all so sad? We are lucky, she told herself again.

∾

Kay waved to Thea, who was back from visiting, leaning on the veranda railing in her best silk chiffon. Thea shaded her eyes to see them, and Kay waved again. Roddy put on a turn of speed to go to his mother, but Kay, hearing Francis calling from the stable, went to see what he wanted.

He beckoned.

"What is it?" she asked.

He turned back to the shadowy interior and she followed, from long habit pausing to tap the horseshoe nailed to the doorway. But it did not help.

"Pilot," Francis said. He was crouched on the planks beside her old dog, without regard for the knees of his good grey suit. "He's not doing well."

Kay went into the twilight. Her good dog Pilot thrust his nose up into her hand, from where he lay on an old horse blanket Francis must have set out for him. His long tail trembled and then gently thumped the floor in greeting. Under his fur she felt the lumpy growths she'd come to expect. Two, three of them—perhaps they were larger. He had been ailing for some time, this was no surprise. But Francis took her hand and held it, and with his other hand drew back the long fur under Pilot's jaw. A greater lump there, and it had opened, oozing pinkish fluid. He had been sore and stiff before she left, but this was very bad.

"It's not the lumps, so much," Francis said. "But this abscess, the open tumour—he's in pain now, Kay. It's time to give him release."

She saw that it must be so. Pilot's eyes looked into hers until the effort of holding his neck was too much and he let his head slump, flump, on the blanket. That was how it was with dogs, they were frailer than humans and aged much more quickly, and the good thing was that one could put them out of their misery. It was all quite rational.

"All right," she said. Would Francis wish her to do it herself? He had taught her to shoot the little rifle. She put her hand under her eye to stop it trembling there. It was very hard for him to fire a rifle now, after the war, so she should do it.

"He's very old for such a big dog," Francis said, looking at her a little anxiously. It made him look like Roddy. "We'll give him a good dinner, and keep him warm, and it will be the best thing."

She nodded, and got up. "I'll find something in the kitchen, then." Best get on with it.

He pulled a scrap of sacking over from the hay bin and sat beside Pilot, one hand buried in the soft mane. His trousers would be ruined.

At the door, she turned back. "Should I tell Roddy?"

"He asked me to have a look at the poor old boy. Ask Thea, as you go by. She'll know."

Whether it would be better for him to know beforehand or afterwards. With people one did not have that choice, to know or not to know. But then parents were always discussing whether or not to tell their children this or that, whether it was good for them to know the truth or whether they should be spared.

At the porch table, Thea had rested her head on one hand bent across her eyes—reading, or asleep? Roddy must have been sent to change his mucky breeches. Thea lifted her head as Kay climbed the stairs and, seeing her, said, "Oh, Kay, will you help Lena bring in lunch? I must go turn Aunt Lydia."

"Let me do that." The cold misery of rolling Aunt Lydia's oblivious sausage-body in the sheets was less disheartening than Lena's conscious dislike.

Lena Hubbard had left the sea as well, and worked for Thea now, her hind end still a mute reproach to Kay. Nothing was known of Hubbard's whereabouts; Lena had come back to Yarmouth, destitute, a week before Olive left for her long-promised six month's tour of Europe, just as Thea and Francis were about to take on Aunt Lydia's invalid care in Olive's absence. Kay had begged them not to hire Lena, but of course that was no use.

Now Thea caught Kay's sleeve gently. "What would you like me to do? Leave her to rely on the parish?" She meant Lena, not Aunt Lydia. Abandoning Aunt Lydia was not even imaginable.

"No," Kay had to say, and again, "No!"

Thea looked up, her eyes still in her hand's shadow, considering her as Father used to. "You still must work to correct your temper, and a reminder in the house can do no harm."

The cruel justice of this left Kay with nothing to say—indeed, let the breath out of her chest so that she had to walk to the end of the porch to find more air to fill it. But she could not be angry with Thea.

She was not allowed to be angry anywhere, with anyone, was the truth of it, and that alone made her want to screech like a harbour gull. She made her fingers into talons and flexed them, and went in through the glass doors at the end of the veranda to turn Aunt Lydia.

The shade, and the heat, the smell, the quietness, all magnified the clunk of the clock on the mantel in the dark-panelled room that had once been the dining room. The great body lying there, not quite a husk. Olive had been right to worry, long ago, that Kay might send her mother apoplectic. But it was not Kay that felled Aunt Lydia, it was the war, and Forrest lost in France. Nobody blamed poor Olive for leaving; she had managed all that time alone, six years of ministering to an unresponding lump. When she came back, Thea had said, they would make sure she had daily help; with any luck, Lena could be persuaded to stay with her. But now Olive was not coming back.

With practised moves, Kay stripped the top sheet off and pulled a clean sheet over Aunt Lydia's bulk, tucking half of it in on the wall side; rolled the body forward onto the clean half and slid the soiled half out with a jerk. Not as efficiently as Thea did it, but her clumsiness caused no stirring from Aunt Lydia. Tuck, tuck, and then she allowed the bulk to roll back, and roll a quarter turn again to give a fresh side to the bed. Old sores that Thea had found when they first came were healed now. But indeed, it must have been very hard for Olive all alone.

Kay pulled the nightgown into place down the thin old bluish legs, set the bolsters to brace the body and tucked the sheets in carefully to keep it suspended on its side—on *her* side.

It was not necessary to think of this body as a woman; Kay felt sure that whatever had made Aunt Lydia herself had left this mortal shell long before. She had no wish to remember her aunt in true vivid life, grown more cranky and difficult with age. Even Francis had disliked her, and she was his aunt too, by marriage. But he had agreed that they must relieve Olive, and had not protested at moving out to Lake Milo for six months or however long the

European tour would take. He did have some relief: from time to time he stayed at the house in Yarmouth, attending to business that could not be delayed. His affairs were mysterious to Kay—holdings in various ships, interests in others; not always successful, she supposed, from the Elm Street house, which was smaller and less opulently furnished than Marion Hilton's father's place. Shipping was chancy business.

To relieve the gloom and silence, Kay opened the curtains to the afternoon light, although Lena would certainly close them again, left the French door to the veranda ajar and lifted the heavy sash of the west window halfway. Light brought a pale pearl-glow to Aunt Lydia's arm, extending limply from the linen sleeve. Outside in the sunlight Thea looked pale too. Was she ill?

Kay curbed her sudden fear—it was Pilot who was ill. She went to forage in the kitchen, where she found cold beef and warmed a dish. Out in the stable, the dog was sleeping. She knelt on the straw beside him and stroked his great head without waking him.

Francis, still sitting vigil, said he would stay with him. "We'll wait till morning, in case there's any change," he said. He'd made himself a cot of horse blankets, and she could tell Thea he would not come in for dinner. "Pilot is saving me from those damned Cryptosporidians," he said. "Faithful to the last."

There being nothing she could do, Kay went up and sat on the windowsill to watch Thea dress for dinner, going into costume as a matron of Yarmouth. She had been so pure, so much better, so far removed from ordinary women—now here she was, Secretary of the Krito-sophians, in a tambour lace dress over dove-grey satin, putting cold cream on her face that Kay had watched her buy in Paris for twenty-five dollars. Twenty-five dollars, for half a teacupful! Where was her noble charity now?

The burden of scorn was heavy to bear, and Kay knew it was unfair. It had been a relief to run off to Bar Harbor with Francis, and watch Olive with her captive Mr. Dawlish. Olive had offered her a room at the hotel for an extended visit. "If you're getting ready to take life seriously," she said, which made Kay laugh a little, interiorly.

What was she to take seriously? She had no skill worth flogging, beyond hitting a golf ball; there was no one to marry. For a while it had looked as if she might be assumed into an engagement with another Wetmore cousin, Terence, but that had come to nothing. Because there was nothing in it. It was all right for Terence—back from France with new determination, he had married (to the dismay of his mother) Doris Sweeney, who was a telephone operator, and gone to live in Hebron with Doris's family. It was a great relief to Kay not to have people throwing them together anymore, and Doris was quite nice and kind.

Marion Hilton drove out to dinner with the Krito-sophian ladies, two of whom were her aunts, another her future mother-in-law. Safely engaged to Murray Judge (after a short, exciting romance with an unsuitable American), she was in line for membership. Worthy, round-faced, worried, nice—though she could not stop herself from occasional piercing honesty. She'd have to curb that, to fit into the Krito-sophian circle.

Drinking sweet sherry in the drawing room before dinner, they sat a little removed from the older women. Marion stared at Kay with the ordinary rudeness of a childhood friend. "I like your Boston frock!"

Kay smoothed her dress. Francis had taken her to Filene's, for their usual annual visit. Fawn linen, very nice.

"But what happened to your eye? What have you done to it?"

Her hand went up to the bruise. "Hit myself, just before the wedding. I was adjusting—some strap, you know, and my hand slipped, and I gave myself a knuckle punch. My eye swelled up horribly."

"No, it's black—above your eye—"

"Oh, that—it's just a mole."

"Oh my, are you worried about it?" Marion's own eyes, sky blue, could barely focus close up; that only added to her dreamy look. She was such a pretty girl.

"It's nothing. It does keep growing, though." Kay stood. "Let me refill your glass."

Soon she would be so ugly she'd be unable to go out in public at all. At the drinks cart, Kay pulled her dress, which had rucked up behind, over her lumpy waist and straight-down hips again. There was something stark and comforting about being ugly in this world, about not conforming to the way people want you to look.

Or she could shake herself out of this ill temper and spare a thought for Thea, who did not point out one's blemishes and was kindness itself. Kay would take her a glass of sherry.

But it was time to troop into the new dining room, which had been the sitting room before Aunt Lydia could not go upstairs. Thea gestured around the table and seated the Krito-sophians in an order that would make them agree with their neighbours, more or less, and only talk each other's ears off. Very skilfully done; Kay saluted her with her eyebrows in South Pacific fashion.

Lena Hubbard went in and out with the soup tureen and the biscuits, Jerry Melanson carried the roast, and the customary heavy meal lifted on the evening tide and got under way.

Sharp-tongued Miss Yarrow congratulated Kay on her cultural achievements. "I understand that you could give us all some pointers in the use of the Latin tongue!" Since Miss Yarrow was the new Latin teacher at the Yarmouth high school, that was very condescending.

"I am better at Greek," Kay heard her own mouth say, and then she felt heat rising in her cheeks and added, "It is not boasting, but only that I was lucky enough to have had a good teacher."

Miss Yarrow *hmmph*ed, perhaps taking that as an insult. Conscious that she herself was scowling, Kay turned to Mrs. Judge and asked how her daughter was finding normal school in Truro. The conversation veered onto various offspring and supposed friends of Kay; all the Krito-sophians had much to say about Higher Education and Life Paths.

Safe for a while, Kay cut her portion of meat into neat pieces and stared down at her plate. Roddy was too far away to talk to, and she disliked everyone else around the table. Her stomach was sullen, aware of Pilot out in the stable, and what must be done, but she put a forkful into her mouth anyway.

At last they retired to the front parlour and sat in little groups, and Thea asked Kay to play. She went obediently to the piano. Roddy came to turn the pages for her, so they were at least removed from the general talk. He leaned against her on the piano bench, knowing about Pilot and needing comfort. She played a selection of moderately difficult pieces, not nearly so well as Thea would have done, and endured the ignorant praise of her technique.

The conversation became general, and Miss Yarrow, sitting on Kay's right, had a question about the rites of the South Sea Islanders.

"I am no authority. I do not know anything at all about the South Sea Islanders," Kay said. "I have seen the sea, that is all a person like me can say." She went to the mantel, tidying the china figures there to give herself something to do.

"Well! I had hoped your journeying would be more salutary. They say that travel ought to broaden the mind, you know." Miss Yarrow's little eyes drilled test holes into Kay's blank face, seeking some ore or other.

Kay hated her. And everyone.

Thea said, "Don't listen to Kay, Miss Yarrow. She learned a great deal on all our travels and never stopped studying for a moment. Her piano, and literature, and Latin, and an enormous amount of Greek—enough for a boy!"

To shield Kay, though any defence would be wasted on Miss Yarrow, Thea added seriously, "Here is what *I* know of the Islanders, Miss Yarrow: that they are not unlike the Indian people my father worked with in the West. They, like us, are a portion of that fallen race for whom Christ died, they have souls to be saved or lost."

Miss Yarrow drew back her head on her thin neck.

But Thea continued, gravely. "They are accessible to the Grace of God. They have intellects of a superior kind, which receive instruction readily. The people in all those islands are remarkably skilful in all kinds of handiwork, and they are as capable of improvement in their social condition as any other race—or more so, due to the benefits of their geography."

All that sounded to Kay very much like Father holding forth to Dr. Bryce when the doctor had come to inspect the school. Boasting of the cleverness of his charges as if they were pets, except of course that he judged them to have souls, which he believed dogs did not.

As the word *dogs* appeared in Kay's mind, a bitter flame ignited in her stomach. But she could do nothing about that.

She could do nothing about anything! She was a mediocre pianist, she knew very little Latin—and anyway, the world had no purpose for that except to turn one into a wizened-up Miss Yarrow—and she had entirely failed to learn Greek, even with the best of teachers.

Miss Yarrow pressed on, getting Thea to her real question. "And what of that *young fellow* you brought home? Where has he gone off to?"

Before the question was finished, Thea had already picked up the big silver tray and was taking quick steps to the door. "Lena! Oh, there you are— Take this, will you, and where—will you send Roddy to me?"

He had slipped out the window at the end of Kay's playing. She thought he had gone down to find his father, in the barn with Pilot.

Relieved of the tray, Thea turned back and crossed the drawing room to the open French doors. "Rod? Roddy?"

She stepped out onto the veranda, looking in her lace dress like a picture from a magazine, a lovely mother searching for her child. She worked too hard and never rested, but she was still a delight to look at, long and graceful in her body. Life was very unfair, that sisters could be so unalike.

"Aren left us," Kay told Miss Yarrow. Since Thea was not going to answer. "Not finding the people of Yarmouth to his liking, he went to Halifax and found work there."

"That's gratitude for you," said Miss Yarrow.

In late evening, as if they were on the deck of the *Morning Light* again, Kay and Thea sat on the veranda in their nightdresses looking at the moon over the orchard. Kay had been crying, but had stopped now.

"Why can we let Pilot die, but not Aunt Lydia?" she asked.

Thea gave the question room, but at last said, "People believe that pain, the act of suffering, brings human beings closer to God. We cannot know what value her suffering may have."

What value might Pilot's suffering have? Kay wondered.

Thea said, "God disposes. It would be a sin for any human being to presume to know when someone should die."

"I think God has forgotten to take Aunt Lydia."

Thea rocked to and fro slowly, gently, making no noise. It was mostly her work that kept the old lady alive, feeding and turning and tending to her, and Kay ought not to carp about that long tenderness. If she could keep tending Pilot, she would.

"We are to do it in the morning," she said.

"I know. I will take Roddy in to see Dr. McKee, to spare him watching, as he would no doubt feel he must. There never was such a boy for feeling responsible. He is to be given a trial of asthma cigarettes, and perhaps that scientific excitement will take his mind from it."

Kay almost laughed to think of Roddy puffing away behind the barn, as if they were pilfered cigars. But the barn made her think of target practice there with the rifle, and she set her thoughts away from that.

"It is a pretty moon," she said out loud.

"It is," said Thea.

They had learned silence during the war, and it was still useful.

2

Pilot

Francis had taught her to shoot before he went away to France. He said Thea was too gentle, and Roddy was too young, but now that all the men were going overseas, someone ought to know how to handle a gun. Kay felt a dark mantle of duty fall on her then: if the Germans came over the sea and landed their U-boats at Meteghan and made their sneaking way overland, it was she who would fend them off with the hunting rifle.

At six in the morning, she could not wait any longer, nor excuse herself from the task. She got up and dressed quietly, and washed her face.

She took the rifle down from the summer kitchen doorway, breaking it open and checking to see that it was clean. It was, but she used her handkerchief to worry at a smudge of oil. The cartridges were on the shelf over the icebox. No need to keep them handy any longer, but they had never gone back to their original home in the barn.

Francis was in the barn already. The plate of beef on the boards, uneaten. He had slept there, she saw, sitting propped against the stall wall with his legs crossed in front of him and one hand on Pilot's flank.

She should have spelled him off, not for his sake but for her own.

"Those guns were used at Ypres," Francis said, seeing the rifle when she set it carefully on the hayrack. "Ross rifles. By Vimy we had the Lee–Enfield."

That was the most he'd ever said to her about the war. She knelt and buried her hands in Pilot's warm fur.

"The bolts jammed. A boot heel might help, might not."

Kay nodded.

His voice was calm. He had been awake all night, though. "Everything did jam. The Lee–Enfield, even. But some men called the Ross sheer murder. I had forgotten that."

She did not dare to answer, not wanting to make him think more, or not think, or have to react in any way. She had no courage at all where Francis was concerned. But she could be brave enough to do this, in case he could not.

She bent to kiss Pilot and looked into his eyes, and touched his dear head, carefully avoiding his sores. He tried to lick her hand, but his tongue was dry and the movement seemed to hurt him.

"I'll do it," Francis began.

But she said, "No, I can."

She stood and lifted the rifle and checked it again, with her back to her dear dog. "You hold his leg," she said, and then she turned and sighted and shot him once in the back of the head. He moved a little as if he was not dead, so that she lifted the gun again, but the movement stilled. Then he was more still. That was all.

Even as fast as she walked the four miles, she missed the noon DAR train. So she walked along to the South Western station to wait for the two o'clock, which would land her in Halifax after nine.

Nobody she knew was on the train; that was lucky. The engine staggered to a start and pulled out of Yarmouth, slowly at first, then gathering, gathering, like the lump in her chest was gathering. She sat back in the red leather seat, pressing against the slight give of the wicker seatback, and set herself to be still and show nothing.

Three Acadian men sat by themselves at the end of the carriage, playing a silent card game on the table between their seats. Kay had a little French, acquired from books and tested at hotels in Calais and Tahiti, but these men had their own way of speaking, with flattened accents and words from English and other words she'd never learned in France, and she could not keep up. When Acadian carpenters or woodworkers came to the house, she tried sometimes, but they were a separate country. Only the girls who did the wash would speak to her, but their tongues went too fast, as if telling secrets—and Kay was not good at talking to people anyhow, even when they wanted to talk to her.

Thinking of other lands and peoples, with Pilot weighing on her memory and not knowing in what state she might find Aren, Kay sagged into the windowsill and slept. She woke fitfully from station to station, and finally, fully, as the train steamed into Halifax. She had slept on her hat. It was squashed, but she could steam it.

The station was not a bad place to be let off, even in late evening. She was hungry, though. At the terminal gates, she turned and walked down Barrington Street, hoping to find Aren at the victualling yard. He was not there. The man she asked shook his head and would not say more; perhaps he was a war veteran, for he looked distressed when she asked again. Instead, she left the yard and stopped at a milk bar for a bowl of soup. She had the number of the house, Francis had dug it up. Gottingen Street. She would just walk over and find Aren there.

His name was written on a snip of paper slid into a brass holder in the front porch. One of eighteen slots in that tall house. Eighteen, to match his age. Too young to live by himself in this strange place. There was a button to press. She put her finger on it, not hoping for much, but a grating bell sounded, and after a moment she heard feet on stairs, and then the inner door was opening.

When she saw him, her brother, tears started to her eyes. She pushed them back with her fingers. "I'm not crying for you," she said. "We had to shoot Pilot. I had to do it myself. It was only fair, you can't ask Francis to do that anymore."

Aren's eyes filled too, but he let his tears spill out, and then she could too, the two of them crying in the vestibule as if the world was all over at last.

He put his head down into his hands and Kay reached her arms around him, his folded-up elbows tucking into her embrace, and laid her cheek on his warm head. She was still taller than him, at least. She hadn't meant to say it fast like that and shock him, but he always made her tell what was in her mind, whatever it might be. That wish to tell—she did not have that with other people. Because he would listen rightly.

They were half in, half out of the little porch. She had already cried too much and had not much water left in her, so she pressed gently to make him back up, and he shook his head and did. The inner door, on a strong spring, shut behind her foot.

Inside, the narrow hall was shadowy, but Aren led her to the stairs, keeping her hand in his. Three flights up, before he pulled at a door and they went into his new home.

"He was ill, he was in terrible pain so that he could not move—cancer had made great sores on his jaw, and swellings—it all came up quite suddenly, he did not seem really ill before we left for Boston, but we came back to find him so."

There was no more to explain, nothing that could have been done. "Francis says he was old for a big dog . . ."

Her tweed coat hampered her. She shucked out of it, and looked around for a place to put it. There was nowhere in this tiny space, this half room. A partition made of crumbling boards had been added down the middle of an ordinary small bedchamber, leaving half a window and six or seven feet of width. Maybe nine feet in length.

Aren wiped his eyes with one sleeve. He took her coat and found a cloth to brush off the one chair. "Here," he said. "Sit down, stay for a moment."

She had not thought beyond this, beyond telling him and finding some comfort. Where was she to stay tonight? The Barrington
Hotel, down at the corner, perhaps. And never tell Thea. Or if she
ran, she could catch the ten thirty DAR goods train, and be back
for breakfast.

The room was cold. She could not ask for her coat back—Aren
had hung it on the only clothes hook he had, taking his own jacket
off it first and tossing it in the corner.

He was wearing a grey shirt without a collar, and dungarees. His
boots were neatly placed by the door. This was a sailor's berth,
shipshape. Grey blanket on the cot, tucked in with hospital corners,
his sea-chest at the foot, and on it some books. She was amused and
a little comforted to see that he had brought with him his old picture book, *Nursery Lessons, In Words of One Syllable*, with the unsail-
able fishing boat and the good dog Dash and the aunt who gave the
boy his horse. She touched it, saying quietly, "*See here is a fine nag.*"

The floor was stained, but clean. On the green-washed walls he
had pinned a few postcards: the *Morning Light*, the *Belmont*, Captain
Hilton's ship. A photograph of Roddy and Thea. Herself, scowling
in a toga at the high school *tableau vivant*, and there again, shrieking, in the photograph Francis had taken of her when Aren slid the
piglet down into the barrel bath.

She touched the smooth little moon scar on her arm, from
the piglet's sharp hoof. "Are you better here? Happier than in
Yarmouth?"

He lifted his brows, that quick assent. "Good enough, there is
nothing wrong with me."

He was the same person, always merciful to her. To them all.

"I came without telling Thea, or I'd have never got away—but
she'd have sent her love, and a parcel, if she'd known."

"I am all right for cakes," he said. "They feed us well."

Kay hated that he must put a good face on it. Most likely, they
were quite cruel to apprentices at the shipyards. All hard discipline
and men shouting. But a person has to live somehow, of course. Aren

could have chosen school, she told herself; this was his own choice. Only it was not. Staying at school in Yarmouth was impossible. It had been too difficult for her, and she was white and English; he would always be foreign and coloured, no matter how staunchly Thea championed him. Where else could a person go to make a life?

"What have you done with him?"

"Francis got Jerry Melanson to bury him, back in the orchard."

"You did not want to be there for the funeral?"

He was laughing at her now. She caught herself frowning, and let it go. "I would not have held a *funeral*. Only one sacred song and a wreath."

"Well, a grave marker, though." He was serious now.

She nodded, having drawn one on the train. She did not want to show him in case he laughed again. Then she pulled out her note-book, for of course he wouldn't laugh.

He did not. Staring down at the careful lettering she had drawn, he lifted his eyebrows again and again in strong agreement.

Fear not, I will Pilot thee.

She'd drawn a straight marker, no cross, Pilot in her view not being subject to God, but being God's straight emissary. Not requiring salvation, being without sin.

"I wish you would come home, Aren."

He stood up and went to the tiny cupboard. "I am home."

"To your real home, I mean," she said.

At the cupboard, his back to her, he asked in his quiet way, "Where is my real home?"

Then she heard what she had said. How stupid she was. Not Yarmouth, he meant. Where else could be their home now?

"Pulo Anna?"

He laughed at her, a furious burst of bitterness.

She wished she'd never said those words. He was past reaching anyhow. She had wasted her time coming here, and he would never

come back, nor want to. This half room, this ugly life was what he
was choosing. No more business of hers.

He laughed again, amused this time, watching her look around
the room. From a stack in the cupboard he took a celluloid collar and
began to attach it to his shirt. He was not meeting her eyes. But that
was all right, he never did by choice, though he usually would allow
their gaze to rest together. Maybe he was too sad, because of Pilot.

"You caught me as I was going out," he said.

"Out where?"

It was already ten in the evening. No restaurant or place to buy
food would be open now, on a Thursday night.

"To drink."

But—oh, he must mean to a secret place, a silent pig or a speak-
easy, they called them. Not legal, but of course everyone knew where
they were. Mrs. Curtis Surette ran one in Yarmouth. She had not been
there herself, but Marion Hilton had gone to one of Mrs. Surette's
special nights with Murray Judge. Cocktails in china teacups.

This would not be one of those places. Anyway, Aren was too
young for drinking. But she did not know what his life was like now,
or what it had been like for the last two years. He was a good deal
older now than Jack and Arthur had been when they came aboard
so drunk one night that Mr. Best whipped them at the mast next
day to teach them manners.

"How do you know where to go?"

He laughed, a short bark. "Follow any sailor!"

"Is that what it is like, being a workingman in Halifax?"

"They've no choice—a sailor isn't going to stay in dry dock for
long."

Marion Hilton had gone to one, after all. "What happens if the
police raid?"

"You get arrested—give a false name, and they let you go in the
morning."

A night in pokey would be a thing to experience. That would
top Marion Hilton.

He picked up his jacket from the floor and beat at it, not to much purpose. "I'm off," he said. "Come if you like. I have a friend to meet. You can meet her too."

Kay looked around the half room and put on her squashed hat.

The streets were wet, shining black and gold in the light from a few bright windows. The electric street lights did not cast much glow this foggy night, but served as direction pointers. They walked more or less together, Kay straggling behind sometimes when she thought perhaps she should not go after all. Then her courage, or her stubbornness, would come inching back, and she'd run to catch him up.

After a considerable damp tramp, Aren turned in at a narrow corridor between buildings and down some metal stairs into the first establishment, where a large man took his money and opened a wine-dark metal door.

It was darker inside than out. Aren stood poised a moment, holding Kay with a touch on her arm, and then started forward through crowded tables.

She followed close, not wanting to be alone in that strange place. All the people there were darkly clothed and grimy, some of them clearly black-gang men from steamers, marked by oiled-in coal dust that would never wash off. The women, not very many of them, hung over the tables, breasts dangling under not enough fabric. They were not pretty, exactly, but their lack of care had a crazy attraction; Kay felt it herself. A sour disorder in the dress, that wantonness. They laughed and talked too loud, to be heard over the din.

After speaking to one woman, Aren turned back and pushed Kay toward the door again.

"Not here," he shouted into her ear above the din. "Cherry says to try Isadore's."

Each place after that one was worse. The raucous noise everywhere was surprising. Kay was not shocked, and certainly heard nothing she hadn't heard already from a thousand sailors, but she had thought speakeasies would be hushed places, to avoid detection. These closed-in rooms, each with a smoke veil hovering three feet down from the low ceiling, were tighter and hotter than she'd expected. She hadn't thought about that part, the smell of other people, none of them in very good health. Worse than below decks, worse than any crew mess she'd looked in on. But she'd been lucky, always to sail on respectable vessels. So had Aren.

And the drink, not a good smell either. Bootleg rum, or something water-coloured and tasteless that (when Aren passed her a tot to try) hit the back of the tongue and then the throat with a scrape like paint thinner. Everyone was pretty much half-poisoned, it seemed to her. The older men drank warm yellow beer in thick-bottomed glasses. Kay felt her insides curdle at the sight of it, horrible stuff.

In each place, different but the same, Aren led the way through the press of people and stopped at one table or another to ask after the girl, Merissa. One woman had seen her, she thought. "Out Bedford way, she was."

Aren shook his head and said that must have been her sister, whose fellow lived in Africville.

The woman nodded and shook her head, first nodding and then shaking, very drunk. She demanded abruptly, "Where you from?"

"I am from the South Seas," Aren said. "From an island called Pulo Anna."

"Yeah, I seed you was different from these other fellas . . ."

Aren shook his head, giving it up, and they went out.

In the fourth place, Jerry Joe's, a player piano played at top speed, a man standing beside it banging on a drum. That was the loudest place yet.

Kay had put her *First Greek Book* in her pocket to read on the train, thinking that perhaps she might find solace there in Cyrus's old campaign, and it clunked against the table.

Aren saw it peeking from her coat pocket and laughed. "Your vademecum."

She tried to shove it deeper, but he took it from her and flipped through the pages, shaking his head. "That old language is not even real, nothing they wrote is real any longer," he said.

She was aware of that, and aware besides that she didn't even read Greek now. "But I could have, if I had worked harder," she said, not explaining, stiff with him now. She slid the book deep into her pocket.

"Here we only speak the words we need to speak," he said. "*Piss, cunt, money.*"

What had happened to her brother?

Just then, a drunk fell stiff as a plank and landed on the floor beside them, feet twitching. His shirt was open wide and his narrow chest fluttered pearly white beneath a tide line of dirt. An eddy of filth and ash from below the tables swirled around his head.

A man came from the bar counter and hauled the drunk away, pulling under the arms so the fellow looked to have fallen sweetly asleep.

Aren handed Kay another drink, saying she might like this better—it was sweeter, but still tasted raw and dangerous.

"What is it?" she asked him.

"Spruce beer, maybe?" His eyes kept roaming, checking. "Or needle beer. Don't ask." Then his eyes fixed, gladly, and his arm flew up to wave at someone.

At a table by the back wall sat a girl, her black hair half bright orange from dye, hanging in matted locks around her lacquered face. Under thick-drawn eyebrows her mostly closed eyes were ringed with black and her lips were painted bright, strong pink, showing bluish underneath the paint. She had a dainty nose and a full chin, but a very sullen expression.

"Merissa!" Aren called.

A man knocked Kay's elbow. "There's a fellow calling you," he told her, indicating a man at the other side of the room. "Why aren't you answering him?"

"Why don't you answer him?" said a woman on her left. "Too proud for it?"

"I don't know him," Kay said. She frowned at the woman, who was colossal.

"Are ya sure?"

"Perfectly sure!" But in her heart Kay felt some doubt—she was so short-sighted it might have been someone she knew, someone from Yarmouth, from the South End, or a sailor.

The people wouldn't let it go. They started shouting to the man by the door, "Joey! That you, Joey Cremo? This lady say she doesn' know you!"

Well, she did not know a Joey Cremo. For a moment he had the look of Jacky Judge, but he was younger than Jacky must now be, just a boy. He came over, smiling, a bit shy, and took off his hat. He had such a soft look—like the boy she once imagined would bring her groceries, when she was living on a solitary island . . . The thought of Arthur Wetmore surfaced for a moment, but she pushed that aside.

"Oh," he said. "I thought for sure you was my cousin! I do beg your pardon, Miss."

"He begs her *pardon!*" the first man shouted. "Buy'n a drink!"

This was uncomfortable. Kay lifted her glass as if to toast him, to say she already had one, thank you, and drank the spruce beer down. It made her choke, but she swallowed more, still choking, and laughed. She felt the bruise below her eye. Still tender. That swollen eye was why she fit in here.

The boy's name was Augustine Muise. The large woman was Doraine, and the shouter said he himself was Old Joe Brooks, and he seemed to know Aren, so they all sat at a table in the smoky noise while Aren and the red-haired girl talked together by the wall for a long time. Someone gave Kay another glass of spruce beer. She tried to pay for it, but could not find her purse in her pocket. Oh dear. She turned to Aren, worried—

"I've got it. You dropped it a time ago," he said, "in Tom Poulette's place."

He held out her little brown purse, and she fished in it for a fifty-cent piece. The price of drink was criminal here, but of course it would be. How could Aren afford it?

Merissa was sitting on his lap now. Kay did not like that at all. She was tired.

Then there was a cloudy time, walking through the streets making too much noise. Kay tried to shush Aren, for he would get in worse trouble than she would. Merissa, the girl, kept hanging on his arm laughing, with her head rolling around. She had a loose way of hanging and strutting that Kay did not like but Aren seemed to find hilarious.

A gang of sailors in duck pants and sweaters rolled past, and one man stopped to look back at them.

Then he turned and ran back to grab at Aren, shouting, "Get away from these girls! You're a foul bastard and will take them your way to hell!"

It made no sense to Kay, what he said, nor to Aren, apparently.

"We bunked on the *Alhambra*, you know me!" the man shouted. "Off Manila in '19!" It seemed to enrage him when Aren shrugged and moved aside, lifting a shoulder to prevent the man from grabbing at his neck.

Kay waded in then, though she had nothing to fight him with. The other men from the ship were laughing and chivvying their mate. Seeing a long piece of lath there on the ground, Kay picked it up and swung it like a mashie, as if to take the man's feet out from under him, but it broke on his ankles and the men all laughed.

Aren laughed too and put his hands up, making peace with them. He called over his shoulder not to take them on, that it was not worth it. "Not worth the fight," he said. Or did he say, *I'm not worth a fight?*

Then someone spotted a dock guard coming and the gang of men went reeling off in another direction, still laughing at the broken lath.

Aren loped ahead to catch up to Merissa, and Kay had only a splinter in her palm for her trouble.

They ended up in another place, a cellar, with men sleeping against the wall. People were smoking at a stove, passing a stubby pipe around, and Kay did not like that either. She was glad of her dark coat that let her slide into the background, glad of her lack of prettiness.

The men swayed toward and away from Merissa; some of her clothes seemed to have got lost. Aren stood back by the cellar door, leaning against the wall and laughing sometimes, but keeping a grip on Kay's hand too. He wanted to leave and Merissa did not, but in the end he won, and they were walking again . . .

Kay did not know the route they took, but when they stopped tramping, they were at the foot of the stone steps at Aren's house. In the dim hall, Merissa went ahead of them up all those stairs, shoes clacking all three flights up, swaying exaggeratedly, looking back over her shoulder at them. Aren told Kay she was to sleep in his bed, that he would find another bunk. "There's an empty room down the hall," he said, "but it will be a sty."

Merissa hung in the doorway waiting for him, and when Aren was satisfied that Kay was safe, they left her there.

"Lock the door," he whispered through the crack before he shut it.

She did. Then she was alone in that half room. She did not take off her clothes, but slid her shoes together in front of the door so she could find them.

It was no longer entirely dark. She lay down on his bed and heard strange noises, sounds she did not want to hear. She heard Aren's voice and then high laughing, and strange crows from that girl, and huffing noises. It was miserable to hear them together. It was none of her business. She stuffed her fingers in her ears and waited for sleep to hide her.

Without a perceptible interval, without dreams or thinking, it was bright morning. She'd forgotten to wind her watch, but it was still ticking: just after seven. She wound it carefully, her fingers not working very well.

Standing, she made the bed; the sheets were worn thin as silk. She put her shoes back on and tidied her hair, and pulled her coat around her—little purse back in the pocket, yes, with her Greek book, and a still-clean handkerchief. There was no water in the room, and she did not dare explore the hallway to find the pipe. Gently, gently, she unlocked the door and turned the handle, and stepped out.

Aren opened a door nearby. "Goodbye," he said.

"Goodbye."

At the head of the steep-pitched stairs, she turned. He was still watching her.

"I'll come and see you again," she said. "We miss you so much—we are always looking for you."

He touched his fingers to his lips and blew, as she had taught him to do on the *Morning Light*, and turned back into that other room.

The stairs were steep and the stairwell so ill-lit that she had to take her time going down the three flights. She'd already missed the early train, she'd have to take the DAR train through Wolfville to get home by supper.

Almost at the bottom of the stairs, the outer door opened and in came a woman Kay knew: Esther Field, who had been in her class at school. Her father was the Baptist minister at the South End church in Yarmouth.

Esther looked up and cocked her head under her neat blue hat. "Why, Kay!"

"Hello," Kay said, stopping on the stairs. "Do you live here too?"

Esther smiled, taking that as a pleasantry. "No, I am a district visitor these days, and this rooming house is on my beat. I go round Saturday mornings to look in on a few church families and elderly people, see that they are getting good nutrition, you know, and arrange help for those who need it. You've come to see your nephew?"

Trust Esther to remember Kay's relationship with Aren perfectly—she'd won the History Prize at school, and was a scholarship student at Queen's University. Now doing good works in Halifax, while Kay did what? Went to weddings.

She liked Esther, but she did not want to talk to her this morning, with her tongue still furred and Aren upstairs in bad straits, and also with that Merissa girl who might start shouting any moment. She stood back against the wall for Esther to pass on the narrow stairs.

"I know you can't be happy to see him out of work," Esther said.

So that was the truth of it.

"But you can't do more than a person will let you. He's chosen this himself."

Kay looked at her.

"You mustn't blame yourselves, you and your family. It's not anything you did," Esther said, her voice cooler, eyes assessing Kay's face and hat and life.

But it was, it was exactly something that they had done.

Going through the Public Gardens, Kay stopped to lean on the railings and watch the grebes and waterhens, and bright-coloured mallards with their retiring wives. "*I come from haunts of coot and hern,*" she said out loud, and strode out more purposefully for the train station. Even the rails followed the rhythm, and all day long she could not get that poem out of her tired head, listening to the clicks tricking over the tracks, "*For men may come and men may go, but I go on forever.*"

Aren was never coming back. He would become one of those men in the cellar, lying against the wall, smoking a long pipe. He would fight with that beat-up, damaged girl and live in poverty and misery—not that he could not have money if he wanted it, but he had told Thea he would not take any. How was he living, if he'd left the job Francis had found him? Most likely running rum, and that would be a bad business—jail if he was ever caught.

What she had liked least about him was the patience in his eyes, that said this was what he expected, all he would ever expect.

Down the Annapolis Valley, the sentence made by the tracks'

clacking changed, as it often does when the train rounds a bend, or when one is tired. *Not worth a fight not worth a fight not worth a fight* they said again and again, while Kay tried to find a place on the windowsill that did not hurt her head.

3

Lake Milo

She jumped off at the Milton station at 4 p.m. on Saturday, planning to walk or—because she was very tired—to sit on the station fence till someone from Lake Milo came by. Along came Donny Sweeney from the ice factory, who offered to take her out in his trap after he'd off-loaded the cheese, so that was longer to wait.

She got him to let her out before the turning, cut across and walked over the fields and into the orchard. Somewhere back here, Jerry Melanson had buried Pilot. There, there was the mound. And there was Roddy, staring at a grave-marker stick, already made and carved, not very neatly. Not a cross, Kay saw. Roddy shared her mind on that, then. When she got close enough to read, she saw that it said,

PILOT

HOME FROM THE SEA

Which was what she had thought about Francis.

Hearing her approach, the boy turned as she came near, unsurprised. "Did you go to see him?"

Kay nodded. Her head still ached. "I saw his room, and met some of his friends."

"But why— Why he hasn't been back?" It seemed like Roddy had been wanting to ask that for a long time. "We want him around here, he is— I love him."

A hard thing for a nine-year-old boy to say. Kay could not think of anything to tell him.

His white, knobby hands, big for his age, trembled as they adjusted the grave stick again. "It was Eleanor King, wasn't it? The fellows were saying at school that my brother had tried to go with her, and her father and brother ran him off."

She knew what *the fellows were saying* must mean. They had been making fun of him, or of Aren to get to him, which was worse. She must think of something useful to tell him.

"I don't think it was exactly that they ran him off," she said. In her inner ear she heard Aren saying *don't take them on, I am not worth a fight.* She could not tell Roddy the real story, the sudden, ridiculous drama of Eleanor's mother reading her diary, all those six months of 1920 scribbled with June-mooning over Aren, and the men bounding down the hill to confront Aren where he sat with Eleanor eating ice cream by the bronze horse, the mother following along clucking like a hen. And Eleanor meekly going home with them, after the months of passionate secret vows. Or Mr. King saying he'd be damned if he'd have a damned darky in the family—and Kay at the counter of the luncheonette while all this was going on, Aren standing there alone until she went to be with him and shouted a few things back at Mr. King, which even Thea had not asked her to apologize for.

She said, "Mr. King was angry because Eleanor had not let him know that she was going to the dance with Aren. He is a stupid man and takes a long time to wrap his head around new things. And Eleanor is foolish and silly, and had not grown up." That was the crux of it.

"She is married now."

She was, to James Fitzgerald. Not a bad person, a junior engineer on the DAR line. Eleanor was still pretty and wobbly, no more able to stand up to James than she had been to her father. But being her father's daughter, she was too stupid for Aren, and Kay could not be exactly sad that it had all been stopped. Except that it had led to Aren leaving, and nothing was any good when he was gone and unhappy and not ever coming back. And also, Merissa Peck! She was even less possible than Eleanor King had been. Aren was perhaps only being kind to her—she was impossible—but he would probably love her soon, if he did not now, for her trouble and hurt as much as anything else.

"You smell right bad," Roddy said as they walked back down the orchard. "What even *is* that smell?"

She sniffed her sleeve, breathing in deep. "Drinks, meat, smoke, sadness." None of it smelled like Aren, his good smell of salt water and rope and sun.

Roddy went to the stables. Kay slipped in the side way to avoid Lena Hubbard and reached the bathroom before Thea could hear her, or smell her. Her fawn linen dress was probably ruined, now she came to look at it, but she washed it in the sink, tiptoed to her room and hung it in the closet to drip onto the strip of old linoleum there. Still faintly fragrant of tobacco and depravity.

On Sunday morning, the Reverend Arnold Archibald preached about the heathen. It was Missionary Sunday and he exhorted the congregation to "give up to your uttermost and then give more."

The only way to save poor heathen souls from damnation was to enlighten them with the gospel, he said, and ended on a joke: "It reminds one of the missionary who was tasked to translate the Nunc Dimittis—*Lord, now lettest thou thy servant depart in peace*—into the backward tongue of an African tribe, and could get no nearer than *Big Boss, kick us out gently.*"

Ha ha ha, the congregation chortled as one.

Kay thought of walking out, but then there would be explanations to give, and she would become inarticulate or weep with fury. Instead, she waited for the Communion prayers and the confession, where she could speak to God frankly. The prayers wound on and on in Archibald's florid rendering, so unlike Mr. Brimner's brisk, sane exhortations. Beside Kay, thin and stiff in his tweed knicker suit, Roddy kept kicking the kneeler very delicately, leaning his head on the pew back, unable to bear the frustration. Kay too tapped her shoe against it until her big toe hurt, even though she had learned better over long years of attendance at both services every Sunday.

Finally they were dismissed. At the door, Mr. Archibald pressed Thea's hand, thanking her for the invitation to midday dinner. A large meal that Kay could not avoid by a walk in the fields. He pressed Kay's hand too, fleetingly, before reaching for Aunty Bob, who had some money to give to the mission.

Kay could have given some, too, if she'd been inclined. She had no admiration for missionaries, but she was all right for cash. She was not earning her keep, but the trust from Father's part of the English estates was at last wound up, and Kay would have an annuity. If she lived modestly, she would not have to work, though she might need to supplement her living by teaching piano, or tutoring high school boys in Latin for pin money.

She and Roddy and Thea went out into the glassy northern sunlight and Kay thought of the sun she wanted, that hot glow of the tropics, light everywhere, needing no visible source.

Virginia Archibald had a serious disposition. She was a little older than Kay, but they had been in the same class at school, which meant that she remembered the various ways Kay had made a fool of herself: knowing too much and not understanding to keep quiet; fighting in the schoolyard whenever Aren was threatened, or even when he was not; angry weeping at the top of the class when ordered to describe her experiences in the West; clumsiness at double-dutch skipping. All the myriad infelicities of her conduct at school and her inability to fit in or bend to custom or demonstrate school spirit.

And of course Kay too remembered things, like the time Virginia had burnt off all her hair on one side with a too-hot curling iron, and left the other side long for a week before accepting that there was nothing to be done but cut it all even with her ears. Or the truly hideous lilac taffeta dress Mrs. Archibald's wealthy mother had sent for matriculation, which Virginia had had to wear, although it was far too long for the fashion and smelled of moth. So they were cautious with each other as they sat down to midday dinner.

Virginia taught early grades at Yarmouth Elementary School. She was cultivating an interest in folklore and the old songs, which she was determined to write down. It would be a perfectly good life. Kay did not at all dislike her.

But she disliked Mr. Archibald (perhaps mostly for his failure to be Mr. Brimner), and also his wife. Mrs. Archibald was careful of her social standing and liked to place people, ideally below herself. Also, she had known Father, and always told Kay how much she resembled him. Now she did so again, climbing up the veranda steps. She and her husband sat unswinging on the wicker swing, with Virginia beside them on a flowered hassock, smiling vaguely at the general air, all sipping at sherry and making mouths as if it was a little too strong. Thea engaged them in conversation about Giving Sunday and what the missions might expect this year.

Depressed, Kay sat on the veranda steps with Roddy until the dinner bell rang.

Virginia leapt up to help Lena with the plates, so Kay had to do so, too. Thea brought in the asparagus, the first from the glasshouse, arrayed on the *famille rose*, the greatly loved platter that Francis had given her in Shanghai, arrayed with the emperor's hunt. She had brought it out from Elm Street when Olive announced her engagement and it became clear that the family would be at Orchard House for some time. Francis smiled to see it, helping himself to asparagus, but could not be persuaded to tell the story of its acquisition, only smiling again and shaking his head. It was one of his silent days.

To cover the slight awkwardness, Thea told Mrs. Archibald that even though Aunt Lydia had such lovely things, it seemed a pity to leave all their own sea bounty gathering dust on Elm Street.

"I see the famous Hundred Faces fan has replaced your aunt's silver epergne on the fireplace mantel," Mr. Archibald said. "Fifty Chinese faces on each side, quite a treasure!"

Thea did not correct him; neither did Kay.

Roddy was newer to life and could not contain himself. "Forty-nine on the second side, actually," he said. "You see, the one who holds the fan becomes a part of it—you yourself are the hundredth face! It is a capital joke."

Helping herself to salad, Mrs. Archibald said, "I find foreign humour opaque."

Virginia asked Kay, "What do you hear from Aren? I hope he is very well."

She probably did hope so. Kay wondered what would happen if she said, *He is living in squalor on Gottingen Street and drinking too much and I don't know what he does for money.*

"What an act of Christian charity that was," began Mr. Archibald, "to bring that young fellow out of darkness into the light!"

Francis looked up from the pie he was dissecting. "Hardly darkness. The light in the South Seas is particularly radiant." It was the first thing he'd said that afternoon.

"We all thought it was just wonderful of you to take him on," Mr. Archibald continued.

Mrs. Archibald leaned forward. "His leaving almost reads, I must say, as ingratitude."

"Nothing of the sort," Francis said, too loud at the end of the table. "A young man has his way to make in the world—eighteen is high time to be out and exploring."

Roddy was white and tense, and Thea had put her handkerchief to her eyes. Muttering, "I will see about the tea, excuse me, please!" Kay pushed back her chair and took her plate to the kitchen.

Lena Hubbard was eating her dinner at the table there, raw pink arms splayed on the table. She cast a sideways eye at Kay but turned away to press another piece of pie on Jerry Melanson. Jerry winked at Kay, holding his plate to say he did not mind if he did, and then she was past them and out the back door into the air.

To her surprise, Virginia came after her, running down the back lawn in her Sunday shoes. "I'm sorry about Mother," she said, when she got near enough.

Kay said, "It's all right."

"She doesn't—she didn't know him as a person. The way I did. I wondered about him, that's all, but I'm sorry I asked it at the table."

Kay shook her head. "It was kind of you to ask."

"And the fan! How could Father forget the hundredth face? I remember so well when your sister displayed it at the girls' social tea during the war. It always makes me think of an exquisite porcelain face, you know, delicately flirting behind the fan. You are so lucky to have travelled widely and known such an ancient culture!"

A sick wave of anger rose again within Kay. It was all of a piece: whether the Archibalds thought foreigners were dirty or exquisite, they were not people, not real, only stories. But Virginia was not bad-hearted, only ignorant. Untravelled, as she'd said.

Kay took her arm and said, "I suppose I must go back and make that tea. Tell me, how can you bear to teach? Do you love your students? Or do you take the strap to them with abandon and make their hands burn, like old Mrs. Richards?"

After supper that evening, Kay and Thea sat on the veranda, as had become their habit here at Orchard House. Thea looked very tired, very drawn. Kay wondered if she was ill, or just sick of troubles. In a moment of impatience, she wished Thea would go ahead and die, then, if she was going to leave her anyway. Or Roddy, if he was. Coming down to breakfast each morning, wondering which chairs will be empty, or whether Aunt Lydia had finally yielded into dust in the back dining room. What was the point of loving people, anyway? Better to separate oneself from all that.

But not yet, not yet. While you had people, you should talk to them.

"I have some questions for you," Kay said.

Thea nodded. "When did you ever not? As long as you do not ask Mr. Archibald . . ."

"Just listen," Kay said. "You have to answer. Were we right?"

"Right to do what?"

"Were we right—did we have the right, or perhaps even the duty—to take Pilot from New Zealand?"

"Yes! That is a nonsensical question. He was starving in that mining camp—and besides, he was a present from the entrepreneurial dentist, who I believe lost his shirt on those kauri trees, in the end."

The next question was harder to ask: "Were we right—did we have the right—to take Aren?"

After a moment, Thea said, "He was starving too—gaunt with it, they all were. Do you not remember? The men devoured a bushel of bread, and kept crying *poor, poor* and clutching their stomachs."

"Still, was it right, to take a child from his people?"

Thea shook her head and got up from the rocker. "You make me tired, Kay," she said. "You have a way of simplifying an argument that ignores the complexity of life."

"The question is answered, then."

Thea shook her head again. She leaned on the porch railing, trailing her finger along the lilac leaf that overhung it. Tight purple buds had formed; they would be open soon.

Kay did not know how to go on. Perhaps there was a difference between animals and humans. Pilot had been content to be one of their pack, content at sea or on land, only asking to be near them; Aren had needed his own people to find his way in the world.

"Dear Kay, do you always have to be questioning? Why can you not accept that there might be some things we do not know yet, or can never know, because we are human—because you are human, and not God Himself?"

"I can't leave things alone. I have to ask—the questions just arise."

Thea shook her head, not smiling. "It's not a virtue to be curious."

"I think it is!"

"Virtue involves service to others, not vulgar prying into every tiny crack that does not concern you. Virtue would lead you to a greater peacefulness in your own heart."

Kay felt Thea's great eyes upon her, pinning her, putting everything she thought or felt (could not help thinking and feeling, after all) to the test. She could have turned away, gone up to bed. But she loved her sister and did not wish to be misunderstood by her.

Leaning forward to see better in the twilight, Kay said, "I don't care about virtue, or whatever people say is virtue. I care about being kind, about people being kind to each other. I care about saying what is true and not pretending what's false."

She waited, but Thea said nothing.

Kay went on. "At Olive's wedding, I thought, I don't want to care what people think of me anymore. Maybe I never did care about it much, because, except for you, the people whose good opinion I wanted were taken away, or died. I don't care about being demure and pretty, because I'm not pretty anyway. If you look at it coldly, you must admit I have very little prospect of not being chaste."

Thea put out her hand, shaking her head, about to recite for Kay all the ways that mere prettiness did not matter.

But that was not the point! Kay rushed on, to stop her: "All I mean is, that sort of thing doesn't matter to me. I don't care what other people do with their own virtue, or not-virtue—unless they are unkind to others while they do it. All I care about is kindness, I can boil it right down to that. "

Thea did not answer. Her forehead had the U-shaped wrinkle Kay seemed so often to provoke, caused by carefully trying to understand the inexplicable. Or pretending to consider the virtues of her wrong argument. After a long moment, she said, quite quietly, "If you gave yourself to the teachings of our Saviour— You do pray every night, don't you, dear heart?"

Only Mr. Brimner, her long-lost friend, was able to mention God without causing bile to rise up in the back of Kay's throat. "I'm trying to tell you, I don't *care* about God, He means nothing to me—I don't know if He is real or invented. All I know is the world we live on, sail on, stand on. I can use that as God, if you like. Church means nothing to me either, but I see that it sustains you, and Mr. Brimner gave his life to it, so I carry on attending, to be kind to you both."

Thea had tears in her eyes again, because she believed that God was listening to Kay and was being very much hurt by what she said.

Kay tried again. "Long ago, when I said I wished I had the service by heart so that I did not have to hold up the prayer book, you said that it was better not to know it by rote, but to consider and mean the words of Communion freshly every time."

"Did I say that?"

"Yes, and I thought it was very wise."

Thea laughed a little. "I am glad to seem wise to you!"

"You always do," Kay said, surprised.

"But you do not heed my wisdom much." She laid her hand on Kay's brown forearm.

"I do! I run my life by it! But if I think differently, I must attend to my own thoughts too."

"You are so like Father," Thea said.

And then Kay could not talk to her any longer. "I'll get Aunt Lydia's milk," she said, and walked down the veranda to the far end by the kitchen door, first checking that Lena Hubbard was not there to sour everything even more.

It was time for them to be apart, Kay thought. High time for her to be out exploring. Thea loved her, but was tired of her too. You tire even those who love you best, if you are the kind of person Kay knew herself to be, unsatisfied, restless, exhausting. In the ordinary way she would have been married off by now, gone from Thea's immediate vicinity, and perhaps be easier to bear. And she was no doubt a bad influence on Roddy, who was also willing to argue with his mother, although not yet with Francis. Not that Francis was a stern father, or brother.

She went to the back rooms in search of him, to ask which route would be best. She could not tell Thea what was in her mind, but she could tell Francis.

Francis was sitting in the accounts room without the lamps lit. Easy to talk in that shaded room. They did not even have to look at each other, there was no need. He was so quick to respond that Kay wondered if he might have thought of this for Aren himself.

"I can put him in the way of passage Tuesday evening, when the *Prince Arthur* comes in for Boston. Kinney will find us a ship in Boston."

"He needs to leave from Halifax." If she tried to make him come to Yarmouth, he would not.

"Ah. Well, I'd talk to Hilton, in Halifax, get him onto one of the Lakes. *Lake of Flowers*, that's one of his. Or there's the *Constellation*—when did I see that she is leaving . . ." He ran a finger down the sailing list on his desk. "Monday evening! That is quick. Might be for the best. It will be the luck of the draw. Hilton will see him fitted up and find something for Aren to do below decks. He knows his way round a ship, he'll be useful."

"But I want him to have proper passage, and a cabin."

Francis shook his head. "It's best if he finds a berth below."

"He's my brother. He'll be travelling with me."

"Oh, you are going too, are you?"

Kay looked at him, without answering.

After a pause, Francis said, "Do you want to fight the world, or do you want to send Aren back to his people?"

"I can't send him back alone. I don't think he'd make it."

Francis shook his head, agreeing. "Doubt it."

"He's not feckless or—or irresponsible, it's not that."

Francis seemed surprised. "Of course not! Only he's sad, and ashamed of himself these days, and it takes a certain gall to get around the world at a young age. Gall like yours."

Kay decided that he'd meant that to please her, although his flat, expressionless face did not change.

"I had it too," he said. "A good supply of gall." He turned to open the cupboard and pulled his strongbox out of the shelf, unlocked it and lifted the papers. "You know where you're headed?" He counted out bills to a hundred dollars, fit them together, tapped them against the desk to order their edges and then continued: "Pulo Anna, the Sonsorol group, south of Palau . . ."

Kay nodded. She and Aren had found Palau on the globe so often that its name had worn off.

"This will not see you the whole way there," he said. "But it's all I've got on hand. I'll arrange a bank draft in Wellington for the same again."

She began to protest, but Francis raised a hand. "When you run out, wire me, and I'll arrange your passage home—and Aren's too, if that's how it transpires."

"Must I get a passport for him?"

"He'll stay on the ship most of the time—the seamen's book will be enough."

"That's good, then."

She did not know how to ask him not to tell Thea what she planned to do.

He put the bills in a little leather wallet and handed it across the desk. "I'm off to Elm Street for the night," he said. "Things to do in town in the morning—afraid I won't have time to discuss this with Thea before I go. But I'll have a word with Jerry Melanson and he'll run you in to meet the ten fifteen, if that suits you."

Kay nodded, and held out her hand. They were formal with each other always, and did not hug or kiss, but his clasp was strong and warm. "Thank you," she said.

"Give Aren my blessing, if it's any use to him," Francis told her. "He has a home here too, whenever we are fortunate enough to see him again."

———

Kay ran quietly up the attic stairs. Dust motes moved restlessly in the last glimmer of sun through the slanted stomacher windows. Her small steamer trunk—very light, with nothing in it. She could carry it down easily, and she could ask Jerry Melanson to take it to the wagon for her once it was packed.

There on a shelf was her mother's old valise. She put her hand through its black bone handle, felt again the clasp of a hand, like her mother's hand holding hers. It was small—she opened the trunk and put the valise inside. It would do to hold her books.

She packed her dinner dress and two lawn dresses, white and grey-striped, and a blue serge smock, and then went to the closet and shook out the fawn linen. It had hung itself dry into an almost unwrinkled state. That went in too. She could wear her brown twill for the train. Two cotton nightdresses, underclothes, cotton hose. She packed her silk stockings and took them out again. Then she packed them again. Before they got there, all that way across the world, she might need silk stockings somewhere. But very little else. The small green pocket *Odyssey* Mr. Brimner had given her, her note-book, two books to read on the long way over (*Middlemarch*, good and long, and *Penny Plain* for light relief); her sponge bag, with her sponge from Eleuthera and a bar of the rose soap Thea had bought last year in Paris. Who knew when she would have good French soap again. The silver cup from Dawlish was on the dresser, and she added it.

Her blue linen coat and skirt, in case there was church, and two pairs of shoes—there. Three of the trunk's fitted drawers were empty. Never mind—if the trunk was lighter, Jerry would not make noise carting it down the kitchen stairs. She went down that way to see if he was still in the kitchen. He was not, and nor was Lena Hubbard, thank goodness. Seeing smoke rising on the back step from his pipe, she stepped out and asked Jerry to help her in a while. No need to ask him not to tell; he never spoke unless spoken to, and only would answer a direct question with yes or no.

Back in her room, she remembered her toothbrush, the nice red one she'd bought at Filene's in Boston, and added it to her sponge bag. Then, meaning to find Thea, but not to say goodbye, she opened the door again—and there was Roddy, standing in his pyjamas, his hair an upright shock. He saw the packed trunk, not yet closed.

"Are you going away?" he asked, quiet in the evening hall.

"Yes," she said. She would not lie outright.

He stood thinking. "With Aren too?"

"Yes," she said. "But I can't tell Thea."

He shook his head.

She looked at him, helpless to explain. "I'm sorry—I have to go, we have to."

He nodded this time. He did not ask anything at all, the dear and private heart.

"I wish you could come with us—it would be so useful to have you! But you must finish school, that is the first thing."

He clenched his fists. "I don't want to stay in school, school is stupid. I would learn much more by going with you. You hated school, and Aren never even finished. Why must I?"

"You can't understand how it was for us. People feel they know you, because you're from here."

"I was not born at sea," he said sadly.

"Well, neither were we, that does not matter a tick—but your parents are Yarmouth-born and ours were not."

"But I am odd, you know."

She laughed. She did know. "I wish I could take you," she said.

"Perhaps you will let me know where you settle, then, and I will come and meet you," he said, as if confirming a dinner engagement.

She laughed, as quiet as he was. "I will write to you, I promise."

He shook his head. "With your scrawly hand? You might as well write in Greek. Please ask Aren to transcribe your letters!" He came forward in a rush and hugged her, and then vanished down the dark hallway.

Nine o'clock. Time. Kay went to Thea's room and found her in bed already, propped on cushions with her pink leather-bound New Testament. "Francis went to town," she said, moving the marker. "I've taken a holiday and put myself to bed early."

"That's good. You work too hard, you must be careful not to exhaust yourself."

"Nonsense!" Thea patted the bed. "Sit down, you haven't told me enough about Aren, how he looks, how he is. Is he very thin?"

"No, I think he is in good health. Good spirits," Kay said, lying carefully. She must not say anything portentous, or show sadness.

"I must go down to Halifax myself, and try to persuade him to come home," Thea said.

Kay bent to kiss her foot, and the humped length of her shin beneath the blankets. "He loves you," she said. "And he said he misses Roddy something fierce." A small lie; not a lie, because true.

She bent over the bed again to kiss her sister's damask cheek, wishing she could just tell her everything but knowing she could not, and said, "Sleep well, dear Thetty."

Thea caught her hand and kissed it. "You never call me that anymore. You were the sweetest little girl, Kay, so funny and bright. I often thought of that when you were having such a difficult— well. You were always very decisive. Such terrific frowning when your will was crossed. Your eyebrows made little ridges!"

Kay got up, patting Thea's hand, no longer gripped by an agony of wishing to tell. Being told how grouchy you have always been is enough to cure a person of sentimentality.

Now it was time.

Jerry Melanson strained at the trunk, caught it in both hands and headed down the back staircase. Kay raced down the front stairs to delay Lena Hubbard, in case she might be coming early from Aunt Lydia's room, where she spent the evenings seeing to the old body.

Pushing the door just ajar, Kay saw her humming to herself, busy with a cloth at the medicine table, wiping bottles, leaving everything clean and orderly. She did her job neatly. Kay stood watching for a moment.

Lena turned from the bottles to the bed. "One more half hitch for the old bitch," she said under her breath, and she caught Aunt Lydia roughly around the waist and rolled her over a quarter, shoving a long pillow along her back to hold her in place.

A moaning exhalation came from the body's mouth. Lena smacked the old woman's leg and said, "None of your noise, now."

Backing quickly away into the telephone alcove under the stairs, Kay found she had no breath. The ordinary cruelty of it shocked and did not shock her. Lena had always been one who liked to have power over others. And Aunt Lydia could not know. Did that make it all right to hurt her? Why lavish care on this old, empty body, yet consign Pilot to death?

She should tell Thea about it. But if Lena had to leave, Thea would have no help at all, and that was not tenable. All right, it meant that Kay would have to come home soon and be the help.

But first, she could go back to sea.

4

The Constellation

At 6 a.m., a white sky, bright even for May. The train shuddered into the station and Kay moved gingerly, shifting her legs to see if anything was still asleep before gathering herself and rising. Three or four other sad souls who'd made the overnight run in the one passenger carriage were stretching and finding their hats. She left her trunk in the luggage bay and walked down the timber pier, searching for the Hilton office. She'd been there once with Francis, but could not quite remember the spot.

A long line of clattering cars went screeling along black rails into dark sheds, pushed rather than pulled by a wheezing engine car. In shadowy corners, dock boys were sleeping, two or three leaning up against each other, caps down and hands shoved into their armpits for warmth. Any of them could have been Aren.

Seagulls wheeled where she walked, hoping for cake, perhaps. One big white bird stood plump ahead of her and refused to move as she bore down on it, until Kay stamped her blue boot and it deigned to lift off on spreading, lazy wings, crying *sheeee, who does she think she is?*

———

All right, that was done. With some relief, she stood outside on the boardwalk again. Captain Hilton's office had been stuffy, all the windows painted shut. Probably he'd had enough sea air to last his lifetime.

Francis had telephoned ahead last evening, and Captain Hilton greeted her by saying he had found accommodation for them on the *Constellation* (she thought perhaps it was by turfing an officer out of a berth), sailing at 4 p.m. Two fares, one way, came to seventy-five dollars, by Hilton's favourable reckoning.

She was worried about money: she did not intend to wire Francis for more, ever, and they would need to charter a boat at the other end, or live for who knew how long while they worked out what to do. So before going to find Aren, she took her luggage to a little shop she'd often noticed on visits to Halifax, a dusty emporium of bits and bobs with a discreet sign in the window: WE BUY FOR CASH. She must always have known she would be needing this shop.

Two men stood behind the counter, not eccentric or Dickensian, only businessmen. One with a hand-held tally, like an abacus in a Chinese shop. They bought the silver cup—that brought five dollars. Her silver brush set, ten. Her pearls, which had been Aunt Queen's, with knots between each one, for forty.

That was more like it, but still not enough. She sold them her broadcloth coat with the muskrat collar, and her watch, and in the end her steamer trunk. A suitcase would do for her, and they offered one they had on hand as part of the deal, a lady's case in strong butterscotch leather. Her clothes fitted easily in the case, her books in the blue valise. And of course this divestiture was not permanent, she could come back and have nice things again, anything she ever wanted or needed. She had ninety-five dollars extra now, so they were altogether a hundred and thirty to the good. She did the arithmetic again. Or rather, a hundred and twenty. Enough, anyway, to feel beforehand with the world.

Since they'd only offered a dollar and a half for it, she kept the pearl pin that Francis had given her that Christmas in Shanghai.

She wondered if Francis had ever yet remembered that she was with him in Boston when he bought it for Thea, to celebrate the baby who died in Eleuthera. She tumbled her things from the trunk into the cases (slightly sad to let the steamer trunk go, a very fancy one from Paris) and went back out to the cabbie, patiently waiting, and directed him on to Gottingen Street. There, she could unload for herself—which made her glad to be freed of the trunk after all. She arranged her two cases on the stoop, hemming herself in.

She had to wait for an hour, but at last Aren came whistling around the corner.

She stood up to wave.

"What's this, have you run away?" he asked when he was close enough not to shout. He had his key out to open the door.

"I didn't want to bring it all upstairs," she said.

Now that she'd come to the point, she did not know how to broach the subject.

He forestalled her. "Don't worry, I'm in work again. I went cap in hand to Belliveau at the yards and he took me back, working nights. I'm on my feet again, you can count on that."

She flushed. "Did you think— I was not critical of you, only a bit worried."

"I know," he said. "I was angry, in a slump, you know how that is. But I have pulled on my bootstraps and I am on my way up again."

They stood there on the stoop, silent for a moment.

Putting his key into his pocket again, he said, as if it was no matter, "What have you got in those cases?"

Kay looked up and down the street. No helpful people, no stray dogs. Better come out with it. "I had an idea," she said.

Aren cocked his head and looked blank, waiting.

"I thought we could go home."

He waited. Giving her nothing.

"To your real home, I mean."

He looked up to check her face then.

"I have berths for us on the *Constellation*, for New Zealand, sailing at seven."

He laughed. "The *Constellation*! I've just been victualling her."

Then he was silent.

She couldn't breathe. She did not know what would work to persuade him.

"It's the best thing—the only thing that makes sense!" she said in a rush. "I've been thinking and thinking—it's no good for you here, there's nothing—"

She stopped herself. She could not interpret his face. She could not translate it.

After a minute, she said, "Well, anyway, I thought we could just go back."

He stood looking up Gottingen Street, grey and damp. Black ooze running down one gutter, rain beginning overhead. He was still the younger brother, she thought. He would be ruled by her.

"I don't know what Belliveau will have to say about me running out on him again," he said at last.

Leaving the big suitcase at the bottom of the stairs, Kay went up to help Aren pack. There was not much to stow in his sea-chest. When the little room was empty, Aren looked around it. "I did not like it here," he said.

"I am glad to be back on our travels," Kay said, voicing her inmost thought.

A voice came scrawling up the stairs, calling *Aaaaaaaa-ren!* in red ink. That girl, the one with the bruised mouth and the matted red hair.

Aren locked the door of the room. "Landlady has a skeleton key," he said, and slid the key under the door. "Why don't you wait here for a minute until I go talk to Merissa?"

She was glad to let him go down alone, although ashamed of her cowardice. He set the sea-chest on his shoulder and trotted down the stairs, very fit still, though still shadowed under the eyes from rough living.

In a minute Kay heard him talking down below. She could not make out the words. There was a pause, and a longer pause, and then a burst of indeterminate screaming and thumping. She peeped over the balustrade, careful not to be seen.

"You scum-bucket!" the girl shouted. That was the intelligible part; the rest was lost in a long wail and in the whirling of her hands pounding on every part of Aren she could reach. "You can't go! You can't!" Fury breaking outward in every direction, her hard shoes kicking at the stairs and the banisters, and from the sounds of it connecting with Aren's legs once or twice. He held her off at arm's length and tried to set the sea-chest on the step, but she wind-milled in again, crying, "No! No! No! You are a pig! I hate you! You must not go! You can't!"

Aren got the sea-chest down and put his arms around her, his dark hair mixing with her red locks, and held her, whispering in her ear, holding her tighter when she struggled to get free. Kay crept down one flight of stairs while they were occupied, and looked again over the railing.

The girl was crying now, her body sagging in Aren's arms. Her face tilted upward in exaggerated mourning, eyes searching, brows arced up in the centre like a tragedy mask. Kay pulled her head back.

For the best, she thought.

Kay had let the cab go hours ago, and the suitcase, valise and sea-chest were too much to manage on foot. Aren stopped a kid running along the road and asked him to find them a cart. He gave the boy a dime and Kay said that was the last they'd see of that, but soon enough a dray cart turned up the street and the driver whistled down to ask if it was them that needed a lift. At the docks, Aren helped her jump down from the cart and snagged a porter to take the suitcase and the valise, showing him the tags: "For Ward, K. Ward!"

Kay expected him to follow the porter along with her, but he shouldered his sea-chest once again.

"You made a mistake there," he said matter-of-factly. He was not scolding her. "I am not cabin material, even on a tramp. I'll find Hilton and get that straightened out."

"I meant to do it," Kay said. "I won't have you in steerage."

"No such thing on a tramp, only first and second—and anyhow, that's not what I mean. I'll find myself a job and we'll save the price."

"*No!*"

"*Yes!*" he said, aping her tone. "This time, it is you who doesn't know what is right."

She wanted to stamp her foot, for all the good that would do. "Don't you see? It's important."

"It might be important for you, but for my sake, this will be better."

He would not change his mind when in that mood. She breathed out through her nose and said, "If you must, you must."

"Indeed, I must."

He kissed her cheek and went off through the crowd, back toward the Hilton office, and she was left to make her own way through the embarkation shed.

At the counter, two nicely dressed girls laughed with each other, filling out their embarkation forms opposite Kay. One dark, one very fair, of the same height and slenderness, in the same elegant clothing. Under OCCUPATION, after some repartee, they put *Spinster*, so Kay did too. She had no occupation and it did not seem to her that she ever would.

Pride, she had that. So she did not simper at the girls or try to be friends with them. Besides, she had a friend, she had a brother. And she had Roddy too—she would write him a postcard now, before she forgot. In the waiting room, she chose one with the Citadel on it, he would like that.

We sail this evening. I will miss you and I promise to write
each week.

    Give Thea my love when it seems like good timing.

    Don't forget to write to me, too! always your loving Kay

Then, with more difficulty, she composed a telegram to Thea. It
would not be delivered till the morning, when Jerry Melanson's
second cousin rode out on his bicycle from the telegraph office.

I AM SORRY BUT I HAVE GONE TO TAKE AREN
BACK TO HIS HOME. HE IS TOO SAD HERE.
I WILL WRITE FROM NEW ZEALAND. WE SAIL
THIS EVENING. LOVE FROM KAY.

Thirty-two words! It cost her almost a dollar to send.

Then, since she was being so practical, she sent a cable to Mr.
Brimner—this one much shorter, since the fee to Tonga was for-
midable. As if it cost any more to beam around the seas—well,
perhaps it did have to go from shore to shore more times, or whatever the cable wires did. She sent the cable to "English Church,
Ha'ano," hoping that it would reach him. Knowing that it must be
read by many other eyes than his, she was careful what she said.
Ten words only:

COMING TONGA. WILL WRITE FROM NZ.
SAILING TONIGHT. LOVE KAY.

That was all right. All her necessary tasks completed, she bent
to pick up her— Oh! the porter had taken the valise and the case.
Well then. Off she was.

Going up the gangplank, she had the loveliest tremble in her
middle, the subtle, excitable apprehension of a journey long desired.

———

Kay's cabin suited her very well. It was on the promenade deck and had a proper window that opened, not a port, which she would have had to beg the steward to open for her, and which would most times be denied in case of heavy water. She opened the window at once, and let in the soft, faintly stinking harbour air.

It was a single, with one fixed bunk that functioned as a sofa during the day, but she needed no more. Built-in shelves with leather fittings to hold books and toiletries secure; there was a tiny washbasin closet, with a dinky little tap. Cold water only, but she was perfectly happy to wash her face in cold water. She unpacked her case and her valise while the ship's engines changed their note and began to thrum, thrum, in a purposeful way, and by the time the big vessel eased away from the dock (to a very few cheers from dockside friends) she was finished, and sitting calmly on her sofa like an old hand when the steward knocked to inform her that she was down for the first seating, and would be at the captain's table. That arrangement must be courtesy of Captain Hilton, and due to her long friendship with Marion. She would send Marion a card too, to let her know how kind her father had been.

The dining room was low-ceilinged but long, and ringed with mirrors. The radio played quiet music in one corner, where the carpet had been taken up to provide a tiny dance floor. One couple was already seated at the head table: a slight naval man and his companion, a middle-aged, middle-sized, middle-coloured woman in a serviceable navy satin dress, chosen to look well with a uniform beside it.

As Kay was finding her name card, the captain came to the table and introduced himself. "Captain Richard Bathurst—I sailed with your brother a time or two in our younger days."

Kay said she knew Francis would be very happy to hear that, and the captain said he had already sent a message through "internal channels" (which she supposed to mean by way of Captain Hilton) that he was happy to have aboard any relative of Grant's, and he heard that they had his son as well, down in the engine rooms, and that was a very good thing too. "A *very good thing*," he repeated, glowering at Kay as if she had argued.

She nodded, not knowing what to say.

"Fellow down there is my first lieutenant, Mr. Johns, and that's his wife, of course."

Mr. and Mrs. Johns gave Kay a nod, and both would have spoken except that they were interrupted by the arrival of the two girls from the embarkation shed, who were introduced by Mr. Johns as Elizabeth Spiers and Julia Speedwell.

Elsie, as she said to call her, was writing an article about travelling by tramp steamer; Julia was sailing along as her companion and support. Julia was engaged to be married. Elsie said this was her last hurrah as a free woman. That was a joke, but they both looked very well off, and likely the rest of their lives would be taken up with clothes and children and ministering to their husbands, helping them in their careers by entertaining well in large, high-ceilinged rooms. Marion Hilton would be in their club. They were both very pretty and their shoes were simply beautiful.

Elsie and Julia pretended to be over-awed by Captain Bathurst, but Kay had met men of his ilk in various harbours, and did not find him such a stern example of the genus. He struck her as having a sense of humour—and if he knew anything about Aren's origin, he had some kindness as well.

The first lieutenant, Mr. Johns, was an accommodating man who clearly liked the ladies; his wife was along on the voyage for the third time. Julia asked if Mr. Johns needed minding, and Mrs. Johns did not find that amusing. She told the girls many interesting things over supper. Kay recognized this desire to inform, and resolved to squelch it in herself.

Mrs. Johns had never been squelched—her mild colouring was deceptive. "You'd be astonished to know, Miss Spiers, Miss Speedwell, how much has crept into our language from the seafaring man! For instance, you know that *by* means *into* the wind, while *large* means *with* the wind—therefore, *by and large* includes all possible situations—as in, the *Constellation* handles well both *by* and *large*. Is that not just fascinating?" Mrs. Johns waved her vichyssoise spoon to indicate that she had more bons mots to impart and would continue.

Her husband leapt in before her: "Or *groggy*—that's referring to having drunk too much grog, you know!"

The captain suddenly commanded his first lieutenant to *splice the main brace*! Kay laughed, knowing what that meant: it was the order to send out an extra issue of grog. Mr. Johns passed the wine bottle down the table, but Captain Bathurst had already hailed a waiter.

Mrs. Johns did not pause in her lecture. "When we say *hand over fist*, you know, that's as a sailor climbs the shrouds, hand over hand, steadily upwards."

Elsie had taken out a notebook and was scribbling on the narrow pages.

"And here's another: when you do a thing *handsomely*, although we don't use that as we once did, that's *slowly*, you know, as if you was hauling in a line. Hand by hand, do you see? Steady and even."

Dinner was four courses. With Mrs. Johns, it was not unlike an evening with the Krito-sophians.

Aren came to her cabin door at midnight and gave their secret knock: *pompholugo paphlasma*. She had not yet settled for the night— she had only reorganized her clothes in the locker and the fitted drawers, and rearranged her books on the shelf, and plumped the cushion on the bunk two or three times. Then she sat at peace in the loved sensation of smooth motion over yielding, buoying, deep, eternally swaying ocean. How did anyone ever live on land?

Aren was black with oil already and would not sit on the bed— he'd brought a scrap of matting that he set on the carpet and sat upon cross-legged. "I'm a freezer-greaser," he told her, boasting. "Oiling the engines for the refrigerators, not a bad gig."

"I will feed you extras from the dining room." She drew out her dinner haul, shanghaied in a napkin: a soft bun filled with chicken salad and two lemon cakes.

"I've got the run of the refrigerators—I'll be living on ice cream," he said, but he ate the bun and one of the cakes, to please her. He left the other on her bedside table. "Save this one for your night lunch."

She told him about Elsie and Julia from the embarkation shed, and what the captain had said, and the first lieutenant's prosy wife's pronouncements; he told her nothing at all, except that he had a comfortable bunk and trim arrangements. "The crew's all right, so far," he said. "Nobody *we* know, but many who knew the *Morning Light*, and Francis. I'm in solid on the strength of my connexions."

"Do you have anything to read down there?"

He laughed at that. "Whenever there's light, I'll be working, and when it's dark, I'll sleep, and if the engineer ever gives me a moment off, I'll find a lifeboat, like Seaton."

Kay felt sick that she was in this cozy room and he stuck below in the black heat of the engines.

Seeing her frown, he laughed again. "I don't like to laze about," he said. "Anyway, it's no more than most people do every day all over the world, and I can think, can't I?"

"Does the engineer know—" No, she could not ask that, whether he'd mentioned that he had a weak chest.

Aren frowned. "You're not going to be boring, are you?"

She shook her head.

He jumped to his feet. "All right, let me wash my face and I'll find my bunk, and see you when I can," he said. He splashed some water into the steel bowl from the little tap. "All the modern conveniences!"

She had a towel ready, but he wiped his sleeve across his face.

"Mustn't be too dainty down below, or the fellows will rag me," he said, like Roddy would, and was out the door and gone.

The engine noise was audible, here in the cabin, a constant burr to rest your mind against. And Aren would be down there keeping the long screw going through the swell. Or at least, keeping the refrigerators cool. She had never been on a ship with a refrigeration room. Maybe sometime he could take her down to see. She'd been awake for such a long time, it seemed like a very great effort to take off her dress and hang it up and find her nightdress, and she did not even bother to wash her face but lay down and wept for her dear dog Pilot, who had died so short a time ago and whom she missed especially here at sea. Then she ate her midnight cake.

At first light, Aren found her at the railing of the promenade deck, and motioned her to follow. He led her up a narrow stair to the weather deck, and gave a quick yank on one of the ropes holding the canvas cover on the second starboard lifeboat, so that it folded back halfway. He handed her up and jumped in after, and there they sat, playing Seaton, enjoying the salt wind and the air.

"Passenger boats are strange," Aren said. "The work is all done hole-and-corner, in the hope that no one will see how hard they work, below."

"It makes me uncomfortable," Kay said. "Though I know that is absurd—I've been a passenger all my life."

"Now you have reached the acme of your profession." He settled into the curve of the prow and bit into one of the apples she'd brought from her cabin, stored up from dinner.

She wondered if he was glad to be going on this journey, but did not want to ask. "I am glad to be here," she said instead.

"I am sorry for Merissa Peck," he said.

Kay had almost managed to forget her. Hungry again, she took a bite of the other apple.

"But it would not have been kind to take her so far away, in uncertain circumstances," Aren said, when he was halfway through his apple.

"I did not see her at her best."

"If you'd met her in Tonga or in Fiji, you would think her very fine and strong-minded. She's like you, except poor."

Kay supposed she was to take that as a compliment.

Below them, the stewards moved along, setting up the deck chairs for the passengers.

"Go down and put dibs on a chair," Aren said, pushing her with his foot. "I'm going to nap here for a while—the man next to me snored fearfully all night."

Kay slid gingerly out onto the metal foot of the lifeboat launcher, jumped down and took the stairs to Promenade deck as if she had simply been enjoying the sunshine above.

"Chair for you, Miss? You're up early!" said the steward, a wiry man of little height with a bright eye.

"May I?"

"Miss Ward, ain't it, if you'll pardon me? Got you listed as Cabin 6, which means this chair here, if that suits?"

She sat, and swivelled to let her feet fall on the slanting footrest. "Blanket?"

The air was brisk still, so she took the blanket.

"I'm Handy, Miss."

She nodded, thinking he certainly was, then realized it was his name. "Thank you, Mr. Handy."

"Breakfast at eight, Miss," Handy said, and went on down the line of chairs.

Kay sat staring out into the far distance, that prospect only available at sea, or (her practical mind inserted) sometimes from a balcony looking out to sea. Like the view out across the prairie from the upper windows at Blade Lake. The long view, the only view she wanted.

Up and down deck, other passengers appeared, in cruise wear or overcoats, depending on their experience and expectation and hardiness. One lady wore furs, although it was only rabbit fur dressed to look like muskrat. Some seemed to be in summer kit. Kay was glad she'd sold her coat. She thought warmly of the little roll of dollars in her brown purse.

The girls from dinner came along to find their chairs, Julia very correct in a navy steamer coat, Elsie more frivolous in a cardigan, a red wool scarf tucked around her neck against the wind.

"Aren't the mornings beautifully fresh?" she called to Kay.

Kay nodded, and pulled the rug up around the cheek that faced them. She wished she'd brought her book. Now those girls would think they had to speak to her.

At the noon bell, Julia stood and stretched, and asked Kay if she would walk in to luncheon with them. This was a strange life, this passenger business. Being with a large set of people all day long, people you did not know or particularly like, involved multiple courtesies that Kay had not bargained for. She had thought she would just read all the time, yet here she was foisted into social occasions, over and over.

Seeing tape pasted down the middle of the passageway, Kay kept to the left, the dry side. Julia and Elsie walked all over until Kay put out a hand and tugged gently at Elsie's sleeve to nudge her over. The seaman on his knees swabbing ahead looked up and gave them a grateful grin.

"If there's tape, they're waxing," Kay said, trying not to sound like Mrs. Johns. "They work one side all the way down and then do the other, so we can still walk along."

"Clever!"

It was only practical, but Elsie demanded to know how Kay knew so much about "shipboard culture," left her no time to answer, and then talked all through lunch about the exigencies and cleverness of life at sea. Mrs. Johns having come down with seasickness, there was no one to compete with her.

The *Constellation*, a British-India cargo steamer of four thousand tons, had been a coast-to-coaster for forty years, and a beauty in her time, Lieutenant Johns assured Kay. Even now, sagging after the war and firmly into middle age, Elsie called her "a capital ship for an ocean trip, with everything trim about her."

Not quite trim, to Kay's cooler eye. A good old ship, battered but sturdy. The passengers were undemanding, many of them British and American missionaries coming from or heading back to India and points along the way, and a sprinkling of other travellers: people with a little money, but not enough for a liner passage. The *Constellation* also carried cargo, ferrying silk and spice to the west, and everything from typewriters to trucks back to New Zealand and Australia.

Sheep grazed in pens on the main deck. Elsie mourned them extravagantly. "Look at them, poor things. Doomed to die, one by one, to feed the native crew. And looking as if they knew it." Kay doubted the mutton was only for the crew. Aren did not like it, so she hoped it was not their only food. She pointed out the ducks on the poop deck, and they were a great hit with Elsie and Julia.

Besides the livestock, between decks, and wherever there was a nook or cranny, coal for the engines was piled—tons of it, the heaps covered with tarpaulin. Francis had said that the journey of a steamer was a constant tug-of-war between coal and time: will there be enough coal to get the ship to shore, or will the woodwork have to be fed into the furnace? Once in a while shipmasters had had to pull up and burn the floorboards to get to harbour.

❧

When the telegram broke the news that Kay had gone, and where, Thea quarrelled with Francis for the first time in their married life.

Dropping the telegram on the dining table as if it burned her, she mowed into the drawing room, where Francis was sitting with the morning paper. She was already shouting incoherently.

Francis, pointing at Roddy's brown foot deep in the window seat, motioned to her to temper her voice, but she could suffer no restraint, telling herself in a lightning flare that Roddy ought to know what had happened—in fact she was sure he *did* know, for he and Kay were always hand in glove, always running away into the orchard to keep secrets—

But what did that matter, it was Francis who must have made this wild goose chase possible, must have funded it, and encouraged Kay, and—

Had he seen Aren? Had he gone to Halifax behind her back and—

Thea stood still, her legs shaking with rage and despair. She could not remember ever being so angry. In a wild rush that felt like freedom after chains, she flew out at Francis hammer and tongs, at last, about why Aren had not been happy and what had happened to make everything so difficult. At first it was a flood of mixed-up words, all *no* and *why* and *how could you* and *what gave you the right*—but once that first spate slowed, she shook her head sharply and found her sense again, and stopped Francis when he made to answer.

"Don't you dare say that we should not have taken him from that island, as Kay believes. He would have starved—you know those men were at the breaking point. Even so, he was never strong, because of that early deprivation—*that* is to blame for his TB, and perhaps he had already been exposed to the bacillus, and would have died of it all unknowing in that backward place. And if we had not taken him? Who else might they have sold him to next, for ship's boy or worse!"

He said nothing.

"Answer me!" she demanded. Her voice was unrecognizable to herself.

But Francis would not fight. He stood on the drawing room carpet like a schoolboy called to account, and refused to quarrel.

She battered herself on the blank wall of his refusal, crying, "He was happy with us—do you question that? On all our voyages, he was the happiest boy, until the war— It all went wrong when you left us to go to France."

That was something she had never said before. She had not questioned Francis's decision at the time. But it was a decision—he had enlisted, he had chosen to go, although at an age when most men would have stayed to support their family. Leaving her and

Kay to manage everything alone, without word or letter for months at a time, not knowing if he ever would come back, and all for some idea of glory.

"No, not that," Francis said. "Don't go blaming the war. The trouble was there before I left. I myself sorted out a few things at the school, if you recall."

"Between voyages!"

Because he was never there, not there to help her, or to guide his sons. Roddy was all right, would be all right because he was one of them, a Grant, and a Wetmore. It was Aren who had needed a father.

But it was she who had insisted that he go to school, had made him go when he'd asked to please stay home. He had to finish his education properly, and learn to be with other boys. Then Roddy's failing health had claimed her attention, and his weak leg, and the brace for all that time, the worry over whether he would ever walk. Aren was always so patient and good with him, was one of the reasons Roddy was stronger now—was Roddy to lose his brother, too?

Francis did not answer her. He did not speak at all, letting her run her anger out.

Bile rose again in the back of her throat. This anger business was horrible, she wished she was free of it. But Kay's telegram rose in her mind again, and her head went up in flames again, so that it was all she could do to stand still and not lash out in every direction. How much anger had she been swallowing all this time?

She shuddered again under the onslaught of old time, old fears, and flung at Francis, desiring to spear him in place on Aunt Lydia's Turkey carpet, "Anyone could see he was unhappy, yet you have not lifted a hand to help him, except by sending him away to Halifax and helping him to a life of hardship and suffering."

He did not waver at her attack, but stood solid and calm, as if her madness gave him stability. "Apprenticeship is hardly that!" he said. "It is a straight path to a good career, for a lad who knows the ropes."

In her fury, Thea did not address the instigating incident—the reprehensible behaviour of the King family over boy-and-girl foolishness, or any of the miseries she knew Aren had suffered at school, the Acadian boys throwing stones at him and calling names that first year, or the bad business of Ernest Bain and the stolen books—but skipped back to earlier wrongs.

"You wanted to take him for a cabin boy—" That first day, she meant, the day they bought him. Found him.

"Yes, and it might have been the better for him."

"There was no reason to separate him from us, from his family—" She bit her lip until it bled, thinking of having separated Aren from his original family. As maybe Francis was thinking now.

"There is always reason to separate a boy from his family," Francis said. Comforting her, even in this whirlwind. "I was ten when I went to sea, and I did very well."

"You were a sturdy boy. His lungs were compromised, and he could not thrive. As well take Roddy!"

"Aren was—is—much sturdier than you believe. A wild child, and a man now, fitted to survive. So is Roddy—he'd do very well in a ship's company. You underrate his strength."

Her hands had made themselves into fists, sharp-knuckled weapons. She locked them into a hand clasp so they would not fly out at him. "If you do it, if you work hole-and-corner with Roddy, knowing what he suffers—"

"No, no," he protested. "I would not go against you in that way, I swear it." He was almost laughing, perhaps readying himself to catch her fists if need be.

But her fine fire had burnt down. She turned away, sick at heart, unable to argue with his fixed idea. "You should not have encouraged Kay."

"I did no encouraging. I made her safer in what she was determined to do. You'd sooner have had her ship as a stewardess?"

"No!"

"Indeed. There was little enough I could do for them, in any case."

"Do you even know what ship they are on?"

"The *Constellation*, bound for Wellington. Cable them on board, if you like to throw your coin away, or a letter will reach port before them. Write to Pitcairn and it might catch them earlier, if you like."

That was an absurdity. Half the time ships could not approach Pitcairn and had to hand on the mailbag, untouched, to the next ship.

But Thea went off anyway, to go upstairs and write to Kay in this first burst of urgent disapproval. She would wait a day before posting the letter, but she could start a blistering note tonight with all her rage intact.

At the newel post she turned back to tell Francis another thing; turning, she saw back into the drawing room, where Roddy had crept out of the window seat and slid his hand into his father's.

"It was a good thing that you helped Kay," she heard Roddy say in a low voice. "I wished I could go along, but she said I was too young still, I must finish school."

"It's a tough life, old man," Francis said, cupping the dear head with his other hand.

Thea turned again and went upstairs.

5

At Sea

May 21, a beautiful shining day. It had taken a week to go from New York to Panama. There was a sameness to the days on a steamer that Kay could not remember under sail, when every day was changeable, dependent on the wind.

In the ladies' bath she found a great horned beetle living under the slats by the tub, but refrained from mentioning it to the American girls, who would have squawked. Perhaps it was only lively in the very early morning, when she had her own bath. It stayed for some days, clicking and rushing, and then was gone. She hoped it had not gone down the drain and into the sea, poor thing.

She was lonely, although she mostly preferred to be alone. She worried about Aren. He usually managed to sneak away for half an hour in a day; once, he fell asleep on his little bit of matting on the floor of her cabin, and she stayed perfectly still for an hour to let him rest. He was working hard in the belly of the ship, maybe harder than he had worked for a while, but he showed her the muscle in his arm proudly, and he did not seem at all unhappy to be down among the workingmen.

So Kay stayed above in the strange limbo of passenger life. Sometimes she talked to the American girls and sometimes she kept aloof.

The Canal made an excitement in the sameness, and she stood
at the railing with Julia while they waited and waited to go through.
For a while they were held up in the bay that served as the waiting
room for the Canal, twisting in and out between the boats. Then
the *Constellation* sidled up to load again at the coaling docks outside
the town of Colón, and the passengers were allowed off for a brief
shopping trip. Kay was persuaded to go ashore with Elsie and Julia
on a quest for sweet exotic treats. After a donkey-cart ride through
sweltering, dusty streets, they carried slabs of chocolate and long
packages of cakes back to the girls' cabin, which they had made
homelike by littering it with scarves and gaily coloured lingerie.
Sitting on the rug as Elsie and Julia chattered, Kay felt like a
donkey among show ponies. Elsie read them the draft of her article. She was a flamboyant writer, partial to phrases like *the rose-light
of a tropical morning.*

With a slight headache from the chocolate, Kay found a postcard and posted it to Marion before they left the dock at Colón,
saying she missed her, which would probably seem flamboyant to
Marion. The postcard had a startling painting of a swaying Spanish
lady, to give Murray Judge and the Krito-sophians something to
discuss at the next meeting.

She should have written properly to Mr. Brimner, but that was
a longer proposition. She drew out and reread his last letter, so as
to have an answer ready to post from Wellington.

> The movement of the sea today recalls an old note I found
> in Prior's notebook on waves, while he was recuperating at
> Eastbourne, one wintry English summer: "The laps of
> running foam striking the sea-wall double on themselves
> and return in nearly the same order and shape in which
> they came. This is mechanical reflection and is the same as
> optical: indeed *all nature* is mechanical, but then it is not
> seen that mechanics contain that which is beyond
> mechanics."

I see that daily here—how the waves double on themselves and return in nearly the same order and shape in
which they came. Beyond mechanics.

This doubling recalls Prior to my mind, of course, but
it also recalls you and Aren (and your sister and Francis)
to my mind—how we double on ourselves and return,
return, and how the waves are usefully able to be bent into
many such metaphorical shapes to convey the wishes and
desires of humans for the company of each other.

The first time she read that, last month, she did not know they
would be returning.

But you must know I am not lonely here on Haʻano, nor in
the least alone! My doorstep is stomped at every hour
with some visitor or other, and I am glad to be of service
and equally glad to be left alone as the evening shutters
quickly down.

Here is Sione now, pounding on my door to say the
cricket game is on, and I must go and bowl. Our main
expense with the school is cricket bats; please thank your
sister and Francis for their kind Christmas gift and tell
them every penny went toward replacing broken bats.

Late that night, Aren tapped at her cabin door and slipped inside,
but he would not even sit, saying he would soon be missed down
below. She gave him the chocolate she had got him on the excursion, and he thanked her but said he would keep it in her sink
cupboard.

"It gets so infernally hot down there, it would melt in a moment,"
he said.

She searched his face again for signs of strain or misery, and he
laughed at her and doused his head under her cold tap and dirtied

her last clean towel. He told her not to eat his chocolate under pain of death, and went away again.

Thinking of Marion Hilton, perhaps, made Kay dream of Corcovado. She hardly ever dreamed of land. In dusk or dawnlight she climbed and climbed, following Marion's white lawn dress, her brown legs and half boots up through a green sea of leaves and up again, up to the highest promontory, Aren unseen behind her following too, climbing too fast for his poor lungs.

All the next day, the ship swayed and hesitated through the Canal, and Kay stood as long as she could at the rail to watch this narrow wonder of engineering, of man's strange imagination and determination, that had cut a continent in two and saved who knew how many boys from drowning at Cape Horn. At last, at evening, they were out, past the peaks of Darien and sailing free, into the midst of a blinding, stinging sunset shower, out into the blue Pacific—on the other side of the world.

Besides the girls and Mrs. Johns, there were a sprinkling of other passengers. A man called Johnny Ace, owner of a troupe of famous performing poodles, was taking his wife and brother home to Australia because he had not heard a kookaburra laugh for seven years. Mrs. Ace, a short woman with a beaming smile, was almost entirely silent; the younger Mr. Ace, they discovered, was not sullen but only cripplingly shy. Johnny Ace made the dogs perform on the hatches one day for Elsie and Julia to see; but most of the tricks required balancing, and that day the ship leaned to every wave, so it wasn't a great success. The dogs were mostly kept penned, because they were too valuable to risk on deck. They were not very friendly, and seemed to regard themselves as professionals who had no need to slum by fawning like regular pets. They made Kay sad anyhow, missing her Pilot.

There was a dark-haired, saturnine fellow called Cliffe who wrote scenarios for the movies. When he wasn't whistle-snoring in a deck chair, he was forever trying to remember the name of a poem that sounded like a French patisserie. Elsie teased him at every meal with various possible names—"The Croissant Heart" or "*Brisée, Brisée, Brisée,* on thy cold grey stones, O Sea . . ."—and spent hours coming up with new ones, taking it as a challenge, but Mr. Cliffe seemed to be seriously disturbed by not being able to recall it. He felt it was a sign of the wilting of the brain tissues, and he worried that he would not be able to write any more scenarios. Kay found him incomprehensible and his self-dramatizing a little false.

The last passenger, Mrs. Mannering, was a missionary going out to join her husband in India. Elsie called her the Early Victorian. "Not that she was born in the Victorian era, for she is young and pretty, look how those swooping braids tremble about her face. But she weeps and swoons and is afraid of mice—in *this* day and age, I ask you!"

Kay could not imagine how Mrs. Mannering would manage in India, if a mere mouse upset her. Her conversation consisted of *praise God* and *no thank you.*

All those passengers sat at the other long table, leaving Kay and the two American girls at the captain's table with Mrs. Johns and whichever of his men were on table duty that evening. The captain quite often begged off and dined in his quarters, not being a naturally gregarious man. He reminded Kay of the woodchuck in the back garden of Francis's house on Elm Street, who had staked out a certain territory by the creek and stalked it every evening, not fighting unless made to fight.

After finishing her seafoam cake, Kay got up to leave the table, asking, as was correct, "May I be excused, Captain?"

Mrs. Johns, recovered from her *mal de mer*, enlightened the American girls as to dining protocol aboard ship. "It is from the mess, you know," she fluted. "You will be acknowledged by the senior officer present with a nod or a reply such as *Very well,* and you may then leave the mess, remembering to put your rolled napkin back in its place."

Behind her, Kay heard the captain get up noisily from his own chair and stomp off. There were no reused napkins on the *Constellation*, wherever else Mrs. Johns might have shipped.

Many nights, they slept on deck. The passengers were allowed—encouraged—to do that once the ship got into the hot latitudes. The first time it was suggested, Kay joined the other passengers lining up at their deck chairs to be bundled into blankets by Mr. Handy and the other deck steward. Each one in turn stood waiting while extra padding was added to the chair, then was eased back and tucked in all round by swift, practised hands. It was a little mannequin factory, assembling sleeping Eaton Beauty dolls and lying them in their boxes.

As the stewards worked their way toward her, Kay found herself tense and could not think why. But once she was wrapped and supine like the others, she realized that it was ominously reminiscent of the TB ward in New York, where she had only been allowed to visit Aren once. And possibly earlier wards, which she had not thought of for ages. After that first night, Kay did not sleep in her deck chair like the others; she waited until the coast was clear and went up to the lifeboat above, where Aren had arranged a nest for them, using cushions from the stewards' secret trove. There they lay with the cover folded back, listening to the desultory conversation of the passengers on the deck below, and the Indian sailors at their prayers.

"We are Seatons now," Aren said, and she laughed and stuck one leg over the oarlock. "He was a man of many ways. I remember the day of meeting him, the day I came."

"Yes," she said. "I remember that day too."

"That was a day." He was sitting upright, staring out to the barely marked horizon.

After a moment, she asked, "Do you remember other people, I mean, from—before us?" She knew he did not like to talk of that. But perhaps they must, now.

"I remember. An old man, who taught me things. I do not have a name for him."

She waited, as quiet and still as she might be.

"A man who was my . . . A man coming into the boat, holding my knee when I bled. And a woman."

Kay was so sorry she had asked. She turned her head away and buried it in the cushions. It was too much to make him say those things out loud.

The next night, Kay brought oranges from the dining room and the chocolate from Colón. She was not sure Aren would come, but his hand appeared at the edge of the lifeboat, and then his dear cropped head, and all the rest of him unfolding over the edge and collapsing into the cushions, sighing with tiredness.

She peeled the oranges, letting the orange oil spray up into the black tropical sky, and handed Aren segments one by one, alternating with chocolate. The moon had risen over the dark border of the water, its road just setting out toward them. No wind that night.

Below, she heard Elsie say, "Look, look, Julia—the sea and the heavens, they are like two black bowls touching edge to edge."

Elsie really ought to be a travel writer, Kay decided. She ought to publish that article and then write many books, and make Julia go with her all over the world instead of letting her marry her stolid fiancé, to whose photo Kay had taken an instant dislike.

It was very hot.

The head chef came out on deck, a hulking, white, pasty man, like a great soft puppet made out of cake, a damp cigarette smouldering in his mouth. He walked across to the bridge with a tray for the duty officers. On his way back, he paused below the lifeboat and one beefy arm reached up, pale, frond-like fingers proffering a dish of ice cream with two spoons.

"Thanks, Frans," whispered Aren.

The chef said, "No need to sank me." He was a man who enjoyed procuring happiness.

Kay had had ice cream at dinner, so she pushed the bowl back when Aren offered it, and he dug in willingly. Despite his claim to the freedom of the refrigerators, he was not eating enough.

It was irritating that some people were naturally skinny and others plump. Kay's own plumpness was a certain source of sorrow to her, mostly as it stood opposed to Thea's slenderness. On the other hand, she did maintain a certain discipline. If I was not so very careful, she thought, I would weigh five hundred pounds—nobody ever takes into account how hard I've worked to be only *this* plump.

On the deck below the lifeboat, the girls were laughing together. Elsie had a game going that Julia had a hopeless passion for Mr. Cliffe, and was giving her advice on how to attract the Older Man. It was not fitting, Kay thought. And then thought what a prude and a prig she had turned out to be.

She hated everything. She hated most of all that she had a deck chair with her name on it and Aren had a face covered in engine grease. It was the way of the world, and there was no way she could see to get out of it, but that too made her despair; a person of some education, willing to think, should be able to find a way.

Aren scraped his spoon around the edge of the bowl and lay back on the pillows.

"What do you suppose it will cost to charter a boat in Fiji?" she asked him.

He rolled his head away from her.

"Will a hundred dollars do it, do you think?"

He glanced back at her and away again, before saying, "*I* don't know! Do you suppose I am an expert in boat charters?"

"Well, there must be someone you could ask, someone who would know down below, or the mate, or someone?"

"Stop talking," he said. "Stop talking about things! Since we cannot do anything about it until Wellington at the earliest—and the only things to do are to charter or buy passage, and we don't know and can't find out yet which is going to be possible—could we just not talk?"

So Kay stopped, even though the thinking would not ever stop inside her own head.

In the steam room, where the passengers went when the bath was not sufficient to remove the grime of the steamer's gritty smoke, steam bathers sat on benches in a series of white-tiled rooms, each warmer than the last. The final room was so hot it was simply wreaths of smoke. Alone in the far corner of the last room one afternoon, Kay saw the American girls come in, laughing with each other over some remembered joke and dancing with their towels like vaudeville girls. Between her lashes Kay saw a face appearing in the steam when Elsie's towel unfastened, the face of Elsie's body—the nipples dark pupils glancing from round white eyes, the tiny navel nose, the dark triangular mouth below.

If I were a man, she thought, that is the form and shape I would choose for a wife. So it was a good thing she was not a man. Because Elsie would not be a good wife at all, she was too talkative and too fond of a joke.

Thinking again, Kay thought as she had before that she would not be chosen for any man's wife herself—she was too ornery, too fond of her own opinion, and she did not have that smiling loveliness of body that might make up for a general prickliness of disposition.

She sat very still. The girls soon got too hot and left without noticing her, and she sat on a little longer, although she was by then so much steamed that her fingers were wrinkly.

In the ladies' change room, she stood by the mirror half-dressed (combinations on for modesty's sake, and also to avoid looking at the undressed sofa cushion of her body in the glass). Her braids had matted in the steam and heat, it would take an hour to undo and brush and untangle and rebraid them, and they would still be dun-coloured and plain. Mrs. Mannering the Early Victorian had beautiful glossy braids, great ropes of bronze silk bound about her brow, more pre-Raphaelite than Victorian. She would be a great success with the older Krito-sophians. None of the girls in Yarmouth had bobbed hair, nor would for ages. Fashions from elsewhere always took years longer to filter through the shrouds.

She pulled one braid out straight, away from her head. Two feet long. The manicure tools were on the counter there, and a larger pair of scissors in the sewing box. Without thinking much more than that, she took the big scissors and lopped off her braid, close to her head.

That was one. Like Virginia Archibald when she burned her hair, should she leave the other side long for a week?

She held out the other braid and set the scissors to it, as the door opened behind her and Elsie appeared in the glass.

Afraid that she might try to stop her—but it would be no use anyway, since one braid was gone—Kay sawed at the braid from an angle and managed to cut it through. "There," she said. She dropped the two braids into the wastebasket and turned to find her dress and stockings.

Elsie stared at her, struck dumb.

Kay slipped her white lawn dress over her head—how light and airy her head felt!—and shook out her hair again. She looked in the mirror. Well, it was not elegant, but she had her manicure scissors in her cabin. She would get Aren to straighten it out for her. Perhaps a little fringe would be nice. She gave Elsie a friendly smile, and left.

All the way down the corridor she was smiling, she could not stop for joy. Now she could be herself. Not like them, but like herself. The air floated around her neck!

She had no regrets. Her short hair felt lovely in the back, free and cool. It made a nice shape to change the roundness of her face; and, released from its braid, the hair began to curl, as it had not since she was a child.

When she met him at the lifeboat in the evening, Aren liked it too. He fluffed it up at the nape of her neck and laughed at her pleasure.

She realized that she was vain and foolish, but she did not even mind. She was better, lighter, now. "I am trying to be myself as well as I can," she told him.

"That's a full-time job," Aren said.

Abruptly, the weather soured. The sea rose up on its tail and raged like a pig in a tantrum, drawing an unbearable squealing of metal and rope even from the sturdy *Constellation*. The first wild night, Elsie and Julia still slept on deck to avoid the close heat of their cabin, but during the night the wind tore the blankets from their cots, and at the breakfast table Elsie made a great tale of how they had waked up clutching, the blankets slipping and slithering across the decks like great water snakes.

Kay did not know why the stewards had not bustled to gather them in; perhaps they had not believed the girls meant to stay out all night. But it was exciting, to be out in real weather. She heard Seaton sending her back inside from a storm in the forties below Australia, his cracked voice crying from his lifeboat, *Lubber!*

Safe in the coffee room, Elsie read from the draft of her article: "*We rescued them, and later woke again as our cots raced each other into the scuppers, and our poor cold feet stuck out over the rail and caught an icy blast of wind and rain. We rolled and rolled, we pitched and tossed. One kept saying to oneself*"—and here she sang—"'*When the ship goes* wop *with a wiggle between, When the steward falls into the soup tureen.*'"

Kay laughed. This storm *was* like that song. It was all comedy, slapstick: the wild whirl of the propeller leaping high out of the water, and the occasional crash of dishes sliding from the pantry shelves, always followed by a dismal moan from some responsible steward or other. It went on and on. She didn't mind the storm at all.

Even with the comic relief that Elsie provided (not from her writing, but from the infectious and understanding hilarity that welled up like a spring in her), Kay felt dislodged, disjointed. Perhaps it was only the remnant of the storm, the wild variations of pressure. Or maybe it was because the aftermath of the storm on an aging vessel meant that Aren was stuck below decks constantly, fighting breakdowns with the engineers, and Kay was lonely.

She used to be good at being by herself. She'd lost the long view she had in childhood, sitting in the attic window or at the lip of the long coulee; she'd lost the solitude-in-company of life on the *Morning Light* and the companionable aloneness of being a child with Aren, the protective freedom of the enclosing ramparts of school books that opened into another, wider world. In Nova Scotia, in Yarmouth, everything was close, too close to breathe.

She had not talked to Aren in three days. This had to be remedied.

She brushed her cropped hair with both hands and went down into the hold, where she spent a frustrating hour winding through metal corridors and tapping on doors with gradually lessening strength of purpose, being directed and redirected through to successively lower decks, until finally one dark-greased oval door opened a crack to emit a great bellow of heat, and Aren's face looked out, and hissed at her to go away, that he was fine, he would find her later.

Of course he was. He was not in hell or Gogol's lower depths but only helping a steamship run, after all, so she went up to her cabin and washed her hands and face and lay down on her bunk to have a short weep over her own useless stupidity.

Then she found that she had got her period, and some of the interior turmoil and self-recrimination was explained. She was still a woman, subject to her body, even if her hair was short.

One evening at sunset, when the wind had blown forever and there was no warm corner left to hide in, land appeared on the starboard bow, tumbled white blocks on the horizon. The mountains of New Zealand. Elsie waxed rhapsodic, addressing the "snow-capped mountains rising out of the sea, far, far off, but coming nearer." And then scribbled that down too.

The sun came up next morning, as suns have done for eons, making a spectacle of itself and of the sea. Kay pulled herself out of her bunk and dressed in a flash, and went up to see what all this shining was about.

"It's like the hymn—*Rise, crowned with light,*" Elsie sang, while Julia stood silent, transfixed, at the railing.

They were going into Lyttelton Harbour, between cliffs, the sea and cliffs equally opulent, the sea plated in pearly gold from the early sun, the hills veiled with yellow gorse.

Elsie sang on: "*Exalt thy towering head and lift thine eyes! See heaven its sparkling portals wide display, and break upon thee in a flood of day.*"

Julia joined her, taking the tenor line. "*See a long race thy spacious courts adorn: see future sons, and daughters yet unborn, in crowding ranks on every side arise, demanding life, impatient for the skies.*"

"I don't suppose you would know that one," Elsie said kindly to Kay. "It's Lutheran—American, like me and Julia."

Unable to resist, Kay lifted her own chin and sang, "*See barbarous nations at thy gates attend, walk in thy light and in thy temple bend.*" It had been the anthem last Easter, when Virginia Archibald had for a few weeks persuaded her to join the choir. That had not been a success; Kay's voice had volume but not beauty, and she could not bear to sing in company. But when Miss Coots the organist fell ill on Maundy Thursday, Kay took her place and saved the day, in a minor way.

"Derived from an eclogue of Pope's," Julia said, confident in her American education.

"Derived from Virgil," Kay corrected her, and then wished she had not. But she pushed doggedly on, explaining, because it was quite funny really: "An eclogue of Virgil's celebrating the expected birth of a longed-for child who was to bring good fortune—but the baby Virgil expected was the child of Marc Antony and Octavia."

The girls looked at her blankly.

Oh, Mr. Brimner, Mr. Brimner, you have not fitted me for ordinary chat.
This interesting footnote to history made Julia and Elsie stop talking to Kay, and she deserved it. Nobody needs to know everything
you know, she told herself.

She stood alone, watching New Zealand come into view.
Unfolding hills rolling down, down, nudging the sea with their
knees. Like the softer parts of Nova Scotia, along the south shore,
but with even less barrier between land and sea.

Behind her, Elsie's pleasant trilling voice took up the thread
again and pointed out to Julia, as she wrote her notes, how the
sunrise was lighting the tops of the hills with crimson, leaving the
hidden parts in darkness "like valleys of mystery or death—look,
the glow, creeping down, on and on, until the world is shining!"

She was such a flowery, overflowing person. At first Kay had
disliked all that orotundity, but she had come to enjoy it, and
would have liked to tell Elsie so. But it was impossible to tell
people what one admired in them; or inadvisable, in case one's
enthusiasm put them off.

The inner harbour approached, and then they were in its shade,
the bare black outlines of the hills ("crowned," Elsie said, "with red
and gold"), and then the sun came up over the tallest hill and
everything was both glowing and ordinary.

Kay went below to find some breakfast.

6

Wellington

A day later, after refuelling at Lyttelton, they sailed into Wellington, on the North Island, the end of their voyage on the *Constellation*. Mr. Cliffe the screenwriter came up on deck that morning looking radiantly happy. Elsie asked him what had happened to make this change and he said, "*Lalla Rookh!*"

"Of course!" cried Elsie, and Julia said, "For us, that name will belong to you forever."

Then it was Kay's turn not to know things, but Elsie kindly told her, aside, that *Lalla Rookh* was a terrible junky Oriental-romance poem, very old and stale, that she was better off not knowing. Kay felt forgiven.

The bustle of disembarking took them all unprepared, even though they'd seen the land approaching for a day. The girls rushed down to finish packing, and Kay went after them more slowly, having less to pack. The air was sweet and clean here, and it would be good to get off this boat.

At the poste restante in Wellington, as well as the bank draft Francis had promised, there were letters from Nova Scotia, one for Kay and another for Aren. Thea's blue-spiked handwriting gave Kay a deep sway of vertigo, from missing her sister, however much she dreaded opening the letter.

> Dear Kay, although it pains me to call you "dear" at this moment, for I am very gravely disappointed

There she had crossed out ~~disappointed~~ and written *Angry*, with a capital *A*.

> Angry with you. With Francis too, believe me, but I will not speak of that.
> And with Aren, for agreeing to this very foolish plan, and for leaving his post in Halifax. It took considerable arranging for Francis to find him that berth and it reflects badly on him when Aren drops everything to run to the other end of the earth on a wild goose chase.
> It is all so useless! you don't know what pain you may be letting him in for, or how sad you will cause him to be, perhaps for the rest of his life. I do not know why you can never be persuaded to leave well alone but always must go prying into things and trying to discover the roots of things.
> But that is not at all what I want to tell you.
> Since you have done this ill-judged thing, you are to keep a close guard over Aren and never leave him, <u>nor abandon him to the good graces of some strangers.</u>

Kay laughed at the irony of that, and again at Thea's furious, oblivious underlining, which had scratched right through the paper.

> If I could come haring after you, I would, but I cannot leave Francis nor Roddy—and then there is Aunt Lydia, who needs sameness and quiet and good nursing.

She won't get that from Lena Hubbard, Kay thought. But she was glad (wasn't she?) that she had not told Thea about Lena man-handling the poor old body.

> You will remember that I have been writing to Dorothy Fruelock all this time—she is back in the village of Pangai, widowed now; her daughters married one after another, and only Pansy is left to keep her mother company.
>
> I did not mention it before, and have only mentioned it to_ you now, but before Rev. Fruelock passed on, they spent some intervening years in the Diocese of Papua, serving on Palau and the Sonsorol islands, one of which you will remember is Pulo Anna. She has news of Aren's people. I have written to ask her to talk to you if you think it wise to see her.
>
> And I do beg you to consider well whether or not it is_ wise. Aren has a loving family and home in us, and for good or ill we are the only family he truly remembers. We have seen him through sickness and health, and have loved him all this time.

Well, Kay would not argue with Thea about any of that. Good intent—was it enough? Kay did not think so any longer. What news could this be, that Mrs. Fruelock had?

Thea expostulated and condemned and lectured and prayed—even wept, it looked like from the blots on page three—and finally arrived at acceptance of the journey, exhorting Kay to make certain that Aren had suitable clothing and was well supplied with every ointment and remedy for malaria, coughs, fevers, bruising, et cetera. Aren had been given a similar list to supply to Kay, includ-ing making sure that she ate her greens and roughage, "for other-wise her system simply ceases to function," and recommending Jervin's cod liver oil for such an eventuality.

Kay wrote her sister a careful reply, promising to take every care of Aren and to make certain he knew that they were his real family—which she knew to be both wrong and true. She wrote down all the things she had been thinking as they sailed, until it seemed to her that she could write nothing more. She signed the letter affectionately, knowing it would be many weeks before Thea could read her reasoning, and hoped, in a postscript, *that my dearest sister will forgive me, if I cannot agree with your thinking.* And then added another, *p.p.s. And that you will also forgive me if you cannot agree with mine.*

Aren came in to find her in the hotel's writing room, and handed her a sealed letter to enclose in her packet. "I have promised to keep you regular," he said. He caught the ink-eradicator bottle she threw at him, and went off whistling.

She did not know whether or not to tell him what Thea had said about Mrs. Fruelock. She would think about that.

They had a week to wait in Wellington for the next steamer, the *Tofua*, which would take them to Nuku'alofa, then up to Ha'apai to Pangai, to meet Mr. Brimner. If he got Kay's cable and was still alive, which she told herself was not sensible to think about. Doing them one last favour, Captain Hilton had cabled ahead to reserve a cabin on the *Tofua* for Kay; the returned fare for Aren's passage from Halifax paid for his. He consented to a cabin, but he handed Kay fifty dollars, his pay for working on the *Constellation*, and would not take it back. With the bank draft Francis had sent and the money she had left, that would let them find some way onward, Kay felt sure. Although she could not yet imagine what way.

Aren had come out of the ship's refrigerator rooms in a deeply filthy condition. The first order of business was to get him thoroughly cleaned. The little town of Wellington had proper steam baths; Kay looked him over the first time, and sent him through again.

As they were walking up Cuba Street after Aren's second time through the baths, they met Elsie and Julia.

Kay saw how surprised they were to find her with a young man, and for a flashing instant also saw, in the angled window of a shop—as if outside her body, as if through Elsie's eyes—herself and Aren standing together on the grey street, the same height, with the same guarded expression. A compact, nicely made young man with a cap of clean black hair and a calm face, standing with a girl he knew and trusted. Her short, free hair and the quietude she had learned from him made her look like him, like someone who could be trusted.

Strengthened by that, she grinned at the girls, saying, "This is my brother, Aren—Aren, Julia and Elsie sat at my table on the *Constellation*. Aren worked his passage over in the engine room," she added, daring those girls to say something wrong.

"Well, Aren!" said Elsie. "Pleased to meet you!"

"Captain Bathurst mentioned your brother on the very first day," Julia said, smiling. "But I instantly forgot—how nice to meet you finally," she said. She put out her hand.

All right, they had done pretty well. We can still be friends, Kay thought.

"Do you plan to stay in New Zealand for some time?" Aren asked, after the hand shaking had been accomplished.

Elsie made a face, and Julia said firmly, "Yes, we do."

"Because Julia wants a rest from seafaring," Elsie said, "and I have to file some copy with my paper or I'll lose the whole reason for coming."

"And also the payment," Julia reminded her.

"So we're here for a month, but then—on to Samoa!"

"We have never been to Samoa," Aren said. "I envy you."

"We're going to Tonga on the *Tofua*, a week from tomorrow," Kay said.

"Oh, Tonga! And Fiji too? Our ship—what is it, Julia? the *Matua*, I think?—stops at both islands, but we won't stay on. We're heading for Stevenson's grave, you know."

Kay did know, having been told early in the voyage what the end point was, but Aren had never heard. "Why Stevenson?" he asked Elsie.

"Oh—everything! His life, his vision, *Treasure Island*."

"*Dr. Jekyll and Mr. Hyde* for me," Julia said.

"I learned to read from *Treasure Island*," Aren said.

Julia said, "It is a very good primer." She took Kay's arm and they all set off to walk together along the broad pounded-dirt sidewalk. "Are you staying at the Royal Oak?" That was the hotel where the *Constellation*'s cart had deposited passengers after disembarking.

"We must move today," Kay said. "It is above our budget."

Elsie clapped her hands and said, "Come with us, then! We're moving up into the hills this afternoon, to a small inn called the Blue Moon, recommended by a woman at my paper. It's a quarter the price and all-found, and it looks sweetly pretty, as my aunts would say."

The landlady looked doubtful about a coloured guest at first, so that Kay wished to smack her face, but with Julia and Elsie's introduction (and perhaps at a higher rate—Kay could not tell and decided not to ask) they were able to get lodging at the Blue Moon. Kay and Aren had two little rooms side by side, each almost filled by platform cots with mosquito netting, like beds in Bali. As soon as he'd dropped his sea-chest in a corner, Aren took himself off into the garden out the glass door that showed a path into the hills, and Kay let him go.

Julia and Elsie were waiting in the shadowy hall when she came out of Aren's room.

"Mrs. Thorpe was horrible," Julia said.

"There is a lot of that around," Kay said. She wondered what Julia had to say about it.

"It's worse in the States," Julia said. "But things are going to change."

"Oh yes?"

Elsie looked at her. "You're prickly about it, of course. Was your brother adopted, or are you blood relations?"

Kay looked at her. "It does not matter which, but he was adopted."

Julia said, "It does not matter which."

And then Kay went to her own room and lay down on the little bed and thought of as little as she could for a while.

While they waited for the *Tofua* to steam down, they spent their days paddling up the small river near the Blue Moon. Elsie and Julia said it reminded them of England, overhung with willow trees and lined along the banks with wattle fence. The view along the water beneath the willow branches did look like pictures Kay had seen of the joys of punting on the Thames.

Elsie boasted of her skill with little boats, and indeed she did not upset hers. When the flatboat wallowed in a shallow stretch, a couple of small boys came out and helped Aren tow them up the rapids. On the way back, Elsie made them stop for tea (which came with hot buttered scones, as if they really were in England) in a tea house set back from the bank of the river. Most of the people they met in Wellington still called England *home*; yet most of those had been away from England twenty or thirty years and had no idea of going back. Used to the same sort of thing in Nova Scotia, Kay had no sympathy with this colonial view. She thought the sooner these New Zealanders got over making their country a copy of England, the better. The American girls thought it was awfully quaint.

They saw only a few Maori people. The one or two they passed walking on the roads looked to Kay like people she had known in the West. For a few nights she dreamed of being back at Blade Lake, until in one dream Miss Ramsay chased her and Annie down the upper hallway, where they found Mary—she woke then and would not think of it again nor dream again, although she could not go back to sleep.

After a while she got up and went out the glass door into the garden and walked slowly upward in the very early morning, before dawn was even picking at the edge of the mountains. The mountains loomed over everything here; that too reminded her of Blade Lake, although here they were even closer. Little, big: it was as if the mountains had zoomed in closer while she was sleeping, and had got into her dreams that way.

Aren stayed at the hotel peaceably enough, but he would not go for walks with Kay. She could not fault him for this. Here, he would not be taken for a Maori, or even for a Tongan, but for a Bornean or a Fijian—and decent clothing might not be enough to keep him from trouble.

She wished the boat would hurry up.

One afternoon, Elsie came in from a solitary row in the boat with a sad bruise on her cheek, telling a miserable story: "I'd moored at a bridge to walk up on the bank and have my tea, and just as I was getting back in to float away again, something hard hit me on the side of the head. It hurt, and I looked down—and there was a large stone in the bottom of the boat!"

Aren was angry. He wanted to go back to the bridge and find out who had hurt her, but Elsie would not let him go; she would not even tell him which branch of the little river she had been on.

"I was angry too, at first, and frightened," she admitted. "But true pilgrims are often stoned in foreign lands."

It was such a strange thing to have happened. Kay worried that it was because Elsie had been seen being friendly with Aren.

The day after the stone-throwing incident, the American girls decided to take the train to Auckland, planning to meet the *Matua* there instead. Elsie's desire to reach the gravestone of Robert Louis Stevenson baffled Kay, however much one might enjoy *Treasure Island*. In a rush of affectionate embraces, both promised to write to Kay and visit "when she was back at home" whenever that vague time and wherever that place might be.

She stood on the hotel steps watching them climb into the pony trap, thinking, Goodbye, then, who cares about you. But when their luggage was all loaded in and they turned to wave, she ran down the steps and kissed each one in turn, calling, *Goodbye, goodbye!* as the trap sped away.

Things were more peaceful after they left; she did not miss them after all. But she was surprised to hear herself saying things in their voices, or rising from a chair the way Julia did. She was a copycat, with no instinct for womanhood of her own.

Aren said they were good, kind girls she would do well to emulate, and would not listen when she told him how silly they often were. He wrote a long letter to Roddy with illustrations, including one of Elsie's boat with a great hole in it from the stone, with indignant imprecations at the stone thrower, so that Kay wondered if he might have liked Elsie, and was glad he was too young for her—because how might that have gone, between them?

Finally, the morning came for their own departure. Kay woke at dawn and went for a long walk in the pretty valley, and then sat on at the breakfast table among the eggshells, smoking a thin cigarette as she had learned to do from Julia. Her suitcase and the blue valise stood in the hall waiting for the cart.

At last she heard the wheels on the driveway, and Aren came with his sea-chest, and they rode down to the docks as the *Tofua* steamed up the bay.

The *Tofua* had a master rather than a captain. It did not matter, though, because passengers had no reason to speak to the officers of that ship; it being a dedicated passenger ship, they were kept quite separate. Aren and Kay became acquainted with several of the men, though, because one of their old friends was on board, Jimmy Giles from Christchurch, New Zealand, who had joined the *Morning Light* many years ago as a boy, after Arthur Wetmore was lost, and was now second engineer on the *Tofua*.

In his off-hours they had a good visit with him, in his preferred spot in the saloon bar, right at the rear of the ship on the top deck. The *Constellation* had had no such amenities. As they talked about

Aren's work on the refrigerators, Jimmy invited them both down to the engine room to have a look around.

It was nothing compared with the sail system of a barque, of course, but the *Tofua* was very interesting below decks, even though Kay could not make herself go down into the shaft tunnel. She peered into it obediently when Jimmy opened the hatch: a long, reddish-dark hole showing the whole structure of the hull, with the ribs and the actual bottom of the ship clearly visible. She put her hand out to a great round coupling with big bolts, until Jimmy Giles said "Hot!" and she snatched her hand back.

The coupling joined parts of the shaft together; Aren showed her how. "It must be very accurately aligned so there's no movement—the shaft is in a direct line from the engine crankshaft to the propeller." He was interested in all this! She had not understood that before.

They went back up to the saloon bar and Kay had another cocktail for the relief of not being in that long, rusted hole. It was good to see Jimmy firmly settled in the South Pacific now, happy on this banana boat run, with one brother to visit in Wallis and Futuna and another he saw more often, who lived in Ha'apai on the island of Lifuka, near Pangai village. Jimmy knew Mrs. Fruelock well, and was acquainted with Mr. Brimner. Both Jimmy's brothers were married to island women, and running fishing boats.

Jimmy told them about the *Tofua*'s life as a troop transport during the war, a thousand soldiers crammed into the space a hundred passengers now knocked around in. He was glad to hear that Francis had come through the war and was in good health, more or less. "More or less is how it is with most of us, Ma'am," he told Kay. He would not stop using *Ma'am* for her, which made her uncomfortable but clearly felt better for him.

The refitted *Tofua* was proud, even grand, for a small passenger ship. Each cabin had eiderdown quilts in tidy rolls on two bunks, which could be folded out of the way by day to make more room. The natty little cupboards and closet fitted Kay's clothes perfectly, and each room had the comfort of running water in a little hand basin. She was sad that this would not be home for very long, because she liked it almost as well as her cabin on the *Morning Light*.

The music room, which served as the main lounge, was nicely furnished with sofas and chairs made of sycamore wood and upholstered in rose-pink raised velvet. The ladies' lounge was also pinkish, and usually full of women playing cards—contract bridge was an addiction on this run. The dining room was plain but well lit, with white linens on small tables, room for a hundred passengers with no necessity for double seating. There was a barbershop, a clothes press service, a library and a doctor on board. And nothing to do but enjoy this opulence. Except, of course, it was not real luxury: this was the South Pacific, after all. Cockroaches and little green lizards raced over Kay's bunk, and she expected that at night rats would hold revel up and down the black-and-white tiles of the hall.

After her exploring, Kay fetched up at the starboard railing, staring east, away from the land, into the afternoon indigo of the waves in case she might see a whale or two, now they were in leviathan waters again.

Aren had gone below to be introduced to a few fellows by Jimmy Giles; Kay was all alone for the first time in a good while. She had not exactly belonged with Elsie and Julia, but they had been good company, and she did not expect she would ever know any people like them again. She turned from the rail and climbed steel stairs to the highest deck where passengers were allowed, and sat on the farthest forward bench she could find, taking off her hat to let the wind play in her cropped hair as it would.

It was not long before Aren found her there and sat quiet beside her. He put a hand to her elbow after a while, saying, "I keep looking for whales, but I have not seen any."

"We haven't been keeping watch—you were working too hard, on the *Constellation*, and I was distracted by those girls."

But they were likely to see some now. She scanned the waves, looking for darker patches.

He said, "I like it when your eyes squint because you are looking at far distances. Perhaps you need spectacles, though."

"Or a pair of smoked glasses, like Mr. Brimner had."

"You are beginning to look like yourself again," he said.

She hated it when Thea said that! But she did not mind it at all from Aren. That was unfair, except she knew Thea saw some imaginary self, the docile child she had never been except when sleeping, and Aren was seeing her without pretense. She smiled at him, her wind-chapped mouth stretching. "Let me guess: sunburnt and disapproving?"

He stood and reached for her hand. "Come take a turn around the promenade deck before dinner—five times around equals one mile," he reminded her.

So they walked two miles, and sat down to their brown soup with a good appetite.

They were not alone at their table; the stewards gave them different company each night. Tonight it was Miss Vera Pike, a tall, thin, mild and elderly Canadian, retired from teaching at the celebrated Bishop Strachan School in Ontario, on her way to Fiji to teach literature in the Anglican girls' school in Suva, and her arthritic older sister, Miss Pauline (introduced by Miss Vera as "the well-known watercolourist"), who would also teach, as an auxiliary. They seemed to see this next part of their lives as a reward for service, and were extremely cheerful—*most* interested to hear that Kay had lived at an Anglican school for the first part of her life, and even more intensely keen to know what it had been like to minister to the Indians.

Kay did not like talking about the school, and would not have disclosed it except that she hated to feel ashamed of it either, or to hide the facts of her life.

"Do tell us what it was like to live right amongst the Indians! I expect you had some grand adventures in the wilderness, and came to know some of them very well."

Kay's mind slid into the wolf willows, trailing after Annie, Annie turning and laughing, her face all soft, smooth lines, so much loved. She did not think of her so often anymore, her dear friend who had helped her to live, so it was good to say, "I did, yes, very well."

Miss Vera intervened. "We must not pester her, Pauline."

Kay did not dislike these exclaiming old ladies as she did the Krito-sophians. At least these two were trying to do some practical good, however strange it might seem, when you thought about it, to teach watercolour and English poesy to Fijian girls. And maybe some of those girls would love painting and poems.

"I have heard it said," Miss Pauline said, "that when the child lives with its parents, who are of course—" She broke off, and looked doubtfully around the table. "Forgive me. I forget what I was going to say."

"That is a very widely accepted view," Miss Vera said. "That Indian children should be withdrawn as much as possible from the parental influence, put in schools removed from their families and the desperation of their lives, where they may acquire the habits and modes of thought—" Then it was Miss Vera's turn to break off.

The truth was, Kay saw (and it was strangely easier to see it here on shipboard than in the close confines of Yarmouth, where she had a thousand reasons for resentment)—the truth was that these ladies could see perfectly well that Aren was a human like themselves; only at a distance could they believe that he would be better off made into something different.

"I imagine the Plains Indians to be the noblest of all the heathen races," Miss Pauline said. "From what I have read in the mission news, they are bravery itself, pitting their little ponies against those great buffalo."

"Now, Pauline, that places a burden upon Miss Ward, who can hardly say that they are *not*, whatever her own experience may be."

"I don't know about bravery or nobility. I only know—the people I knew," Kay said. "The people I knew were kind and clever, and loved their families, and loved the country around them, where they have lived for thousands of years. I only knew children who had been taken away from their people, and were frightened and lonely." Perhaps she should not say this to Christian women, but Miss Vera and Miss Pauline seemed sensible. "I do not think the school was a good place, even though my father and my sister worked hard to make it so."

Knowing that Aren watched her, she was aware that she had never said so much out loud in front of him. She had told him about Annie, and Mary and the others, and Miss Ramsay once or twice, after a bad dream; she had talked a little about her father too. But maybe he did not know what they had done there. The habit of silence about the bad winter when so many children died had been deeply instilled in her—and his own tuberculosis and the circumstances of their taking him away had made it seem strange and even cruel to talk about the school in front of him. Because the school was strange and cruel.

"My sister Thea had a great love of the people, and could tell you more about them," she said. "I was only a child; perhaps I saw the thing through the wrong lens, the wrong end of the telescope—being so close, and having friends among the children. But I now think it is not natural or good for children to live in those conditions."

"Oh well, of course! Well, yes!" said Miss Vera, and both sisters nodded quickly.

"*Our* school," Miss Pauline added, stumbling in to please, "is a *day* school."

By their nervousness, Kay knew that she had been too strong in her opinions yet again. She thought she might like to turn all the tables upside down and run through the dining room shouting.

Meanwhile, Aren watched them all, eating his vol-au-vent with neat elegance.

The contract bridge fad among the ladies made for a quiet run up to Auckland. After supper, Kay was inveigled into a four with the

Pike sisters before she could wriggle out of it, and then was out-manoeuvred by the pug-faced lady who marshalled the table, who directed her to sit on the sofa. Being short already, she hated sinking on the sofa side—it made her feel like a child. Although she enjoyed bridge played with speed and skill, she was not Miss Vera's partner but was paired with Miss Pauline, a nervous, fluting player. And the talk round the table was tedious. The pug-faced lady, Mrs. Robinette, was very keen, and inclined to instruct. There were many such tutelary women at sea, Kay thought.

"Third player plays high," Mrs. Robinette told Miss Pauline; and after she flubbed a trick and wanted to change her mind, "At *my* table, a card laid is a card played."

Instead of playing another rubber, Kay said she must write to her sister, and escaped to a writing table away from the bridge games—and since she had thought of it, did write to Thea, giving the details of this new ship.

> . . . Aren relented and took a cabin in second this time; his is near enough to mine that we can halloo out our portholes to each other. Some people from the islands choose a cheaper ticket, which entitles them to deck-space only—they sing in the evenings and it is very reminiscent of our olden days, and I think quite beautiful. You will not be surprised to hear that some of the English people complain.
>
> Tell Francis we were surprised to find Jimmy Giles on board the Tofua, he is second engineer on this voyage but hoping to make first next time. He invited us down to the engine room to have a look around, and we came back to dinner smeared but happy. I saw the shaft tunnel!
>
> Aren continues in good health and good spirits, as I am myself. I hope to meet Mr. Brimner in Ha'apai, because this banana boat stops there. I wrote to ask him if he could come over to see us, and I will see if there is a photographer to take a snapshot of us three to send back to you.

I miss you very much, being back at sea. I hope you are
not missing me too much.

                              your loving sister, Kay

The Misses Pike had disturbed her thoughts, asking about the
school. It had always troubled her that Thea in some way believed
that Aren was sent by God to—what? To try her, to offer redemp-
tion or forgive her for all those deaths?

Well, she could post the letter in Auckland. She went to her cabin
for an envelope and then set off to find Aren, knowing he would be
listening to the singers on the deck. He was—he looked, at least—
happy and calm. She slid into a space on the rail beside him.

It was a beautiful night. The Milky Way was a long, glimmering
snail trail winding up the sky. It reminded her of a night on the
Morning Light, somewhere along the forties on a still night, the stars
bending near the earth, the Milky Way incandescent. She had stood
at that other rail, on that other ship, asking, What is infinity?

Thea had said it was all God's love et cetera, Mr. Wright talked
a little astronomy, and Kay herself stared into the reaches of the
blackness, the universe stretching out on either side, every side,
into never a border, no end to it, because what would be outside?
Turtles all the way down, each ancient turtle carved with Captain
Cook's initials, scars so old that they mean nothing among all the
other scars . . .

She was tired. She hugged Aren's arm for a moment, and took
herself off to bed.

7

Auckland

The *Tofua* reached Auckland early on July 11. Full summer in Yarmouth; mid-winter in Auckland, but it felt like a sparkling autumn morning. Watching the city near, Kay's memory was full of Pilot, her dear dog, at Piha beach, by the dentist's rattle-trap railway along the cliffs. Perhaps those crazy cars still screamed around the curves. Handing her a bit of fur and fluff on a whim, that shaky man had given Kay great stability. Her companion, her first friend in the new life, before even Aren. Well, she would not continue on that rickety train of thought, it would just land her in the salty deeps.

The *Tofua* would stay in dock until four, loading passengers and goods bound for the outer islands, and Kay persuaded Aren to walk along the harbour with her while they waited. Thinking he would stand out in the city, he was reluctant. She said, "Things are different here. You may be yourself here without disguise."

He shook his head, saying that was not necessarily true. "And besides, all humans are always in disguise of some sort."

But he put on his good jacket and came with her down the gangplank, weaving their way among the thronging people who were coming up (a few English and American, but mostly Maori and Pacific Islanders, taking deck passage). The dock was equally crowded with people carrying huge packages for their friends. Some of the bundles leaked blood—there was a great appetite for beef on the islands.

They braced themselves to burrow through the crowd of dauntingly large Pacific Islanders, and inevitably were separated, each threading a path through the mass until they reached the wharf and relative safety and found each other.

And Kay also found, standing quietly on the Auckland pier, thin in the middle of that sturdy, milling crowd, wearing his grey linen jacket and looking up through green-smoked glasses, her dear friend, Mr. Brimner.

He was unchanged. Except as Kay looked again, looked longer, he was changed very much. He was younger, because she was older. His face was the same: serious, broad-browed, tender-skinned still, but he had achieved some truce with the sun and was now an even biscuit tone, several shades less pale. He looked at rest, in some ineffable way.

She walked—ran—the few remaining paces between them, to clasp the hands he held out, warm and strongly responding. Her friend, the one who knew her best, so far from home, and so unexpectedly! This was why she could not send Aren alone.

"Kay! My dear Kay!" He took her hands and then her elbows, gratefully shaking them and then her hands, and turned to her brother. "And Aren, how *tall* you are!"

Aren laughed, and stood taller. No one ever said that to him.

At Mr. Brimner's lead, they turned to walk up out of the thronging crowd to find some peaceful place. His straw hat could not be the same one, but his smoked spectacles certainly were. He took them off as they climbed up to the shaded porch of a nearby hotel, and then Kay could see the whole of his face.

She wished to say, "I am overwhelmed with happiness," but instead, in case she had been staring, she looked down at the boards of the porch. Each board perfect, the dark interstices cool and perfect. Mr. Brimner's boots were very worn, but clean and polished to a cheerful sheen.

He turned aside to speak to the waiter; Kay and Aren found a table with wicker chairs. A long box of flowering thyme ran along the railing, a scented barrier between porch and road.

"What a comfortable spot," Mr. Brimner said, returning to them.

Kay asked, almost stern in her effort to keep her happiness contained, "But how do you come to be here? You must tell us everything, and where you are going—but we only have an hour or two before the *Tofua* leaves again! How do you come to be in Auckland? Have you been moved here? Or posted for a locum?"

"No, no," he said, having tried to interrupt several times. "Let me explain, I beg you! Nothing of the sort. I am still at Ha'ano. I only arrived two days ago."

Quicker off the mark, Aren said, "You are here to meet us?"

"I did not hear from you," Kay said. "I thought my cable had gone astray."

"Receiving your cable very late (after some not-surprising mishaps), I counted the days. There are limited ways to arrive at Tonga, and a limited schedule of ships. I calculated that if you were not on the *Tofua*, you'd be on the *Matua*, a week from now, and I ran!"

A pitcher of cold tea and a plate of sandwiches came. Waving away Kay's purse, Mr. Brimner had coin ready to pay the waiter. Aren, the younger brother, let them argue over it and tucked in to the lunch as if he had not just had breakfast.

Mr. Brimner said he had put up at the diocesan centre and had a little holiday. "I do not know Auckland well—but I remembered our trip to the dentist, last time!"

She laughed, and then, because of course he would remember, told him briefly, "I had to put Pilot down, just before we left. He was very sick." She was surprised to find that her eyes were welling with tears again, seeing his still body in the straw. Aren put his warm hand on her arm and handed her a clean handkerchief.

"I am sorry for him, and for you." Kindly giving her time to stop crying, Mr. Brimner said, "In his honour, all unknowing, I went out through the forest to Piha beach yesterday. It is still very beautiful . . ."

Then he said, to Aren, "But why are you here? Kay's cable gave only the bare fact that you were coming."

Kay looked at Aren, but he said nothing. "Well, we are set for Nuku'alofa first, perhaps looking to charter a boat from there, or from Fiji, or at least— Oh, it is so frustrating not to know, Aren! I wish you would not keep putting off . . ."

There was a little silence.

Steadfastly not looking at her, Aren told Mr. Brimner, "Kay decided I should go home. To Pulo Anna," he added, to explain what *home* might mean. He put the last sandwich in his mouth.

That gave her a shock, hearing it stated straight out. Had he not wanted to come?

After a moment, Mr. Brimner asked it out loud. "Did you need persuading?"

"It was a good idea," Aren said. He looked over their heads at the hotel wall beyond. "But I did not think of it."

"Had something happened that made you wish to leave Nova Scotia?"

"I was not being a good citizen," Aren said. He pushed his chair back and said, "I will go for a walk, I think, and stretch my legs farther than the ship allows. I'll meet you back there at four, Kay."

Kay and Mr. Brimner sat in silence after he left, and Kay struggled with a bloom of shame. Consciousness of having *managed* things, and people, swept through her. Some people required that direction, but never Aren. When people around you were quiet and accepting, you had to be doubly, trebly careful not to impinge on their independence.

Mr. Brimner took up his satchel from beside his chair. "Let me show you something," he said.

He pulled out a padded manila envelope, and from it eased a dark-blue box sleeve. He looked at it briefly, fondly, saying, "Please note, a most elegant quarter-morocco solander box . . ." From that, at last, he pulled out a book with a grey cover and blue leather along the narrow spine. He passed it across the table to her.

The cover read, *Poems of Charles Leland Prior · now first published · edited with notes by Rev. Henry Brimner*

"You have finished it!"

"It is finished."

A nonsensical thing struck her first: she had not known that Mr. Brimner's name was Henry. She opened the stiff cover and admired the water-marbled end papers and the thick cream pages, and turned one or two to see the poems, set out on the page (she caught herself thinking) like in a real book.

"It is quite beautiful," she said.

"I think so."

"You have done justice to your friend."

Mr. Brimner's smile widened again, amplifying beautifully into an accepting, grateful, acknowledging beam.

The hotel clock struck, and looking up, Kay saw there was only half an hour till the *Tofua* left again. She handed the book back and pointed to the clock. "I am afraid we must be back at the ship soon. And you must need to return to your—" Not parish, precisely, because there was no church? "To your home."

He smiled at her, the unfolding, understanding benediction she remembered very well. "It *is* my home. I would like you to see Ha'ano again, because I know it better. But just now I will go with you and Aren, I think. It strikes me that you may need some companionship."

"Oh."

Her relief and gratitude was so great that Kay could not say anything more.

Then as was only practical, and not managing, she said, "Well, you must go and get your things, for the *Tofua* leaves at four."

Mr. Brimner clapped his hands on his jacket and his small satchel. "All that is mine I carry with me, like Cicero's Bias: *omnia mecum porto mea*. And do you know, Seneca tells exactly the same tale of Stilpon, also running from the destruction of his city, but arranges it slightly differently, which is a lesson to all us translators: *Omnia mea mecum sunt . . .*"

"*All my things are with me,*" Kay said. "I think that is better, and cleaner, but it may not have as nice a rhythm."

Talking in this enjoyable way, they progressed along the pier until they came to Aren, waiting in the shadow of a baggage shed. He put an arm around Kay's shoulder and she hugged his waist, and they were of one mind again.

Going up the gangplank, Mr. Brimner said, "I must see the purser. If there are no cabins left, I shall travel as a deck passenger. Ten years have made me a Tongan, you'll find."

Aren said, with a friendly air, "There is an empty bunk in my cabin. I would be honoured to have your company, if that suits you."

Kay loved his calm courtesy, matching Mr. Brimner's. After all, those two did not know each other as well as she knew each of them.

They found a place at the rail to look down on the city once more and the crowded quay. A momentary pause, one last shuffling and calling farewell of visitors and hangers-on, and then the engine note changed, the gangplank came up and the ropes went slithering through watery sky, and they were steaming again out of Auckland harbour.

They parted, Aren taking Mr. Brimner to the purser's cubbyhole to arrange things, and Kay saying she would meet them on B deck before dinner.

It was useful to have a friend in the crew. Jimmy Giles had a word with the purser, and the purser had a word with the steward, and the upshot was that the cabin arrangement was fixed up easily; when they went in to dinner, Kay found that they had been moved to a table for six. The Misses Pike were there before them. The sixth chair had a name holder but no name; Jimmy stopped by and said he'd take his supper with them if he had time, tomorrow night.

Mr. Brimner came to dinner late, explaining as he slid his chair in that he had been caught up in a religious conversation from which it was difficult to extricate himself. "We have on board the Roman Catholic bishop of Cape Town—perhaps you have seen his entourage on the promenade deck?"

Kay laughed and shook her head.

"He keeps to the shade, I believe. He travels with several priests, mostly good fellows. Their presence gives us, according to sea superstition, promise of a good passage. It is a curious fact that, like Jonah, Anglican clergy are generally credited with bringing *bad* weather."

Kay introduced Mr. Brimner to the Misses Pike. They had brightened at his approach, being quite accustomed to clergymen at table, and clearly expecting him to be a less uncomfortable companion than either Kay or Aren.

Which he was, since he gave them his unassuming and friendly smile and asked after their selves, their souls and families, each in turn, keeping himself to himself in a quiet way. They had not seen even a photograph of the school to which they were bound; Mr. Brimner, who had visited it while doing a locum in Suva ten years before, was able to assure them that it was well run and well funded, and that the students were (or at least had been ten years ago) delightful. Various teachers would have changed, more than likely, because time, like an ever-rolling stream, et cetera, but he had heard very good reports of its continued stability and success. The Misses Pike breathed a double sigh of relief and asked if Mr. Brimner would care to play a rubber of bridge, and since all the tables were being turned to that purpose, it was difficult to refuse. He winked at Kay and said that he and Kay would engage to take their money if they insisted.

He shuffled and cut the cards like a professional, and Aren pulled a hard chair over to his elbow, ready to enjoy the show. The first hand went quickly, because between them Mr. Brimner and Kay had all the trumps, so that Kay wondered if he had stacked the deck. He was a surprising person in many ways.

"And the last four hearts are ours—hard lines, Miss Pike! I call that too bad, don't you?"

Miss Pike the younger pushed out her lips. "I did not have a single decent card."

"Nor I, not one," said Miss Pike the elder.

"Are you going to deal?" Miss Vera demanded.

"I deal them like this, since I'm left-handed," Miss Pauline said, placing each card separately onto one of four piles.

At the end of a century, she pushed the piles around the table, picked up her own packet and began to assemble them painstakingly into a fan. "Sorry to be so slow, but I really must put them in the proper order, so I can see what I've got . . ."

Another century went by as she took, placed, took, placed, her cards, the end of the fan growing. Her broad face glowed above the cards, the hundredth of the Hundred Faces fan.

At last Kay prompted, "Miss Pike?"

"Oh! It's me . . . Well, let me see, one spade."

Mr. Brimner passed.

Miss Vera said, "Now, don't scream, Pauline—seven spades."

Her sister screamed.

The worst of it was that since Miss Pauline had first bid spades, she was the one to play the hand, and was forever asking, "Is it dummy or me to lead?"

Patiently, Mr. Brimner would tell her, "You're on the table, Miss Pike."

"Oh, dear. Well, how about—" Then she would rootle in her hand, reorganizing the cards, snick, snick, snick, and finally lay a card. Saying this would drive her mad, Vera left to find more candied nuts, but Aren stayed on, watching quizzically as Miss Pike laid out every spade, one by one, to take a grand slam, which Vera returned in time to witness.

At the end of an hour, Mr. Brimner tallied the points and found—without giving exact scores, but how terribly sad—that he and Kay had only *just* failed to win the rubber, and therefore owed their opponents, "penny a point, let me see: forty cents." They would have their revenge another night, he said, pulling the coins from his pocket.

The loss gave them licence to get up gracefully from the table.

"I have defrauded the poor," Mr. Brimner said as they made their way out, "since that would have gone into the collection box."

"But your sanity is of more value to your people in the long run," Kay said. "I will add forty cents to the next collection box I see, to make up for the deception."

Collecting Aren from the bar corner where he had retreated to talk to Jimmy Giles, they made their way out onto the shelter deck.

The night air was soft and fragrant, as if nearby islands sent out a faint scent. Kay felt transported in an alchemical way back to the deck of the *Morning Light*. If Thea and Francis came walking along, it would be perfect, she thought. And Roddy could come too. She cupped one hand from the breeze to light a cigarette.

"Will you be promoted to Nuku'alofa one day?" Kay hoped it was not painful to ask.

"Ha'ano is my place for now," he said. "But the bishop is leaving us, and I may do better with the next. If not, I am content to stay with my—with the people who have been kind to me. My Tongan family. I might even refuse to be lifted up to Nuku'alofan heights."

Aren clasped his arm, condoling and congratulating at once.

They leaned comfortably against the railing in the silky dark while Mr. Brimner talked about his island, and the people there; adding in explanation a brief synopsis of his life before Ha'ano, which Kay had never heard before—she had never thought to ask, in the old days on the *Morning Light*. His parents' early deaths, his scholarship, his time at Cambridge reading classics, his decision to study for the priesthood at Oxford: all those led to the circumstances of his friendship with Prior. Then a curacy near Prior's parish, and the increasing relationship with Prior's mother, a woman he came to admire and respect, he said, almost as much as he did his friend. And her request that he be the one to edit Prior's work.

"It was all due to poor Prior dying so suddenly. He was well, if tired from overwork, and then he was a little poorly—and the next day he died, to the great dismay of all his friends and of course the devastation of his mother. I did not have time to tell him how deeply I respected his work—none of us did! And he had no time to send the poems out into the wider world, although he meant to do so. The habit of perfection made it difficult for him to relinquish his work."

"Why are the poems so good?" Aren asked.

Mr. Brimner leaned farther forward on the rail, outward, as if the answer was at some other shore. "He— Well! You may read my introduction for a longer answer. They are unusual, even difficult. Ahead of his time. He illuminates a different landscape, an inward, introspective view—but I find odd points of reference to this world, our world here:

> *God, lover of souls, swaying considerate scales,*
> *Complete thy creature dear O where it fails,*
> *Being mighty a master, being a father and fond.*

"The first few times of reading that, in Prior's black-blotched hand, I confess I thought he was referring to some sea creature swaying kindly fish scales in the deeps—*considerate scales.*" He laughed a little. "I struggled to understand—you will already have realized that he is speaking of God's thumb cheating the scales of justice in our favour."

Being a father and fond—Kay liked that vision of God.

"And yet," Mr. Brimner said, "it is a relief not to be expecting the next black-bordered letter, the next set of notes on my edits. I loved them both, mother and son, but they are fixed in time, caught in the week before Prior's illness. My own vision, my ordinary life, has"—he waved an arm around him, at the ship and the sky and the ocean—"well, has transubstantiated, if that is not blasphemy. Only the appearance of me remains."

Kay said, "Remember Arion the singer and the dolphin who carried him safely to Corinth? Reading Plutarch at last, I found this, that you told us once: *To the dolphin alone, beyond all other, nature has granted what the best philosophers seek: friendship for no advantage* . . . You gave that to Prior—friendship for no advantage."

Aren leaned backwards on the rail, tilting his head to look at the starry sky. "Are you still very sad about him?" he asked.

Mr. Brimner looked surprised. "Did I seem so sad, in those olden days?"

"Well, underneath," Kay said.

"I'm sorry to have burdened you with that. I was only conscious of responsibility. Since he had died and I was still alive."

"You must show Aren your book! It has a half-quarto morocco cover in blue, Aren."

"Quarter-morocco," murmured Mr. Brimner.

Aren said, "May I only look from a distance, or is it available for actual reading?"

Waving grandly with his pipe, Mr. Brimner said it *required* to be read, by both of them, and he would be honoured to give them each a copy when his box arrived, when there were proper books and not just grey-cardboard pamphlets, which he trusted would be soon.

"We have already received a first review," he added. "From the critic Theodore Maynard. Allow me to quote: *A shy mid-Victorian priest has proven more modern than the most freakish modern would dare to be* . . . *the poems are the last word in technical development.*"

He beamed at them again, the pleasure of having squired his friend's work into the world almost too great for one face to contain.

Then the drinks cart went rolling by and they followed it into the saloon bar for a nightcap, which Mr. Brimner said was a toast to Prior and, besides, a shipboard habit that none of them would indulge in real life.

Returning to her cabin late and slightly tipsy, Kay found that the
steward had left a letter from the poste restante bag in Auckland.
From Thea, of course, a postscript to her first letter, sent after the
first fire of her shock and unhappiness had burned down.

> I did not trouble you with this at the time, because
> you were only a child, but it weighs heavily on my mind
> now. When you were both so ill, after Shanghai en route
> for Manila, you know, one night I went to Aren's cabin to
> check his fever, and I found him standing on his bunk
> looking out the port.
>
> "When do they come?" he asked me. I asked who he
> meant. He stared at me, too fevered to make sense. "They
> come to get me," he said. "When will they come? I must
> go now."
>
> I sat with him, but he did not want to be comforted, he
> only wanted to stand at the port and try to see. Francis came
> to find me, and he carried the little fellow up on deck to be
> able to see better in the air—I do not know what he told him,
> but it comforted Aren enough that he could sleep. I thought
> at the time he was delirious and perhaps referring to angels.
> That was what I told myself. Now I know, can admit, that he
> meant his parents, of course.

Of course he did. Kay turned the page—Thea's handwriting,
usually so smooth and controlled, was hard to read here.

> He did not yet know the word for mother—there
> had been no reason to teach him that word yet. I had not
> intentionally left it out of our lessons, but I was never,
> could never be his mother, and so I did not pretend to be.
> He only knew "Aunt" from that book you loved so much
> in Corcovado, and it was you he knew as his Aunt. I still
> do not know what relation he thought I bore him then,

but I hope that it had in it some kindness at least, and care for him.

This was a strange understanding for Thea to come to now. Kay felt sorry for her.

I was not his mother, but he was my son, and so he still is, as much as Roddy is. Last night Roddy had a fever and sat up straight in bed, asking, "When will they come back?" and my heart was crushed in my chest. He misses you, of course he does, because you are his own family, and I hope that you both will come back as soon as you are able.

Kay wrote back to Thea quickly, meaning to send it from Nuku'alofa,

You became Aren's mother, as you were my mother. As you are Roddy's loving mother. I know you meant it only for good. It is not your fault ~~that it was not right,~~

She crossed that out.

that it has not been good for Aren

She crossed that out as well. Neither said what she meant. There was time before they reached Nuku'alofa; she would wait to finish this.

8

Nuku'alofa

The *Tofua* took nearly a week to reach Tonga, first stopping at the Cook Islands for passengers to disembark and embark. Often in the distance, and sometimes nearby, they saw humpback whales—almost always two or three, because they love to travel together, Mr. Brimner said, having learned more about whales during his time in Tonga.

They were still, always, a shocking size. Leviathan, gleaming blue-black in the depths, greyish-white showing underneath when one rolled into a turn or came to the surface for air—or when they rose like swallows with wings spread in the play and display of breaching. Once they had breathed, they might stay underwater ten or twenty minutes, or an hour, as they chose; the game was to spot where they came up again. In the olden days, Kay had thought she would always be sailing among them.

The dining room was well run, and the menu on the second evening included Tartines à la Yarmouth, which turned out to be clam fritters with pinkish sauce. A small band played the tango in the saloon bar, where the Misses Pike, at loose ends between rubbers of bridge, took it in turn to dance with Aren and Mr. Brimner. Between those mild excitements, Kay and Mr.

Brimner talked and thought and walked many miles around the promenade deck.

Aren listened to Kay talk about how they might go on to Pulo Anna, without taking part. But Jimmy Giles joined naturally in the conversation, since he knew the island routes, and he abused his privilege to send several cables to his brother John in Pangai, part-owner of a fishing boat that made longer voyages from time to time.

Days came and went in orderly sequence, clouds processing across the long sky from morning till night, till at the end of one afternoon there was a green hill in the distance.

This was the island of 'Eua, which sounded to Kay like the name of the first land that ever came out of the sea. She had wanted to stop there long ago, on her first voyage—and now they would, for most of the day, while the *Tofua* let off passengers and took on more. The green island was lit by white sunlight, no half-lights or shadows. Untarnished, just born—she heard herself empurpling her thoughts, like Elsie Spiers. Or like Tennyson: *In the afternoon they came unto a land in which it seemed always afternoon.* Heavy-flowered heat wound round the ship as it slowed, and they saw schools of jewelled fishes in the water near the shore, almost as clear as the water in Eleuthera (the place that stood in Kay's mind for heaven, perhaps because Thea had buried her first child there), but darker green than that sea's pellucid blue.

White-sailed schooners crowded the pier at 'Eua, coming and going. The *Tofua* anchored out beyond the tiny harbour at 'Ohonua, and boats ran back and forth, first with the many deck passengers who were getting off and getting on, then more and smaller boats loaded with fruit and coconuts. It was a family-home week, which also meant it was time for some funerals, and many of the houses near the shore were in mourning, wrapped from side to side in huge swaths of black cloth.

Mr. Brimner, Kay and Aren, wanting to explore the town for an hour or so, went over on the first boat with Jimmy Giles, and he promised to make sure they got back on the last boat. They walked

up the long tamped-dirt street. Yellow trumpet flowers hung from
the roofs of the houses; little black pigs ran in and out of doorways,
chased by children in raggedy drawers. One of the boys shinned up
a tree to please the people from the ship, and dropped down green
coconuts for them to drink. There was a surprise, too: a tiny bookshop, where Kay bought a mystery novel called *Gore of Babylon*. She
could not resist—it had a knife-wielding vicar on the cover, locked
in the embrace of a red-haired woman in a saturated-red dress.

But even standing on the dirt road, with nothing to hurry for,
Kay felt a hungry need to get on with it, to get to Tonga, and on to
Pangai, to get John Giles's boat and go beyond into what they
needed to find.

On the shore, they saw a man carrying an oar. Kay told Mr.
Brimner of Francis's joking threat to walk inland carrying an oar
until someone asked him, "What's that on your shoulder?" and
there settle down—and how she'd shown him that joke in the
Odyssey, at least a variation. "*I will tell you an obvious marker*—at least,
that is how I translated σῆμα," she said, checking with her teacher.
"But perhaps it ought to be *sign? Whenever some traveller meets you and
asks why you have a winnowing fan on your fine shoulder, at that very point
drive the well-shaped oar into the ground.*"

Aren had heard this before; seeing his patient expression, Kay
turned to Mr. Brimner to apologize for having perhaps already told
the joke to him too, in a long-ago letter, but he said that he had the
most obliging memory and never minded being told good stories
again. As a true classicist must not.

"We must read together again, dear Kay," he said.

This was a generous offer, but of course he had no duty to tutor
her now. "Your passage was paid that way long ago," she said, "but
I will be delighted to read with you again!" She did not add "Mr.
Brimner" because that seemed too distant. But to say "Henry" was
too close.

Evening came down like a blind being pulled as the *Tofua*
steamed toward the main island of Tongatapu, lying flatter than

'Eua, a low, straggling coastline. Looking back, they saw 'Eua's palm trees as black outlines against the moon, and heard the low singing of mourners who would sit vigil at church all night. Or was that singing coming from Tongatapu already?

The ship stayed at anchor off Nuku'alofa for the night—the rising and falling cadence of hymns audible from shore all night long—and very early in the morning the boats began to go back and forth to the wharf. Kay stared at the scruffy shoreline of Nuku'alofa. There were still wading women, going out to check the progress of the leaves for weaving mats. Always women at that work, tending and checking. She stood recalling their last visit here, when they had not even known Aren yet. The thing in Tonga that she had most loved, of all the things she saw then, was the *'esi maka faaki-nanga*, the stone to lean against, from where the king had struck the knees of his visitors. She had loved sitting there beside Miss Winifred Small's tender and affectionate knees, safe from the unpredictable power of kings.

As they were rowed shoreward, the first person she could make out on the wharf looked familiar. Coming closer, Kay saw that it really was a friend: as if she had come out of a dream again, it was Lisia, Miss Winifred's companion. She was waving and jumping at the steel guardrail, displaying undignified and gratifying joy at the sight of Kay.

"Miss Winifred is here!" Lisia shouted as soon as she might be heard across the water. "She has come to meet you, *herself*!"

This was obviously a great honour, and Kay felt it. She did not need to remind Mr. Brimner who Miss Winifred was, but told Aren how lucky they were to know such a great lady.

At her open carriage, which was painted so nicely it could not be called a cart, Miss Winifred Small held down a hand to them, offering leis of fragrant maile leaves to refresh them after their journey, and saying, "Mālō 'etau lava!"

"Mālō! Mālō 'e lelei," Kay replied.

"Mrs. Thea, your dear sister, cabled to say you would be on this boat," Miss Winifred said, "so I had Lisia harness King George and bring us down, in order that we would not miss a moment of your company."

Miss Winifred had grown very large, these last ten years, and only more beautiful. Kay stood on the step and stretched up to her old friend, who enveloped her in a warm embrace smelling of clean clothes and sandalwood.

"You must meet my brother, Aren!" Kay stepped back to bring him for inspection. Miss Winifred gave him a generous smile and set a graceful hand on his head. "And you know our friend Mr. Brimner—"

"I have known Henry these ten years!" Miss Winifred waved at Mr. Brimner and motioned him forward. "And will enlist him now for my purposes."

With a hand on the edge of the cart, Mr. Brimner said, "Miss Winifred and I meet often, dear Kay. Though a confirmed Wesleyan, I assure you, she is a force in the nation."

"You must stay for a proper visit," said Miss Winifred, not heeding this flattery. "I do not know what you may be planning, but you cannot proceed on the *Tofua* today! We will arrange things better."

Kay lifted her hands, helpless against the ship's schedule, but Miss Winifred had gestured and Lisia was already running back to the boat. "I have instructed her to get you a wharf ticket, so you may stay for a week, until the *Matua* comes. It's just as good a boat, I promise you, but you must let me have a little time to enjoy your company."

The *Matua* was the ship that Elsie and Julia were to travel on to Samoa. For a moment Kay thought it would be nice to see them again, before remembering that they were going in a different direction altogether.

Here was Lisia coming back across the pavement, and Jimmy Giles following close behind—he must have come over on the second boat. He was waving the long-awaited cable from his brother John. "It is all fixed," he said to Aren as he reached him. "You sail Tuesday after next, out of Pangai. That gives John time to provision the boat and find a crew."

Aren clasped Jimmy's hand and thanked him, and so did Mr. Brimner, and the three of them stepped aside a little to learn more, while Kay turned back to tell Miss Winifred of their plans.

"We did not know if Mr. Giles's brother could—but he can! So we will go on from Pangai in his fishing boat, up to the Solomons and then on to Micronesia to the Palau group, where Aren was born. We are going to his island."

"Well, that is an Odyssey," she said.

That made Kay laugh—she had not thought of that. "I hope it does not take ten years!" she said. "But if we have a week to wait, I think we might find a guest house here and wait for the *Matua* to take us on to Pangai!"

Miss Winifred would have none of that and insisted they were to be her guests, it was all planned. "Lisia's little daughter is back at the house right now seeing that the beds are well aired."

The first thing was to go back to the *Tofua* with the second boat for their things. Mr. Brimner, as always, had his possessions ready in a flash; Aren shouldered his seabag. But in the rush to get their luggage packed and taken off, and retrieved from the quayside melee of gigantic parcels of food and clothing bound for the outer islands, Kay forgot to look in the cupboard over her sink, and truly regretted losing the red toothbrush she'd bought in Boston.

Back on shore, they bowled along in a hired cart past the Queen's palace and down Vuna Road, looking for Miss Winifred's white clapboard house "with gingerbread decorations over the door," built since Kay's last visit, and even since Mr. Brimner had last been to Nuku'alofa.

Keeping her eyes open for the house, Kay saw a man loping past along the side of the road, and twisted back to look again. Aren was looking back, too.

"That man! Was that Seaton?" Aren asked.

"I think it was," Kay said, and Mr. Brimner nodded.

Aren stood up in the cart and called after him. "Hi! Seaton!" he cried. "Seeeee-ton!"

But the man did not turn or stop in his easy striding. His legs were newel posts, smooth as mahogany and covered with black decorations, and he wore a white cap on his head.

"Well, if it was him, I will find him later," said Aren, sitting back again.

And that must be the house—yes, Miss Winifred's, the driver agreed, yes, yes. He waited for them to get down, and for payment, and then backed his old cart and made off. In the distance they saw him pull up by the running man, and let him up for the ride back to town.

After their little party was settled, Mr. Brimner explained to Miss Winifred their plans for Aren's trip: he knew John Giles well, whose wife Lotoua came from Ha'ano and was his neighbour Mahina's sister. "They are Fifitas," he said.

As if that explained everything, Miss Winifred nodded, saying, "Sione's daughters."

So there was an island code of understanding—like in Yarmouth, Kay thought.

"Jimmy Giles sent his brother a cable proposing that John cease from fishing for a few weeks and instead ferry the little party up to the Palau islands north of Papua New Guinea. A big trip for a small schooner, but not impracticable, if John were willing," Mr. Brimner told Miss Winifred. It took some time for John to think about the route, and another day of waiting to hear what Lotoua had to say about it. "Perhaps helped by my suggestion that Lotoua might go over to Ha'ano for a holiday, and stay in my little house."

With one eye on Aren, playing a juggling game in the distance with Lisia's younger daughter Joy, Miss Winifred said, "And do you expect this home-return to make him happy?"

Kay did not know what to answer.

Mr. Brimner saved her. "*Casus ubique valet,*" he said. "*Semper tibi pendeat hamus . . .*" He gave Kay a bright glance, as one prompting a star pupil.

She laughed. "All right, that is enough for me."

Miss Winifred said testily, "What, what? You must not speak in secret languages!"

Kay translated, as Mr. Brimner had meant her to. "It is a tag from Ovid: *Chance rules everything. Keep dangling your hook, and in an eddy where you least expect it—a fish!*"

Miss Winifred was not much mollified. "That is only ordinary sense. I will speak in Tongan and then you will be the ones who cannot keep up!" After a moment, she said, "It will be an expensive trip, Henry."

"It will cost a certain amount, but I have some savings—I have not been able to spend any money at all in these last few years, except for postage and my clerical collars, which are sent from London at hideous expense."

Miss Winifred laughed, but Kay shook her head sternly at Mr. Brimner. "It will be all right. I have received my inheritance, and Aren has money of his own. My brother Francis will wire us the funds."

"Well, I am a passenger, and will contribute my share," Mr. Brimner said.

Miss Winifred hauled herself out of her chair. "I leave you and Henry to quarrel it out," she said. "From the kitchen smell, dinner is either ready or ruined—I will investigate."

The household was not exactly what they were used to, but warm and comfortable. Lisia and her daughters Eponie and Joy lived with Miss Winifred, mostly as friends, Kay thought, and very slightly as live-in help, except that Lisia was more like an unmarried sister than a poor relation. But it was Miss Winifred who had never married. She did not understand the relationships, or Miss Winifred's complicated history, and she thought (congratulating herself on thinking this, then scolding herself for thinking she was so wise) that perhaps she had better just listen and wait and not jump to any conclusions.

As the night wind cooled, she adjusted the louvres in her window and settled herself into the comfortable bed Lisia and Eponie had made up for her. Grateful for this peaceful room, and for not being on a ship for a little while, she said her prayers, asking God to keep Roddy and Francis and Thea safe. She would write tomorrow and tell Thea everything, everything.

She closed her eyes and tried not to think, but just to listen to the far-off singing.

Next morning, Aren went out searching for Seaton, who Miss Winifred confirmed was an off-and-on inhabitant of Nuku'alofa. He had most likely been out odd-jobbing farther down Vuna Road, and might be there again today.

"He is a codger," she declared. "Well known throughout the region, an easygoing fellow of regular habits, kava-drunk in the same place every Saturday night—I will point you to it if you have not found him by then, but he will not be hard to find. He is a knowing man, if he will not move faster than he pleases."

Kay would have liked to go with Aren, but this seemed to be his own quest. She stood on the gingerbread porch looking after him as he strode down the road toward the town.

After breakfast, Mr. Brimner left too, saying he might be gone most of the day; it was his bounden duty to visit the Nuku'alofa priest-in-charge, Mr. Hill's replacement, whom he had not yet met.

Miss Winifred waved him off without regret and said that Lisia and Kay should find their hats and they would go into the country to see the sights without him, since Henry had had his fill long ago, and Kay must have forgotten everything by now.

Jouncing down the dirt road, coming back from the rather unimpressive and marshy site of Captain Cook's famous landing on Tonga, the cart gave a wild swerve, as Lisia manoeuvred to avoid something tiny—what? Oh, it was a puppy, lost on the road, looking half-starved.

She pulled up and Kay jumped down to gather up the little bundle. So small, so new! His breath smelled like a skunk, even here where there were no skunks. She turned him up in her arms so he could look at her. His fur was mixed black and cream, a dark mask over his face giving him a rakish look. He was nothing like her dog Pilot, of course, but he had a bright, curious eye. He nipped her finger gently with his sharp little teeth, and then licked her hand to make up for it.

Then another came romping out from a hedge, and another, and soon there were six pups playing in the road, and the mother nosing after them.

A bright-eyed child ran out into the road, entirely without caution, but Kay supposed there was no motor traffic to be careful of.

"Whose is this puppy, child?" Lisia demanded.

"Our puppy!" the girl said.

"Will you sell him to me?" Kay asked.

Her sister had come out behind her. "We get you a good one!" she shouted, running back to where the litter had returned to their food.

"No, no," Kay protested, but the younger girl tore the pup from her arms, and then both children were gone back to a house a little way removed from the road.

A woman came to the door then, and Lisia went to speak to her, and Kay saw her hold out some notes, which the woman counted quickly with her fingers. Then she let the door hang while she went back into the dark interior, and in a moment one of the girls came out carrying two hastily brushed puppies, fatter than the one from the road.

"Are they old enough, do you think?" Kay asked Lisia, and she nodded, shrugging.

"Close enough, anyhow."

The girl lifted the two pups by the scruff of their necks and said, "Choose!" and Kay did not know what to do. Then a third pup— oh, it was the dark-faced, inquisitive one she had picked up on the road—wormed his way through the girl's legs and yipped, demanding to be picked up.

"This one," Kay said.

Of course, he was flea-ridden. Kay ought to have realized, before hugging him close to her bosom all the way home to Nuku'alofa. Lisia did the debugging. Sitting wide-legged on the back step, she tore the brown, fibrous part off a coconut, and with her big knife hacked at the nut to get at the white meat of it, and grated that against a rough board to shred it.

That took a long time, so Kay went off to change and wash her dress, arriving back in time to watch Lisia pick up the fibrous mass she had discarded and make it into a kind of sieve for the grated coconut, wringing out the milk into a large wooden bowl. The grated coconut went in there too, and last of all the puppy. He did not like it! As the women scrubbed, he tried to climb out, over and over, hooking one paw over the edge and mewling piteously, but they would not let him out until Lisia pronounced the treatment complete. When Kay asked her about it, she said only, "It is somehow antiseptic is all I know, the old women tell us to do it."

Whatever the cause, the milky liquid in the bowl was soon speckled with myriad fleas, which were at least no longer on the puppy. They washed him in clean water and towelled him dry, and then combed him all out again. He was too young to bark, but only expressed his dislike and disapproval by opening and closing his wedge-shaped mouth with great melodramatic stretches in a soft, yowling song, interspersed with mild, piglike grunting.

"*Si'i mafu*," Lisia said, bending to kiss one clean paw, and stroked his fluffing fur. "Sorry we have been so rough with you, little heart!"

Kay asked, "*Mafu* is heart? Little *mafu* . . ."

Back from his adventures, Aren came around the garden gate. When he saw the pup curled in Kay's arms, he laughed, and recited, "*When Ann had a bun or cake, she would give some to Dash.* That is a large dog for you to be fond of, Kay!"

So he was Dash.

———

Kay took little Dash with her to her bedroom, although the idea of a dog in a bedroom was clearly incomprehensible to Lisia, who courteously said nothing, but looked a little shocked.

In the distance, the funeral singing came winding out of every church of every denomination, as it did all day and all night. And there were so many churches. Whenever she paused to think, Kay became aware of that contrapuntal continuo. She did not dislike it, but it made her a little anxious.

The third time she was woken by Dash's whining, Kay stumbled to the door to let him out and found Aren coming up the white stone path from the lane behind the house.

"Where have you been all this time?" she asked, surprised.

"I have been with Seaton all this time," he said. He had a strange, flattened expression, and she thought he must have been drinking kava with some of the men. He picked up Dash and petted the little dog until it curled into his arm and went back to sleep. "Sit out with me for a little," he said.

They found a low stone bench along the path and sat together, nestling the dog between them for warmth.

"Seaton is not—" Kay began, but she did not know what she meant to say.

Aren turned his head. "A good influence?"

She laughed. "No, that is not what I was thinking. But maybe not reliable?"

"I needed to see him. I needed to talk to someone like him. Like me."

She sat quiet, waiting. She did not like that he thought he was like Seaton, a sea-crazed wanderer, jetsam of the waters.

"He gave me good advice, he gave me a Tongan proverb to live by: *Tā ki tahi, tā ki ʻuta.* It means, Perform in the ocean, perform in the land."

"And what does that mean?"

"That—that the person who acquires the *tā*, the rhythm, to perform or work or do things in many places, the ocean *and* the land, is a well-rounded person."

"That is only ordinary sense," she said, as Miss Winifred had said to her and Mr. Brimner about Ovid. She ran to help Dash negotiate a stile, where he had got caught, and then came back to sit beside Aren on the bench, cradling the puppy in her arms and stroking his soft nose.

"Have you considered," Aren said, forming the words carefully, "have you thought, what if they do not want me on my island? What if—"

She moved, wanting to speak, but he stopped her with a look.

"What if I cannot speak to them, and I am not one of them anymore?"

The singing around them swelled up to the end of some hymn.

"Seaton says maybe I should stay here—he will find me work and teach me how to fix things in the town."

Gathering her courage and remembering that Aren was perhaps quite drunk, Kay said, "They will want you. Of course they will want you. And you will learn to speak to them again. Look how quickly you learned to speak to me."

"That is true," he said. He seemed quite struck by that. "I am a fast learner. And I am very brave, as you recall."

She nodded. Then she took his arm and helped him up the stairs and into bed, and let him sleep it off.

9

Pangai

The time had come to set out. Because Queen Salote was visiting the island group of Ha'apai—"Or I would have introduced you at the palace," said Miss Winifred sadly—the ferry schedule was upset. The boat left Nuku'alofa at midnight, stopping at Nomuka at five, at Ha'afeva at nine, and reaching Pangai wharf on the large island of Lifuka before lunch.

"This is not one of your New Zealand boats," Miss Winifred cautioned them. "There will be no pleasant cabin, only a bench. But you are hardy and young, and you know the Pacific, so I am not concerned." Kay took this as a serious compliment.

Aren sat on the top of the cart, Mr. Brimner on the bench. There had been a slight pother about Dash and how to transport him, easily solved by making a cloth lid for a market basket; Kay sat in back with him to soothe him if he was afraid. "Dash, little *mafu*," she whispered through the cloth. "It will be all right."

They bundled into the boat—which, being much smaller than the *Tofua*, had moored right at the wharf—and, moving through the crowd of Tongans (who had to be distributed carefully by the sailors, or their mass might make the boat list one way or the other), found some spare acreage of deck and made themselves partly comfortable. Mr. Brimner was greeted with joy by many of the passengers and exchanged pleasantries with them in Tongan. Kay held the basket on her lap, one hand inside to stroke her little dog. Leaning against Aren, guarded by Mr. Brimner on her other side, she managed to sleep most of the way to Nomuka.

There she darted off to let Dash have a run, worrying in the heavy tropical darkness that she might miss the ferry leaving—though she knew perfectly well that Aren and Mr. Brimner would not let it leave without her. She looked up for a moment into a sky so dazzlingly starred that she forgot to worry, and only picked up Dash when he came to nibble at her shoe.

It was bright daylight before Ha'afeva, so that was an easier stop. They got off with the crowd of passengers to buy a cup of fruit juice from the vendor by the pier, and Kay took Dash down to the beach to let him run and play. When the ferry whistle blew, he came eagerly at her call and settled back into his basket. It was good that he was so young, because he slept a lot and only chewed one of the handles of the basket beyond repair. She was proud of him.

At noon, as promised, they reached Pangai. The jetty and the trees and houses in the village were hung with bright bunting and banners as if to welcome them—but it was for Queen Salote's visit, of course. John Giles was the first order of business, but Aren and Mr. Brimner would see him; there was nothing for Kay to help with there.

"Mrs. Fruelock lives in the same house you will remember, down that angled road," Mr. Brimner said. "Would you care to go there for the afternoon? I think she would be grateful for a visit, and her daughter Pansy—only a little younger than you—is a kindly person too."

Kay was ragged around the edges from the overnight trip, and it would only be sensible to let Dash run free in the walled garden she remembered between the house and the schoolrooms. Since their route to John Giles's place went past the Fruelock house, she had company for the walk; she felt quite wilted by the sun, for the first time in this hemisphere.

Mr. Brimner waited by the gate while Kay knocked at the Fruelocks' door. At the sight of the young woman who opened it, he lifted his hat and waved and shouted an introduction. "This is Miss Ward, whom you may remember—please tell your mother I'll be back to visit when our business with John Giles is done."

Kay turned back to the girl, whose golden-brown hair hung loose in waves over her shoulders. She tried to resolve that open, bright face with the little girl she had met long ago, but could not pull the child back to mind well enough.

She put out her hand anyway. "I think you are Pansy? I am Kay. We met long ago, when we both were children, while I was travelling with my sister and her husband on his ship, the *Morning Light*."

The girl turned to call over her shoulder, "Mother! Mother! Thea's sister has come!" Then she took Kay's hand, gently pulling her in. "We are so happy to see you! If you knew how few white women come to visit—not that it makes you odd or anything, but it will be a great excitement in the town. Everyone will come to take a look at the *papalangi*!"

Kay blinked a little, unsure what was required of her. "Well, I am not very interesting," she said. "But my brother— Well, Mr. Brimner said I ought to wait here for them, if that is all right. May I take my little dog into your garden?"

The girl, Pansy, stood back to show the way. "Of course! Right through the passage, there, all on the flags, and you may leave the door unlatched—I will find Mother and come right out to you. Let me take your bag—oh, no, that is the dog! Well, this one?"

Kay gave up her blue valise and took the basket through as she had been directed, out into the sunlit square of paving stones. In a shaded area at one end, assorted chairs had been set round a long table. She set down the basket and opened the lid, and Dash climbed cautiously out, and made for the edge of the garden to lift his leg—which he was not yet very good at, sometimes overbalancing and landing in a confused heap.

This was a pleasant, quiet arbour. Leaves and vines covered the lattice over most of one end, and the variegation of light and dark, mixed with a slight trilling from the birds overhead, made Kay feel more peaceful. She sat for a moment in one of the wicker chairs.

From a doze of rippling light she woke to Pansy coming out into the garden, her mother in tow. Dorothy Fruelock came forward gladly, with a hand stretched out.

"Why, Miss Grant—no, Miss— I ought to recall!"

"Ward," Kay said, "It is Ward. But I hope you will call me Kay, everybody does."

Kay had half-expected widowhood to have left Mrs. Fruelock wan or listless. But she was herself, looking no older, no different in any way. Her black skirt made an elegant swish as she settled into the wicker chair nearest to Kay.

Pansy sat in the rocking chair, poised on its edge as if for flight. She said she'd left the kettle to boil and would run in and out and not to mind her—then hearing the whistle she jumped up and ran back to the kitchen regions.

With the same calm vitality Kay remembered, Mrs. Fruelock talked first of her husband and his death. "It was a sudden infection, one of the ordinary, terrible things that happen in the tropics, and we must not repine," his widow said. "We became more used to dying during the war; perhaps that makes the ordinary deaths less desolating."

"My sister said the chief difference, after the war was over, was coming to realize that the young men around us would continue to be there—in the town instead of in foreign graves—and we would have to get used to their presence and learn to live with them again."

"She has a deep store of wisdom. You must be missing her."

Kay said, "I miss her very much."

Returning with a tray, Pansy put a cup of tea beside Kay, and gave another to her mother.

Mrs. Fruelock said, "All my daughters have married, did you know? Your sister must have told you—all except my dear Pansy."

Yes, Thea had told her, Kay agreed. "They were all such beautiful girls, who could be surprised." To Pansy, in companionship, she said, "I am not married either."

"I am glad Pansy remains to me for now," her mother said. "There were a great many young men killed out here, and of course Australians too, but she is not to be the prop of my old age, I tell her. I am not at all old, and will not be for a very long time!"

Kay agreed with that too. Pansy gave a sighing laugh and handed round the cakes.

A knock came from the inner hall, and she went to admit Aren and Mr. Brimner, far sooner than Kay had expected. Calling, "It's Henry and Aren, Mama!" Pansy brought them out to the courtyard.

They came in laughing, and Kay saw from his intent glance that Aren was very taken with Pansy and (it seemed to her) so was she with him. She had not thought that Pansy was like her sister Rose. But she clearly was not, so maybe this was different. Who was she to say? Seeing Aren's pleasure in Pansy, his delicate flirting as she showed him where to stow his seabag, Kay thought again that she knew nothing, nothing. And did not know what authority she'd thought she had back in Halifax either, to think that Merissa Peck was not his other half, his predestined soul— when she herself had no more understanding of these things than a cat, or a bird in a tree.

Tea was offered and refused with thanks, cakes refused in turn. Then there was a tiny silence, an expectation.

"Well. Now we can have our *real* conversation," Mrs. Fruelock said. "Henry, you come in too, and I will gather my wits around me." She took Aren's arm and led him to the arbour. "See, here is a fine chair, come and sit."

"*See here is a fine nag*," Aren whispered to Kay, as he was led to the settee.

Mr. Brimner sat in one of the chairs near the trunk of the big shade tree, and waited.

"First let me say, my dears," said Mrs. Fruelock, "I have had a cable from Thea, asking me to speak to you before you travelled on, and I fear you will not be glad to hear my news."

Nobody moved or spoke, and in a moment she went on.

"You know that three or four years after Henry was installed in Ha'ano, Mr. Fruelock went to the Diocese of Papua New Guinea. After that, for several years, the people here in Pangai were forced to endure that crawling viper Mr. Piper-Ffrench, once he was ridden off Tongatapu, but that is not to the point. Eric—my husband—quarrelled with Bishop Willis over many aspects of their calling, but the Anglo-Catholic mission to Papua was the real impetus for his change. We went to Palau, the largest island in the chain that includes Pulo Anna."

There was something for Aren here, Kay understood, something difficult. The angle of the sun meant she could not see her brother's face, only the stillness of his head.

"We went to Palau in 1916, in the middle of the war," Mrs. Fruelock said. "Goodness, it seems like longer than six years ago, does it not? A lifetime ago."

Mr. Brimner set his teacup on the little table and leaned forward, elbows on his thin knees. "Everything was confused and confusing—time seemed to stretch out during the war."

"That was two years after the German Administration ended and the Japanese took over; and it was four years after a typhoon had washed out Pulo Anna and a nearby island, Merir. The Germans did send a boat and took some people off, I believe to Koror, but not many . . . My memory may be failing me, but in any case, it was not many people, two or three at the most. And the famine afterwards took the rest of them." Turning to Aren, she said, with some formality, "I am so sorry, my dear."

Aren's fine chair sat directly beneath the orange wheel of sun lowering behind the black garden wall. His face, his eyes were hidden from Kay.

"I went with Eric to inspect the damage, and what we saw was terrible. The men sailing the boat had sleeves wet with tears they kept dashing from their eyes to see the way forward. Eric himself had to go below at one point and pray—the whole beach was littered with bodies, long dead and rotted. That was at Merir."

Mr. Brimner moved softly, taking a cane chair to sit near Aren, within arm's reach. He said to Mrs. Fruelock, "We are hampered by not knowing precisely what Aren's family arrangements were, whether he had already lost his parents. Perhaps because of his long illness, he does not remember those old days properly."

Kay wished she could go to Aren herself, but Mr. Brimner was filling the purpose and she did not matter. She sat still.

Mrs. Fruelock said, "Perhaps I can help with that, at least."

She folded her hands again, as if praying, on the long thighs beneath her grey cotton dress, and told them that she and her husband had heard, even several years later, of a boy being taken away by a ship.

"Of course, we had no notion, hearing the tale, that it involved people with whom we were acquainted. But the story was still talked of in the islands, the boy who was taken for tobacco. The boy's mother, her terrible scolding of the brother who had let him go, and the white people's ship that sailed away with him." She looked up at them. "Reng, he was called. And that boy was Aren. I wrote to Thea of it long ago, when we first corresponded and I realized what ship that must be, but perhaps she did not wish"— she paused—" . . . to cause you pain."

Or did not wish to look at what they had done.

Or, Kay quickly told herself, she had looked squarely at it, and knew it could not be remedied, and that the only help for Aren was to bring him up as well as she could.

"We went back to the islands, not long before Eric died," said Mrs. Fruelock. "There was no one there at all. On Pulo Anna there are graves, great stone slabs in a glade of rhododendrons. It might be possible to find someone among the various islands who knows whose graves they are."

She fell silent then. This was the only fragment she could offer.

Mrs. Fruelock did not seem to be in distress—at least, not that Kay could see—but Pansy poured a glass of water for her and crouched by her feet, watching her mother. Perhaps she had been dreading this visit.

Aren stood up from his chair. "I do not know what to think of this," he said.

He took a step, as if he would walk down the garden, but checked himself and stood motionless. Kay moved then, and went to him, but was afraid to put her arm around him in case he shook her off. She stood beside him, waiting for him to think. Above them in the lacy trees, bats flitted like thoughts you could not quite remember.

Mr. Brimner picked up his hat and said, "I think we must go now. John Giles will be waiting at the jetty."

Aren moved then, and they followed him across the flags and went back through into the house.

As they went, Mrs. Fruelock put a trembling hand on Kay's arm. For the first time, she looked older. "I know this must be a sad disappointment to him," she said quietly. "But I look at it as a blessing, not only that he was reared in a Christian home but that he was saved from flood and famine. I hope he may come to see it that way."

Kay bit her tongue, until a little gush of blood welled into her mouth. She shook or nodded her head, she hardly knew which, and went.

Pansy helped them gather their things. She was the kindest, most companionable girl—she rounded up Dash and bundled him into the basket with a steak bone to chew on, and she found their other things without fuss, and stayed in the doorway waving until they turned the corner to the harbour.

Kay and Aren and Mr. Brimner walked down to the jetty in silence. John Giles's boat was moored there, rocking in the low afternoon light, ready to take them to the ghost island, Pulo Anna.

Kay tried to still the frantic beating of her heart, the panic of guilt and grief that had seized her. She had been a child—she would not usurp the act of taking Aren—but now she could not bear even to have witnessed it. What had anything they had done added to his life?

She did not know. Feeling suddenly very unsettled, she turned away and was vilely sick into a ditch. Aren halted, and Mr. Brimner pulled out a handkerchief. After the heaving stopped, she straightened herself, saying, "I'm sorry—do carry on, I will be right there."

She waited a moment to see if there was more to come, and then stumbled down the path to the pier. There was the little boat making ready to set out. But they would stop soon, at Ha'ano, because John Giles's wife was going to stay with her sister there. Clutching at that ordinary detail, Kay went up the little gangplank and onto the boat in a strange, unmoored state, wobbling as the deck wobbled with her added weight.

The boat seemed small and makeshift after their long journey by steamer, but they stowed their things away in two tiny slanted forward cabins with bunks, where everything was clean as a whistle, and then went back up on deck for the short sail to Ha'ano. Dash slumped at her feet with his bone.

As they were making ready, Pansy came hurrying down the slope toward the pier, calling out to them. She held out a folded paper, an envelope. "Mother forgot to give this to Miss Ward," she called over.

Aren stretched to take it from her.

"A letter for Miss Ward, for Kay. It came to us yesterday. In the worry, she forgot it."

Aren handed the envelope to Kay. She turned it over in her hands, but as the boat swung, the writing did not stay still. She could not make it out, and could not force her eyes to make the effort. She put it in her pocket. "Thank her for me," she called back to Pansy, "and thank you for catching us."

Pansy stood waving as John Giles untied the ropes and went to the tiller.

Aren waved back, setting one hip on the rail, and rode easily as the boat swayed away from the pier. Then he leaned over to Kay, looking into her eyes to see if she was all right, and recited from their old book: "*How hard the wind blows! and how the little boats rock to and fro! It must be sad for those poor men who have to earn their bread on the sea—I hope they will bring home a good net full of fish . . .*"

So at least he did not hate her. The boat did look like the one the nursery fishermen had: two short masts, a lugger-style sloop.

John Giles's wife, Lotoua, came up from below, where she had been organizing stores in the lazaret cupboard. Her beaming face reminded Kay of the young dancer shining with oil from long ago. Lotoua knew Mr. Brimner well, of course; they exchanged news and jokes. She was happy to meet Aren and tell him everything she knew or had heard about Micronesia, and with her laughing chatter, the boat became a little party.

While the others talked, Kay subsided onto the boards and put her head in her hands.

She hoped to be unnoticed, but Mr. Brimner came over to commiserate with her. "I have never been able to reconcile to the Tongan diet myself. A chicken, well boiled, is usually acceptable, but those are few on Ha'ano, kept for feast days. Fish, fish stew, those I can manage. Taro is impossible. I have wished not to eat at all sometimes."

He was very thin—she had not noticed before how thin he was. Was he ill too?

It was kind of him to comfort her, but, shivering by the side rail in a hazy blue confusion, all she could think of was what she had done by talking Aren into leaving Nova Scotia—away from Thea, from all of them, Merissa, everyone, everything he'd known for most of his conscious life—in order to stick him back here in the sand as if he was a doll. And all this time there had been no one for him to go home to.

10

Haʻano

Away from land, the water was very still as the afternoon blended down into evening. A breeze barely filled her sails, but the little sloop was light and slippy on the ʻAuhangamea current.

Kay drifted in and out of a cloud. It was late to be setting out, but Haʻano was only a short sail along the coast—hardly even separated from Haʻapai. John Giles said he'd like to stop at the village of Haʻano for the night, to have a visit with his wife's sister before heading out over the long stretch to Papua, and also to find the last crew member, his brother-in-law Fokisi, who was famous for being late, having been born late, and who had missed the boat to Pangai that morning.

Sound came slipping down from the prow, where Aren and Mr. Brimner were talking. Once in a while their voices would make sense. The boat was named the *Lata*. Kay had seen that on the side as she came on board. No bigger than a racing schooner out of Yarmouth, but the men often went on those boats down to Bar Harbor and even to the Bahamas. It would get them to Pulo Anna.

Waking from a daze, she became aware of something odd. At length she realized it was silence. The air was so still, she had thought they might be dead. But it was only that being under sail again, there was no engine noise.

"Noise is the chief thing I notice on returning to the world," Mr. Brimner was saying. Hearing him was why she had noticed it was silent.

"The water and the sky all through," Aren said. She thought he said.

After what seemed like many days and nights, or an hour, they dropped anchor in the little half-moon harbour at Ha'ano, and somehow Kay got down into the dinghy and out again onto the jetty, carrying Dash with her in his basket. Aren had fed him while they were coming over, so the puppy was sleepy again; she was grateful for that.

Aren took the basket from her arms and said not to worry, and a woman called Mahina came down to the water with her little boy Sione, and then they were all being taken somewhere in the darkness and there was a bed.

She woke in the dark and pulled on her dress, and staggered barefoot down to the scrubby beach, talking to Thea. Thea said "No no no, this is terrible, you are ill, I will book you into a hotel, there is one on the next island," and Kay said "Oh no I must not, but if you insist, I will have a bath in a white bathtub."

But it was just a dream, she was having bad dreams again. Thea could not speak to her here or hear her crying on the damp sand. She was alone and always had been.

And then she had to scramble into the bushes as another bout of cramping overtook her poor guts.

The moon was bright, so bright! But no, it was the sun, just rising. When she came out to the sand again, she saw two butterflies tangled in a complicated dance; they were going together, together, together, turning and tumbling in the air in a frenzied dance, mating or perhaps only quarrelling, flying apart and drawn back together.

Nothing was any use. She knew nothing understood nothing nothing made any sense. She made her way back to the bure, and into bed at last in the white cot, and untangled the mosquito netting and lay down—and as soon as she closed her eyes, Mr. Brimner's friend Mahina came to her, looming kindly over the bed. She put a large, warm hand on Kay's head, saying with great concern, "But you must hurry and get well! Queen Salote says you must leave if you are ill, no-one may stay on Ha'ano if they are ill!"

And that was a dream too. But even though she understood, even in the grip of the night terrors, that it was only a dream, Kay resolved to be well. She was soaking wet in her nightdress. But if Queen Salote said she must leave unless she was well, she must be well.

Mr. Brimner and Aren were talking outside her door when she woke again. Aren said he did not think they could go on, with Kay in this fever, and Mr. Brimner said no, I believe you are right. So then Kay did get better.

By focusing her mind on the thing that mattered, which was Aren, she made herself come together into a clump and get up, and she put her dress on again and went out to the stoop where they sat talking in strong daylight.

They turned to look at her, surprised.

"Of course we must go," she said. "Here is John Giles's lovely boat all ready, and we do not want to miss the tide. I have had a very good rest and am feeling much better, only very sorry to have put you all out. I hope we can say goodbye to Lotoua, and to Mahina and her son, before we leave?"

She held herself in well. As well as if she was Thea, in fact. They all looked at her to investigate her health, and she passed inspection.

By a great exercise of will, she continued to feign fitness for travel all through the bustle of embarking. That was all right, she could keep doing that until they got to Pulo Anna. And then she could consider what to do next.

II

Onward

Rapt in conversation with Mr. Brimner, Aren sat on the fo'c'sle roof, legs dangling, looking to Kay like his young uncles had looked ten years before, off Pulo Anna. He was a man now. Bright-eyed, amused, alive—and not as spindly as his uncles had been.

The motion was doing her good, doing them all good. Forward, forward, running along the scudding tips of the waves, the pleasure of that enormous breathing in and breathing out that is the movement of ocean.

She really did feel much better. She had been delirious, on Ha'ano. It was not her old nightmares returning, it was just a fever, and the fever had broken. She had slept for a while in the shade, leaning against the fo'c'sle wall, and she was much better now. But she would stay still for a little.

Rearranging herself on the rolled blanket Fokisi kindly found for her to sit on, she felt a crinkling in her pocket and pulled out the letter that Pansy had run down to hand them at the jetty. It was from Thea, on the thinnest overseas writing paper, the worse for wear from the last few days, but readable.

Dear Kay,

    I am sending this to you because I do not know what to say to Aren.

    By now you will have seen Dorothy Fruelock and you will know about Pulo Anna—please keep this note by you and give it to Aren if you think it will help him. I do not want to impose it on him if you feel it will not, but I am afraid for him. Please write when you can to let me know where you are.

    I write in haste, but send my love, and from Francis & Roddy too.

    I am glad you are with him.

A second note, unsealed, was tucked into the thin folds of the first.

    I am sorry, Aren. I wanted to save you from hurt, but it was wrong to keep the truth from you. I am so sorry about your people. I cannot be sorry we took you, son of my heart. God bless you always, your loving Thea

Kay pulled the frail paper through her fingers, pressing the folds again, reassembling the little package in its envelope. Above her, Aren and Mr. Brimner were talking about fishing and language, about words that Aren remembered from his childhood. Which were pitifully few, but those few strongly grained, some with funny meanings that caught in the mind. Kay listened, thinking about the letter and wondering whether or when she ought to give it to Aren. She thought it might be better to show him Thea's earlier letter, Roddy asking when will they come back? She folded Thea's note small and put it back in her pocket for now.

"*Bub*," Aren was saying, remembering another word. "It means—" He made a rough square with his two hands, fingers spread. "Not square, but parallelogram. Like in geometry at school, and it is two things: both the small fish, bright, straight-lined down one edge—"

John Giles said over his shoulder, "That's a triggerfish, I'll bet you."

"And also the stars, constellation, the fish shape in the sky that we, that you, call—that is called the Southern Cross." He made the shape again. "Small, brightly coloured fish, not very good to eat, I should think, but I don't remember eating one."

Mr. Brimner leaned forward, interested. "It seems you recall things connected with fishing, with the work rather than the eating. When we met long ago, you talked of learning how to fish."

Aren looked out over the water, trying to call memory back. "At night in spring, I went with the men for flying fish. We stood in our canoes with palm torches"—he swept his arm widely—"in a circle, so, when it is dark—only stars, no moon, or the fishing will not work. The men with the nets cannot eat or drink or smoke all day, that smell might warn the fish. The signal comes, and we light the torches from a hidden—" He waited, but the word did not come, so he made a shape with his hands, a small brazier, perhaps. "And then! lights all around, and the fish come to see what is happening."

Surprised, Kay said, "Like when the whales came to watch the eclipse!"

"It is the same curiosity, I guess!" He took up an imaginary net. "The men sweep down with their nets, and they are full of fish— flying fish, but sometimes also shark and needlefish." Some spark of memory had started a fire in his mind. He said, "Also for needle-fish, we fished with a kite."

From the tiller, John Giles said, "I've seen that kite-fishing!"

"More fish with the big kite, a man out in the canoe," Aren said. "But I have fished with the boys, using small kites from the land, with the sticky net made from spiderwebs—we cannot eat oil before it or the sticky part goes slick." As memory came, he wavered in his tenses as he told these things, telling it now as a story, now as a thing that was still happening.

Mr. Brimner had written down the words that Aren recalled, and he read down the list, ending with *bub*, the constellation and the fish.

She and Aren had come here on the *Constellation*, Kay thought. And the name of the mission ship that ferried the Fruelocks around those islands was the *Southern Cross*.

She moved her head to stop that ringing resonance, and said, "Someone told me once—Thea, or perhaps it was Father . . ." She had not thought of that before; she thought she had X'ed out everything he'd told her. "Well, never mind," she went on. "They told me that in the Cree language the word for *seven* means 'enough blankets.' I've lived in the kind of winter that made that word."

"That must be how we understand any language, by living in it," Aren said. "I first understood *spring* by standing in the little spring at the back of the garden on Elm Street, as the ice was melting. That it is both beginning and rising, that it is the season and the water both, life coming up."

Mr. Brimner said, "Prior's brother, who is studying in Hamburg, sent me a fascinating study by a German philosopher named Buber, who believes that human relation is the original unity, perhaps even *is* what we understand as God—the self relating to others, recognizing others as human. I find this idea satisfying, and I am far enough from bishops and doctrine to think what I like. Buber says that where we say *far away*, the Zulu language has a word which means—and remember that I am translating a translation here— 'the place where someone cries out: O mother, I am lost!'"

Kay looked over the side into the foaming lace that travelled alongside the little boat, loving Mr. Brimner with all her heart. No one in Nova Scotia talked or thought like him. The interior of his mind was watch-crystal, unmuddied by self or selfishness.

" . . . and I understand that the Tierra del Fuegans have a seven-syllabled word whose literal meaning is, 'They stare at one another, each waiting for the other to volunteer to do what both wish, but are not able to do."

———

Kay woke from unaccustomed daytime sleep, and the boat was still. Rising and subsiding gently on the swell, but no forward movement. Water lapped quietly on the boards she lay against, tucked in her narrow forward bunk in the prow's shape. She sat up, thinking she was mistaken. But no, they were stopped. Now she really did feel better, much better, except for the bad taste in her mouth.

Dash curled back into her pillows and slept on. She left him there, shook out her hair from its sleep-dampness, found the water cask in the galley and then crept up the little ladder from the galley onto the teak boards. No one was there—had they all been swept overboard as she slept? Of course not! There, they were forward, on the port side, all of them at the railing making the boat heel over slightly, staring out to sea.

Then the noise reached through her sleep-fuddled ears, and she saw the spires of foam and leaping white pillars. It was whales, breaching. Five, six, seven humpback whales, playing in the dark-green world.

Aren was not at the rail—he was above, halfway up the mast, wearing only half-breeches, like a true sailor. Spotting her, he came spiralling down and pulled her over to the other side, pointing not back at the breaching show-offs, but downward.

And there was a whale calf, a so-much-smaller whale, scaled down to a size that was almost seeable for human eyes. His mother nudged him and he turned, turned, and one bright eye stared up at Kay and Aren.

He stood back on his tail under the water, surprised to be looked back at, and then surged up so that his head breached, gently, long mouth rising up and up until the round eye was out in the air and could see them unfiltered by foam.

She caught Aren's hand and squeezed it, and he motioned *yes yes yes* with his eyebrows, and reached out a hand to the black-and-grey smoothness, the softer white under the chin—leaning out far—so far that he overbalanced and fell in.

Kay shrieked and clutched uselessly for his waist or legs, but it was a small boat, there was only ten feet to fall, and Aren was already laughing as he went in.

The whale calf turned in a trice, and its mother turned too, so that for a moment Kay feared she would shoulder up and capsize the boat, but she only pushed her calf out of the way and slid back around again, as if not opposed to Aren but careful of her child.

Aren bobbed up again from the deeps and waved to Kay, his face splitting into a great crow of glorious joy. "I am in here with them!" he cried, and she wanted to tear off her own clothes and jump in too, but she could not swim, so she did not.

The commotion drew Mr. Brimner, and then John Giles and Fokisi, away from their lookout to see what was amiss. They all stood along the rail and whooped, Mr. Brimner talking of Leviathan in semi-hysterical language and John shouting down advice to Aren about staying calm and it all being all right, many a man has swum with the whales and boasted of it later . . .

Through all that, Aren dove and rose, the calf examining his legs and hands and back with his great muzzle. At one point Aren surfaced with a great sputtering and shouted, "He likes to stand upside down!"

Then he went back down again. They could see the mother whale sinking deeper, and the calf playing peep-bo behind her, now darting up to investigate Aren and now retreating, so that Aren took longer and longer time between breaths, until Kay began to feel concerned that he would stay down there, become a whale himself and never come back.

At last John gently laid a life preserver down on the surface of the water, and Aren bowed his head to the mother and her child and caught at the white ring and was hauled out of that dangerous beauty and joy, coming up with water and tears streaming down his face until he could leap off the rail and down on the boards, clapping Kay on the shoulders and kissing her cheek.

"I am sorry it was only me and not us both," he said, for only her to hear.

Then he turned to the men and laughed and laughed, telling the feel of the great fin on one's legs, and confessing that the first drop had given him a fright. "I thought I was eaten for sure," he said, quite serious.

"Piss yourself?" John Giles asked him. "I did, the first time I went in with them—but it was worth it."

She woke again—she was sleeping her life away!—to stillness, and rolled out of her bunk to run up and check for whales.

But it was night, late enough that they would not be visible around the boat. As her head rose from the hold, she saw Aren sitting on the little fo'c'sle roof.

He pointed up to the sky, where the Milky Way was arrayed above, a thousand million dots of light, a thousand billion, a long gossamer scarf flung down the blackness. Low on the scarf, the stars of the Southern Cross, the *bub*, showed pink and gold. Dawn must be near.

"We've stopped," she said, very quietly.

"Yes," he said. He reached a hand down for her to climb up and join him.

"I told John Giles that we should turn and make for Ha'ano," he said.

"But that is—"

He said, "I know."

"—long behind us."

"I know," he said again.

Their legs were snug against each other, the fo'c'sle roof being narrow. The mainsail was down, she now saw. Light wind off the water luffed in the jib, the only sail still up.

"I told him he should set the sea anchor, and that tomorrow we'd go back."

She waited.

"We don't need to go there. I don't need to. It's too far to go for a walk among graves, graves of people I don't know, or can't identify. What is lost is lost, for me. That is not necessarily—it is not the end of my life, my soul."

Kay sat still, listening.

"Ever since we found out that they all died, I have been wondering," he said. "Today, when I fell into the water, I thought, I am already home!"

He shifted so he could see her in the starlight, in the pale light spilling from the compass-light. "Do you mind if we don't go to Pulo Anna?"

She moved too, turning to dangle a leg off the roof, and leaned on one hand to look up into the black and dazzling sky. "I wanted to fix what we did, you know. What could be fixed, at least. I know it can't be, but I wanted to take you there, to hear you say, This is where my house was! And to run after you down different paths, for you to show me this, and this, like the spring behind the house on Elm Street or the paths through the orchard at Lake Milo—for you to see it again, to feel that you could walk the whole island in your sleep because you know it so well."

"Yes," Aren said. "I would say, Come, let me show you the beautiful place—the place with two rocks over a water pool, where the boys have been sliding down for so many years that the rock shines. I know it is there." He took her hand. "It is not my home any longer. It can't be, it's gone now, the people are all gone. I have to make my own home."

Kay could not bear that there was no fixing this. In the silence, water lapped at the boards. "What will you do?" she asked him.

"I think I'll stay here. Don't you think?"

"Don't I think you should?"

"Don't you think you should too?"

She did not know what she should do. She could go home, if Yarmouth was her home, and be with Thea, and Francis, and

Roddy. She could go on to Suva and wait for a boat going to San Francisco, and then go home by train, to New York and then to Boston, and catch the *Prince Arthur* for Yarmouth. That would take a long time.

Or she could go north—try to go back to her original home, to Blade Lake. Except the school had closed now and she did not belong there either, and never had truly, except that her father had taken her there. But she could at least see the land again, the beautiful hills gently bending one over the other, coyote-coloured, close-cropped, rising into mountains.

But none of the people there would want her to come back. And no one would know her. She had been a transplant there and was a transplant in Nova Scotia too. It was her home only because it had some people she loved in it.

"I don't have any home. Maybe that is not something I need," she said.

Mr. Brimner had come up on deck, perhaps drawn by their low conversation. He was thin and brown, she saw now, but not unhealthy. That fear had come from her own illness.

"I hoped—I thought you both might spend some little time on Ha'ano," he said. "There is a cottage empty since the government man from Nuku'alofa went back to his third wife. It is fixable. The garden plot is already dug."

Kay got down from the roof and went to the rail. She knew what she would like best.

Mr. Brimner made himself comfortable against the mast, folding his thin arms, his fluff of light hair lifting in the night breeze. "So are we going back?" he asked, generally.

Aren answered, "Yes."

ACKNOWLEDGEMENTS

This book is fiction, but was sparked by a story my childhood piano teacher told of her mother Grace Ladd's purchase of a small boy near Pulo Anna for four pounds of tobacco. I read Grace's letters and her husband Frederick's logs in manuscript, but also relied on Louise Nichol's excellent compilation of the letters in *Quite a Curiosity, the Sea Letters of Grace F. Ladd*, and I recommend it as a fascinating read on its own behalf. Kathryn Ladd, Grace's daughter, was a brilliant piano teacher and a substantial, complicated person. Although I named Kay after her, they are not much alike; and in fact Miss Ladd was born after that original boy had died. As well as the taking of Aren, I've drawn freely on other events and images from Grace Ladd's letters; I took the liberty of combining two of Captain Frederick Ladd's ships, the *Morning Light* and the *Belmont*, into one barque. Another indispensable source for this book was *Words of the Lagoon* by R.E. Johannes, an examination of fishing culture and language in the Palau island group. I used incidents and people, real and imagined, from many other first-hand accounts of travel in the south seas. Some passengers and events on the *Constellation* reflect E.C. Spykman's account of her pilgrimage by steamer to Robert Louis Stevenson's grave on Samoa, a lovely portrait of a journeying girl in 1922. Most of the surnames are invented, but Arthur is named in honour of my Elm Street neighbours, the Wetmore sisters. (The eldest Miss Wetmore gave me sound but depressing advice, writing in my childhood autograph book, "Be good, sweet maid, and let who will be pretty.") Among many other sea-faring diaries, Alice Wetmore's account of their voyages as children in 1903, stopping at Port Elizabeth and Rio de Janeiro, illuminated those places for me. Anyone who has delved into the deeper cut of Gerard Manley Hopkins will recognize lesser-known lines of his attributed to Mr Brimner's friend Prior, who embodies facts of Hopkins's life and early death, and of Hopkins's mother, who after her son's death used black-bordered paper for her correspondence for the rest of her life.

The Commonwealth Foundation gave me my first opportunity to visit New Zealand and the South Pacific, and the SSHRC research fund gave me a second, more comprehensive research trip to Tonga, Fiji, Singapore and Hong Kong. I'm indebted to Dr. Roxanne Harde and Dr. Kim Misfeldt at the Augustana Faculty of the University of Alberta for their support through the SSHRC process. Tia Lalani was a fine research assistant and reader. I gratefully acknowledge the invaluable assistance of the Canada Council and the Alberta Foundation for the Arts. A more comprehensive list of books and research material is posted on my website, marinaendicott.com

I heard Miss Ladd's story of the boy bought for four pounds of tobacco with an instantaneous feeling of revulsion. But what people have done to other people in Canada is no less obviously wrong. The residential school at Blade Lake is fictional, but would have held students from Stoney/Nakoda, Tsuut'ina, Cree, and possibly Blood and Blackfoot peoples. To begin to understand the terrible legacy of residential schools, the best and hardest reading is survivor accounts, and there are so many. I've put a list of links at marinaendicott.com

If not for Dr. Heather Young-Leslie's introduction to her Tongan family, and to the Pacific world, I'd have been sunk. Heta's generous practical and scholarly advice have been invaluable—all errors are of course my own. Grateful thanks to Mahina Tu'akoi and her son Sione for their hospitality and affectionate friendship.

I also thank Ebonie Fifita for introducing me to Nukua'lofa and the rest of Tongatapu, twice, and Mary Rokonadravu for our visit in Suva. I hope to visit you all again someday.

Some of the people I'd like to thank can't hear me any more: my revered Greek teacher, Mrs. Marion Seretis, sadly missed by all who knew her; and Miss Kay Ladd, my earliest mentor.

But many can. Thanks to intrepid Thyra Endicott for coming with me on the little ship; to the learnèd Timothy Endicott for patient re-reading and help with Greek. Thank you to Helen Oyeyemi, Madeleine Thien and Caroline Adderson—it is good to talk with wise friends and great writers. Thanks to my beloved editor, Lynn Henry at Knopf Canada, to the incomparable Jin Auh and Tracy Bohan, and to Jill Bialosky at W. W. Norton for this next voyage of the *Morning Light*. Having listened to endless yarns about the south seas, Rachel and Will are absolved from ever reading this book. Peter did read this one. Like me, it lives because of him.

MARINA ENDICOTT is the author of *Good to a Fault*, which won the Commonwealth Writers' Prize for Best Book, Canada and the Caribbean, and was a finalist for the Scotiabank Giller Prize; *The Little Shadows*, which was longlisted for the Scotiabank Giller Prize and shortlisted for the Governor General's Literary Award; and *Close to Hugh*, which was also longlisted for the Scotiabank Giller Prize. Endicott has been an actor, director, playwright and editor, and now lives in Alberta.

A NOTE ABOUT THE TYPE

The Voyage of the Morning Light has been set in Janson, a misnamed type-
face designed in or about 1690 by Nicholas Kis, a Hungarian in Amsterdam.
In 1919 the original matrices became the property of the Stempel Foundry
in Frankfurt, Germany. Janson is an old-style book face of excellent clar-
ity and sharpness, featuring concave and splayed serifs, and a marked
contrast between thick and thin strokes.